Biz On the Go

"Finally a real-to-life character older women (yep, that's me) can relate to. Biz will make you laugh and cry as she struggles to find God and His purpose in the midst of life changes she can't control. Will she succeed or make a mess of things? You won't want to put this book down or see the story end."

—MARLENE BAGNULL, Author of *Write His Answer*

"Biz McNeely is on a journey of growth and discovery as she faces getting older. All she's had control of in her life spins out of her reach. Ms. Haley does a wonderful job giving Biz a voice and drawing the reader in for the ride as she faces real-life challenges. The struggle to grow emotionally parallels the spiritual struggle Biz undertakes. Barbara Haley has crafted an excellent work of inspirational fiction."

—SUSAN BAGANZ, Author of *Pesto and Potholes*

"Few authors can combine humor, faith and depth of emotion the way Barb Haley does. You will either see yourself in Biz—or wish she lived next door. Both Biz and Barb give us permission to embrace God's love and be the women we were made to be."

—NANCY RUE, Best-Selling Author of over 120 Books for Teens, Tweens and Adults

 On the Go

by

Barbara E. Haley

CHARA
Publishing
Universal City, Texas

Biz On the Go

Book #1 The Second Wind

Copyright ©2018 by Barbara E. Haley

Chara Publishing

ISBN 978-0-9975580-1-2

Cover Illustrations by Ben Kissell
Cover Design by Rick Marschall

Scriptures taken from the HOLY BIBLE, NEW INTERNATIONAL VERSION. Copyright 1973, 1978, 1984. International Bible Society. Used by permission of Zondervan Bible Publishers.

www.barbarahaleybooks.com
haleybarb@yahoo.com

Printed in the United States of America

Dedication

I'm going to let you in on a dirty little secret—the reason I started writing fiction. Back in the 90s I met someone who told me all about a novel he was writing.

Okay. I'll admit. I became a bit puffed up. As in ... *So what? I could write a book if I wanted to.*

My bad, for sure. Had to hit the altar with that attitude. But at least it got me started. I hurried to Barnes and Noble and bought *The Marshall Plan* to learn how to write a novel.

Good grief, I never imagined there was so much to learn. I discovered fiction writing classes online but they were expensive. Not in the budget with two kids in college.

That's when a very special person stepped up. Virginia "Ginny" Merrill paid my tuition, and I decided right then I would someday dedicate my first novel to her.

Over fifteen years later, I've ghostwritten two books, published three books for kids and two books of devotions. But the novel? Just finished it. Finally.

Anyway, I dedicate this book to you, Ginny. Thank you for your love, friendship and encouragement. Thank you for believing in me from the beginning. Of course, that's who you are. An encourager to everyone you meet. You have blessed my life. Thank you for providing the way for me to realize the dream God planted in my heart. You're the best!

CHAPTER 1

Anticipating the stir my visit was bound to create, I squared my shoulders, lifted my chins and marched through the doorway. After all, the company was still mine on paper.

"Be right there." The voice came from behind a door on the left.

Sure my daughter-in-law would adamantly object to what I intended to do, I skipped the small talk. "Just me, Vickie."

The door to my son's office opened, and Robby stepped into the lobby, almost filling the doorway with his stocky six-and-a-half-foot frame. "Hey, Mom. I thought you took a couple of days off to rest."

So, there it was. I was not expected, and most likely, not wanted. But as I said before, this was still my company.

I slid past my son. Just as I suspected, every stinkin' trucker in our employment was there. I walked my eyes around the circle—somewhat amused with the assortment of emotions displayed on their faces. Surprise, of course. And a bit of guilt, embarrassment and discomfort. I took a seat. "Guess I missed the memo about today's meeting."

Robby took his place behind the large mahogany desk. "Let me be honest, Mom."

"Good start."

He smiled slightly—not an I'm-glad-we're-together-on-this gesture, but one riddled with tension. "The guys want to discuss their future employment . . . with me."

That hit hard, like I'd been plowed down by one of my own trucks. Most of these truckers had worked for me for years. Good grief, I'd seen them through divorces and custody battles and chemotherapy. I made sure I had their backs, and they always had mine. Like when they offered to take somebody out who threatened to sue me a few years ago. Not that I accepted their offer, but the thought got me through the mess.

"Discussing the future is always a good thing." My eyes connected with each employee who would reciprocate. "Will it bother anyone if I stay?"

I faced my son. "Robby?"

He shook his head. "Can you step out a minute, Mom?"

"I don't think so."

"Then we might have to reschedule."

A seasoned trucker, two seats to my left, shifted in his seat and crossed his arms. The wiry little man with clumps of grayish hair draped over his balding crown had been with me from the beginning. "Not necessary, Robby."

Pete turned in my direction. "I'm sure I can speak for most all of us truckers. Ms. Biz, there ain't no one we respect more than you when it comes to trucking know-how. Even though you sometimes get all up on your high horse, we know it's because you care more about this company than life itself."

Heat filled my cheeks. "Thanks, Pete."

"None of us want to desert you. We took the coward's way out, expecting Robby to pass the news on to you."

My neck went stiff. I looked to Robby. "Desert me?"

"Things have to change, Mom, or the guys plan to work elsewhere. Some have already accepted other positions."

I stared at the boy—the man—who sat behind the desk. I waited for someone to say he was wrong. But no one spoke, and the silent buzz in the room intensified until I almost plugged my ears to shut it out. I stood and responded with a false bravado to my voice. "Pay raises? That what you need?"

"It's not that easy, Ms. Biz," Pete said. "There's no way you can afford to pay us the wages we can get from larger, consolidated trucking companies. Then there's the flexible hours, the safety incentives, the most recent technology on them trucks and the on-the-job schooling they provide to keep our licenses current."

"It's the whole package," a younger trucker added. "I can't afford not to take advantage of the offer another company made me. I'm giving my notice, today."

Several others nodded.

"Just can't see no way around it," Pete said.

"Right." The company was going down before my eyes and I could do nothing to stop it. I reached for the desk as my hands began to tingle and my breathing became choppy. The room swirled around me.

Truckers jumped to support me and ease me into a chair.

The room cleared. Vickie appeared and insisted that I nibble on a cracker and take small drinks of water.

My breathing slowed. The meeting. The truckers, and . . . their demands for more than I could ever give them. "What am I going to do, Robby?"

I rested a bit in the break room, then spent a few minutes at the bathroom mirror, combing my fingers through my curly gray hair. I looked about as washed up as I felt. Not to worry about smudged mascara, I wore only a thin layer of face makeup. No eye shadow, blush or lipstick. Didn't want to draw attention to myself. Not until I lost a few pounds.

Vickie was busy with a customer when I walked through the lobby toward Robby's office. A ray of sunlight played on her curly Raggedy-Ann orange hair.

"Can you please explain this fee?" the customer said.

Vickie pointed to the invoice. "As you can see here, you never responded to our request that you confirm the order."

I remembered the situation and stepped behind the counter. "Can I help?"

Despite the pleasant look on Vickie's face, her expressive, green eyes spoke clearly. "I've got this, Biz."

But she obviously didn't. Not that I could blame her. She'd only been working the front office for a little over two weeks. Robby's idea when I started getting daily migraines and the doctor insisted I was juggling too many tasks.

I noted the customer's name on the invoice and extended my hand. "Hi, Mr. Ralston. I'm Biz McNeely. How can we resolve this situation to your satisfaction?"

Within minutes, the charge was deleted and our satisfied customer left, thankful for our willingness to work with him.

Vickie, on the other hand, was obviously not happy. In fact, she didn't even look up when I reminded her to delete the charge on the books.

She'd learn, with time. Right now, I needed to settle things with Robby.

I could hear the roar of engines and other shop sounds through Robby's open office window. "You know we pay for air conditioning around here, right?"

Old joke. Everyone knew Robby refused to be cooped up in artificial air all day. I'd forfeited that battle years ago.

"Are you feeling better?"

I nodded and sat in front of the desk. "We need to talk, and not about how I'm feeling."

"Yes. Just let me get a refill on coffee. Want a cup?"

"Sure. Two sugars."

Robby returned and sat next to me. He blew on his drink. "First let me say that we are not finished."

My eyes clogged, despite my resolve to keep a tight rein on my emotions. "But the truckers were right. I can't compete with the larger companies, and I refuse to—"

"Stop there, Mom. We've had this discussion. At this point, you have to face reality. We only have three choices."

"I'll go under before I'll sell out to a consolidated firm. I mean it, Robby."

Robby picked up his pad and rifled through the pages. "We have friends, Mom."

Yeah, that's what I thought, too.

I headed for the country. The one place in all the world that calmed me when life got too big for me to handle. Usually I just crept along the back roads at random. Relaxed into nostalgic scenes of homesteads dotted with faded barns and swinging gates and combines in the fields. Flipped off the air conditioning and rolled down my windows to hear my tires crunch the gravel and inhale the familiar scent of cow manure and freshly mown grass and whatever else goes into the delicious country aroma.

But today was different. Today I drove with purpose. My heart hurt, and I needed to remember better days. Taking a right turn, I drove about a mile down the road and slowed to a crawl as I neared my destination.

A wooden bridge crossed a bubbling creek at the entrance. The driveway wound upward among heavy oak trees to the white two-story house at the top of the hill—the home of my dreams.

Feeling a little foolish, I pulled into the drive and pretended I'd come home. Shut my eyes and allowed myself to imagine that I held the key to my dream.

This house and I had history. As a teen, I babysat here for a family who laughed and loved and forgave mistakes. As I cuddled their tiny children, I dreamed of one day creating a home of my own here, where my children would feel safe and wanted. I listened to their friendly chatter. Watched their gentle touch. And joined them for engaging games of Monopoly and warm chocolate chip cookies at their kitchen table on Sunday afternoons.

They took me in as one of their own, and looking back, I wondered if they knew the conditions I endured every other day of my life.

If only life had turned out differently. If only I hadn't let the business override the true dreams of my heart. I sighed as I shifted my truck into reverse . . . and backed into reality.

I grimaced as I pulled into my drive. Across the street a rusted washing machine had been hauled to the curb, flanked by oily auto parts, a pee-stained baby mattress and a couple of milk crates overflowing with beer bottles. This eyesore would probably remain on the curb for the next three weeks before anyone took time to call the city for a pickup.

My next-door neighbor's garbage can also stood by the curb. Nasty. Cracked plastic. Dribbled food dried to the rim. I wheeled it to the side of the house and walked around back to let myself in. "Hazel. It's me, Biz."

I walked down the dim hallway to the family room. My elderly friend stirred in her recliner. Dressed in gray slacks and a floral-patterned blouse, muted blue in color, she wore a string of pearls around her neck that perfectly accentuated the baby-soft skin on which they rested. Pale pink gloss tinted her lips, and her wispy white hair, coiled neatly in a bun at the nape of her slender neck, spoke of gentle elegance.

"Oh, hi, Biz. Is it lunchtime already?"

I laughed. "Lunchtime and beyond. I thought your granddaughter planned to be home at noon today."

Hazel inched forward in the chair and reached for her walker. "She had to go in early for some extra training. But she promised to come home early this evening."

Wrapping my arms around Hazel's waist, I helped her to her feet and steadied her. "You should have called. I could have come sooner."

Hazel laughed. "No problem, Bizzie. I just appreciate you stopping by when you can."

Slowly, we stepped to the bathroom. I turned on the shower, gently removed Hazel's clothing and soiled diaper, and helped her onto the shower bench. "So what's new on the Soaps?" I stood outside the glass door. "Did Rosalyn tell Miguel the truth, yet?"

Hazel babbled nonstop as she bathed. She always insisted on doing this herself, but by the time she finished, she was exhausted. I dried my friend's frail body, helped her into a fresh nightie and undergarment and shadowed her to the kitchen. Our daily routine . . . for over three years.

"Want some soup and a grilled cheese?"

Hazel nodded. "That sounds wonderful, sweetie."

As a pat of butter melted into softness in the skillet, so my friend's affection oozed through cracks in the walls I'd built to keep people away. Truth was, it never mattered what condition I entered this house. I always left feeling loved and appreciated. Well, at least I would always have that.

When I got home, Robert was in the backyard watering his flowers. I took a migraine tablet and sipped on hot tea as I heated our supper.

By the time Robert came inside, the pain behind my eyes had subsided considerably.

He washed his hands at the sink. "How's Hazel?"

"The doctors said her lungs are almost clear from the pneumonia. She's breathing so much easier."

Robert scooped a hefty helping of coleslaw onto his plate. "Robby says you stopped by the office this afternoon."

My forehead tensed. "Robby explain our dilemma?"

"He started to, but I stopped him. Said I'd rather hear it from you."

"Thanks, honey. I was bamboozled. The truckers hadn't said a word about being unhappy . . . at least not to me. And then Robby tells me he already has a plan that will fix things."

Robert bit into a juicy chicken breast and wiped his chin with his napkin. "A plan?"

"Yes. But I'm not sure where he got the idea I needed him to plan for the future. Good grief, I hired him as an accountant, not a soothsayer."

Robert laughed. His cell phone buzzed, and he checked the screen. "Sorry, honey. I need to take this in my office."

I toyed with my green beans until Robert returned.

"So what do these plans of Robby's look like? Any common sense behind them?"

I shrugged. "I can't fight the fact that the larger, consolidated companies offer a much better benefit package. Robby has contacted other small trucking companies and proposed a sort of merger with them. A consolidation of sorts, but set up to allow individual owners to maintain a high degree of control. Calls it Mom and Pop United."

"What do you think?"

"It looks impressive on paper. But I'm nervous about investing everything I own. So many things could go wrong."

"Good point. Of course, investments always involve risk. Would you really need to put up everything?"

"Robby says I do. We'll need to update technology and order new trucks. And he wants to hire some financial guru who supposedly has a good handle on what's ahead in the trucking industry. How do you even find such a guy?"

Robert stacked our dishes. "It is a lot to think about."

I reached for the empty vegetable bowl, but Robert took it from me. "I'll get these. Your head's really hurting, isn't it?"

"Well, actually … yes. Did I say something, or—"

"I can see it in your eyes. Why don't you go lie down for a while? We can talk later if you want to."

"But I need to make a decision. The guys at the shop are ready to walk out. Robby said it's just a matter of days."

"I'm sure the decision can wait at least a couple of hours while you rest. Want me to run you a bath?"

As I soaked in a tub of bubbles with a hot washcloth over my face, I appreciated Robert's gentleness. But everyone has two sides, and Robert's other side didn't handle conflict well. In fact, one time, when I paid for a new roof at the shop after he suggested just patching the leaks, Robert was clearly offended. He completely avoided me for days.

Fortunately, I'd let Robert know, early in our marriage, that I'd been an abused pawn in my father's control game and didn't intend to let it happen again. Ever.

I could hear Robert whistling as I climbed into bed. He was right about one thing. The decision could wait. Maybe even until the next day . . . after Robert left for work.

My cell phone rang around ten on Tuesday morning. "Hey, Robby."

"Hey, Mom, could you come in to the office today? I'd like to schedule a meeting with some potential investors."

"I'm having lunch with Lettie. I could come after that. But aren't you jumping the gun a bit?"

"Maybe. But I need to proceed with the business side of things. We don't have a lot of time to play with here."

"Why hold a meeting when we don't really know anything for sure?"

"We know for sure that we're about to lose the company. Isn't that enough?"

His irritation was clear. "Listen, Robby. I don't care—"

"Mom."

I stopped.

"I'm sorry. Look, I'm just putting out feelers with this meeting—not making any commitments. The people coming know that. This is common practice. Please trust me."

"So, you've already called the meeting without my approval?"

Silence.

"Never mind, Robby. We'll deal with this when I get there."

CHAPTER 2

My purse rang as I drove the back way to town, and I shoved my hand inside. Lip balm, candy bar wrappers. Finally, I felt the vibrations and pulled it out. "Hello."

"Hola, mi amiga."

I turned off the gravel road onto Highway 10. "Hey, Lettie. Don't tell me you're cancelling."

"No. I'm a block away. But Alyssa and Alexander are with me, and they're getting crabby."

I pressed my lips together and breathed slowly for a second. I needed Lettie's attention today. "Couldn't you tell your daughter no for once?"

A bambino wailed in the background. "Would you rather call it off?"

"I'd rather eat a quiet lunch at Chester's and tell my best friend about the horrible day I had yesterday. Then stop by Walmart for—"

"Do you want to do lunch or not—with the kids? I'm in the parking lot."

"Look in your mirror. I'm right behind you."

I pulled into an open slot, shoved the gearshift into park and climbed out of the truck. "Hang on, girlfriend. Let me help you."

We each hauled a jabbering ten-month-old baby inside and forced their chubby legs into highchairs. They giggled as I tickled their thighs and played Boo! until crackers arrived. "They've grown so much, Lettie. And you've got Alyssa's hair in pigtails already. Look at those ribbons and curls!"

Chester's Café—a real dive, but the food was to die for. Never mind the cracked cement floor and stained paisley wallpaper. What counted were the greasy burgers, fat, crunchy onion rings and sinfully sweet iced tea. Ahhh, my mouth watered as I listened to my lunch sizzle on the grill.

"Thought I was going to run late." Lettie tossed her long black braid over her shoulder and swiped her thick bangs to the side of her face. "Angelica asked me to care for the twins while she shopped. I'm going to surprise her and make a flan during the twins' siesta."

I smiled, secretly envious of Lettie's relationship with her kids. Life was all about work for me. Always had been. "No wonder your kids keep asking you to babysit."

Lettie stuck out her tongue. "Say, did Robert tell you I saw him yesterday at the Taco Shack with some beautiful blonde?"

"Ha-ha. That place is always packed. You have to share a table if you want a seat."

Lettie cocked her head and lifted her eyebrows. "You sure now?"

"What? Something you're not telling me?" Not that I was worried. Robert's interest in the other sex—or any sex, for that matter—had shriveled up and died at least a decade ago. "Did Robert notice you?"

Lettie attempted to hide a smile, but her deep brown eyes danced below dark, bushy eyebrows. "Actually, I made a point to introduce myself to the woman."

"And . . ."

"Not to worry. Just some professor from the university. Kathy Harmin's her name. Robert said they were working on a school project."

"Makes sense." It did make sense, but something niggled at the back of my mind. Robert seldom took a lunch break, let alone went out for a meal.

Lettie glanced at the time as the waitress set our food before us. "I'd say I have fifteen minutes—max—to hear about yesterday. What went wrong? You and Robert mince words?"

I trusted Lettie. Though no one else really understood me, she did. She'd stood by me when the kids were babies and I had no clue how to make them stop crying . . . or how to stop crying, myself, for that matter. She'd taught me to cook when Robert complained about eating T.V. dinners or chicken potpies every evening. Little things . . . Lettie things.

"It's the business." The babies began to fuss. I plunked an ice cube on each tray and handed them spoons as I told Lettie about the truckers' meeting. "Robby insists we need to change everything."

Lettie's piercing gaze demanded my attention. Loving, but firm. "He's right, isn't he? I mean, the trucking industry has outgrown your old-fashioned ways, Biz. You need to let go."

What was the world coming to when even a woman's best friend turned on her? But what would Lettie know? With a doting husband, seven kids and enough grandkids to pack a U-Haul truck, she lived the perfect life. Definitely never had to make the kind of life-and-death decision I faced.

"You okay, Biz?" Lettie turned as Alexander tried to wrestle his way out of the highchair. Lettie pushed him down, hooked the seat belt and handed him a couple of my French fries. "Face it, you would never change a thing unless forced to, would you?"

I feigned a scowl. "I'm a mess, aren't I?"

Lettie refused to meet my gaze.

"What?"

She looked up with a mischievous glint in her eyes. "Una pregunta grande—a loaded question. No matter how I answer, you're sure to be upset."

She was right. I crossed my eyes and bobbed my head at the babies to make them laugh. "Hey, kids. Your Abuela thinks I need a life. But all I've ever known is the trucking company. Could you tell me where to begin?"

Lettie knuckle-rapped the table. "Isn't there something you've always wanted to do when you retired?"

"Oh, sure, I have a dream. I want to buy an island where I can hang out by myself. No expectations. No disappointments."

Lettie opened her mouth to say something but leaped from her chair instead, hoisted a choking Alyssa from the highchair, flipped her upside down and struck her firmly between the shoulder blades. A triangular-shaped wedge of cracker flew across the table and directly into my glass of water.

The baby's screams filled the restaurant. Lettie groaned. "I guess lunch is over."

Alexander sat spellbound, watching his sister arch her back and bob her head from side to side to gain freedom from Lettie's tight grasp.

I handed him another French fry for good behavior, unstrapped him and picked him up. "I'll carry the good one. We can try again next week if you can find a day when none of your kids con you into doing their job."

"Drop it, Biz." Lettie headed out the door. "It's not your business."

I buckled the cute little guy in his car seat and returned to finish my meal. Maybe it wasn't my business, but Lettie was my friend, and it ticked me off when her kids took advantage of her. I pushed my polluted water aside. At least my sandwich hadn't been ruined.

I sank my teeth into the toasted bun and juicy meat. Ahhh. "Elizabeth?"

Nobody who called me friend, called me Elizabeth. I swiveled around.

Olivia Delanie, a woman from church, sauntered over in a darling plaid shirt and white walking shorts. She glanced at Lettie's enchilada platter. "Someone with you?"

I slapped my hand to my lips and answered with a mouthful of half-chewed food. "Lettie. She just left."

Olivia smiled politely, plopped her skinny little bottom down and motioned for the waitress. "I'm famished. Is Lettie okay?"

I nodded and chewed rapidly, whisking a napkin to my face to keep the mustard that dribbled out the side of my mouth from landing on my faded gray Indiana University T-shirt. A gulp of chocolate shake eased my food down the track. I was going to start a serious diet.

Olivia handed Lettie's dish to a waitress. "I'll take a glass of unsweetened tea and a tossed salad with light house dressing, please."

The food on my plate suddenly looked larger than life. I was sure I recognized a reflection of my chins in the pickle slice. Why couldn't Olivia see she was ruining my meal and have the decency to leave?

The waitress returned with Olivia's salad and tea. "Could you put this food in a box to go, please?" I smiled, patting my belly. "I guess my eyes were bigger than my stomach."

"Can I get you anything else?"

"Some diet water?" No. Those words had not come from my mouth. But from the look on the waitress' face, I knew they had. "Just kidding. I'll pick up my food at the register when I pay."

"Sure." The red-faced girl scurried away.

Olivia crisscrossed her fork and knife and sliced her salad into miniscule pieces. "Are you going to sign up for the Golden Oldies ladies' meeting at church this Thursday?"

"Golden Oldies?" I laughed. "I'm actually not as old as I look."

She didn't get it. At least she didn't smile like she got it. She simply wiped her not-even-dirty mouth and said, "Anyone fifty or older is invited."

Okay. So that included me by four years. Not that the group's name thrilled me. Nonetheless, I smiled appropriately. "I'll need to check my calendar. I might have an exercise class or some other fun planned for that morning. Have many signed up?"

"Just about everyone who qualifies." Olivia opened a cracker and waved it in the air as she spoke. "Of course, I'm only forty-seven, but I took the group five years ago when the church was going through some changes and there was no one else available."

I nodded, short on words.

"And then, there's Pastor's wife. She's only forty-four, but naturally, she's expected to attend all ladies' meetings. Right?"

Not in my opinion.

Olivia popped part of the cracker into her mouth and sipped her tea.

I hardly knew Olivia. Until lately, I'd only darkened the church doors on Sunday mornings, weaseling out with Robert while the choir sang amen to the final hymn. Not that I was antisocial. I was simply too busy for chitchat and meaningless relationships.

But a few months ago, Lettie insisted I take one day a week off from work, reasoning that Robby could pretty much run the office. Said I needed to make some new friends—attend Bible study with her at the church. Well, I hadn't actually made it to a Bible study yet. Maybe it was the friend thing I wanted to avoid. Or maybe it was the shame I felt for calling on God only when I was in hot water.

Noticing Olivia's full mouth, I executed my escape. "I hate to scoot out on you like this, but I've got a meeting at the office. I enjoyed visiting with you."

I never allow myself to tell out-and-out lies, but what could I say? I tossed Olivia a final wave, slapped a twenty-dollar bill on the counter and hurried away with my takeout box.

My glasses fogged as I stepped into the stifling heat. And this was only the beginning of June. I might as well cross Lettie off my Fave Five for the next eight weeks. With her grandkids out of school, her house would be busier than a bus depot.

Problem was . . . Lettie was my Fave Five. Numbers one, two, three, four and five. What would I ever do with the long days ahead if I did decide to let Robby run the office?

With one foot on the running board, I wrapped my fingers around the sweltering steering wheel and hiked my oversized load up into the cab, started the engine and flipped the air conditioning vent shut to avoid searing my nose hairs.

I texted Lettie while I waited for the cab to cool. Love you, girlfriend. Sorry for my big mouth.

My stomach ached. Never mind I hadn't eaten much lunch. This pain radiated from a deeper source—like from knowing everything you'd ever worked for was about to go down the drain.

I thought about Robby's plan. My only option, really. But nobody was going to push Biz McNeely around. I might concede . . . but on my terms. Like I was simply ready to move on with life. Good grief. It wasn't like I was signing the place away completely. I'd still have the final say about everything.

No big deal, right? Then why did everything in me want to smash this truck right into a stupid brick wall? I punched the seat beside me.

I had a few minutes before the meeting so I sat down at my desk to flip through a stack of mail.

Robby wandered into my office. "Glad we have a little time to talk about what's about to happen."

"Really going to be that bad?"

Robby lowered himself into a chair. "No. I just want to prepare you for all the legal talk. I've asked Cameron Huff to attend. He's a corporate attorney with experience in consolidations. You remember him from church?"

"Name doesn't ring a bell. Not like I wander far from my pew."

"You're a real puzzle, sometimes, Mom."

"What?"

"Oh, you're so large-and-in-charge around here and then practically shy around people you don't know."

Spot on. But I waved him off. "You're not going to pay this attorney, are you? Because I keep Morris Ellison on retainer. We go way back."

"Yes, and we need to talk about Mr. Ellison."

My spine straightened. "He's not good enough?"

Robby shut his eyes, inhaled and exhaled a long, slow audible breath. "Mom, we're talking 21st century negotiations. W-a-y over Ellison's head. In fact—"

"No." I pounded my desk. "I am not terminating Ellison. For heaven's sakes, he's older than I am. Find something for him to do."

"Okay. Okay." Robby's hands flew in the air, palms forward, as if to push back some invisible force. "I'll give him plenty of paperwork to keep track of."

My mind reeled with unacceptable responses. "I suppose you consider me outdated as well."

Robby's face reddened.

"You know, Robby, your almighty technology might be more efficient, but a machine will never match wisdom gained only by experience."

"Mom." Every muscle in Robby's face appeared tight, as if he were choking on a thought. "I need to ask you a huge favor."

I hated seeing Robby struggle. "What do you need?"

With elbows resting on the arms of his chair, Robby linked his fingers, leaned forward and arched his back until I heard it pop. Then he relaxed and stared at his hands until just a millisecond before he spoke. "When we go into the meeting, can you let me do the talking? Just sit back and listen?"

His suggestion rendered me speechless. Well, that would work. If he could do that again just before the meeting.

Okay, Biz. This isn't funny. Escape route closed. Return to reality immediately.

Robby watched my face carefully. "Before you object, let me try to explain."

He described what he called the legal and financial implications of the corporation he was proposing. Concerns the other small companies would most likely present as well as research he'd done on the current sales market. "You're not up on the latest research, Mom, and you really might cause more damage than good by asking questions or offering your opinions. Does that make any sense at all?"

He had to know this didn't sit well with me.

He stood, not waiting for my answer. "You can write down any ideas or questions you have during the meeting, of course, and talk to me afterward. You know I'm always going to need your help, right?"

"Whatever." And we both knew that meant I would consider his request but could guarantee nothing.

CHAPTER 3

I slipped into the conference room and sat by the door.

A perfectly postured, red-haired woman caught my attention. Dressed in a rust colored jacket, off-white shell, khaki slacks and heels, she appeared to have life together.

Not that she was perfectly shaped or anything—the kind of thing that usually impressed me. She looked to be at least as old as me, if not older. I tried to imagine her with gray hair. No makeup. Hard to tell for sure.

No, the woman's demeanor peaked my interest. She actively participated. Added her input. Spoke words of encouragement and appreciation for comments made.

I flipped to the opening of the document to find her name. Quinn Shoaf—Chief Executive Officer: Harper-Klein Trucking. Indianapolis, Indiana.

Whoo-hoo. The largest firm among us, double the size of mine. Why on earth would she consider this consolidation?

Robby flipped on a PowerPoint slide. "The next issue we need to discuss is where we'll house our central office. I've marked each of our locations on this map, and it's clear to see that Harper-Klein Trucking, in Indianapolis, is the most convenient for all of us. We've run the statistics on cost control, city taxes, building permits and other factors, and, without a doubt, this is our best option."

Heads nodded.

"Take a few moments to discuss this among yourselves before we move on to the next slide."

The room broke into conversation as these bigwigs—money movers who most likely knew nothing at all about how to actually run a trucking company—debated the topic at hand.

I studied the proposal document to avoid eye contact. But Queen Quinn missed the clue.

"Hi, Elizabeth." She extended her hand. "I'm Quinn Shoaf."

I shook her hand. "Biz McNeely."

Quinn sat beside me. "I'll bet you're proud of your son. The consolidation proposal he's put together is one of the best plans I've ever seen. And believe me, I've examined a lot of different options in the last couple of years."

"Really?" I searched her eyes for signs of duplicity but found only genuine enthusiasm. "I'm surprised you'd even consider the venture. Surely you're doing well enough on your own without dragging all these little guys into your fold."

She studied her hands, and I noticed her painted fingernails were clipped short and showed wear and tear. Her jewelry simple—gold posts, a single band on the fourth finger of her left hand and a small cross pin on her lapel. Broke every presumption I'd formed in the last few minutes.

"Aren't you worried they'll pull you down?"

She lifted her warm eyes. "Is that what you're afraid of?"

Excuse me? Who was this woman to invade my personal space in my own conference room? Thankfully, I quickly realized my offense was ungrounded. After all, hadn't I just asked her basically the same question?

"I think so. I've saved my pennies for over twenty-five years, and now my son wants me to trust him with the majority of that investment. Put my retirement fund in jeopardy. How can that be wise?"

Quinn's eyebrows dipped. "Have you looked through the numbers yourself? Is there a specific area of concern?"

Right. Like I would understand if I did examine the figures. Robby hadn't even tried to explain them to me. Was he that sure I was too feeble-minded to understand?

"You know, Quinn, I'm just going to be honest."

She smiled.

"I've run my business old-school. Paper and pencil accounting. Handshake commitments. Telephone communication. Postage stamp billings. It's worked all these years, and I didn't bother to keep updated on technology."

"Of course." Quinn nodded. "Exactly as I began."

"But . . ." I fought to restrain an unexpected gush of emotion . . . "You obviously moved on. Bettered yourself."

Quinn touched my arm. "Moved on, yes. Bettered myself? I'm not sure. Maybe changed with the times. But I, too, have always preferred the old-school methods."

This woman's transparency unnerved me. I looked at the door. "Excuse me. I really ought to check on the office help during this break."

I hightailed it to the break room for a cup of coffee. Everything in me wanted to give up. But I'd fought for the company for too long and I wasn't ready to concede.

The meeting resumed and twenty, nail-biting minutes later, I caved. Robby opened a discussion on whether employee healthcare should be covered at the corporate level or by the individual entities. Most opted for the corporate route, and I saw my life savings going right down the drain for a bunch of truckers and office help I didn't even know.

I would have politely raised my hand to speak, but I knew the chance of Robby calling on me was about as good as locating a matching hubcap for my pickup at a Goodwill store. So I jumped in at the first pause.

"It seems to me we are going to need some fair method of guaranteeing that the larger businesses like my own don't end up carrying the weight for the smaller struggling ones."

Did I say someone pushed the freeze button? Because that's exactly what happened next. Were my words not clear? I opened my mouth to say more, but Robby beat me to it.

"That's a wise consideration, Elizabeth."

Elizabeth? As if he'd somehow entered this world without humbly sliding between my legs? Good grief, was I no longer this kid's mother?

"I can assure you our accountants have already worked this situation out. In fact, if you'll turn to page seven in your proposal copy, you'll find the guidelines spelled out clearly."

Robby smiled around the room as he spoke, ending his charismatic little journey with a simple nod in my direction. Clean. Curt. Message clear.

The kid should have been a politician. But he hadn't won my vote. On the contrary, I was more determined than ever to exercise my God-given right to free speech. Not to mention the fact that I owned the company that would basically be footing the bill for the whole adventure.

Next item on the agenda: updating technology at every level. I listened as long as I could to those highfalutin computer nerds describe what we supposedly needed to succeed. Hard drives, system analysts . . . way beyond me.

Finally, I'd had my fill. My commitment to honor Robby's gag-order no longer made sense.

This time I stood to take the floor. The anxiety in Robby's eyes increased with each step I took toward the front of the room. He stood, too, the look in his eyes silently pleading . . . "Mom—"

But with a nod of my head, I motioned for him to be seated. "As you know, I am the sole owner of this company. Robby will one day sit at the helm, but that transfer of power has yet to happen, and I'm finished pretending I don't have a say in this room. I don't care if I am old-fashioned and undereducated in the field of technology. I know what it takes to run a profitable business. And, while I admire your education and expertise, I'm not willing to sit back and allow you to make critical decisions without my input or approval."

Hear a pin drop? Good grief, you could have heard a tear fall. Which I was afraid would happen soon if I didn't get out of that stuffy room. "You all carry on. I'm leaving, but please remember that the final answer lies in my hands where this company is concerned. Call me when you're ready to talk."

My mind shifted into autopilot. I backed the truck out of the parking lot and pulled onto the two-lane highway. Acrid bile rose into my throat as I tried to wrap my mind around what had just transpired. I refused to give up. I would go back to school . . . hire someone to take care of—

Horns blared around me. I jumped to my senses just in time to realize I'd drifted into the opposite lane. My heart pounded as I swerved back into my lane and pulled off the road. Leaning my head back, I inhaled until the air reached my lungs, then held it there until stillness spread into my extremities. "Oh, God. I need some help here."

Hazel was separating pieces to a puzzle when I arrived that afternoon. I laughed until I peed my pants when I saw the picture on the box. Fats Domino at the keyboard, wearing only sunglasses and a bright red Speedo.

"Where in the world did you get that?"

Hazel grinned. "My son ordered it online. Said I needed to exercise my brain cells more."

I spotted a corner piece and reached over Hazel shoulder to set it aside. "Three hundred pieces. Think you're up to it?"

"Don't guess there's any hurry. Besides, if all I do is sit here and relive the thrill on Blueberry Hill, I'll be exercising brain cells . . . and a few other cells to boot."

I pushed a few blackish puzzle pieces to a pile of similar pieces. "I need a few of your brain cells to help me sort something out, Hazel."

"Life dealing you some bum cards?"

"More like a dead hand. My company isn't doing so well. Only viable option seems to be stepping away from the helm and handing control to my son."

Hazel fit four or five pieces together to start the border. "You don't trust him?"

"I'm not sure, Hazel. It's been so long since I've trusted anyone but myself."

Hazel looked up with warm eyes and placed her frail hand on mine. "You've implied before that you had a painful childhood. That why you don't trust others?"

I could only nod. Though I didn't want to talk about it, I knew the painful childhood experiences had shaped who I was today. Caused me to strike back when I felt threatened.

Hazel returned to her puzzle and worked for several minutes. "I'm here, if and when you want to talk."

I browned some hamburger as I thought about Robby's plan to restructure the company and Hazel's offer to listen to my unreachable pain.

I did need help . . . in so many areas of my life. Why, then, was I dead-set against accepting it? Why did I feel so driven to prove I could live life on my own?

Easing stiff spaghetti noodles into boiling water, I allowed the steam to wet my face. Loosen my tense muscles. "I'm so tired of life, God."

The garage door rumbled open. I turned off the burners and hurried to the basement to transfer a load of laundry to the dryer. And to get my mind on safer ground.

By the time I came upstairs, Robert had changed into shorts and was in the backyard mowing the lawn. Looked like a great night to eat outdoors.

I threw a salad together and carried our dishes to the patio. The fragrance of freshly cut grass and the slow, rhythmic whoosh of the sprinkler melded in my ears, a soothing tonic. I needed this tonight.

Robert offered a short prayer.

"The yard looks gorgeous."

"Thanks." He placed his napkin in his lap and glanced around the yard. "You know, I've done about all I can do with this little patch of grass. I'm itching to do more."

I kept my eyes on my plate so I wouldn't spit excitement all over Robert. "As in finding a home with more backyard?"

"Oh, my, no. More like getting involved in the neighborhood association in hopes of restoring the neighborhood."

So much for moving to the country. I couldn't speak. Simply nodded as I quickly crammed a bite of spaghetti into my mouth. A legitimate excuse for not replying. But a bite that would take extreme effort to swallow. Even as I pushed the gummy mess around in my mouth, a crazy barrage of tears threatened to spill from my eyes.

But I fought back, and, fortunately, Robert missed the entire surge of emotion as he concentrated on his meal. Gave me time to regain my composure . . . and discreetly empty my mouthful into a napkin.

"I still need to edge and trim the bushes. Maybe I'll do that after dinner."

"You definitely have more energy than me."

Robert laughed and reached for the salad dressing. "I just know I need to get it done tonight because I'm going to be busy tomorrow night."

"You have a board meeting?"

"No, a dinner at the university. I didn't mention it?"

"Not that I remember."

"We're awarding scholarships to incoming freshmen. There's an extra seat at the head table. Want to come?"

"Get all dolled up, eat their famous baked chicken and rice plate and listen to speeches all evening? No thanks. Unless you want me there, that is."

"Ooh. You make it sound so exciting. No, you stay home and enjoy your evening. I'll go suffer for both of us."

With a pout on my face, I ran a pretend bow over the pretend violin cradled in my left arm and hummed the first few bars of "Fur Elise."

Robert smiled as he took another slice of garlic bread from the platter. "You do anything interesting today?"

"Robby asked me to attend a meeting of possible investors in his new program."

Robert swatted a honeybee with his rolled-up newspaper and flicked it to the ground. "How did that go?"

My shoulders tensed. "Robby actually asked me to stay quiet during the meeting. Said I needed to catch up on the latest research before I could ask pertinent questions."

Robert scratched his balding head and slid his hand down and across his thick neck. "Sounds wise to me."

I stopped just short of dropping my glass. "Seriously?"

As always, Robert clammed up. He would wait until I repeated myself in a normal tone.

Counting to three had little effect on my flappable temper. Nevertheless, I managed to control my volume. "Why can't you stand up for me just once?"

Robert chewed his food deliberately, washed it down with coffee and fixed his eyes on mine. "You don't need me to stand up for you, Biz. You never have and never will." His words were gentle, but firm. "The truth is, honey, I doubt you'll ever allow yourself to need anyone."

I shoved my napkin onto my plate and stood. "Well, thanks for that, Robert. You've made my day complete."

So much for a tranquil spirit.

I pulled a daily devotional guide from the nightstand drawer when I woke Wednesday morning. Never mind the date was three years old. I hadn't needed help with my life three years ago. The business was running smoothly, and the business was my life.

Surely there was some way to save the company without turning it over to Robby. I'd be glad to promote him. He could call himself Vice President, for all I cared.

I grabbed my cell phone and sent Robby a text to let him know I wouldn't be in for a couple of days. Needed some time to think. Would make my decision and meet with him on Friday.

Hoping to improve my mood, I opened the devotional and read the scripture at the top. "I created your inmost being. You are fearfully and wonderfully made."

"Sure, Lord." I shoved the booklet back in the drawer. "You may have created me that way, but I've obliterated your design with all my screw-ups."

I fumbled through my closet for an old, faded pink and purple muumuu. Talk about comfortable. The girls would love hanging out in this.

I stepped into the floor-length flowered tent, pulled the zipper and headed for the kitchen. Diet Day Number One: tossed salad, apple slices and a cup of coffee. Someday I would look like Olivia.

With nothing else to do, I stretched out on the sofa, flipped the television on and tucked an afghan under my head. My neck went stiff as I considered the truth. I didn't have a life. I knew nothing but the trucking business, and my relationship with my husband and kids was basically null and void.

Fearfully and wonderfully made . . . the words of the devotional came to mind and begged to snuggle into my spirit. I knew God's words were true. He said he created me with a purpose. Was there still hope?

I really didn't like myself. Tears begged to flow, but I couldn't go there. I couldn't allow myself to become undone day after day. Life was too unkind, and I had too many decisions to make. I really did need to stay in control.

CHAPTER 4

"Mom?"

I opened my eyes. Morgan towered over me, her wavy golden hair falling across my shoulder. "Hey, Morgan." I glanced at my watch. Four-thirty, already? "What are you doing here?"

"I just stopped by to borrow your waffle maker."

I must look a sight. I pushed my hair behind my ears.

Morgan confirmed my suspicions. "What on earth is that dreadful getup you're wearing? Don't I remember that thing from my childhood?"

My lip curled. "It's a muumuu—the most comfortable thing I own. Nobody's asking you to wear it."

Morgan tossed her Gucci purse onto a chair. "Thank goodness!"

I followed Morgan into the kitchen where she grabbed a can of V8 juice from the refrigerator. I opted for Oreos.

"Aren't you going to change before Daddy gets home?" She waved her hand across my body like I was a prize on Wheel of Fortune. "He shouldn't be forced to . . ." Morgan set her drink down. "So, I'm just going to be honest, Mom."

"Go ahead, Morgan. You've never held back before."

"Wonder who I learned that from?"

I shrugged. "So?"

Morgan crossed the room and wrapped her arms around me before pushing me back and examining me from head to toe. "You need to fix yourself up, Mom. You can't afford to go any further downhill. I'm off Tuesday. Let's go shopping."

Even as I smiled, I imagined clawing her beguiling brown eyes right out of her head. Twenty-nine years old, and she knew it all. Her and that tall, slim body she'd inherited from her father's side of the family. "We'll see about the shopping. I might be busy."

"Hmmm." She toyed with the cross around her neck. "I've heard that before. Like all my life."

"Oh, please. Kill the drama. I think Dad keeps the waffle maker in the cabinet beside the oven."

"Nope." Morgan slammed the cabinet door. "Got any second guesses? I'm in a hurry."

"Not a clue. Just keep looking."

I left her rummaging through the cabinets and headed to the bedroom where I caught a glimpse of myself in the dresser mirror. So, Robert deserved better? Well, maybe. But there was only so much better things could get at this point. I needed to get serious about my diet.

Morgan hollered goodbye. Something snapped shut in my heart when the front door clicked. Not physically or anything. Just an overwhelming sadness. A sense of being totally alone in the world.

"Crazy woman. You really do need to get a life."

My cell phone buzzed. A text from Hazel's granddaughter. Home Health Care is here for Grandma's therapy and bath. You don't need to come over this evening.

I checked my other messages, expecting one from Robby. But it wasn't there. Had to appreciate him giving me some space. Or maybe he was too angry to talk to me.

Whatever. Maybe I'd surprise Robert and accompany him to his awards dinner. Take the high road. Forgive him for his unkind remark last night about me not needing anyone but myself. Do my part to ease the tension between us.

I laid my black jacket and slacks on the bed along with a light-yellow blouse. Then, on impulse, I dug through my dusty jewelry box for a solitaire diamond necklace Robert gave me for our twentieth wedding anniversary.

After I showered and dressed, I threw on a bit of makeup and attacked my doo with a fistful of mousse. Definitely a better look than the muumuu, and a huge step out of my comfort zone. But maybe that was okay.

I buzzed into the kitchen when I heard the garage door open, stopping short when Robert stepped inside with a Macy's sack under his arm. "Is that for me?"

Robert's pale face went red clear to the roots of his wavy white hair. With the green shirt he was wearing, he would have made a perfect Hallmark Christmas ornament. "Uh, no. It's actually just a new shirt I bought for myself."

"You went shopping?"

Robert set the sack on the table. "Don't make too big of a deal about it, Biz. Someone mentioned Macy's was having a sale, so I stopped by on my way home."

Creepy-crawlies invaded my body as I followed Robert to the bedroom. I wasn't even sure why. Maybe just a gut feeling. "I thought I'd come with you to the awards banquet."

Robert spun on his heel. "You what?"

His eyes showed white clear around the irises as he pressed his right hand to his leg and rubbed his thumb back and forth.

After thirty-four years of marriage, I recognized the gesture. Something was definitely wrong. "You don't want me to go?"

"It's not that." His eyes relaxed as he smiled. "You look beautiful, by the way. I'm sorry this isn't going to work out."

I blushed. "Thanks."

Robert took off his shirt and threw it in the clothes hamper. "Last night you said you didn't want to go."

He closed the door and turned on the shower.

I sat on the bed, my neck muscles tight. Why had Robert reacted like that?

In a few moments, he walked out in a pair of shorts, drying his hair with a blue and white striped towel.

"Why don't you want me to accompany you to the banquet? And why did you go buy a new shirt? You know that isn't like you."

"Good heavens, honey. Stop making such a big deal out of this. I knew you weren't coming, so I invited someone else to sit in your seat at the head table."

I silently counted to three. "Someone else?"

Robert inhaled deeply and released the air in a steady whoosh through clenched teeth. He returned to the bathroom, tossed the towel to the floor and reached for his hairbrush.

I stood in the doorway. "Someone else as in one of your students?"

"Someone else as in a female professor. Kathy Harmin. You remember her, the head of the English department. One of the students plans to dedicate a poem to her."

Taco Shack Kathy Harmin? "So, what about the shirt? You just decide to spruce up a bit more than usual for Kathy Harmin?"

Robert walked to the closet and pulled out a pair of gray dress pants and a matching tie. "The shirt's a joke. We all decided to wear pink tonight because the chancellor shows up that way at every banquet. I didn't own a pink shirt, so I stopped at Macy's."

He threw the hanger on the bed. "Satisfied?"

"Whatever." I tromped to the living room and stared at the news channel until Robert left. Disgusted with myself for dropping the matter so quickly, I padded to the kitchen to heat up my leftovers from Chester's. So much for the diet. It was one thing to cut back. But this kind of stress called for more, and I sure wasn't going to put my health in danger just to lose a few pounds.

As I rinsed my dishes, I spotted a magazine on the counter. Morgan must have forgotten it. The bold headlines read: GLARING SIGNS OF A HOPELESS MARRIAGE!

Three lines in, I realized how easily I could have written the article. I'd lived the life for years. Not that anyone outside the family had caught on. Robert and I weren't total social misfits. We knew how to play the game with neighbors and colleagues—even church members at Heather Ridge Community Church.

I thought about Kathy Harmin as I read, and my body broke into a sweat.

Sign #1: Spouse keeps secrets and is easily irritated when you ask questions.

Sign #2: Spouse answers cell phone in private—a primary sign of marital unfaithfulness.

Sign #3:   Spouse gives up on relationship—exhibits a sudden need for space and appears excessively annoyed, frustrated or unhappy.

Did this writer interview Robert personally?

As the weight of what I assumed was reality pressed in, I suddenly felt old. My eyes burned, and my pulse thumped at my temples. I crept to the bedroom, shut the drapes and climbed into bed. Pulling the cool sheets up around my shoulders, I buried my face in the pillow. First the business. Now my marriage.

Robert moved through the house quietly when he returned. Probably didn't want to wake me and face the music. I waited until he slipped under the covers to ask about his evening. "Did you enjoy your dinner?"

"Mmmm." Robert rolled from his back to his side—away from me.

"Goodnight, honey," I mocked. "Thanks for asking."

I turned on the fan beside the bed. Morning would come, and we'd talk. I snuggled into my pillow. But as I tried to relax, a knot seemed to sink into the deepest cleft of my chest. I'd never felt anything like that before, and it scared me.

"Honey." I tapped Robert's shoulder, but he was already snoring soundly.

I took several deep, slow breaths. No pain shot through my chest, up my neck or down my left arm. Must not be a heart attack. My heart quivered a few times and returned to its normal rhythm, so I shut my eyes and fell asleep.

When the doorbell rang the next morning, I ignored it. Most likely a sales person. I fluffed my pillow and started to drift back to sleep when my cell phone rang. Lettie.

"Hey, girlfriend. What's up?"

"Are you going to let me in?"

"Oh, bother." I forgot about the ladies' meeting. I rushed to the front door. "I promise I'll just be a minute."

"I'm early. Wanted to allow for time in case I needed to drag you to the car."

Five minutes later we stepped out the front door, greeted by the all-too-familiar roar from across the street. The neighbor revved the engine on his silver Dodge Ram. Heavy metal music blasted from the open windows as the guy popped his hood and leaned inside. "Hey, kid," he yelled. "Go get me a beer."

A small child with matted brown hair and ragged clothing deserted the pile of rocks he was collecting near the end of the driveway and toddled into the house.

"Filthy grease monkey," I muttered.

Lettie shook her head. "This is why José and I love living in the country."

I bugged my eyes. "Rub it in. Wish Robert would consider moving."

"Wouldn't that be cool? You know, a house near ours went up for sale last night. Over on Soldiers Home Road."

I grabbed Lettie's arm. "Not the white house on the hill with a creek, is it?"

Lettie looked at me with question in her eyes and nodded. "You know the place?"

I walked to the car in a daze. "I used to babysit there when I was a teenager. I actually used to dream I could live there when I grew up."

Lettie started the engine. "Ah, so you do have a dream."

"As in past tense, Lettie."

She cocked her head in disbelief. "No me mientas, mi amiga—uh . . . don't lie to me, girlfriend."

I laughed. "Okay. I'm going to tell you a secret I've never told anyone."

Lettie gripped the steering wheel in mock anxiety.

"There's a big red barn that goes with the house. I've always dreamed of converting part of it into a guest house and opening a home for troubled girls. Just a few at a time. Offer equestrian therapy. Does that sound totally crazy?"

"No loco. Muy excelente!"

Images of the inside of the house filled my mind. The country kitchen with white cabinets and red checkered curtains covering the window over a corner booth. The wide living room with plush brown carpeting and a brick fireplace at one end. Family pictures covering one whole wall in all sizes and colors of frames. Grandparents. Pets. Vacations. School pictures.

"I don't think the place has changed owners since José and I moved to the country, and that's been almost thirty years ago. The couple who lives there is probably in their seventies. Very active, though. They always put out a huge vegetable garden."

"Yes. That would be the Carleton's. I had no idea they still lived there."

Lettie pulled into the church parking lot and parked in the shade. "The home is beautiful from the outside. I'm sure it will sell quickly."

"Yeah." Discouragement stole my thrill as I acknowledged the probability of her words.

CHAPTER 5

Olivia met us at the door. "I'm so glad you came, Elizabeth." She put her arm around my shoulder. "I'm sure there will be enough food this time, but be a dear and call your reservation in next week, okay?"

"No problem." A smile sweet enough to attract ants crossed my face. "I don't intend to eat, though . . . Fasting, you know."

Olivia nodded, allowing her eyes to run a quick sweep over my body. In an instant, I was sure she knew the truth. I had never fasted a day in my life.

"You really didn't need to explain, dear." Olivia flipped her hand forward so it hung from her wrist like a dead rabbit. "After all, fasting is meant to be a private matter."

"Oh, you're so right." My voice fairly tinkled, so determined was I not to lose control. Not to suck back and shoot a loogie right between her beady brown eyes.

I hooked Lettie's arm instead. "Let's go sit down."

Twenty-some chairs were arranged in a circle, several of them filled with antique mamas—the ladies who actually produced my baby-boomer generation when their husbands returned from the war. These dear saints had to be, what, in their eighties and nineties? Wonder if they missed the thrill.

Olivia perched on the edge of her chair like a bird on a power line. Of course, a bird with absolutely no tail feathers.

"Good morning, ladies. I'm so glad you made it."

One glance at Olivia and I'm ready to diet again. Decked out in knee-length purple spandex shorts and a long, striped tee, she looked like she belonged on Sesame Street. I sucked in my cheeks. Both sets.

Olivia folded her hands. "Why don't we begin by sharing about our families and hobbies? Then we'll have a short devotional and discuss future plans for our group."

I did not want to do this. I shifted in my seat, contemplating an escape. No, Lettie would definitely make a scene. Didn't she realize how uncomfortable I felt in new situations with people I barely knew?

Olivia wet her plum-colored beak with a sip of water and jiggled her dainty behind deeper into the chair. Okay. She was probably just getting comfortable, but she definitely appeared desperate to scratch an itch. Like we didn't recognize the dance? I can guarantee you every woman present had been cursed with the insanity itch at one point or another in her life. I'm talking, "Give me Monistat or give me a gun."

Grrrr. Just the thought made my fingernails curl. I forced my thighs together in an attempt to short-circuit the nerves that were zapping a real number on me and willed myself to pay attention.

"I'm Olivia Buford. I've attended Heather Ridge Community Church for twenty-two years and served as Director of our Women's Ministry for five. I'm also in charge of the Teen Bible Quiz team."

I shut my eyelids to roll my eyes in private.

Olivia leaned forward and shined her pearly whites around the circle like she expected paparazzi to burst in and start snapping pictures. "My two children play instruments with the worship team on Sunday mornings. When I'm not busy here or helping my husband, Mac, with the ranch, I enjoy cross-stitch and reading historical biographies."

We were definitely not cut from the same fabric. Not that I ever thought we were. With wavy layers of auburn hair, just enough derriere to provide a sweet sway and a dimpled smile, Olivia had life made.

Shoot. People would like me better, too, if my body resembled hers.

Heads bobbed as Olivia continued. "I must say, being involved in so many areas of the church is quite exhausting."

"Oh, please," I muttered under my breath. "Bring out the clowns."

Lettie shot me a peripheral glare. "There's no entertainment planned."

Olivia turned to her left. "Would you like to go next, Corrine?"

With lively, almond-shaped eyes the same caramel color as her smooth dark skin and a wide smile, Corrine was born to be on a magazine cover. "My name is Corrine Eddington. I've only attended this church for a few months, so I'm not yet involved in ministry."

I was mesmerized by Corrine's beauty. She wore a short-sleeved, cream-colored jacket and matching top and a strand of turquoise and coral stones. Her shiny black hair appeared to be straightened and lay perfectly in place with bangs straggled across her forehead. Even her voice seemed trained and elegant.

"I teach second grade at Miller Elementary but am eager to retire and spend more time with my new husband." She paused for the oohs and ahhs from the group. "We just celebrated our first anniversary. Davis is absolutely the best thing that has ever happened to me."

My eyes caught Corrine's, and I smiled. No use being ugly, but being hitched for one year was a whole different story than being hitched for thirty-four. Everything wears out eventually.

Olivia placed her hand on Corrine's wrist. "Surely you're not of retirement age, Corrine."

Corrine's eyes sparkled. "Oh, yes, I am. Sixty-two and not ashamed to admit it. Age means nothing to me now that I have such a fabulous future ahead of me."

Olivia refolded her hands. "And you have children?"

I stifled a groan. Enough of the Barbara Walters routine, already.

"Oh, yes," Corinne answered. "My daughter Clarise is twenty-six and is seriously dating the kindest young man around."

Lucky her. Darkness invaded my thoughts as I considered my own daughter, Morgan. What did I wish for her? A life like mine? Trapped in a sensible marriage with no romance—spending every moment of her existence working for the almighty dollar?

My hands itched as I desperately tried to come up with something worth saying about myself. Maybe I should slip out for a drink of water. I stood and . . .

"Biz? Are you okay?"

It took me a moment to realize I'd fainted. Ladies around me speculated.

"She's fasting."

"Yes, I heard. Could be a sugar problem."

"She is quite overweight."

Brilliant deduction. Too bad I wasn't deaf as well. I opened my eyes.

Lettie assisted me to my chair and dug a package of peanut butter crackers from her purse. "You probably need protein."

I popped a cracker into my mouth, catching Olivia's eye in the process. Condescending old bird. Like I didn't know what she was thinking.

But she smiled, and I smiled back.

"I do hope you're okay, Elizabeth. Why don't we save your turn to share for later?"

So maybe it was Elizabeth with Olivia. Didn't intend to call her a friend, anyway. At least she had the kindness to sense my embarrassment. I nodded and the conversation jumped to Lettie.

"I'm Lettie Hernandez. I sing in the choir and lead the nursery. I guess you might say my family is my hobby. With seven grown children, I stay busy watching my grandbabies and running the older grandkids to piano lessons, swimming lessons and t-ball practice. Lettie fumbled with the pages of her Bible. "I'm not sure I'll be able to attend every week, but I'll be here when I can."

I discretely jabbed Lettie as the next lady began. "Might need to tell your kids to make other plans."

Lettie ignored me.

Seven more ladies. I seriously needed to use the bathroom. The next woman caught my attention. A real hoot—long blonde bangs, spritzed into spikes, clung to her round face, while her crown was covered with deep purple curls. I liked her already, and my decision had nothing to do with the fact that she appeared to be a good three inches shorter than me and every bit as heavy. Lord knows, fat women do appreciate like-company.

"My name is Frieda Parker. I recently moved here from Virginia. I'm a critical care nurse at Stafford Memorial Hospital. My spouse died eight years ago, and now that the kids are raised and I've hit the big five-o, I'm actively searching for a new husband."

The simultaneous gasps could have filled an oxygen tank.

"But, dear," one shriveled little saint dared. She had to be in her eighties. Cherry rouge blared from her weathered cheeks. "Why would you want to do that?"

She laughed out loud. A wonderful, bubbly trickle of amusement that made me want to join in. Her amusing hazel eyes reminded me of a blue-light special at K-Mart. I needed to spend some time with this woman. We were sure to be kindred spirits.

"I loved my dear husband, but he drove me nuts most of the time. I wouldn't risk that again for anything in the world. God rest his soul, the man was brain-dead when it came to common sense, and . . ." With a grin as wide as a friendly old Jack-o-lantern, she dropped her voice to a mere whisper. "His manly batteries ran out just as mine reached a full charge."

"Little Sister!" This came from the woman beside her. The thin woman slapped a starched hankie to her chest. "How can you say such a thing? Right here in church!"

Whoo-hoo. Laugh-out-loud, we did.

Obviously on a roll, Little Sister continued. "I'm telling you, thirty years ago that well went dry!"

By now, I was sure mine weren't the only wet pants in the group. Or Depends. Whatever. I scanned the room. Even the seemingly primmest smiled.

Everyone except Olivia. Come to think of it, though, I never had seen a bird smile. She straightened her back, lifted her chin and simply folded her hands in her lap as she waited for the room to quiet.

One by one, the ladies sobered. Like a flippin' evangelist was in the room. Come to Jesus. Fall on your knees. Good grief, you'd think we'd cussed in front of the Pope or something the way those ladies fell in line.

So much for Golden Oldies. Looked more like a room full of Disabled Veterans. Anyway, from that point on, the introductions continued in an appropriate, Christian-woman-like manner. But when I glanced in Little Sister's direction, she winked. How I longed to be sweet like her.

Renee was the last to speak. "I guess you're all aware I'm the pastor's wife."

Complemented by a soft shade of rose lipstick, Renee's smile appeared genuine. Her hair, too. Blonde to the root, the thick waves fell softly around her sun-tanned face and slightly-thick neck. Her appearance and gentle manner suggested a fulfilled, contented lifestyle, but her tiny blue eyes, darting about as she spoke, betrayed that impression.

"My first priority is to care for my dear husband and our seventeen-year-old daughter, Lindsey. After that, I teach a toddler class, try to keep the church kitchen clean, answer phones in the office and deliver meals to shut-ins. If any of you ever need anything, please call, and I'll do my best to help you."

Oh, my. I'd met pleasers before. Made me wonder what dark secrets powered her hidden need to be appreciated and liked. Maybe I'd try to befriend her, now that I had time on my hands.

That thought surprised me. Okay … it actually scared the willies out of me. So not my make and model to show interest in helping someone else, especially with personal issues.

With the introductions complete, Olivia sat up even taller, opened her Bible and read some Scriptures about Jesus rising early to pray. I swear, if she got any straighter, she was going to transform into a life-sized paper doll.

That's where I overshadowed her completely, thanks to the girls. The woman practically had two backs. I crossed my arms, cupped my elbows and squeezed a slight thank you.

The room suddenly went quiet. What had I missed?

There sat the bird, sniffing and wiping her nose, apparently unable to continue speaking. She cleared her throat. "When I think about what Jesus went through for me, I can't help but berate myself for doing so little. Jesus gave his all to crowds of hurting people. He had to be exhausted. Yet he still made time to pray—to be refilled with his Father's power." Olivia swallowed hard. "I'm so guilty of running in my own power instead of allowing God's power to work through me."

She did not just say that. Perfect Olivia? Not happy with herself? Okay, maybe I shouldn't have placed her on a pedestal. Maybe it was my stinkin' insecurity I actually needed to address. But right now I had a bigger problem to deal with.

Olivia droned on about sewing days and a dozen other ideas. Meanwhile, my bladder filled. By the time Olivia finished, my sweaty cotton underwear stuck to me like the wrapper on a stale Tootsie Roll. I'd need to roll them off like a doggone pair of bobby socks.

I forced myself to think along different lines. The thought of rolling my underwear and releasing the pressure was doing a trick on me, and I wasn't sure how much more my mini pad could safely absorb.

For months, I'd considered shucking the stupid things and switching to plain old kitchen sponges. What were we doing to our environment? I don't care if they did come with pretty little wrappers. None of it would decompose. But sponges. We're talking earth-friendly, and way more protection.

"Biz."

Ladies were migrating toward the next room. Meeting must be over. Lettie leaned in my direction. "Girl, where were you? You look like a kid at a rained-out Easter egg hunt."

"I gotta go."

"You okay?"

I ignored her question and headed for the ladies' room.

"Oh, you mean you've got to go . . . go."

Maintaining one extended Kegel, I burst into a stall. With the touch of a master, I rolled my polyester-elastic-waistband slacks, underwear and all, over the hills. Gravity took over, and I plopped my behind onto the stool just in time. "Yes."

"Biz?"

Lettie stuck her black sequined sandal under the door. The same sandals she'd worn for years. The woman had absolutely no taste. At least that's what Morgan said. I didn't care. Lettie sure wouldn't hang with me if stupid stuff like that mattered to her.

"Be out in a minute."

"You're not dizzy again, are you?"

"No. I think I just got too hungry."

Lettie stepped away from the door. "You need to tee a dotter." She was obviously reapplying her lipstick. She smacked her lips and turned on the water. "You know, to be sure nothing else is wrong."

"I will." About to stand, I felt another urge. Post residual flow, my gynecologist called it. A real pain sometimes, but thankfully, we ladies don't end up with a bulls-eye on the front of our clothing. I'm telling you, if I were a man, I'd wrap the thing. I wouldn't take any chances.

Lettie backed up when I came out of the stall so I could wash my hands. I peeked in the mirror to be sure we were alone. "Let's get lunch somewhere else."

"Hmmm?"

"I can't take another minute of this boring meeting. Talk about control. Olivia probably placed scriptural conversation topics on the lunch tables."

Lettie's forehead tightened. Like when your bowels decide to move in the middle of the grocery. You know. You're forced to make this critical decision. Finish shopping, or shove the cart to the side and run for the car. Because nobody in their right mind lets go of that in public. Least not me.

But Lettie didn't budge. I tossed my towel into the trash and turned. "Really, Lettie, aren't you like totally pumped about making quilts? I mean, do these ladies ever have fun?"

"I'm sure Olivia does her best."

"Oh, yeah. Probably followed the same game plan since the group started. We should call ourselves the Left-Behind Girls."

"Biz, why don't we—"

"I'm serious. What about scrapbooking or stamping or just eating out? I'm all about praying together, but I don't think Jesus meant for us to live on our knees. And did you see her face when the little white-haired lady cracked a funny about her erectile-dysfunctional old man? Olivia reacted like a total prude."

Lettie followed me out of the bathroom. "Come on, Biz. Let's go eat."

"Lettuce and fruit? No way. I need something substantial."

"Fine. We'll leave. Let me get our purses." As Lettie disappeared into the next room, the bathroom door opened and Olivia stepped out.

So that's why Lettie was freaking out. I curled my toes and considered slipping my shoes off. Not because I was standing on holy ground, I can assure you. More like because I was about to wade in deep doo-doo.

"Uh, great turnout this morning." I shoved the exit door open. "Enjoy your lunch."

"Elizabeth?"

Oh, bother. Time to face the music. I expected to find Olivia all droopy-winged and pathetic. Feathers ruffled. But she wasn't. Her warm eyes connected with mine, and I felt a little less intimidated by her.

"Do you think we could meet for coffee sometime next week to talk about some of the ideas I heard you mention in the bathroom?"

My eyebrows dipped as I feigned thought. Like next week held a busy schedule to consider. What a joke—my whole life was free right now.

"At your convenience, of course. Would Monday morning work? Say, Chester's at ten?"

"Sure. That's perfect." Talk about an out-of-body experience. Shut up, already. For the life of me, I didn't recognize the stranger who took control of my mouth. But it was too late. Olivia had her purse opened and was noting the time on her phone.

"Ooh. Glad Monday works. It's my only opening."

I was all ready to cancel—for Olivia's sake—but Lettie returned before I had the chance. "Better hurry, Olivia," Lettie teased. "The ladies are looking for you."

"Oh my, I need to pray over the meal." Olivia hustled off to the next room.

"Biz, Biz, Biz." Lettie pushed past me.

I followed Lettie to her car. "So I have a big mouth. Like I don't know that?"

Lettie pulled out of the parking lot. "IHOP sound substantial enough? They're having a sale on crepes."

"Sounds yummy. Look, you probably won't believe it, but I am trying to do better. You should hear the words that did get stuck in my Jesus trap."

CHAPTER 6

Lettie pulled onto Highway 10. She opened her mouth to say something but glanced in my direction and resealed her lips.

So I started her off with a prompt. "The way I see it . . ."

Instantly, her hand popped into the air like a living stop sign. "Kill the Dr. Phil routine."

I giggled.

She joined me. "Honestly, Biz. It's not about your mouth. Don't you get it?"

Only too well. But I didn't know how to fix it. I'd prayed, but nothing changed.

"You've got a critical spirit. No one can ever do anything well enough to please you."

Words percolated in my throat, coated with grounds of bitterness, anger and confusion. "So tell me this. Didn't my devotional say God individually formed me in my mother's womb—designed for a specific purpose? Is there something wrong with disagreeing with others? Taking the lead instead of . . ." I stopped myself.

"Letting people walk all over you?" Lettie pulled into a parking slot at the pancake house. "I'm sure there's a balance."

"Yeah, and I'm sure we both need to find it. Think about how your kids take advantage of you, Lettie."

No answer.

That's the problem with wimpy people. They're all about telling you what's wrong with you, but they fall apart if you reciprocate. Nevertheless, Lettie was my friend. I touched her hand as she yanked the keys from the ignition. "I'm sorry, Lettie. I hate it, but you're right again. I promise to think about what you said."

Lettie stared at the steering wheel for several seconds before she dabbed at her cheek with the tips of her fingers and turned to face me. "Do you think the day will ever come when you can be honest with people, Biz? With me?"

I groped for a response.

"It's like you suck up your true feelings and say only what you think you ought to say. Then those feelings get trapped inside you where they rot and eventually come out in ugly words that hurt people."

"Like Olivia."

"Si. And your family. And . . . your best friend."

The tears rolled out on their own, and I was sure they weren't pretty. Disgust was flat-out ugly, and that was how I felt about myself right then. "If you only knew how badly I want to be someone different, Lettie. But it's not possible. Believe me, I've tried."

Lettie nodded, and we entered the restaurant in silence. I was no longer hungry. Maybe I'd just order some lettuce and fruit.

After a nap, I visited Hazel and worked on the puzzle with her. "So, you've finished the border. Want me to help sort colors?"

"Sounds good to me. But I've got dibs on the red for the Speedo."

I laughed. "You're twisted, old woman."

She slapped my wrist as I reached for a red piece I intended to hand her. "I said those were mine."

Was she serious? Had I hurt her feelings? "You know I was kidding with the twisted remark, right?"

"Oh, you were?" She crossed her eyes and giggled. "Because I was sort of digging the idea."

I smiled. "You ever hold anger inside and have it leak out when you least expect it, Hazel?"

My friend locked a puzzle piece in place and reached for another. "You saying that's what you did just now? You angry with me about something?"

"My goodness, no. Who could ever be angry with you?"

Remorse bled from Hazel's eyes. "At one point, my children. You see, I ruled my household with rage. Refused to accept anything but perfection from them. Chided and belittled them without end."

She stared into the distance. "When my youngest daughter was fifteen, she almost died from a fall. That's when I realized what I was doing and set out to change."

"And she forgave you?"

"Yes, but my sons were older and had already left home. We weren't close for many years."

"That's sad, Hazel. I don't even want to think about what my kids hold against me."

Back home, I started supper. I had so much to think about. Top of the list should have been my marriage, but I was honestly more anxious about my meeting with Robby the next day. Three options. Sell out to one of the large consolidations—Never. Watch the business go under—NOT a good choice. Provide the funds for Robby to create his own consolidation—Mom and Pop United. Seriously, what was there to think about?

Robert's cell phone rang in his office. Normally I wouldn't care. But after reading the article on hopeless marriages, I had to wonder if it might be Kathy Harmin calling. Was she interested in my husband? Wooing him with words of admiration and respect every man craves to hear. Words Robert seldom received at home.

A beep indicated a voice message. I popped into the office and clicked into the voicemail.

"Hi, Robert. This is Kathy. Give me a call if you can sneak away for a few minutes. I'd love to hear about your trip. If not, we'll talk tomorrow."

Sneak away? Had she really said that?

I impulsively deleted the message and returned to the kitchen just as Robert walked in the back door. I should confront him about the phone call. Demand he explain his relationship with Kathy Harmin.

But I couldn't. I was too angry at the moment. Or was I afraid to hear his answers?

Robert forked a pork chop onto my plate before serving himself. "How did the ladies' meeting go today?"

"Not bad." I buttered my corn. "About what I expected. Introductions, devotions, prayer and a discussion about future goals."

That basically covered everything I was prepared to share. Thankfully, Robert must have been hungrier for his dinner than for more information about the meeting because he dropped it at that. Good old Robert. Probably didn't even remember that we weren't on speaking terms when we went to sleep last night.

But that was pretty much how it went after a fight at our house. Compatible dribble. Never getting to the crux of our problems or resolving anything.

Whatever. It was what it was, but there was one issue that I would insist we discussed. Kathy Harmin. "How was the awards dinner last night?"

Robert looked up. "It was nice. Turned out someone didn't show, so you could have come after all. Sorry about all that confusion."

I willed myself to continue the conversation. "And the dedication to Kathy Harmin? Was she pleased to—"

Robert's cell phone rang. I heard a female voice and his face reddened. "Let me call you right back."

He snapped the phone shut. "We've got a problem at work that I need to sort out." He disappeared into his office and shut the door.

I shuddered, remembering sign #2: Spouse always answers cell phone in private.

Looked like my little Kathy Harmin investigation might be postponed, but I'd get to the bottom of it if it was the last thing I did.

On Friday morning, I headed to the office to find out what was going on.

I detested the bitterness that surged through me each time I considered Robby's consolidation plan, but I knew there really was no other solution. I needed to clear the air with Robby. After all, he was my son, and that was more important than the business. At least it should be.

My stomach knotted as I entered the building. I longed to get busy at my desk. My work. My business. If I turned it all over to Robby, I'd have no better reason to wake up in the morning than a cup of coffee and a sweet roll.

The phone rang. I hurried to grab it. "Beemer's Trucking and Storage."

"Hey, I'd recognize that gravelly voice anywhere. That you, Biz McNeely?"

My face relaxed. "None other. What do you need, Charlie?"

"I thought the queen bee gave up her throne. Figured Princess Vickie would pick up."

"Don't go there. You got a problem?"

"Actually, I do. The charges on the invoice I received were half your usual rate. Got any idea what happened?"

"Sure—a simple lack of focus. Decorating the office. Checking Twitter and Facebook. Losing the—"

"Biz?"

"I'll tell her about the invoice. Thanks for your honesty."

"No problem. Go easy on her, Biz. I'm sure she'll catch on soon enough."

"Yeah, I suppose you're right." I hung up and shuffled through some papers.

"What are you doing?"

Oh great. Vickie stood on the other side of the desk. The girl always had been as quiet as a mouse. Vickie Mouse. I attempted to swallow a grin as a tune ran through my mind. V-I-C . . . K-I-E . . . M-O-U-S-E.

This particular mouse was practically steaming, her paws planted firmly on her tiny hips, her squinty eyes trained directly on mine.

I jumped to my feet and distanced myself from the desk. "Vickie, I'm sorry. I was trying to help. The phone rang, and —"

"That's what the answering machine is for." Vickie slipped into her desk chair as I poked my head into my son's office and flipped on the lights. "Where's Robby?"

"He ran to the bank."

"And left you here alone? You think you're ready for that?"

The mouse squealed. Or maybe I imagined it. Anyway, before I had a chance to lick my chops, a squirt of shame spoiled my appetite.

"I really didn't mean that the way it sounded, Vickie . . . I promise."

I walked to the customer side of the counter, grabbed a mini-Snickers bar from the open sack and pulled off the wrapper. "Cute curtains."

Vickie fumbled with a stack of files. In a voice almost too soft to hear—a perfect Vickie Mouse voice, in fact—she thanked me. "And Biz . . . about the lack of focus, checking social media comments . . . you are way off base."

"Yes. I apologize."

Vickie tugged on an earring. "I thought we had an agreement. You were going to give me space, right?"

"Yes, we did. I mean, we do, and I plan to honor it. But I really didn't get a lot of time to train you properly. Like the monthly billing—we only got to go through that one time."

Vickie pointed to the laptop on her desk. "Actually, I bought a program that practically does the work for me."

Seriously? I'd spent twenty-five years developing my accounting books—a perfect system of recording, computing and crosschecking. And now a computer program was going to do all that? "Charlie Neighbors called. Your program only charged him half our usual rate."

"I guess I entered the wrong percentage. An easy fix."

The phone rang. I sighed as Vickie answered it, ashamed of the ugly satisfaction I'd felt pointing out the error. Life demanded change, but change terrified me.

Vickie hung up the phone. "That was the high school. Stephanie isn't feeling well."

"Awww. That's too bad." Though I tried to love all my grandchildren the same, Stephanie was special. She'd been only two years old when her mother, Robby's first wife, decided to run off to California with an old boyfriend. Robby and Stephanie lived in our home for almost three years before Robby married Vickie.

Now, at fifteen, Stephanie touted a major attitude, rarely conceded to anything without a fuss, and took tremendous pleasure in aggravating her younger brothers, eight-year-old Christopher and six-year-old Kyle. "Do you want me to stay here and double check the billing amounts while you go pick her up?"

Vickie opened her laptop and pushed a few buttons. "No. I can take care of the billings. Would you mind picking Stephanie up and dropping her off at the house? Robby should be back when you return."

Fact was, I was much more qualified to check the numbers. But propriety called. I smiled and fished through my purse for my keys. "Of course, I'll run to the school, if that's what will help you the most."

Vickie pressed her lips into a thin line. "Thanks, Biz. I'm sorry if I overreacted. I just feel so intimidated with you around. You can practically run this place with your eyes shut. Surely you made mistakes when you were beginning. Right?"

Ah. Reverse psychology. So Vickie Mouse wasn't afraid to stand up to the cat. Ten points for her. "Mistakes? Sure, I made plenty. The important thing is to learn from them, or they'll eat you alive. Take this billing, for example. You—"

Vickie raised her eyelids and glanced at the door. "Sorry to interrupt, but Stephanie's waiting."

Right. Time to haul this unneeded, intimidating body away. I'd catch up with my son later. I dumped a few more Snickers bars into my purse and purposely let the door hit me in the butt as I left. At least I had somewhere to go. For the time being, anyway.

I would have bet my last dollar Stephanie was faking it when I saw her hunched over and holding her tummy.

"Stephanie doesn't have a fever." The secretary lowered her voice. "She says she has cramps, though, and I know that can be tough for these young girls."

Right. I turned to Stephanie. "Ready to go, sweetie?"

Stephanie kept her head down. But as soon as we got outside, she looked up and grinned. "Granny, I thought Dad said you weren't feeling well."

I gently yanked on a strand of her long blonde hair and laughed. "Yeah, and what about you? You sick?"

"For real. Sick of summer school."

Someone had to be an adult, here. With great effort, I maintained a straight face as we climbed into the truck. "Honey, you've got to take your studies seriously."

Stephanie nodded and turned on the radio, flipping through the stations until she found something loud and obnoxious. "I am trying, Granny, but I had a paper due in the next class, and I don't have it finished. I really did have cramps last night."

"Whatever." I turned the music down. "Tell you what. You pass those two classes with a C or better, and you and I will head for the outlet mall with a wad of money. Sound good?"

CHAPTER 7

Vickie was gone when I returned to the office.

"Hey, Mom." Robby stepped out of his office. "Vickie sent you on a mission of mercy, huh?"

"Funny. She tell you about not charging Charlie enough?"

Robby nodded. "Mistakes happen. No big deal."

This visit was becoming stressful. The Snickers bag called my name. Only two left. I offered the last one to Robby.

"No, thanks. Vickie put me on a health food diet."

"One candy bar isn't going to hurt you."

Robby waved it away.

Fine. I shoved the extra bar in my pocket. "I've been thinking about your plan for the company, Robby, and I honestly don't see any other way our company will survive."

My son's eyes widened. "Are you serious?"

"Yes. You can go ahead with your plans. I'll sign whatever you need me to sign."

Robby cupped his hand over his nose and mouth and paced across the lobby.

What had I put my boy through? Regret shot through my veins, pushing anger and offense further from my heart.

Robby wiped his eyes on his sleeve and turned to face me.

I didn't want to upset his obvious sense of euphoria, but it had to be done before I could leave the building with a clear conscience. "I do have one condition."

Robby pointed to his office with an open hand. "I'm sure we can work out any details."

"No. I don't plan to stay. I'm obviously not needed."

"Mom—"

"No. I just need time to absorb all this change. I know you and Vickie are trying to do the right things around here, but frankly, all the improvements you're making feel like a major slap in the face."

There. I'd said it. And maybe that's all I needed to say because the air actually did feel a bit clearer.

"I'm sorry, Mom." Robby wrapped his arms around me.

I stiffened, and he backed away. "Never mind. With time, I can roll with the punches. But you need to know that I'm not agreeing to bow out of the picture. I'm good with you and Vickie running the office, but I intend to be included in all decision-making. We are clear on that, aren't we?"

Robby's turn to stiffen, his face pale.

"No more secret meetings. No more gag orders. I'm willing and able to learn about this new technology, Robby, and I'll not be shut out of my own company."

"But the migraines . . . the stress. Why can't you just let go, Mom? Stay home where you can get healthy."

Boy-howdy, that made me mad. I stared at my son like he'd just asked me to disappear from the face of the earth. Which, in essence, I guess he had.

I turned my back and walked away. "I know you did not just ask me to stay away from the office."

Robby reached out and stopped me. "C'mon. You know what I'm saying makes sense. You worked hard to make this business what it is today. You deserve to go find yourself a life."

I shook myself free. "I've got a life, thank you."

Robby blocked my way. "Mom. Please don't go away mad."

"I know. Just go away. Right?"

Comic relief. We both knew it. Robby crossed his eyes and smiled the same goofy smile he'd been flashing since he was a toddler.

Ergh. Was it even possible for a man to understand the difference between mad and hurt?

Robby touched my arm as he stepped aside and opened the door. "Look, Mom. We're going to get through this, I promise. Whatever happens, please remember that I love you, okay?"

Love you, too. I wondered how he would feel if I told him what this business really meant to me. And why.

I started the truck and rested my head on the steering wheel. What had Robby meant when he said, "Whatever happens . . .?"

The possibilities nauseated me. Shifting into reverse, I checked my rearview mirror. A sleek red La Ferrari pulled into the other end of the lot and parked. A 2015 V12— Hybrid. Now out of production. Available only to those who had money to burn. So, what was it doing at Beemer's Trucking? And more important . . . who was driving it?

The door opened and Quinn Shoaf emerged. Ms. Harper-Klein Trucking, herself. Dressed in a sophisticated poncho top, skinny black pants and four-inch heels, she exuded elegance in an underdressed sort of way. Perfect for just dropping by the office.

But why? Was Robby holding another investors meeting? Without me? Would this craziness never end?

I grabbed a napkin from the cubby to wipe my sweaty hands as I watched the woman enter the building. I would wait ten minutes to see who else showed up.

Five minutes passed and I noticed truckers exiting the back lot. Workday over. That did it. I was going inside.

Once the parking lot was clear of moving vehicles, I pulled my truck around to the back lot and entered the building through the employees' entrance. Snaking around hallways and through the empty conference room, I slipped into my office unnoticed. The door to Robby's office, next to mine, was closed.

Quietly, I slid my window open. Bingo. Robby's voice came through loud and clear. I assumed the female voice belonged to Quinn Shoaf.

"We were so close," Robby said. "I couldn't believe my ears when she told me she would sign the papers. I thought it was a done deal, Quinn. I really did."

"Then she mentioned the condition? Her being in on all decisions?"

I imagined the scowl on my son's face as he affirmed Quinn's words.

"Did you even try to talk her out of it?"

"No. It's useless to try. I hate to say it, but I think it's time to pursue Plan B. We can't go on like this, and I don't know where else to turn."

Plan B? What was left? Burning the place down? Enough of this eavesdropping. Robby had obviously violated my one condition with this secret meeting, and I was going to put a stop to it.

Without hesitation, I stepped into the hallway and opened the door to Robby's office.

Robby and Quinn, seated at a small corner table under the window, jumped to their feet, their faces flushed. Robby hurried across the room and stood within inches of my face.

"Mom! What are you doing here?"

Suddenly, I didn't know what to say. My own son was undercutting me. "P-Plan B. Something I should know about?"

Robby took my arm and motioned for me to sit in the chair he'd just vacated. In consideration of my shaking legs, I obliged.

Quinn sat, too. She kept her eyes on the floor. My eyes were trained on her. Waiting for her response. Ready for confrontation.

Robby pulled up a third chair and sat between us. Only then did I avert my focus.

He shifted his body in my direction. "Believe it or not, Mom, I'm glad you're here."

"That's a surprise."

Quinn looked up. Locked her eyes on mine. "Let me do this, Robby."

I looked back and forth. Robby nodded.

"We know you aren't ready to give up your trucking company and probably never will be, Elizabeth. But the facts remain. Smaller, independent trucking companies like yours and mine are going under. We can't continue the way we have in the past."

I agreed up to that point. Crossing my arms, I lifted my head a notch higher. "And you have a solution?"

She shook her head. "Robby's solution is the best all the way around. But if you won't agree to sign over complete control to him—"

"—which I won't—"

Robby shut his eyes and his forehead crumpled into a five-lane highway. "Oh, Mom . . ."

I felt sick but determined to hold my own. There was no way I was going to quit just because some beautiful broad threatened me with—

"Elizabeth." Quinn's soft voice and calm demeanor caught me off guard, and believe me, the thing I've feared most, my entire life, was to be caught off guard again. Out of control. A pawn in someone else's hands.

I held my queasy stomach. "Give me just a minute, please."

Robby stood. "Maybe we should finish this discussion at a later time."

"No." The simultaneous reply from Quinn and myself could not have been clearer.

"Please go on," I said to Quinn.

She nodded, the look in her eyes gentle, as if searching for understanding. Maybe, compromise. "I'm just going to lay the cards on the table, Elizabeth. If you do not want to join this consolidation of sorts that Robby has masterfully designed in the best interest of all involved, I'm prepared to employ him myself. Hear me, carefully. Harper-Klein Trucking is ready to back Robby financially and intends to go forward with his plan—with or without you."

My eyes turned to Robby as the truth of her words hit home. "And you'd do that? You'd quit here and go to work for her?"

Robby hesitated, but finally nodded. "I'm sorry, Mom, but I can't just sit around and watch the place go under without at least trying to implement my plan. And I can't have you second guessing my every move, either. You'll have to trust me completely, or I'll take Quinn's offer. The decision is yours."

I shut my eyes and laughed. Louder than I intended to, and I swear I heard myself scream something ugly. Or maybe I imagined it because I also thought I slammed my fist through the wall. But when I opened my eyes, I had done nothing of the kind.

Robby and Quinn stared at me with open mouths.

"Well, I guess I got what I asked for, didn't I? To make the final decision?"

Robby scrunched his eyebrows. "You do understand what I mean, don't you, Mom? Deciding to totally trust me means turning the company over to me completely. For good. No more decisions in your hands."

I nodded. "I really don't want to see the business go under, and I'm too tired to fight you any longer." I wiped tears from my eyes as I focused on a redwood tree outside the window. "What do I need to do to make this official?"

And that was that. I surrendered. Lock, stock and barrel.

Robby was ready. He and his up-to-date attorney had already drawn up the necessary papers. Within minutes, the deal was done. No turning back. I kept half of my savings and would receive dividends when the company got back on its feet. Robby bought the company from me for a whopping price of one dollar . . . with no stipulations.

And I was pushed out of the nest to fly. Or not.

I picked up Steak-and-Shake and texted Robert to suggest he heat up leftovers for dinner. I was going to eat with Hazel.

I dreaded going home. I hated that house more than ever now. Knowing I'd be stuck there every day with nowhere else to go. Or was it life with an allegedly unfaithful husband I loathed facing?

"How about spending the evening watching Netflix?" I asked Hazel as we sat to eat. "Maybe a Jimmy Stewart marathon?"

My friend loved the idea, but I can't say we ever got around to turning the television on. Hazel was much too intuitive and wouldn't let my mood slide.

"So, you want to talk before or after the movies?" Hazel dipped a shoestring French fry in ketchup and popped it in her mouth, waiting for my response with wide, inquisitive eyes.

I finished the last bite of my cheeseburger. "You don't miss a beat, do you?"

She smiled but said nothing. Just lifted the lids on those beautiful blues of hers a little bit higher.

"It really isn't a wonderful life most of the time, is it, Hazel?"

I picked at my fries, stacking them, end over end, to construct a small box. Like the beginning of a log cabin. "I mean, I get why George Bailey wished he'd never been born. Everything he'd ever worked for had gone up in smoke, and there was no turning back. Why go on?"

Hazel wrapped her half-eaten sandwich in the waxed paper it came in. "Easier to quit than face life's problems. That what you're saying?"

"I suppose." I folded my paper French fry pocket in half to form a roof for my cabin and set it atop the fries. "I've made such a mess of my life that I wouldn't even know how to start to make things right. I've hurt so many people—especially those closest to me. And now I've lost the one thing that brought me happiness."

"You signed the business over to your son?"

I nodded, impulsively squishing the tiny French fry cabin between my fingers in a tight fist. I burst into tears as I shoved it in the carry-out sack and stared at my greasy fingers. Violent sobs, as the full impact of what I'd just done really hit home. I covered my face. "Oh, Hazel. I don't think I can go on."

She prayed. "Dear Father in heaven. Draw nigh unto this child of yours. Give her the courage to trust you with her questions and fears. Take the weight of this situation off her shoulders so she can rest."

I envisioned handing my problems to God. Curling my fingers around Hazel's warm hand, I drew strength from my friend as I waited until I could speak without a hitch. "Three years I've known you and we've never talked about God. You're a believer?"

Hazel smiled. "Since before you took your first breath, my sweet thing."

I had to laugh as I wiped my nose on the scratchy napkin. "And here I've been worried sick that you would kick the bucket before I found the courage to lead you to Jesus."

Hazel laughed, too. "My guess is that you know Jesus as your Savior, but not as an intimate friend—someone you can trust without reservation. That's who I want to teach you about before I kick the bucket."

My eyes clamped shut as I fought off another wave of emotion, and I held up the stop-sign hand. "Maybe another time, Hazel. Right now, I think I need to get home. I'm exhausted."

Crickets chirped their greeting as I walked across the patch of grass between our homes. That sweet Hazel sure was bent on calling things exactly as they were. Not that I minded so much . . . not with her, anyway.

CHAPTER 8

I was reading the Saturday morning paper and finishing my cup of coffee when Robert stepped inside from the backyard and slipped his sandals off by the door. "Good morning."

I glanced at the clock. "What's left of it. What do you have planned?"

Robert poured himself some coffee and leaned back against the counter on his elbows with the mug in one hand. "I promised Pastor I'd help him paint his family room today. What about you?"

I shrugged my shoulders and flipped through the funny papers. "Not a whole lot on my schedule these days."

Robert sat across the table from me. "You were at Hazel's quite late last night. Sorry I didn't wait up. Everything okay over there?"

"Hazel's fine." I set the newspaper aside and accidentally tipped over my coffee cup.

Robert grabbed a dishtowel and caught the mess before it ran off the table. Then he sat next to me and took my hand in his. "Biz, your fingers are shaking. Are you okay?"

"No. I'm really not okay at all."

"Robby called last night. Told me what happened at the office."

My lips quivered. I nodded, unable to speak around the knot in my throat.

"He's worried about you, honey, and so am I."

A sarcastic chortle escaped, and I didn't even try to explain it. I didn't really care what anyone thought. A spurt of unexpected audacity, largely tinged with arrogance, stiffened my defeated spine. I swiveled to face my husband and spoke directly into his nervous eyes. "Look. I've done what Robby deemed necessary, so let's leave it at that. Talking about it won't change a thing, and I've got other things to think about."

"Like?"

Like the fact that you gave my seat to your overly-attached colleague at the banquet Wednesday night, received a voicemail message requesting that you sneak out together, and spent all of Thursday evening on the phone with her in your office?

I stood and carried my cup to the sink to rinse it out. "Don't forget that we're going out to that new steakhouse with José and Lettie tonight. Give yourself plenty of time to get home and clean up."

Robert stepped over and placed his cup in the sink. "So that's where we're going to leave this? Just not talk about it?"

I didn't answer. Truth be told, I was afraid to even get started.

Robert accepted my silence. "Right. Guess I'll go jump in the shower, then. You plan to fix breakfast or should I pick up something on my way over to Pastor's house?"

"How about pancakes and bacon?"

"Sounds great."

I fumed as I cracked eggs into a bowl. Pulverized the shells between my fingers before dumping them down the garbage disposal. All I wanted, right now, was for Robert to hear me out. To try to understand where I was coming from.

Self-disgust surfaced, as well, as I flipped the bacon and pancakes and collected our dishes from the cabinet. I would say what Robert wanted to hear, and we'd be on good terms once again. Same old, same old. But my stomach would continue to churn with self-hatred, and migraines would continue to plague my days.

I carried our breakfast to the patio, the crisp morning air thick with the sweet scent of lilac from the bushes lining our property. A robin picked at the dirt in the flower beds, and squirrels scampered from one branch to another in the old oak. The scene, a blaring dichotomy to what crouched within me.

Robert prayed a blessing over the food, and we began to eat.

The Kathy Harmin thing was killing me. Maybe I was wrong, but I'd never be able to let it go if we didn't at least discuss it. Surely Robert could understand that.

"About the night of the banquet. I'm sorry for the way I acted and for implying that . . . well, you know. There's no excuse, but you have to admit—"

"No." Robert set his fork and knife down and placed his large, age-spotted hands flat on the table. "I don't have to admit anything. You've apologized and I accept. I think it's better if we just leave it there and drop the matter."

"I can't." My voice wavered. "That phone call at supper Thursday night. Was that Kathy Harmin?"

Robert's head jerked up. "Yes, but you don't understand, honey. She—"

"Did you spend the evening in your office talking to Kathy Harmin?"

Robert shut his eyes and leaned his head back. "Dear Jesus. Where are you going with this, Biz?"

I felt fire behind my eyes. The onset of another migraine. "I just want the truth."

Robert lowered his chin and met my eyes. "Yes. I was talking to Kathy all evening. We're working together on a writing project the upcoming seniors need to complete in order to graduate. The theme relates to their future goals. That's where my counseling tips come in. Does that make any sense?"

I nodded, my tiny spurt of courage rapidly waning. "But why on earth did she have to call you at home?"

Robert shrugged. "I guess she was bored. Or lonely. Whatever. I didn't mind. Not like I had anything more pressing to do. What's this all about, anyway? What's gotten into you, Biz?"

"I don't know." I lowered my eyes and ran my fingers along the edge of the roughened pine table. "I have this feeling in my gut that something isn't right about that woman, and I'm afraid for you to spend time with her."

There. I'd said it. I wanted to puke, but I'd said it.

Robert came over and gave me a hug. "Let it go, honey. I promise, you have nothing to worry about. Please, let it go."

I rinsed the dishes and loaded the dishwasher after Robert left for the pastor's house. Let it go. Hadn't the tabloid claimed unfaithful spouses would most likely refuse to argue or fight? That they were resigned to the fact the marriage was over? That some might never divorce, but would find ways to meet their needs outside the marriage relationship?

These questions gnawed at me throughout the morning. I could only blame myself for the broken marriage in the first place. I'd been the one to push Robert away when he tried to be strong for me in the beginning. I'd insisted I could take care of myself.

I had no right to complain. But now I wanted more. I desperately wanted the man I had married to be my best friend.

I headed to the basement to work on the laundry. "Well, I tried your advice, Lettie. I voiced my true feelings, but I don't feel one bit better."

I pulled a load of white clothes from the dryer and tossed them into a basket. Then I saw Robert's new pink shirt in the pile of dirty clothes. I grinned as I threw it in the washer. Wouldn't hurt to run Robert's white underwear through another cycle, now would it?

"Hazel?" I called my friend's name as I entered her house. "It's Biz."

Sandy sat at the family room table working on the puzzle. She stood. "Oh, hi, Mrs. McNeely. Grandma's in her room."

I ran my fingers over the large portion of puzzle that had been finished since the night before. "You been doing this all morning?"

"No. Grandma worked pretty late last night. Says she's anxious to move on to more important things."

"I'll just go see what your grandma is up to."

Hazel was parked in her rocker with her eyes closed and her chin resting on her chest. Her breathing seemed heavier than normal.

I sat on the edge of the bed and soaked up her presence.

Hazel stirred and opened her eyes. "Hi, Bizzie. Have you been here long?"

I shook my head. "Sandy says you were up late working on the puzzle."

Hazel blushed. "That thing is addicting, for sure." She adjusted her position and shut the book on her lap. Her Bible. "You feeling any better today, honey?"

"I think so. How about you? Your breathing sounds a little labored."

"It does that when I sleep without the C-Pap machine."

"Okay. Can I get you anything to drink?"

"Not yet. But I'd love to talk to you about something if you have time."

"Sure. Anything wrong?"

"No." Hazel opened her Bible. "I think I have a verse here that might help you find that peace you're looking for."

I settled into the chair. "Great. I find out you're a Christian one day, and you preach to me the next."

"Don't worry, it's quick. Says, 'Trust in the Lord with all your heart and lean not on your own understanding.'"

"O-o-kay. So, where are you going with this?"

Hazel grinned. "You said you hadn't trusted anyone but yourself for quite a while. Well, I'm suggesting you start trusting God. That's the first step to building that relationship with God we talked about."

I felt my face heat. Didn't Hazel know better than discussing religion so openly? "You want me to work up some feeling? Fake it?"

"Absolutely not. Trust has nothing to do with feelings."

"Well, I'm with you there. God let me down pretty bad as a child, Hazel. Just not sure how to trust him after that."

Hazel crossed her arms. "So, for you, the verse would be better if it read, 'Trust not in the Lord with all your heart, but lean on your own understanding?'"

No answer for that one.

"Did God or people let you down, Biz?"

I had to think about that. "Both, I guess. But God could have rescued me, couldn't he?"

"Oh, sure. If we were a bunch of puppets, he could have reached down and switched you to another family. Life happens, honey. There is sin and pain in the world. For everyone."

That made sense. "But I didn't see it that way as a child."

"No, you were too young." Hazel reached for her walker. "Sorry to cut this conversation short, but my bowels are talking."

I helped her to her feet and followed her to the bathroom.

She turned at the door. "This might take awhile. Sandy can help me with my bath tonight. Why don't you go on home and think about letting go of your childhood view of God? Ask him to show you who he really is?"

Yeah. Now that would be a big load to dump—might take awhile.

By afternoon, Robert was whistling "Dixie" again. The man definitely deserved an award for the Best Repressed Actor of the Year.

He flipped on the television. "What time do we need to leave for dinner?"

"The reservations are for six. Five thirty good?"

He nodded. "Oh, I forgot to tell you. José invited Olivia and Mac to join us tonight."

My jaw clenched.

"I'm anxious to spend some time with Mac. Hopefully we can convince him to start attending church."

"Be sure to sit next to him at the table." That would ensure I'd be two seats away from Olivia. I dreaded the small talk, and . . . God-forbid, the important stuff. Made me think . . . "Robert, can we just keep the lid on the business deal I signed with Robby? Not sure I'm ready to talk about it openly yet."

Robert nodded. "I get that."

I showered and dressed in my favorite black jacket and slacks. Not that I had a choice. Other than my jeans and sweats, these were the only pants that still fit. I knew what I needed to do, and it had nothing to do with buying larger pants.

Mac helped Olivia out of a shiny red Chevy Silverado 1500 as we pulled into the steak house parking lot.

"Hey, Mac." Robert crossed the lot to shake Mac's hand. "This the new truck José told me about?"

I sized up Mac's figure. Nice—in a rugged sort of way. Of course, I'd have shot Robert dead if he tried to wear a cowboy hat and boots to a fine restaurant like Perrigo's. Wasn't like we lived out west. We're talking Indiana.

Olivia stood next to her husband, smoothing nonexistent wrinkles from the front of her sleeveless dress, a deep cranberry-red print that beautifully complimented her pale skin. She smiled as I approached. "Hi, Elizabeth. Isn't this heat dreadful?"

So we agreed on at least one thing. I nodded. I was starting to like this Elizabeth thing a little. Might switch to it altogether if I ever got my act together in life. "Let's go find a table. These guys could talk forever about a new truck."

Truth be told, I was probably more intrigued with the 6.6L turbo-diesel engine than Robert. My cell phone buzzed as the waiter led us to a table for six in the center of the room and set menus before us. I smiled my thanks and glanced at my phone as I sat. A text from Lettie—Running late. Be there in 5.

Where are you?

Relax. Order our iced tea.

Right. I put the phone in my purse and studied the menu to avoid conversation. What was taking Mac and Robert so long?

"The guys have hit it off quickly. Your husband into trucks, too?"

I lifted my head. "Not really. But he's a talker—any subject. No telling how long he'll fire questions at Mac."

Olivia studied her beautifully manicured nails. "Since we have a few minutes to ourselves, I'd like to apologize for appearing to be such a prude at Thursday's meeting. Truth is, my mind was elsewhere and I missed Gracie's comment completely. After the meeting, I was puzzled when she apologized for what she said. Gracie repeated the comment, and I laughed hysterically. I love that little lady, don't you?"

Okay. So we agreed on two things. And I'd been totally wrong about Olivia's reasoning. I believe that particular sin would fall under the do not judge one another command.

Thankfully, the waiter arrived with our drinks, and I quietly excused myself to go to the bathroom where I took some extra time for a genuine come-to-Jesus meeting about my attitude. Hazel's words plagued me. Did I really believe I was more worthy of trust than God, himself?

The men came inside and Lettie and José arrived. I reread the menu as the others rambled on about corn crops and the need for rain. Olivia held her own.

Much as I tried, I couldn't keep my eyes off the juicy ribeye steak pictured so cleverly in the center of the menu. I should just order it. Forget Olivia. Not like she couldn't see I was fat.

I promptly changed my mind when Olivia and Lettie ordered grilled chicken salads, though. Grrrr. And I thought Lettie was my friend. Didn't she realize she set me up?

While Lettie engaged the others with stories about her grandchildren, José surprised me by slipping a chunk of his steak onto my plate. He was a true friend.

As I sliced the meat into small chunks and mixed it with my greens, a bit of dressing splashed over the side of my dish. Unfortunately, I dragged my wrist through it, put my hand in my lap and transferred the mess to my slacks. I dabbed at the stain with a napkin until Mac's voice pulled me from my dilemma.

"Sorry to eat and run." Mac pushed his empty plate back. "Next time we'll plan earlier so I can round up some help to feed the livestock."

"No problem." José stood and extended his hand. "Just glad you were able to come."

Olivia blushed.

Probably embarrassed Mac would agree to dinner out when he refused to attend church on Sunday. With a tinge of compassion for Olivia, I realized how blessed I was to be married to a man who put God first in his life. Or did he?

With a spark in her eye, Lettie motioned for the waiter. "Now, I'm ready for dessert."

Shock must have registered on my face because Lettie laughed. "Que? You think I wanted to order that salad?"

For one of the few times in my life, I was speechless. Robert and José joined in the laughter. What was this—a joke on Biz?

"Oh, Biz," Lettie said. "Sorry I didn't call. I told José I wasn't about to eat a fattening meal in front of Olivia. She's way too perfectly shaped, don't you think?"

Robert reddened and turned away. He'd noticed, too. Double grrrr.

Lettie ordered a chocolate cake and ice cream dessert with four spoons. "I want to learn how to make this."

José winked at his wife. "Lettie is going to start a catering service."

I laughed. "When did you decide this?"

José cupped his hand over Lettie's. "A dream from years ago. You do know her cooking's what I fell in love with first, don't you?"

Lettie jabbed him in the side. "José wants me to do something for myself."

I shrugged. "Yeah, like in between babysitting the bambinos and babysitting the bambinos?"

Lettie dropped her smile. "I know you're right. I hate the idea of telling the kids I can't help them when they need me."

I threw my hands up in defeat. "Not to worry, then. You've already got a catering job. You're just not getting paid for it."

Lettie frowned and pointed a finger at me. "I didn't mean catering to my family, Biz McNeely, so you can keep your comments to yourself. I meant a real job, like decorating wedding cakes and catering banquets and parties."

Sounded like a life to me. But the thought of Lettie saying no to one of her kids concerned me. "I guess you realize the can of worms you're thinking about opening."

"That's just gross, Biz. Why would I serve worms?"

José laughed and smothered his wife in a hug. Pulling a strand of hair aside, he whispered into her ear and she smiled.

But as our eyes connected, her smile morphed into a distinct look of chagrin. "I know it won't be easy, but at least I'm willing to try."

And what about me? I'd been trying so hard all evening to guard my lips. Would I ever be able to seal the rotten can of worms that fed my negative attitude? Lettie's words still hung in the air. I reached out to embrace them. I, too, wanted to change.

Robert checked the time. "Nine o'clock, already. We'd better get going."

I was more than ready. Stepping close to Lettie on our way out of the restaurant, I touched her arm. "I was wrong to say what I did, Lettie. Will you please forgive me?"

She turned to face me, forgiveness in her eyes. "Of course, but don't be surprised if you bite into a piece of my apple pie one day and find a worm."

I pretended to gag. "Better than half a worm, I guess."

CHAPTER 9

Robert waited for the traffic light to turn green. "You enjoy the meal?"

"Hardly. Mind stopping to order me a hamburger?"

"Honey, you just had dessert. You sure you want to do this?" Robert's voice contained not a drop of sarcasm.

Made me want to change my mind just to show him I could do it, but I was too hungry. "I'm serious about the diet, Robert, but that salad and dessert didn't fill me up. I need something substantial, or I'm liable to snack all night long."

Robert pulled into the drive-up lane at Wendy's. "No problem."

"Can I help you?"

Robert looked in my direction as the metal box waited for an answer.

"A double cheeseburger and fries, please," I shouted past Robert's shoulder. "And plenty of ketchup."

Robert eased the car up to the next window, paid, and handed the sack to me. He raised the window as he pulled back into traffic. "I really believe you can do this diet thing, honey. I'm proud of you for trying."

I stared into the night, wishing that just once, Robert would struggle with something he set out to do. The car hit a pothole and the ketchup packets slid from my lap to the floor. I'd retrieve them when we got home.

We drove several blocks before Robert broke the silence. "I need to talk to you about something, Biz."

"Not tonight, honey. I'm exhausted, and my head is killing me."

Robert tapped the steering wheel with his thumb. "It's important."

"Can't we talk in the morning?"

We turned into the driveway. Robert's thumb stopped in mid-air as if I'd just blown his fuse. "You know, Biz. The word important used to mean something." He pulled the keys from the ignition. "Will the day ever come when you really care about anything I have to say?"

He climbed out of the car, shut the door softly and went inside. Mr. Self-Control.

I popped a fry in my mouth and reached below the seat for the ketchup. Unfortunately, the packets were not all I came across.

The bag of food slipped from my lap, and fries spilled onto the floor mat as I stared at the silver-spangled, black cosmetic bag in my hand. Was this what Robert wanted to talk about?

The smell of greasy fries and ground beef turned my stomach. I shifted in my seat and opened the door for some fresh air, shutting my eyes for a moment before I looked down and pulled the zipper on the bag.

The satin bag held a tube of Clinique lipstick, a small vial of Victoria Secret's Very Sexy Summer perfume, a compact mirror and a comb. My stomach lurched. I grabbed the

Wendy's bag from the floor and hurled into it. Again. And again. Despite the cool evening air circulating around me, my face burned. The stench of vomit caused my stomach to roil again. I crawled from the car and leaned against the door frame until my knees steadied.

What was I going to do? Robert wanted to talk. Well, I was ready, and believe me I totally cared what he had to say.

But as I picked up the fries and dumped everything into the trashcan at the side of the house, I changed my mind. I would hide the cosmetic bag. Make Robert come crawling to ask me about it.

Well, I could hope. Whatever the case, I couldn't talk about the mess tonight because now my head really did hurt.

I'm not sure what actually woke me the next morning—the aroma of fresh coffee or the sound of Robert whistling "Amazing Grace."

Appropriate song. I considered pulling the cosmetic bag out of my purse and confronting him right then. But Sunday was Sunday, and my husband and I had an appearance to make.

"Oh great." I'd forgotten to wash my black slacks. That could only mean one thing, a dress and—Ugh!

I fished to the bottom of my underwear drawer until my fingers touched a satin-covered control panel and rubber ribbing. I locked the bedroom door, stripped to my undies and tackled the enemy. Sat on the bed, stuck my feet in the holes and tugged. Halfway up my thighs, the wretched thing stopped.

I walked my fingers down my hips and seized the slippery devil. Breathe. Breathe. Yank. Breathe. Breathe. Yank.

The girdle reached an impasse—my behind. I arched backward at the waist and pulled. "I . . . can do . . . all things." And somehow, I did. The girdle rolled over my tail, bypassed my tummy, and slipped into place.

"Ahhh." The extra control felt strangely good. I slipped the dress over my head and checked myself in the mirror. Definitely not sleek nor slender, but maybe I didn't need to diet after all. I could just shop for larger clothing and a more agreeable girdle.

Olivia caught me as I headed into the sanctuary. "I'm so sorry, Elizabeth. I'm going to have to cancel our breakfast plans for tomorrow. I hope we can reschedule."

Fat chance. I might be slow, but I didn't usually make the same mistake twice. "No problem."

By the time church ended, my girdle pinched my body mercilessly.

I followed Robert to the car. "Hurry, Biz. Robby and Vickie want us to meet them for lunch."

I reached for my shoulder belt. "I wished I'd known. I never would have worn this girdle. Now I won't even be able to enjoy my meal."

"I'm sure you'll manage. Take the thing off in the bathroom and shove it in your purse."

"Good idea."

Robert smiled. "Forget the diet, too. Today is your day."

What in tarnation was he talking about?

I found out when I stepped inside the restaurant and noted a huge banner hung across the back corner of the room.

Congratulations on your retirement, Ms. Biz!

Several tables had been pushed together. Former employees, sporting corny smiles, filled the chairs. Robby and the others stood and clapped as Robert guided me through the room and pulled out a chair at the head of the table.

"Sit down," I ordered brusquely. "No need for all this fuss."

Everyone laughed and did as they were told. Pete, to my left, whispered, "It's good to hear you barking commands again, boss. We've been missing you."

Was there an emergency exit?

Robby offered thanks, and the waiters served heaping dishes of roast beef, mashed potatoes, white gravy, corn-on-the-cob and warm, melt-in-your-mouth buttered biscuits. Now this was my type of meal.

"What'ya gonna do with all your free time, Ms. Biz?" Pete asked.

My gut ached. "Whatever I want, I reckon."

Pete laughed. "Nothing new, there."

I concentrated on my dinner, successfully squelching further discussion on the matter. "Where are the kids?" I asked Robert.

"Stephanie went home from church with a friend, and Vickie sent Christopher and Kyle to the lake with her parents.

"What about Morgan? Anyone call her?"

Robert nodded. "She tried to get off, but couldn't. The managers take turns working Sundays, and this was her week."

"She shouldn't be working on the Sabbath."

Robert ran his thumb along the rim of his plate. He detested arguing about the children.

Not that I cared. I detested discovering cosmetic bags hidden in my husband's car.

Vickie carried out a cake baked in the shape of an 18-wheeler, and for some reason, the frivolous thing almost did me in. Trucking had been my life. How I longed to return to easier times. Sit around cups of coffee with the guys, each trucker topping the last one's tale.

Those nutty truckers spoke a few words on my behalf. I was humbled and embarrassed. Robby stood when they finished.

"First of all, I want to thank Mom for her trust in me. She's always insisted I could do anything I wanted to do, but I was never sure that included running the business her father left her."

Robby stepped around the corner of the table and placed a hand on my shoulder. As I looked into his eyes, I saw the baby I gave birth to thirty-two years ago—his first steps, first day of school, first t-ball game. Then I drew a blank. Of course. That's when I had taken over the company. I squeezed Robby's fingers, determined, in the future, to get to know my son better.

Robby leaned down to kiss my forehead. "Be careful, Mom. You're dangerously close to showing us your soft side."

Everyone laughed. "In all the years I've known ya, Ms. Biz, I must say I've never seen that side," Pete joked.

"Don't feel bad." Robby returned to his seat. "My sister and I only saw it when we were on our deathbeds."

Throughout the years, I'd imagined this day. My retirement—a time to celebrate accomplishments. I worked hard, and the company had prospered. But what had I forfeited in the process? I smiled, but burned with shame, as I watched Robby and Vickie interact with the truckers.

"I don't understand how you put up with all these men," one trucker's wife said to Vickie. "Sometimes I think one man is too many."

Robby took his wife's hand. "Vickie's good at anything she puts her mind to. She cooks, keeps a clean house and is always there when I need her." Leaning closer to the others, he whispered, "She's everything my mom never was."

Unfortunately, the room grew quiet just as he spoke, and his words hung in the air for all to consider.

I'm not sure what I wish would have happened next. Maybe Robby running to my side. Insisting his words had been a joke. Promising the others that I'd been a terrific mom. None. Of. That. Happened.

Robby apologized for his comment. Didn't detract it, but apologized for how it sounded. Then he grinned and added, "But Vickie really should be everything to me. I mean … she's my helpmate, after all. Mom was just a . . . parent."

Folks laughed and the tension lifted.

Meanwhile, the scrumptious dinner and chocolate cake settled like a rack of spare tires in my gut. Indigestion sliced through my chest, shooting spurts of acid into my throat.

A couple of Tums and a nap. That's what I needed. I would turn the air conditioning down, cover up with a fuzzy throw and sleep the afternoon away. I'd be fine when I awoke—probably even hungry again.

I tried to shut out Robby's words as we waited on the waitress to bring some takeaway boxes. She's everything my mom never was. Surely, he was just trying to get a laugh. That was it. Robby had always loved the spotlight.

And besides, I told my mortified, cowering self, I was just his parent. Right?

"Oh!" Climbing into the car, I became painfully aware I hadn't removed my girdle. The rubber leg grippers had rolled end over end until they'd cut into the tender creases between my legs and my torso.

Robert cleared his throat, pulling me from my thoughts. "I really need to talk to you, Biz, as soon as possible."

Yeah, I need to talk to you, too. About a little black cosmetic bag and some Sexy Summer perfume. Got anything to say about that? And what about the floozy who left it in your car? Kathy Harmin, perhaps?

I couldn't deal with Robert right now. I pulled out my cell phone and tapped in Morgan's number. "Just a minute, honey. I need to check on Morgan."

"Fine." Robert threw his hand in the air. "Just don't say I didn't try to tell you."

Morgan didn't answer, and I was about to click off when I heard her pick up.

"Dis is Moigan's pone, but I'n not Moigan."

Obviously not. "Who is this?"

No answer.

"Hel-l-l-o-o-o. Is anyone there?"

"Mrs. McNeely?"

The invisible child turned into a man. "Yes."

"This is Tony Martinez. Morgan's not here right now, but I will be glad to take a message."

"Where did you say she's gone?"

"She forgot her phone. She should be here in a few minutes, though. We want to make the movies by two."

"The child who answered the phone, he's your son?"

Robert shot a puzzled look in my direction as he pulled in the driveway. I shrugged.

"Yes, ma'am," the man said. "I have him on the weekends. Morgan never mentioned he lived with us?"

"Us?" Awkward silence.

Robert left the car running and went inside. I flipped the car's air on full blast and willed my blood pressure down. "You're living with Morgan?"

Tony laughed. "Yes, I moved in about a month ago. I'm surprised Morgan didn't—"

"You married?"

"Divorced, or in the process, anyway. My ex and I tried to work things out, but once I met your daughter, I decided my marriage wasn't worth saving. Why put up with a bossy nag when charming women like Morgan are out there? Right?"

No. Definitely not right. Marriage is a life commitment.

"Mrs. McNeely? Did I say something wrong? I'm sorry if I—Oh, here's Morgan."

The phone crackled. "It's your mom."

I could imagine my daughter's face.

"Mom?"

"It's not nice to roll your eyes at your mother, Morgan."

She laughed. "You're good."

"What's up with this Tony guy?"

No answer.

"Good grief, Morgan, he's married. Didn't I raise you any better than that?"

"So you would approve if I lived with a single man?"

"That's not what I meant, and I sure hope Tony the Tiger isn't filling your tank."

"I refuse to go there with you, Mother. What did you call about? I'm sort of in a hurry."

The Tony subject was obviously closed. At least for the time being. "You missed my retirement party."

"Oh, that. I meant to FaceTime you and tell you congratulations. I'm really sorry. I got busy at work and forgot."

"Yeah, and why were you at work on a Sunday, anyway? You need to be in church."

"Look, Mom. You really need to back off and let me live my own life. Nothing I do is ever enough to satisfy you."

"Because I don't believe in premarital sex?"

"Because I want to make my own decisions in life and not be expected to justify them to you. Talk to you later, Mom."

And with that, she clicked off.

Whatever. I felt a tug in my chest. Did Morgan not realize that a marriage based solely on attraction was destined for failure? But then, I hated to admit it, but at least she had someone to love on her and laugh with her and . . . I forced myself to stop.

Climbing out of the car was going to be a trick. Given the fact that the tourniquet I was wearing had put my entire lower half to sleep, I wondered if my legs would even support me.

To make matters worse, my Barbie-doll neighbor stepped out of her house just as I cut off the engine and opened my door. She waved her hand back and forth like a windshield wiper on steroids. "Hey."

I hastily slapped my cell phone to my ear and shot her a courtesy nod. I was in no mood to chat—even if the dog she had on a leash was absolutely adorable with its shiny caramel-colored coat, droopy ears, and humongous chocolate-brown eyes.

CHAPTER 10

Robbie's call woke me from my nap.

"Hey, Mom. This is Robby. Can you do me a favor?"

"Possibly."

"Stephanie spent the afternoon with Lindsey Dempsey. We're out at the lake house and would love to stay through the evening. Could you pick Stephanie up and bring her to your house? We'll stop by for her on our way home. She has summer school tomorrow."

"Sure. When will she be ready?"

"We were supposed to pick her up ten minutes ago."

I grinned. "So, super-wife Vickie can't be in all places at all times for all people?"

"Mom? Is there a problem?"

Busted. "I'm sorry, Robby. Just overreacting to the comment you made at the party, I think."

"I'm really sorry about that, Mom."

"Yeah, well, never mind. Stephanie can spend the night. We'll run by the house and pick up some clothes for summer school."

As soon as I hung up, the phone rang again.

"Mom," Robby said. "You didn't let me tell you where to go."

Thankfully, my Jesus-filter caught a snarky reply that came to mind. "I have a pencil. Give me the address."

Though the Dempsey's had pastored the church for almost two years, I hardly knew them. The congregation ran around six hundred on a good Sunday. Renee always sat front row, center section, while Robert and I sat back row, to the left.

I pulled into a fairly new subdivision, found their street and turned into the drive.

Renee opened the door, still dressed in the pink and brown dress she'd worn to church. She'd pushed her dark, shoulder length hair behind her ears. Wispy bangs softened her otherwise strong cheekbones and jawline. Though she sported a bit of a full figure, Renee was absolutely beautiful.

"Hi, Biz. Please come in."

Renee clutched the folds of her dress in her fingers as she led the way to a small den. We took our seats in a pair of cherry Victorian armchairs upholstered in pale blue brocade. Between us, an end table held a pastel-colored carnival lamp. A dark spinet piano occupied most of the opposite wall, while tiny clear Christmas lights flickered on an artificial ficus tree in the corner.

"This room is beautiful. I see you're into antiques."

"These are the pieces my great-grandmother left me when she died a few years ago."

"The tan walls accentuate the furniture very nicely."

Renee's eyes flittered to the front door as I spoke. "I was excited when my husband decided to build this house. He wouldn't move the furniture into the parsonage because it was so small. I worried when we had to put everything in storage."

I nodded, wondering what would happen if Robert ever tried to stop me from doing something I really wanted to do. Muscles tightened in the back of my neck. No man was ever going to control my life again. Images of my mother cowering under my father's commands flashed through my mind.

The girls returned a few minutes later, and Stephanie and I headed for home.

"I can't believe Mom and Dad went to the lake without me." Stephanie closed her eyes.

I reached over and rested my hand on hers. "Sleepy?"

"Hmp-mm. Just wishing I was at the lake."

"Lindsey could have gone with you."

Stephanie's head popped up, and she laughed, rolling her eyes. "I don't think so. She couldn't have even gone shopping today if her dad had known about it."

Red flags shot up so fast I almost swerved off the road. "She went behind her father's back?"

"Don't freak, Granny. She didn't lie to him or anything."

"So . . ."

"So, she just didn't tell him. It's a system she and her mom worked out. Totally sweet. Lindsey's allowed to do whatever she wants when her dad isn't home."

"Like?"

"Like if he leaves the house early, she can wear makeup to school, but if he's still there when she's getting ready, she brings her stuff in her backpack and puts it on at school. And she always washes it off last hour after P.E. because her dad comes home early a lot of times."

"Do the other kids know about this?"

Stephanie jerked her head to the side and shot me one of those, "Are you serious?" looks. "They call her Cami at school—that's short for chameleon."

"I see." Actually, I did see, and I wondered if Robby and Vickie had any idea what kind of influence the seventeen-year-old pastor's daughter was having on Stephanie.

"Granny, you're scowling. You're not going to, like, tell Pastor about this, are you? Cause if you do—"

I patted her hand. "I wouldn't dream of it, honey."

I persuaded Stephanie to join me when I brought restaurant leftovers to Hazel's that evening. We played a game of Scrabble. Stephanie surprised me with a win after playing two seven-letter words in one game. I sure wouldn't have pegged her as a vocabulary buff.

Stephanie dumped the Scrabble tiles back into the velvet bag they came in. "Want to learn a new game called Crazy Scrabble?" she asked Sandy. "It's great for just two people."

I nudged Hazel. "Guess that's our clue to leave."

Hazel pulled her walker close and swiveled in her chair before standing. "Fine with me. I'm ready for my bath and an early bedtime."

I stayed close to my friend. She seemed weaker than normal. Didn't even argue when I stepped inside the shower to wash and rinse her hair for her. No light conversation. Nothing.

Something wasn't right. I helped Hazel into bed and checked her forehead for temperature.

"I'm fine." She touched my hand. "Just really tired. I hope it's not that pneumonia coming back."

I checked the water level on her C-Pap, handed her the mask and kissed her cheek. "Sleep well, my sweet angel."

A horn honked in the driveway around seven o'clock on Monday morning.

Robert flipped to his back and stretched. "Vickie called after you went to bed last night. She's picking Stephanie up for school."

"What?" I sat up and swung my legs over the side of the bed. "I told Robby I'd take Stephanie to school."

"Vickie wants to be sure Stephanie is wearing something appropriate."

"Oh, bother." I heard the front door slam as I slipped into my housecoat. I peeked out my window and burst out laughing. "You gotta love that kid."

Sometime in the night, Stephanie had dyed her long, kinky blonde hair jet black and was wearing black lipstick and fingernail polish, a skin-tight black tank top and a black denim skirt so short it practically showed her behind with every step.

"What's so funny?" Robert stepped up behind me just as Stephanie bent over to climb into the car. "Oh my! She didn't—"

"Mmm-hm, she did. That's my girl. I do believe we were cast from the exact same mold."

"Why on earth do you encourage her, Biz?"

"You think I was aware she was going to dye her hair and dress like that?"

"It wouldn't surprise me."

There were so many things I wanted to say. But if I even started to open my mouth, I was going to blurt out all kinds of ugly questions. Like why Robert always assumed the worst about me. Why he couldn't accept me the way I was. And why he was . . . why he was allowing himself to develop a relationship with another woman.

Robert disappeared into the bathroom, and I climbed back into bed and pulled the pillow over my head.

Robby called later that morning. "Did you help her do it, Mom?"

"Good morning, son."

"It is not a good morning. Vickie swears you encouraged Stephanie to dye her hair. Tell me that's not so, Mom, or I'll have to . . ."

I waited, but he didn't finish his sentence. My lips twitched. "Why don't you ask Stephanie if I encouraged her?"

"Like Stephanie is going to talk to us. The girl has done nothing but roll her eyes and glare at us since she got home. Makes me want to slap her silly."

"Robby, that wouldn't do any good."

"Yes, I know that, Mother. She's been grounded from everything. Probably until Jesus comes if Vickie has anything to say about it."

"If?"

Robby lowered his voice. "Don't go there, Mom. Do you know where she got all the stuff? We've never seen the clothes she had on, and I know she couldn't afford to buy new ones."

"My guess is Lindsey Dempsey. The girls went to the mall yesterday afternoon. Has Vickie spoken to Renee?"

"I don't know. She just told me to drop Christopher and Kyle off at her parents' house on my way to work. Vickie took Stephanie to a beauty shop to see if the damage could be undone."

"Do you honestly believe I had a part in this, Robby?"

He paused. "I'm sorry, Mom, but I need for you to say you didn't. Vickie will ask."

"And keeping Vickie happy warrants attacking your mother's integrity?"

I slammed the receiver to the counter, not waiting for an answer. Why did everyone always assume the worst about me?

My stomach growled and I thought of the leftover cake in the frig. But, no. I was determined to show Robert I could lose weight, even if it killed me. Just before I killed him, in fact . . . after he explained how the little black bag found its way into his car.

I needed to get to the store and stock up on fresh fruit and vegetables, fish, diet sodas and a stack of frozen Weight Watcher meals. I could do this.

Lettie pulled into the drive just as I finished putting the cold groceries away. I closed the tailgate on the truck. Across the lawn, my thirty-something-going-on-sixteen-year-old neighbor waved. Decked out in a hot pink halter top, blue jean cutoffs and spiked sandals, she practically pranced behind her self-propelled lawnmower.

"Good heavens. If she attached a rake to that rear end, she could do the whole job at once. You think?"

"Sí." Lettie climbed from her car, and I noticed her reddened eyes—her spirits obviously sagging as low as my neighbor's halter top.

"You okay?"

She shook her head and followed me to the front porch where we sat together on the white wooden swing, gently gliding back and forth. Hemmed in by plush mature shrubs on every side, I waited until my friend was ready to share what troubled her.

Lettie shoved a legal-sized envelope into my hand. "I don't think I can do this."

Twisting sideways, I attempted to shift my clammy steel-enforced bra into a more comfortable position. Like that could happen. I glanced at the return address. "Application for a catering license?"

Lettie nodded, throwing her long black braid over her shoulder and pushing her bangs to the side. Even at fifty-four, Lettie's dark pixie-shaped face showed few wrinkles.

"Okay. You said you want me to be more honest, so I'll admit that I am so-o-o jealous that you have a future to look forward to. My life seems totally empty right now."

"Si. I understand. But God, he has a plan for your future, too. I will pray and ask him to show us what it is."

"Thanks, Lettie. Now tell me why on earth this application is not a good thing?"

Lettie's cheeks reddened. "I'm just nervous about how the kids will react."

I bit my tongue to keep from verbalizing my thoughts. My honest—ugly—thoughts that I somehow knew weren't the kind Lettie wanted me to share. Why couldn't I empathize with Lettie? Why were my thoughts always so critical?

"Biz?" Lettie nudged me with her elbow. "Are you listening?"

"Sorry."

We rocked in silence for a few minutes. I considered telling Lettie about the cosmetic bag but decided against it. Lettie had a way of insisting my mountains were molehills. I didn't want to argue this one.

I patted her knee. "You know, your kids will eventually get used to the change. Probably even be happy for you."

"I suppose."

We heard a car pull into the drive next door. Lettie glanced in that direction. "Say, how's Hazel doing lately?"

"Better since her granddaughter moved in a few weeks ago. I thought, for sure, she was headed for an assisted living center. But as it is, Sandy works the early dinner shift at Red Lobster. She keeps Hazel company throughout the day and at bedtime."

"That's good. And you still stop by to help her bathe?"

"Yeah. I thought Sandy might start doing that, too, but Hazel vetoed that idea. Can't blame her—trying to hang on to her integrity as long as she can, I guess."

Lettie nodded. "My guess is that Hazel enjoys your company and wants to be sure you don't stop coming to see her every day. She needs you, you know."

My cheeks grew warm. "Well, maybe that, too."

I wiped the sweat off my neck, unfastened two more buttons on my blouse and fanned the fabric away from my skin. "Let's go inside for a glass of tea. This heat is killing me, and"—I glanced down—"the girls are dying for a breath of fresh air. If you know what I mean."

"Sí." Lettie grinned and stood. "Go on in and set the girls free. I need to get home anyway. All the kids are coming for dinner, and I promised them tamales."

Lettie did not know what I was talking about. How could a thirty-six-B have any idea what a forty-six-D endured? Besides, there wasn't a drop of perspiration anywhere on her body. Someday I would look like that.

I put away the rest of the groceries and hid a handful of candy bars I'd thrown into the cart at the last minute. I was committed to this diet, but I also knew emergencies would arise that only chocolate could resolve.

I showered, praying God would strengthen and comfort Lettie as she prepared for this new season in her life. "And Lord, show me what you have for me, too. I know I'm a mess, but surely you have some paperwork for me to keep track of or something."

After a banana and a quick nap, I started a load of laundry. I couldn't risk another outing without my black slacks because, believe me, that girdle had enjoyed its last ride.

Maybe I should take Morgan up on her offer to shop. Wouldn't hurt to pick up another pair of black slacks. Of course, I'd have to do some sweet-talking to get Morgan back into my good graces.

I came upstairs, fished my cell phone from my purse and pushed M for Morgan. She didn't answer, so I tried her work number.

"Bobbie's Boutique."

"Morgan McNeely, please."

"I'm sorry, she's not working today. Would you like to leave a message?"

A wild idea popped into my head, but I immediately sensed a check in my spirit. "Uh, no, thank-you. I'll try to reach her on her cell."

I sensed a foreign, but oh, so pleasurable, sense of accomplishment as I ended the call. As badly as I'd wanted to ask for the shop owner in hopes of discussing Morgan's work schedule, I'd stopped myself. And like the stinkin' girdle I'd successfully wrangled into the day before, the control felt strangely good.

CHAPTER 11

I tried Morgan's cell phone again. This time the live-in answered.

"Yo, Mrs. McNeely."

"Hello, Tony. Morgan there?"

"No, she's getting her hair cut. Then we're gonna hit the beach."

So much for shopping. "You have the same days off?"

"Uh . . . I'm not working right now. But I'm definitely looking every day."

"Like today?"

"Well, you know what they say: 'All work and no play . . .' Actually, I have no idea how that ends. You?"

I crossed my fingers. "I believe it ends with something about making responsibility a priority. Morgan's surely not paying your bills, is she?"

"No, ma'am. Not for long, anyway. I'll be working again soon. Got a few tickets to take care of and all before anyone will hire me. No big deal."

"Right. Well, please tell Morgan I called."

"Sure thing."

I dropped the phone in my purse and headed for the truck. I definitely needed to find something new to wear to the Golden Oldies meeting. I could shop without Morgan.

Thirty minutes later I stood in a dressing room, surrounded by black. Slacks, tops, jackets, even a dress or two hung on the hooks waiting to be evaluated on my body. I was only going to do this shopping gig one time. Trying on clothes in front of a three-way-mirror was not my idea of fun.

To make matters worse, nothing fit. My blobby body refused to slide into one size, but swam in the next. I felt claustrophobic and obese, but I knew what to do. I jumped into the truck and headed for Dairy Queen. A hot fudge sundae every afternoon would do the trick. In no time at all, I'd be perfect for the larger size.

But I couldn't do it. One glimpse of my pooched cheeks in the rearview mirror and a familiar wave of self-disgust shot through me like acid indigestion after a chili burrito. How pathetic—I couldn't even find fat clothes that fit.

Resigned to change, I popped into a corner drugstore and filled my basket with diet shakes, organic breakfast bars and sugar-free chocolate candy. My stomach growled as I walked to the truck.

No time like the present. I ripped open the bag of sugar-free bonbons, unwrapped one and popped it into my mouth. Sweet. I could do this retirement thing—sitting back, watching the tube and snacking on bonbons.

Who was I kidding? Sitting around was definitely not my style. Made me think of Charlie and other customers. Was Vickie taking care of them?

I should find out. It was a bit of a drive to Indy, but my truck practically steered itself to Tires Warehouse on the northwest loop. Good grief. I hadn't had my tires rotated for ages. Might as well give Charlie my business now that I was no longer welcome at my own . . . at Beemer's Trucking.

I parked in the service lane and handed my keys to the attendant. "Oil change and tire rotation, please."

"Hey, Biz."

I turned toward the familiar voice. "Well, Charlie Neighbors. How's the working world treating you?"

Charlie was dressed in stained but clean overalls and a blue denim work shirt. Gray-white stubble peppered his ruddy cheeks and, as always, he balanced a toothpick between his lips as he spoke out one side of his mouth. "Things are great, but how about you? You enjoying your free time?"

Regret cramped my tummy. "Retired life isn't all it's cracked up to be. But, say, I'm glad I happened to see you. Did Vickie ever get your invoice straightened out?"

Charlie kicked at the pavement with the toe of his boot. "I best not go there with you. Robby wouldn't like it much."

Ugh. I could almost feel steam misting from my ears. Half afraid I would start to whistle, I knew I should drop the issue. "No problem, but can't you just put my mind at ease?"

I nudged Charlie with an elbow. "Look, I'm sure you still do coffee with the boys on Friday mornings, so what's the word? They satisfied with the service they're getting?"

Charlie kept his head low. "Uh, sure. A lot of guys think Vickie's some kind of mind reader." He faced me. "Almost freaky how she prepares things before we even ask."

So Vickie was on top of things.

"Not what you wanted to hear, Biz-girl?" Charlie kept his voice soft.

I laughed. "Of course, it's what I want to hear. In fact"—I grabbed Charlie's elbow and led him under the shadow of the building's overhang where we were less likely to be overheard. "We go way back, right, Charlie?"

Charlie stepped back a few paces and glanced around. "Look, Biz. This makes me real uncomfortable. Kind of a fine line between loyalty and integrity here. Give me a break?"

I dropped my eyes. "Sorry, Charlie. I just thought maybe you could give me a call every now and then to let me know how things are going. You know, just friend to friend. No one else would find out."

Charlie shook his head and placed his oil-creased hand on my shoulder. "Sorry, Biz. Can't do it." He turned to walk away as a technician drove my truck up. "Looks like we've got you taken care of." Charlie turned to the serviceman. "This one's on the house, Sal."

"Thanks, Charlie." I climbed into the truck and pulled away. Charlie had put me in my place. Did the right thing. Unlike me.

And I was sick of me. I pulled into Sonic and ordered a Diet Limeade. "I'm so sorry, God. I don't want to control my life anymore. I want to do things your way."

I wasn't even sure what that meant, but the peace that filled me at that moment led me to believe I was moving in the right direction. Perhaps Hazel could tell me more.

I stripped the bed in the guest room, dropping a pillowcase on the floor. As I bent to retrieve it, my fingers came across something solid just under the edge of the bed.

Oh my. Talk about decision time. I knew what I should do. But minutes later, I was stretched across the mattress cover, wishing I'd never broken the cover of Stephanie's diary. Definitely too much information for a take-charge grandmother like me.

I'm an outsider—not even a part of this family. I can't stand them. Not even Daddy. And then . . . *Do you ever think about me, Mommy? Why did you leave me?*

Pulling a pillow over my head, I shut my burning eyes and attempted to relax the muscles around my forehead. But I couldn't shut out my thoughts. Oh, God. Please help me figure out what to do with this thing.

Robert came home early and brought company—our new neighbor.

Thank God, I was wearing a bra. Close up, her age showed—slight bags under her eyes, a shadow of growth on her upper lip, and pucker lines extending from her lips like rays of sunlight. Smoker lines. I extended my hand. "Hi. My name is Biz."

"Oh, what an interesting name." She shook my hand. "I'm Marissa Hocking. I rented the house next door."

"Biz just retired from a taxing job," Robert said. "She's home during the day now, if you ever need anything."

Thanks, Robert. Like I wanted this woman on my doorstep every morning. She'd probably expect us to feed her between paydays and cart her around when her car was on the blink and thaw her water pipes when they froze.

Robert elbowed me discreetly. He was telling Marissa about his counseling job at the university.

"Sounds challenging." Her voice carried a slight southern lilt. "I'm in counseling, too."

My tummy churned and something shifted. I crossed my ankles and squeezed my cheeks. The drop would have to wait. I didn't want to miss a word this woman said.

Marissa continued. "I was so glad to find a house near the hospital. I just signed on with Karrol and Yates at Stafford Memorial. I need to be close for emergencies."

Was the woman suicidal? "I know a nurse who works at Stafford Memorial. She might work for the doctors you'll be seeing. Her name is Frieda—"

Marissa interrupted with a light laugh. "No, I'll be counseling hospital patients."

Robert beamed. "You're a psychologist?"

"Actually, a psychiatrist."

I groaned silently. Not so much that I was wrong about Marissa. More like I was about to drop something nasty right there on my kitchen floor. "Excuse me."

I hurried to the bathroom, and as those stinking diet candies made their way to daylight again, I thought about Marissa. *Actually, a psychiatrist.*

A shrink was a shrink. She definitely wouldn't need our help, though. Probably had some interesting stories to tell. Maybe we could invite her over for a meal or out to eat. She was probably some exotic chef who would choke on the plain meals we fixed.

When I returned to the kitchen, Marissa offered an understanding smile. Good grief. Now she was all up into my business just because she had a Ph.D. after her name?

The woman shifted her leather bag from one shoulder to the other. "I don't want to keep you, so let me explain why I dropped by. I work on Thursday evenings and wondered if you might take my puppy potty during the afternoon. I'll be glad to pay for your service."

"That won't be necessary," Robert said. "Thursday is my early day. I'm glad to help."

Marissa caught my eye. "That okay with you, Biz?"

I was impressed. "Of course. That's what neighbors are for, right?"

Marissa set a key on the counter. "What a relief to meet kind neighbors. You know how some folks assume the worst before you even introduce yourself."

I faked a smile. Could shrinks read minds?

Sandy texted just after Marissa left. No need to come. Grandma has a temperature. Home Health Care here overnight.

I texted back. Let me know if you need anything.

The air had cooled considerably, so Robert and I ate on the patio. Hopefully, rain was on the way. My mind was on overload. The whole Kathy Harmin thing. The cosmetic bag. The business. Stephanie's diary. And now, sweet Hazel.

"You okay, honey?"

Robert's words pulled me back. "Yes. Just worried about Hazel. She seemed so down and out last night. I'd hate it if that pneumonia was back."

"You need to go spend time with her this evening?"

"No. The nurse is there. I'll go by in the morning."

Robert smiled. "It's kind of nice that you don't have to worry about going into work, isn't it?"

"Yes, I have to admit that I'm starting to appreciate sleeping in and not worrying about that rat race."

Robert nearly choked. "You serious?"

"Yes. Of course, I'm bored silly and need to find something to occupy my time. But I didn't realize how much stress I was under."

Robert gave me a thumbs-up. "Speaking of the rat race, my supervisor needs me to take a short trip north to check on our satellite campus near Chicago. Seems proctors are overlooking illegal practices in the testing lab."

My mind immediately veered into the Kathy Harmin lane. "You travelling alone?"

"Yes. I leave early tomorrow morning and should be gone a few days."

I sighed, not sure whether I was more relieved that he was going alone or that he didn't pick up on my suspicion. "I saw Charlie Neighbors today. Asked him how the transition was going."

Robert's eyes narrowed like he was having trouble seeing across the table. "You did what?"

"Relax, Robert. It's called casual conversation."

Robert filled his cheeks and released the air slowly, like a pinched balloon.

"I can't help but worry about the place."

"Give the kids a chance, honey. They'll do fine."

A mouthful of casserole clogged my throat. Humble pie. How did Robert do that? Treat me so kindly just moments after he was obviously ticked about my conversation with Charlie. How did a person shake off anger just like that?

A light breeze blew my napkin to the ground. As I bent to retrieve it, I noticed Robert's thumb sliding along the top of his pants leg.

So, maybe he hadn't shaken the anger.

He pushed his chair back and folded his hands on the table.

"I talked to Morgan and Robby today," Robert began. "They're tired of your interference. I realize you're trying to find your way after retiring, but attempting to run the kids' lives is not the best route."

"Run their lives? They said that?"

"You're surprised?"

"More like irked. First of all, why didn't they come to me? And who am I, that all of you interpret my motherly advice as interference? Does my word mean that little?"

I was shouting. Robert twirled his thumbs, the rest of his fingers still tightly folded together.

An ant crawled across the table. Bad timing. I smooshed the thing and wiped my finger on a napkin. Called for a bit of soap and water, but I wasn't about to leave my post.

Robert set our dishes to the side. Then he pulled a slip of paper from his shirt pocket, unfolded it and scanned the contents. "We need to talk about some things, Biz."

My battle buddies fell back, leaving me defenseless right there on the front line. Well, my grandpa always told me never to let a bully know I was afraid. To stand tall, even if I had just wet my pants. I squared my shoulders and crossed my arms. "Where would you like to begin?"

He laid the paper on the table. "We need to finish talking about the kids. Then there's something work-related I need to discuss with you, and . . . I'd really like to talk about where our marriage is headed—or not headed."

Did I mention I just wet my pants? This was turning into a serious discussion. Well, you'd better believe we were going to add Kathy Harmin and the cosmetic bag to the list. If he—

"Biz, I'd really like to pray together before we go any further." He reached for my hand, but I pulled back. No warm fuzzies traveling through my fingers.

Robert simply bowed his head and asked God to bless our conversation, our home and our marriage. He lifted his head. "I can sense your anger. And I want you to know that was not my intent."

"Anger," I repeated. "I don't know what to say, Robert. I've got so many doggone feelings messing with my head right now that I feel dizzy. I'll do better with the kids, though. I promise."

"Just like that?"

"To tell you the truth, Robert, I'm not sure what I'm supposed to do differently. But both kids have practically written me off, anyway, so there shouldn't be any more problems." I focused on Robert's hands to avoid his eyes. "Now, what's next on your let's-fix-Biz list?"

Robert didn't answer immediately. I looked up and caught his emotionally-torn gaze. "Never mind," he whispered. He folded the list and dropped it back into his pocket. "I guess this isn't the right time."

"I'm trying, Robert. But it feels like you're attacking me. Can you blame me for reacting defensively?"

He shook his head. "I'm not attacking you. But if this is the best we can do at communicating, I see very little hope for improving our marriage or our family."

"I'm sorry you see it that way." I was proud of myself for not spouting any of the snarky comments that had come to mind, but I didn't need to press my luck. The Kathy Harmin and cosmetic bag talk would have to wait. "I'm going in to take a bath and try to get rid of this headache."

"Sure. Run away from the truth. Just don't expect God to help us with what we aren't even willing to face."

He refused to stop pushing my buttons. "And by we, I'm sure you mean me. Right?"

Robert massaged the back of his neck. "Actually, what I mean is that I'm sick of living like this, Biz. Something has to change, or this marriage is not going to survive."

CHAPTER 12

I reheated a cup of stale coffee in the microwave Tuesday morning and headed outside with my phone and my Bible. Dark clouds huddled in the sky and a cool breeze swept across the patio. I could almost smell the coming rain.

Gazing at the colorful display of flowers, I appreciated Robert's care and diligence with the yard. He was a good guy, and as much as I hated to admit it, spot on about me being all up into the kids' business.

What was it he had suggested . . . our marriage was not going to survive? My stomach twisted. Was he involved with Kathy Harmin and comparing the two relationships? Trying to make a last-ditch effort to save his marriage before cutting things off and committing to the other woman?

"Something has to change," he'd said. And that something was me.

I took a gulp of hot coffee and thought about Hazel's verse. I opened my phone and Googled Trust in the Lord.

The verse popped up—Proverbs 3:5. "Trust in the Lord with all your heart and lean not on your own understanding." I pulled a scrap of paper from the back of my Bible and copied that verse and the next. "In all your ways submit to him, and he will make your paths straight."

Submit. Oooh, strong word. But if I ever needed someone to step in and make my path straight, it was now.

The phone rang and startled me. Coffee splashed onto my paper. I shook it gently. "Hello."

"Mom. This is Robby. We need to talk."

His voice sounded controlled. Irritated. "What about?"

"I'd rather not say. Can you come by this morning?"

Blotting the slip of paper with a napkin, I set it in the sunlight to dry. "Sure. I'll leave in about thirty minutes."

I looked at the stained paper, messy as my life. Maybe I was too far gone for change. I crumpled the paper and went inside to shower.

As I pulled onto the highway, I thought about the words in Stephanie's diary. I'm an outsider—not even a part of this family. Why doesn't Daddy ever stand up for me? Why does he always give in to Mom? Why does she hate me so much?

The words that haunted me the most came last. The ink on the page had been smudged, the paper bubbled. But the question was clear. Why did you leave me, Mommy?

I shook the steering wheel. Why did there have to be so much pain in the world?

Vickie's sister, Jackie, sat at the front desk when I arrived. She was a cute girl with a tiny snub nose and large brown eyes, set off with thick mascara and eyeliner. She'd pulled her light brown hair into a high ponytail and wore a red Purdue T-shirt with matching loop earrings the size of piston rings. "Hey, Biz. Can I get you some coffee?"

"No, thanks. Vickie sick today?"

Jackie grinned and waved her hand over the cluttered desktop. "Yeah. That's the story I heard."

Robby opened his office door. He looked past me with bloodshot eyes. "No calls, Jackie."

Jackie saluted. "Yes, sir, Robster." Then she grinned at me. "You can go on in, Mrs. McNeely."

Robby shoved some paperwork into a basket and pulled a yellow legal pad from the drawer. "Why'd you drive to see Charlie, Mom? Couldn't you leave well enough alone?"

Charlie. The fink had ratted on me. "What could I do, Robby? You won't tell me a thing. I can't run a business for twenty-five years and then simply forget about it."

Robby fidgeted with his pen. Probably trying to regain control of his emotions before speaking. Had I gone overboard? Was an addendum in order?

"I'm not falling apart or anything, but—"

"Reel it in, Mom. I'm not biting. We agreed that I'm in charge around here. Remember?"

Appropriate words were on the tip of my tongue, but suddenly, I didn't want to fight. Maybe it was God. Or maybe I was just ready to give up. Until I thought of Stephanie.

Ugly surfaced. "This the kind of control you use around home? Is this why Stephanie can't stand her family?"

I honestly don't think the guy knew what hit him. He was down in a flash. "Stephanie? She told you that?"

"Those were her words." I totally had the floor now. But the victory didn't taste so sweet. What had I done?

Robby glanced at his watch. "Vickie should be back from her doctor's appointment any minute. She needs to hear this." He pulled his cell phone from his belt clip.

"No! I won't talk in front of Vickie."

Robby pounded his desk and stood. He swiveled around to stare out the window, now shaded with mini-blinds and bordered with a navy plaid valance. The grimy white walls had been painted a light gray. Gave the room a touch of class. I had to give one thing to Vickie—she could decorate. But that didn't mean she knew beans about running my business or mothering my granddaughter.

Robby touched my knee. Brought me back to the office. He sat beside me on a second black plastic chair. Surely Vickie realized how cheap plastic looked. Even I could envision comfortable leather chairs with chrome trim. Very contemporary. Very—

"Mom. What else did Stephanie say?"

"First, I'll tell you why I don't want Vickie here, Robby."

Shaking his head, he rubbed his thumb up and down his pants leg, just like his dad. I'd never seen him do that before. "I realize you and Vickie aren't the best of friends, Mom, but she's my wife. Doesn't that count for anything?"

"I'm not sure if it does or not. What I do know is that the two of you seem oblivious to Stephanie's heartache."

"Oh God, help me." Robby crossed the room to face the far wall, his hands cradling the top of his head. Finally, he turned, dragging some imaginary lint from both eyes.

"I'm sorry, son."

He nodded, swallowing as he stepped to the door and grasped the handle. "You are sorry, Mom. You've done a lot of things to undermine my marriage, but never anything as destructive as this. I'm not sure what you think you're doing, but you've gone too far this time."

He didn't understand. I really was sorry. I seriously hadn't meant to start trouble. I just wanted Stephanie to get some help. But what had I been thinking? Of course, Robby would take offense. "Robby, can't you see—"

Robby cut me short. "For your information, you've probably turned our daughter against us at a time when she needs us more than ever."

"Robby, please. If you'll just let me—"

"Let you what? Keep trashing my wife? No way. God, himself, will have to convince me there is any sane reason to spend time with you, Mom. I'm done putting up with your interference. Please just leave me and my family alone."

He stormed out the door and disappeared into the shop.

My fingers twitched as the shock of what had just happened faded and life trickled back into my body. I'd go home. And I wouldn't return until I actually approved of who I was and what I was doing.

"Oh, God, no." I pulled into the driveway and jumped from the truck. "Please, no!"

An ambulance, the engine running, was parked in Hazel's driveway. I rounded the bush that separated our properties just as emergency personnel wheeled my friend out the front door on a stretcher. "Hazel," I yelled, relieved not to see a body bag on that cart. "What happened?"

My friend didn't respond. Her ashen face, partially covered with an oxygen mask appeared swollen, her eyes like sunken thumbprints in a soft cake of mud. Cocooned in blankets and straps, she looked as lost and helpless as I felt.

I shivered. "Please protect my friend, Lord."

Young Sandy scrambled to the ambulance. "She's fallen, and they think she's broken her hip," Sandy called in my direction. "Her vital signs are fluctuating. I'll call you as soon as I know anything."

And with that, they sped away, the siren blaring. The red light atop the vehicle swirling brightly. I clutched my stomach as I watched the ambulance until I could see it no longer.

Marissa stood in my driveway. "Biz, are you okay?"

I stared at Marissa. I didn't want her there. I wanted to be alone to process what I'd just experienced. To find some way to make up to God for all the wrong I'd done so he'd listen to my prayers. And not let Hazel die.

"Can I give you a ride to the hospital, Biz?"

"No, I'll be fine." My fingers shook as I dug through my pocket for my keys and tried to single out the one to the truck. "It's just that Hazel . . . I thought she was going to be fine . . . I planned to sit with her today." I bent over the hood of my truck, buried my head in my arms, and bawled. "Oh, God," I pleaded. "Please don't let her die."

Despite Marissa's pleas, I drove myself to the Emergency Room and waited to be allowed to visit Hazel. While I waited, I texted Lettie to let her know what was happening and to ask for her prayers. I was so afraid mine wouldn't be enough.

Sandy came out just as I finished and sat beside me. "They say she had a stroke at home. That's why she fell."

Hazel was going to die. Somehow, I knew it, and I wanted to run as far and as fast as I could. Pretend Hazel just moved out of my life. But Hazel was my friend. For once, I would do the right thing. "Can I see her, Sandy?"

Sandy nodded. "Hazel had another stroke on the way to the hospital and the doctors don't think she'll even make it through the night. One son is flying in this afternoon from Chicago, the other later tonight from Michigan."

Sandy's eyes searched my face, and I knew she was afraid to say the words. I took her hands in mine. "So, she's dying?"

Sandy collapsed into my open arms, muffling her cries into my shoulder. "I can't do this, Mrs. McNeely. I can't watch her die."

I pulled the girl so close her pulse vibrated against my breast. "I'm here, Sandy."

Sandy lifted her head and wiped her face with the tips of her fingers. We pushed through the heavy doors to the inner parts of the Emergency Room. A nurse looked at me with question as we neared Hazel's cubicle.

"I'm sorry. But only family—"

Sandy didn't hesitate. "This is Biz McNeely. Hazel's adopted daughter."

Laugh or cry. I wasn't sure which to do first.

Machines blinked and beeped over Hazel's bed. I slid my hand under Hazel's and watched for a response. A twitch of the eye. A muscle spasm in her jaw. But there was nothing.

Sandy broke the silence. "Do you mind sitting here for a few minutes while I use the bathroom?"

"Of course. And here . . ." I pulled a few dollar bills from my pants pocket and tucked them into Sandy's hand. "Get yourself a snack and something to drink. Take your time."

I sat and listened to the suction and release of the ventilator that breathed for my friend. Her complexion had returned to a rosy color, but I knew that was misleading. Artificially induced.

"Oh, Hazel." I took her fingers in mine. "Please don't leave us. Please fight. Sandy needs you . . . I need you.

"I'm working on the trust thing with God, Hazel. Read the verse in my Bible this morning and discovered the next verse about submitting and allowing God to make my path straight. That really possible? I mean, my path has to be more twisted than a stinkin' braided rug."

My eyes glided over Hazel's facial features in a painstakingly slow journey. I wanted to remember her velvet skin. Her slightly crooked, scarred right eyebrow. Her downy white hair. I unfastened the pearl-lined clips from her disheveled strands and finger-combed each hair perfectly into place. Then I replaced the clips and kissed her cheek. "I love you, my friend."

Sandy and I sat together that afternoon until one of Hazel's sons arrived. We laughed. And cried. And told Hazel stories. Then we simply sat in silence and contemplated the inevitable.

Not that it mattered one iota in the wide scheme of things, but I couldn't stop obsessing over the fact that Hazel would never finish her puzzle. She rested peacefully, plastic tubing sending liquids through her veins and monitors ticking out her vital signs. I didn't understand the particulars, just that my friend was on her way out of this world. I knew that as sure as I knew Fats Domino sang the rhythm-and-blues. What I didn't know was how I would ever live without that bundle of sweetness next door.

The call came just a little after midnight. Hazel had opened her eyes. Recognized her sons and Sandy. Tolerated a few ice chips and a sip of water.

She showed signs of slight paralysis on the left side and wasn't talking yet, but her vitals were strong. Doctors said it looked like she could possibly pull through.

I fell back into my pillow and cried as if my own life had been handed back to me. And in a way, I think I experienced a sort of spiritual transfusion. Fresh blood pumped through my veins, and I longed to know this God who listened to my prayer and helped my friend. This God who knew my heart and loved me anyway. This God who wanted me to trust him.

The next morning Sandy met me just outside the fourth-floor elevator. "Thanks for coming, Mrs. McNeely. Grandma is actually saying a few words this morning."

"This is so unbelievable, Sandy. Is she awake?"

Sandy led the way to a small sitting room just off the main hallway. "I don't want you to be caught off guard."

Sandy's delay in answering frightened me. I'd often heard of patients making a remarkable recovery just before death. I steadied myself in the doorway. "What is it, Sandy?"

"Breathe, Mrs. McNeely." Sandy took a deep breath with me. "Grandma is okay. The doctors are in with her."

I raised my face and blew a prayer of thanksgiving toward heaven.

Sandy touched my arm. "Sorry to scare you. It's just that recovery is going to take a long time. She can't use her left side at all and her speech is slurred."

"And . . .?"

"And my uncles are having her transferred to a hospital in Michigan—this afternoon."

"Are they with her now?"

Sandy shook her head. "They left to get some lunch. I'll stay here and let you have some time alone with Grandma."

I hugged Sandy and walked toward Hazel's room. So God was taking her from me after all.

Hazel was nodding off when I entered. The nurse explained that the physical therapist was on his way, so she'd just given Hazel a dose of pain medicine.

"Hey, Hazel." I sat by the bed. "You look comfortable."

Hazel opened her eyes and turned her head in my direction. "Love you," she mouthed. Her right hand rested on the bed. She lifted a couple of fingers and I wrapped mine around hers.

"Love you, too." There was so much I wanted to say and so little time. What was most important?

"San—" Hazel couldn't finish the word.

"Sandy?" I stood. "You want me to go get Sandy?"

"No." Hazel separated her fingers from mine, then jabbed her index finger into the palm of my hand repeatedly. "San—Biz."

Hazel's eyes searched mine as she struggled to lift her head.

"No." I gently eased her head back to the pillow and leaned close to her ear. "Save your strength."

She shook her head ever so slightly.

I smiled at her spunk.

"Go- - God loves you." Her soft, scratchy voice vibrated in my ears and traveled straight to my heart like a bullet in the wind. Lodged there forever.

Then my friend shut her eyes and said no more.

The nurse wrapped a blood pressure cuff around Hazel's arm and smiled. "Don't worry. She's just asleep."

My heart did a few flip-flops, and I knew I had to get out of there. I'd had very little experience saying goodbye to folks and wasn't quite sure how to handle the emotions. I kissed Hazel on the cheek and promised to pray for her every day.

She stirred but didn't open her eyes. That was okay. I would always have her words in my heart. And her love.

CHAPTER 13

Not quite ready to pick up life where I'd left it outside the doors to the hospital, I headed off in search of a strong cup of coffee and maybe a sandwich. I found the cafeteria, but lunch hours wouldn't begin for another thirty minutes.

The chapel was situated right next to the cafeteria. I pushed the double doors open, relieved to find the small room empty. I had no strength to form words for conversation and just wanted a few moments to bask in Hazel's endearing love. Cement it in my memory.

A pulpit and a keyboard stood on a carpeted platform at the front. Burning candles lined the window ledges, and a dozen or so pews filled the rest of the space. Tranquil music playing from overhead speakers filled the room with an aura of reverence.

I slipped into the back pew and knelt on the padded kneeler. Resting my forehead on the next pew, I shut my eyes and let the music minister to my weary emotions. *God loves you so much.* Hazel loved me . . . with God's love. Just like Grandpa. And Lettie.

My knees ached. I pushed myself into the pew and focused my eyes on the cross hanging in front of the stained-glass window.

Jesus. I sensed his presence. Felt him calling me to talk to him. To let him share my pain. Good grief, when a bold spray of sunlight pierced the lighter hues of stained glass and warmed my face, I could almost imagine his smile.

"Okay, Jesus. It's just you and me, here."

Awkward permeated my being, but I forced myself to continue.

"I know you're changing me on the inside, Lord. I can feel myself sort of thawing out. I recognize your love and your desire to work in my life. But I don't know how to translate that into real life. Words and decisions.

"Hazel says I'm supposed to throw out my childish view of you so . . . I know that, as a child, I saw you as a giant power in the sky. Beyond my reach. My Sunday school teachers said you loved me. Died for me."

I searched for a flaw in the sterile room. The thoughts converging on me were filthy, and I didn't want to mess up the beauty of everything-God.

But what had my teachers said? Christ died for me and for my sins. My ugly. Christ's death on the cross was anything but pristine.

Shutting my eyes, I continued with pure, childlike honesty. "Lord, I begged you to make my dad stop beating my mom and me. I begged you to make my parents love me. But you never answered, and little by little, I grew to resent you. I detested myself because I couldn't figure out how to be good enough to get your attention. No matter how hard I tried, it was never enough."

Sobs racked my body. Jesus didn't turn his face. Rather, he wrapped me in his arms and assured me that there was never a day in my life that he didn't have his hand on me. You may not understand, my child. But you can trust in my love—my perfect love.

And just like that, I envisioned Christ with new eyes. He wasn't waiting on me to make myself worthy of his love. He loved me right where I was. That was the unconditional love my devotional had talked about.

His love didn't waver, even when I totally messed up in life. Like I had with Robby. I was so proud of my son. His plan for the company was truly exceptional, and I was learning to trust him. Why couldn't I do the same where Stephanie was concerned?

I wanted to vomit, so heavy was the disgust I felt for myself at that moment.

"Mrs. McNeely?"

I jumped when someone touched my shoulder and handed me a few tissues. I wiped my eyes, then the snot that had run down my chin and onto my fingers. "I'm sorry."

A gentleman wearing blue jeans and a Detroit Tigers jersey stood in the aisle. "Please don't apologize." He grinned. "I spent about an hour here in the middle of the night in the same condition."

He extended his hand. Oooh. I waved it away as I recognized his deep blue eyes. "You must be Hazel's son?"

"Yes, Walter Vick. And you are Biz?"

I nodded and scooted over. "Want to sit down?"

Walter shook his head. "How about a piece of pie in the cafeteria?"

After a quick trip to the restroom to wash my hands, I opted for a tub of yogurt with granola topping and a cup of coffee. As we were seated, my phone buzzed with a text from Lettie. You still at the hospital?

In the cafeteria. You here?

Si. Be right down.

I returned to the cafeteria line and ordered an iced tea for Lettie. She stepped in the door as I finished paying. "You want anything to eat?"

"No. José and I just finished a big breakfast."

I handed her the drink. "I'm sitting over here with one of Hazel's sons."

Walter stood as we approached and introduced himself to Lettie. He waited for us to be seated first. I liked that.

"Walter is from Michigan. Hazel's elder son."

Lettie nodded. "So how many siblings do you have?"

My stomach growled. I peeled the lid from my yogurt and stirred in the granola pieces.

Walter swallowed a mouthful of apple pie and drank a sip of water. "Just two. A younger brother from Chicago and a younger sister from New Orleans. We were all born here in Indiana, but Mom moved us to Michigan when our dad was killed."

Lettie cocked her head. "Oh, I'm sorry."

"It was a long time ago. And then, about three years ago, Mom got it into her head to move back to Indiana where all her friends lived. We were afraid she'd be devastated when she realized how many of them had already passed on, but not so. The woman doesn't have a shy bone in her body. Returned to her old church and befriended her friends' second and third generations. It's been really good for her."

Wow. I hadn't known that about her. "And Sandy. Will she stay here when you move your mom to Michigan?"

Walter's forehead wrinkled, and he sighed. "That's up in the air, right now. How much do you know about Sandy?"

"Just that she came to visit a month ago."

Walter laughed. "Mom always has been tight-lipped. I'm surprised you know anything about her."

"Actually, I don't know much for the three years we've been neighbors. She has a way of turning the topic around when it gravitates to her." I grinned. "I really didn't even realize how true that was. But she knows a lot about me. That woman's an incredible listener with a way of making a person feel totally comfortable."

"Yes, that she is. Well, the fact is, Sandy is my sister's child. But she's currently a ward of the court because of some past behavior. She's been living with her grandmother as an alternative to juvenile detention or some sort of expensive boot camp for troubled kids."

My stomach ached. How many people in my life had I just sort of hovered over and never gotten to know?

Walter's phone buzzed. He glanced at the screen. "I need to get back upstairs soon. The desk nurse needs me to sign some paperwork so we can get going."

I couldn't bear the thought of Walter walking out of the cafe because that meant . . . "What will become of Sandy now?"

"I'm going to take her with me. Try to get it approved through the court. My kids are grown and my wife and I have plenty of room in our home for her. Plus, she'll get to visit Mom as often as she likes."

I sighed. "Sounds like a wonderful plan."

Walter tipped his head, his eyes wide. "Well, it wouldn't hurt to say a little prayer that everything works out. You see, Sandy belongs to my sister and she detests my brother and me. She'll likely fight to have Sandy sent to a Juvenile Center before letting us have her."

Walter's phone buzzed again, and he shrugged. "Time's up. Gotta go."

He reached across the table and took my hand. "Before I do, though, I'll tell you why I came to find you in the chapel. Every time I called Mom, she mentioned what a wonderful friend you were and how you faithfully cared for her. My brother and I will be eternally grateful for that. Without your help, Mom could never have seen her dream fulfilled to live in Indiana again before she died. When that house came available, I bought it for her immediately. You see, my parents lived in that house, and Mom gave birth to all three of their children there."

Lettie and I gasped.

Walter nodded. "So, you see what an answer you've been to our prayers."

Lettie picked up her purse. "Do you want me to come to the house with you, Biz?"

"No, thanks. I think I'd rather be alone for the evening."

As I walked to my car, I thought about Sandy. How I wished I could take her home with me. Girls like Sandy needed a place to call home. Someone to love them and accept them for who they were, regardless of their past. Someone to believe in them as they reached for a better future.

I spent some time on the patio that evening. The pungent, but pleasant scent of the citrus candle I lit to scare away mosquitoes steadied my nerves. Why couldn't life really be like this? A hot cup of coffee. A refreshing breeze tantalizing my senses. A comfortable silence.

Why did there always have to be drama behind the scenes? Would there ever come a time when I could totally relax and trust in the moment?

I could pretend. Imagine that Robert and I were more than compatible. Like we had a marriage like José and Lettie. That we genuinely cared for each other and enjoyed spending time together. Maybe even bought the house in the country, worked together and resolved our differences as a family.

The thickness in my throat swelled when I glanced over at Hazel's backyard. "Be with her, Lord. Give her peace. Please work a miracle so Sandy can live with her uncle."

My shoulders felt lighter as I carried my cup inside and ran a hot bath. Was this what it meant to give my burdens to God?

As I soaked in the bubbles, I considered bringing my marriage and family burdens to God, also. But I couldn't. I wasn't at all sure I could leave them there, and I didn't want to fail God again.

Robert called as I climbed into bed.

"Hi, Biz. You doing okay?"

"No. Not really. Hazel had a stroke yesterday."

"Oh, Biz. Is she . . .?"

I reached for a tissue. "She made it. Partially paralyzed, but she's alive and her long-term prognosis is good."

"Thank God. Now she'll need you more than ever."

"No. Her sons flew down last night. They transferred her to a rehab center in Michigan this afternoon She's gone."

"I'm sorry, honey. Did you call Lettie?"

"Yes. She came up to the hospital."

"Couldn't ask for a better friend than Lettie, could you?"

"Nope." I propped my pillow and snuggled under the covers. "Lettie told me something exciting this morning. The house I showed you years ago is for sale. The one where I used to babysit."

"With the creek?"

"Uh, huh."

"That's a beautiful home with lots of acreage."

"I was wondering if we could check it out when you get back."

Robert paused. "You're not suggesting we consider buying the place, are you?"

"Actually, I am. Lettie and I could hardly hold a conversation on the front porch with that hippie mechanic across the street. I can't stand this neighborhood, Robert."

"I do remember better days."

Was Robert softening? "People leave their trash cans out by the curb for days, and the lawns are a mess. Pitiful excuse for a neighborhood."

Robert yawned. "It's late, Biz, and I have a long drive home tomorrow. We need to talk about so many things. I'm really sorry I left things as they were before I went out of town. I understand how you might have perceived my words as an attack, and I'm sorry for that, as well. Our marriage definitely needs help, but I'm not ready to give up. Are you?"

"No. But I'm not ready to accept all the blame, either. I have a list of my own, you know."

"Yes, I'm sure you do. Well, when I get home we'll cover both our lists and then talk about buying a new house."

Frieda sat next to me at the meeting the next morning. "Any more fainting spells?"

I rolled my eyes.

"Were you really fasting?"

Merriment shined from Frieda's eyes. The woman totally had my number. "Just trying to cut back."

"Been there. Like when you supersize your meal at McDonalds, and the guy behind the counter asks if you're sure."

I laughed. "Yeah, or when you go to the doctor and the nurse hands you two sheets instead of one?"

My new friend laughed like an intoxicated hyena. "I am so with you, sister."

At ten minutes after the hour, Olivia still hadn't shown. Renee fidgeted in her seat, alternating her gaze between the door and the clock on the wall at the back of the room.

Someone needed to get the ball rolling or we were going to be there all day. On impulse, I spoke. "Olivia has obviously been delayed. Why don't we go ahead and get the prayer stuff out of the way? Does anyone want to share a need?"

The ladies shared requests, and as I encouraged others to join in, I remembered how much I enjoyed being in charge.

I asked Lettie to lead us in prayer. Olivia hurried in the door just as we finished. "I'm so sorry I'm late." She shared a short devotional about commitment. "In the past, our Bible study attendance has fizzled after just a few weeks. I sincerely hope you're ready to make a commitment, because we have a lot of work to do in our church and community."

Corrine raised her hand from the elbow up like a silly second grader, not speaking until Olivia nodded permission. "If I'm going to commit to every week, I think it's important that we stay on track and not waste time with trivial prattle. Stick to productive discussion."

I stifled a groan. Well, excu-u-se us, Ms. Too-Busy-with-Your-Exciting-New-Husband.

Fortunately, Olivia was more gracious. Probably why God had her in charge instead of me. "I think you're right. We'll fellowship during lunch. Sound good, ladies?"

Heads bobbed like the room had just turned into a giant rocking horse.

Olivia beamed. The woman obviously loved control as much as I did. "I believe God spoke to me about reshaping our vision and goals. Titus instructs us to teach the younger women in the church. How do you think we can do this best?"

Okay, who was Titus? I couldn't remember Robert mentioning his name. Lettie flipped through her Bible. Oh, that Titus. Guess I would have to spend more time in my Bible if I didn't want to make a fool of myself.

Little Sister giggled. "Well, I don't know about the rest of you, but at eighty years old, I'm not sure I could even relate to the younger girls. Their world is so different than mine."

I agreed. "I also think we should concentrate on getting acquainted with each other before we reach out to the kids."

Once again, heads nodded.

I was on a roll. "Why don't we meet at someone's house next week for brunch instead of coming to the church? I'm sure Lettie will make her famous breakfast tacos for us."

Lettie pretended to be put out but burst into a smile a few seconds later. "Sounds like a plan—as long as you don't mind driving to the country."

Cheerful conversation filled the room. This was the happiest I'd seen the ladies.

Olivia smiled, but her shoulders stiffened. *Oooh, I felt a veto coming. I should definitely keep my mouth shut for the rest of the meeting.*

Turns out I should have opted for silence sooner. As the ladies migrated to the lunch tables, Olivia asked to speak to me privately, leading the way to an empty classroom.

Hoping for backup, I glanced around for Lettie or Frieda. No luck.

Olivia began with a smile. "Thank you for getting the meeting started, Elizabeth. I took Mac's mother to a doctor's appointment, and you know how those go."

"Glad to help." I turned to leave.

"There is one more thing."

Drats.

Olivia fidgeted with her cross necklace. "I want you to know I'm trying my best to make the meetings interesting, but I refuse to make that my first priority. After all, we're not here to be entertained, but to do the Lord's work. Would you agree?"

I nodded—not so much because I agreed, but because I wasn't sure how to put my feelings into words. *Was it wrong to enjoy doing the Lord's work?*

I put on my best Christian sister voice. "I appreciate all you do for the church, Olivia. I can't imagine what it's like to juggle so many plates. I mean, I'm sure you must inadvertently drop one here and there—like being late for the meeting today."

Olivia cleared her throat as red shot up her neck. "Well, in the future, I need for you to check with me before sharing your ideas with the group. Pastor placed me in leadership to avoid sticky situations like this."

Pour on the humility, Lord, before I totally put this bird in her flippin' cage. Inhale . . . Exhale . . . Smile . . . Ready.

"I apologize, Olivia. I didn't realize the discussion was sticky. Wouldn't you agree most of the ladies loved the idea?"

"I did see that. But we are to please God, not people. The ladies may love the idea, but I need to pray and confirm the Lord's will before we finalize any plans."

Stinkin' bird patted me on the shoulder.

"I'll clear this matter up during lunch, and I promise to pray about having a brunch in the future. So, are we good on this?"

Oh, yeah. Smear doo in my face. Preen those victory feathers. I might not know my scriptures so well, but I knew when I'd been slammed against a wall, and believe me, it didn't feel so Christian-like.

CHAPTER 14

Lettie caught my arm as I bolted for the door. "I thought we were staying for lunch. Olivia correct you for forgetting to call in your reservation again?"

"No lunch for me. I just had my fill."

I hurtled out the door and leaned against the building—spewing a few less-than-Christian words I'd involuntarily picked up at the shop.

Lettie must have had the sense to go back inside for our purses because the next thing I knew, she was herding me to the car. She glanced over as she turned the key in the ignition. "Talk to me."

I slammed my hand against the dash and relayed Olivia's words. "This is exactly why I've avoided Christian fellowship all these years."

Lettie pulled into a Sonic, and we slurped on Diet Limeades while we talked. The whole mess didn't sound nearly so serious when I shared it with Lettie. "Not sure why that woman set me off so bad."

"This isn't just about Olivia, Biz. This is your childhood coming out. Pain that's been bottled up for way too long."

"Maybe. Anyway, I'm probably making too much of it all."

Lettie shook her head. "I don't think so. Look, Biz. You're probably not going to want to hear this, but try to remember that 'hurting people hurt people.'"

No, the words did not help. "Are you asking me to punch your lights out, girlfriend?"

We laughed until the car rocked and we had used every napkin we could find to wipe our eyes and noses. I pulled my head back and scrunched my eyes. "Like Olivia Delanie has any idea what a tough day looks like—her and her perfect body and family."

"How do you know that, Biz? You have some supernatural ability to view her personal life?"

"What's your point?"

"I've just been wondering why you've taken such a strong dislike to Olivia from day one? What's she ever done to you?"

"Besides reading me the riot act today?"

"Don't avoid the question."

I tried laughing her seriousness away, but Lettie didn't cave. "You know what, Lettie. I honestly don't know the answer. I just know Olivia makes me feel like a fat slob when I'm around her."

"And that's her fault because . . ."

I ignored the interruption. "And when she spouts all those holy words at the meetings, it makes me feel like a doggone heathen, and I'm not. I may not—"

"Biz." Lettie held up the stop sign hand. "You really can't see what's happening here?"

I frowned. "No, I can't. Please enlighten me, wise sage."

"Save your snarky comments. I'm just trying to help."

"I know. I'm sorry."

"You're playing the comparison game and basing your feelings on your feelings. When—"

"Wait . . . Say that again in English."

We laughed.

"Okay. When you're around Olivia, her strengths make you painfully aware of your weaknesses—or what you perceive to be your weaknesses. Like your desire to lose weight and to know your Bible better."

"Whatever. I love the way you're turning me into the problem instead of the victim, here. Can we just head home?"

Boy-howdy. I was exhausted by the time Lettie dropped me off. I can't imagine how I used to manage twelve-hour workdays.

Took me a while to fall to sleep. The argument with Olivia caught me off guard. I thought we had really started connecting. But as soon as she started criticizing me, my defenses shot up and I turned incredibly ugly. So frustrating. Why couldn't I learn to simply disagree nicely like a normal person?

Renee called later in the day.

"Pastor and I wondered if you and Robert would like to go to Casey's Steak House on Saturday night."

"Sounds fun. I'll check with Robert."

"No need. Todd texted him a few minutes ago. Robert said he's game if you are."

"Sounds like we're on, then. See you there."

Seemed odd Renee didn't even mention the ladies' meeting. I headed to the kitchen to start supper. Had Olivia discussed my faux pas with the other ladies after I left?

Robert arrived home right at dinner time. I waited until he downed half a plate of lasagna before approaching him about the house.

"Honey, I know we need to talk about a lot of things, but I'm afraid the house will sell in the meantime, and it means so much to me. Would it hurt to just walk through it?"

"We'd get a realtor on our backs."

"And …?"

He set his fork down. "Okay, I'd love to move, too. But it's just not wise with me approaching retirement. Besides, that house is much too big for us. Why don't you see if Robby and Vickie would be interested in the place?"

Yeah, like when hell freezes over. This was my house.

I waited until Robert was busy in his office to tackle the guest room. I pulled ragged blankets, sleeping bags and extra pillows out of the closet and made a mental note to arrange pick up by the Salvation Army. I stacked everything in a huge pile in the corner and set to work sweeping the closet floor, clearing the cobwebs and washing down the shelves.

Exhausted from climbing up and down the ladder, I decided to take a break. I stuck my head inside the door to Robert's office. "Want an English muffin and a cup of coffee?"

We carried our snack to the living room. "I think I've discovered what I want to do with all my extra time."

Robert walked to the door of the guest room and looked inside. "Yeah, I heard you messing around in here. So, you're going to do some deep housecleaning?"

I nodded. "Robert, I really want that house in the country. I know it doesn't make sense, but I've dreamed of living there for years, and I know it will sell fast. Can you please consider looking at it? We could always use my savings to buy it."

Robert sat down and stared into his coffee. "Biz, I hate to disappoint you, but this isn't the right time. There are other homes in the country. We'll look when I retire."

"I don't want any other house in the country. Don't you understand, Robert? This one has emotional ties."

Robert shut his eyes and shook his head. "I'm sorry, Biz. I just can't go there. You know there's more to it."

"As in . . .?"

He looked at the floor. "As in, is this marriage going to last? I'm serious, Biz. I don't see us ever divorcing, but we may be looking at separation until we can work on things. Primarily, our ability to communicate."

"You're that unhappy?"

"Not on the surface. We get along pretty well. But I want more out of life. I'm tired of shoving my frustration when you won't listen to me."

He traced the edge of the sofa cushion with his thumb. "For heaven's sake, Biz. I'm a counselor. I make a living helping people sort out their thoughts and goals. Others listen and respect my insight and advice. But not you. You always have to one-up anything I say, and I'm sick of it. Marriage doesn't have to be a competition. It's time to get on the same side or give up."

Time to one-up him with my own list? Probably not.

We finished our snack in silence. Then Robert showered and went to bed.

The money in savings was mine. I could always do this on my own.

But what about trusting God? What if Robert eventually left me for Kathy Harmin? I would need the savings as I grew older. There was no good solution. Except . . .

I knelt by my chair. Forget the pain in my knees. I wanted God to know I was serious. "Lord, I thought I wanted this house more than anything in my life. But now I see my marriage crumbling before my eyes and I've got to wonder what good a home will be without our family to fill it?

"I'll admit that, right now, the house means more to me than my marriage. But it shouldn't be that way, should it? That's not the dream I've held close to my heart for years. I've longed for the whole package."

My forehead tensed as I pictured my family at the country house at Christmas time. Snow covered the ground. The large pine next to the barn sparkled with glistening lights. We laughed as the grandkids built a snowman and made snow angels. I hurried inside to remove the cookies from the oven and heat milk for hot chocolate.

Picturesque? Maybe. But was this what true love looked like? I remembered what Hazel told me about my relationship with God. About surrendering old beliefs and getting to know who God really was.

I would start there with Robert. Get to know him. Learn to communicate. To listen without making assumptions. I wiped tears from my cheeks, grabbed the chair frame for support and pushed myself to my feet. My body didn't shiver, and I didn't hear a voice from Heaven. But I now knew what I wanted. The house, yes. But love in my marriage and family first.

And for this, I knew I could trust God.

He might say no to the house. I would accept his answer. But on the off chance that he might say yes, I planned to be ready.

So . . . back to work. Dresser drawers came next. Cancelled checks, guidebooks for discarded appliances, yellowed linen tablecloths and napkins, long white tapered candles. Two drawers completely full of Christmas cards and gifts we neither wanted nor needed—my way of cleaning up after the holidays.

Absolutely nothing for the To Keep stack. That was good. I stacked all the new stuff on top of the dresser and tossed the trash in a pile on the floor.

My back and feet ached. Good grief, I hadn't done this much physical labor since I gave birth to Morgan.

Thankfully, a spurt of fresh energy kicked in as I made up the bed. I glanced around, filled with a peaceful sense of accomplishment and pride, despite the fact the room actually fared worse than when I started. No one else might be able to tell it, but organization was happening. I'd accomplished a lot for one night.

Ah, Friday morning. Coffee and sticky buns with Lettie—a la no grandkids. Not exactly diet food, so we decided to split one and forego the butter. My face twisted in wry amusement as I swallowed the first bite and pushed the plate away. "This isn't worth it. Think I'll save my calories until I can have the real deal."

Lettie laughed and forked my share onto her plate. "Tastes fine to me. By the way, have you heard how Hazel is doing?"

"Yes. Sandy texted me to say they arrived in Michigan and Hazel is doing well in the hospital. Doctors want to regulate her meds and start her on physical therapy before they send her to rehab."

"Good to hear. And Sandy?"

"I didn't ask." I sweetened my coffee with Splenda and added a couple of ice cubes from my water glass. "I did ask Robert about the house in the country."

"And?"

"He said we needed to wait until he retired to move.

Lettie finished the last of the sticky bun. "Maybe he's right. Can you imagine how hard it's going to be to move after living in your house for all these years?"

I couldn't look Lettie in the eyes. "I should have known you'd support Robert."

"I didn't do that. I'm just trying to look at it from both sides."

I looked up. "I prayed about it, Lettie."

She smiled.

"God's doing something special in me lately. He helped me realize that my marriage is more important than getting this new house. I'm going to try to be a better wife to Robert."

"And if you don't get the house? Will you be okay with that?"

"I want to be."

Lettie pushed some buttons on her cell phone. "I don't want you to accuse me of spouting holy words, but there's a perfect verse for you."

I sat up straight and folded my hands in mock reverence.

Lettie laughed. "Here it is in 1 Samuel 16. Verse seven. It says, 'The Lord does not look at the things people look at. People look at the outward appearance, but the Lord looks at the heart.'"

Okay, that made my eyes run. "I remember that verse. But, honestly, Lettie, I'm not sure my heart's much better than my flesh at this point."

She shrugged. "Maybe there's more than one part to the heart? Like there's the evil that is stored there, but also the desire to improve? I think you need to give yourself grace, Biz. Changing your heart is a process."

"But I've tried for so long."

"You can't do it alone. But you're on the right track. Remember, there's also a verse where God says, 'I will take your heart of stone and give you a heart of flesh.'"

I was hungry to know more. "That's reassuring, isn't it? That God plans to do the work. Maybe the Bible is where I should be looking for my new life."

We laughed at the simple, and yet, profound truth nestled in my words. "Hey, Lettie. How about we do breakfast and talk like this every Friday morning?"

Lettie picked up her phone and keys. "Sounds good to me."

As long as your kids don't need you, that is. I winced as the snarky dig ran through my mind.

Lettie pulled up in front of the house just as Morgan swung into the drive, stepped from her car, and slammed the door.

"To what might I owe this privilege?" I mused. "Isn't Mother's Day always on a Sunday?"

Lettie cocked her head and gave me the eagle eye.

"I know, I know. I'll be sweet. See you later."

I so didn't feel like dealing with Morgan. The girl made me a nervous wreck when she got in one of her holier-than-thou moods.

Morgan paced the living room. I shut the door, and she halted her march, initiated eye-to-eye combat and attacked with a fury known only to a totally ticked woman. "Where in the world do you get off sticking your nose into my life again?"

"Are you asking me or the neighborhood?"

She dropped her mascara-caked, desert-fatigue-brown weapons, plunked down into the recliner and switched from megaphone to monotone. Each word seemed to require a breath of its own. "The way you talked to Tony."

"Morgan, you're blowing this way out of proportion. All I did was—"

Morgan lunged to her feet, towering over me like a drill sergeant on a first-day recruit. "All you did was imply that Tony was a total loser. Well, let me tell you. If I want to spend my money on a loser, that's my business. I sure don't need you trying to play the doting mother. You failed that role years ago."

"Morgan, please."

"Save it." She turned her back and headed for the front door. "I like my life, and my friends accept me just like I am. You are way too high maintenance."

One more closed door in my life.

My head hurt, and I wanted a nap, but I needed to talk to Robert. He would understand. He'd call Morgan and fix everything, because that's what Robert did.

CHAPTER 15

I took the back stairs, hoping to find Robert alone in his office. Never expecting to hear a high-pitched voice, dripping with sex appeal, beyond his closed door.

"Robert, you are such a dear."

That wasn't the voice of a young whiney student. More like the total woman. With no effort, my creative mind paired the voice with images from a book I'd read in the seventies, and I pictured the woman wrapped in nothing but glittery Saran Wrap and Stilettos.

I stole a quick glance toward the adjoining observation room. Dark. Empty. I slipped inside and peered through the one-way window. Kathy Harmin, head of the English department, lunch companion, stood beside my husband pointing to a map and several brochures spread out on his desk.

Robert turned his head and the woman plastered a smooch on his cheek.

"Oh, Robert, this is going to be so much fun."

Robert rolled his chair backward while the petite blonde propped herself on the desktop. She crossed her legs, adjusted her mid-length skirt and leaned back on the palms of her hands—bust extended and taut.

I wanted to puke. What if a coworker walked in? Duh, what if Robert's wife was in the next room?

Robert stood and turned his back to the slippery eel— unaware that he now peered in my direction. What I wouldn't have given for a super-soaker able to penetrate glass. Maybe fill the thing with vinegar. Or tear gas. Mow 'em both down with one satisfying round.

"So, Maui would be your first choice?" she asked.

They were planning a trip? My head went dizzy and my elbow hit the glass with a solid thud as I plummeted to the floor.

Life happened. Fast. Someone flipped on the overhead fluorescent lights, and a sea of black dots swam before my eyes. Robert was in my face.

"Biz! Are you okay?"

"Sure." My voice dragged. I glanced around. We were alone. Professor Harlot had disappeared.

Robert's thumb twitched against his pants leg. I used the chair for support as I pulled myself to my knees. Robert took my arm and hoisted me to my feet. His hands felt clammy, his breathing labored. "I'll drive you home."

Yeah, and stay just long enough to pack your bags. I didn't say it. Something about the concern in his warm eyes stopped me. "No need. I've got errands to run."

I lied. I had no errands to run. Whatever. Dishonesty was mere dribble compared to what I'd just seen.

"You don't understand." Robert touched my arm. "What you think you saw—"

"Is what I saw." I pulled away, dabbed at a bit of nonexistent lipstick on his cheek and headed for the door. "By the way, would Maui be your first choice?"

Thankfully, Robert didn't follow me. I tossed my purse across the front seat and slammed my hand against the steering wheel. "This isn't fair, God! I'll admit I did things wrong, but even I don't deserve this."

Marissa stepped outside with Boomer as I pulled in the drive.

"Hi, Biz. How's it going?"

Oddly enough, I longed to tell her exactly how it was going. Who else would ask? Who else cared? I wanted to verbally tear Robert to shreds so someone would realize what a bum he was. But as angry as I was, I couldn't allow myself to malign my husband's character before I learned all the facts. "I'm doing okay. How about you?"

"Tired, as usual. But I took today off. Needed a long weekend to rest."

She'd probably want company. I sensed a dirty look forming on my lips and managed to turn it around. "You got plans?"

"Nope. I just want to sleep and watch movies with Boomer." The pup sat obediently at her ankles, staring into Marissa's eyes like some lovesick sailor. I swear the mutt actually smiled when Marissa bent to pat his head. "Anyway, I just wanted to tell you that you don't need to let Boomer out next Thursday. Tell Robert—Biz, you're crying."

"Sorry." I practically gurgled my words. "I just had a really bad day."

"Can I—"

"No, I'll be fine." I smiled, despite my pain. "Enjoy your break."

Not waiting for a response, I hurried into the house to wash my face and . . . plot my revenge. Shallow breaths clogged around the knot in my throat as I replayed what I'd seen at the office. Kathy's full lips on Robert's face. Her voluptuous body propped on his desk.

Feeling lightheaded, I lowered the toilet lid and sat. The woman had forced herself on my husband. Would Robert eventually give in to her advances?

Could I blame him? I'd never been good in bed. Probably never would be. At least not until I found some way to let go of the memories of that heinous night so many years ago when a young man, a friend, forced himself upon my body and stole my virginity.

My stomach muscles contracted as if a wire were being coiled around my waist. Tighter and tighter—until I doubled with the pain. Oh, God. Would I ever truly recover from that night?

My grandpa came to me after the truth was known. He held me in his arms. Kissed my forehead and stroked my unkempt hair. "Don't let your heart grow cold, sweet thing," he'd said. "Leave the revenge to God. He will heap coals of fire on that son-of-the-devil's head."

But that never happened. My father made sure of it. He saw an opportunity to make good on the situation and greedily took advantage of it.

I dropped my head into my hands. "You let me down, Lord. You allowed them both to use me." I swallowed hard, leaning against the wall. "You didn't take revenge."

What was I to do with all the fury I still held inside? I couldn't just deny its presence, or I would surely turn my back on God again.

A picture came to mind. Christ on the cross. Beaten. Bleeding and dying.

And a message. I am not shocked with your anger, sweet Biz. I created you with the ability to feel, and I understand why you're angry. Revenge is mine, yes. But even when you cannot see my hand at work or comprehend my ways, you can trust in my promises. Trust in me.

I dragged myself to bed, too exhausted to respond.

I woke several hours later. I lay there for a long time, allowing the stillness of night to comfort my bruised soul. My eyes burned and tears threatened to spill once again, but I was too tired to cry. Tired enough to sleep. Forever.

Robert was home. I heard the faint buzz of the evening news in the next room and smelled fresh coffee. Robert never drank coffee after noon. He must have brewed it for me.

"No, no, no." I moaned into my pillow. "Don't be nice to me. I want to hate you." But my steam dissipated. I kept picturing Robert turning away from the wicked predator who'd slapped her lips to his face and perched herself on his desk. He'd done the right thing.

I considered staying in bed for the night. But someone had to take the high road. I dragged myself out of bed. "Lord, please help me trust you through this. I have no clue how to handle the rage burning in my breast."

I slipped past Robert on my way to the kitchen. A Wendy's bag on the counter held a double cheeseburger and large fries.

Robert called to me from the living room. "There's a chocolate shake in the freezer."

He thought that would fix things? I poured a cup of coffee and headed for the living room, my gut filled with dread.

Robert clicked off the television as soon as I sat down.

No pretending tonight.

He looked up, his eyes swollen. "Are you okay?"

Never been better. Sarcasm. That's all I could come up with?

But for some reason, I didn't want to fight. Honestly, I just wanted this to all go away like it had never really happened.

Robert uncrossed his legs and placed his hands on his knees. "You scared me when I found you collapsed at the office."

"And you said marriage didn't need to be a competition. Well, from what I saw, the game is on."

"I'm sorry you saw what you did."

His words stoked bedded coals, and I felt a bit more ugly trickle in. "Just sorry I saw it?"

"You know I didn't mean that."

I thought about what I needed to say. "Look, Robert. I don't want to fight. But I know what I saw. A beautiful blonde, oversexed colleague determined to win your affections, to say the least."

Robert's eyes popped up faster than a Chinese firecracker. "Are you talking about Kathy?"

Now I wanted to puke. All over Robert. Was he seriously blind to the woman's intentions? Did he need a complete testosterone infusion?

I laughed. Not a perfect time for humor, but I couldn't stop myself. Irony like this was hard to come by.

"What on earth is funny about all this?"

I couldn't tell him. Not in a million years. Giddy—that's the only way to describe my mood. Not happy-giddy, but avoidance-giddy.

"Let me know when you're ready to talk seriously, Biz. I need to discuss something important with you."

"Oh, right! Like something more important than what happened this afternoon?"

My hands shook as I slid the end table drawer open, removed the black cosmetic bag, and fired it at Robert like a missile. "Why don't we start with this?"

Robert let the bag fall to the floor. "I have no idea what that thing is."

"How did I know that would be your answer?"

Robert threw his hands in the air. "You're not even talking sense, now, Biz. It's a bad situation, but I did nothing to encourage it. I promise."

Sharp replies bombarded my Jesus-filter. Well-deserved attacks, in my opinion. I'd like to say God helped me keep my mouth shut, but I honestly think it was more about a mental delay in choosing which retort to discharge first.

Robert turned to leave. "Maybe we can talk tomorrow. Or we could always shove the whole mess under the rug like we've done with every other issue we haven't agreed on over the years."

I picked up the stupid cosmetic bag and shoved it in my purse, my body still charged with adrenaline. I would get to the bottom of this. Robert may wish the evidence would disappear, but that wasn't going to happen.

After a trip to the bathroom, I decided to start on the basement. My body ached from all the cleaning I'd done the night before, but I sure wasn't going to be able to sleep. Might as well get some work done. I armed myself with cleaning rags, a bucket and a tall glass of ice water.

Shelves that once housed games, Barbie doll cases and Lego buckets were now cluttered with cardboard boxes covered in dust, grime and occasional roach shells and mouse turds. Ooooh.

I dusted off one of the chairs to the red chrome table in the corner and sat. Hazy light from the corner streetlight shone through the windows, still covered with faded Christmas wrap Morgan taped up years ago when she and her friends held their secret Nancy Drew Club meetings down here.

My washer and dryer stood on the far wall. To reach them, I had to navigate through cardboard boxes, rubber tubs and odd furniture.

Where would I begin? I sipped my water and shut my eyes. If only I could just wish this mess away. Or blow the place up and claim it was an accident.

Wouldn't work. I could never learn how to build a bomb in time.

Why should I finish, anyway? Surely Robert would never consider buying the house in the country now. I could easily see us going our separate ways, and in that case . . . well, in that case, I sure wasn't staying in this house by myself!

The thought of moving—anywhere—reenergized me. I ripped paper off the windows, shoved and stacked boxes and tubs into one central area and attacked the spider community with a rag-covered broom.

By now, I was sweating like a racehorse in Africa, and my nose was a regular faucet. I needed to get away from the dust.

Robert's snoring didn't miss a beat when I showered. Amazing that he could sleep at all after what happened today.

I retrieved the chocolate shake from the freezer and set it on the counter to thaw while I waited for my Wendy's hamburger and fries to heat in the microwave. After practically inhaling my food, I nuked the shake for a few seconds and sipped on it while I gathered expired boxed and canned goods from the pantry and stuffed them into a garbage bag. By the time I'd finished the shake, two of the four pantry shelves were clean.

Time for bed. The thought of sleeping with Robert made me sick. I headed for the guest room and groaned when I flipped on the light. Piles of trash and unwanted bedding covered the floor. Empty dresser drawers hung open, and a bucket of cold, greenish-gray wash water sat just inside the closet door. The room reeked of lemon scented cleaning solution and stale sleeping bags, but at least the bed was made.

After raising the window a crack, I climbed into bed and turned off the light. I couldn't bear to look at the mess. Chaos. Just like my life.

Within minutes, a steady rain bounced off the aluminum window awning. Distant images flittered through my mind. Memories of the rainy night I was rushed to the hospital to deliver my first child. Danny Cooke's baby. The excruciating pain of rejection and injustice remained lodged in my chest.

I had no idea how God could ever fix this situation, but I would leave it with him, along with the need to take revenge. I'd do as Grandpa pleaded so many years ago.

Grandpa. Warmth radiated my being with memories of him. He'd introduced me to God as a child, read me Bible stories and knelt by my bed to teach me to pray. Grandpa was the only person I'd ever known who genuinely loved me, and I'd always pictured God as a mightier, holier version of Grandpa.

Until God let Grandpa die.

I was away having my baby so I didn't get to tell Grandpa goodbye. Church folks explained that God needed Grandpa in heaven, but their words only made me angrier. Why would God—who could create anything he wanted—need to take my grandpa? How could that kind of God claim to love me?

The wind changed, blowing the summer rain onto my bare arm—a welcome relief in the musty room. As I rolled to my side, the drops washed my face.

"Oh, Jesus." I buried my face in the pillow as I realized this was where a piece of my childish views of God had originated. Old people die. Everyone dies. God didn't take Grandpa because he needed him in Heaven more than I needed him on earth.

I breathed in new life as I rejected this lie I'd believed since childhood and replaced it with truth. My body relaxed into the arms of a heavenly Father who understood me, inside and out, and loved me anyway. "I miss Grandpa, Lord. Will you tell him for me?"

The thought brought joy. God might or might not tell Grandpa, but I'd left it in God's hands and trusted his answer. And that felt very good.

As my eyes grew accustomed to the dark, I reexamined the chaos around me. Chaos, yes. But change was happening. And that was definitely okay.

And just maybe, with God's help, the chaos in my marriage and relationships with my kids could change, too.

CHAPTER 16

A jackhammer punched at my skull when I woke Saturday morning. I rolled to the wall and threw an arm over my face. Starting at the crown of my head, I willed my muscles to relax. Forehead. Eyes. Cheeks. Mouth. Chins. Neck. Back to the top.

The pain refused to retreat. Next step: caffeine.

Nibbling on a blueberry bagel, I waited for my coffee to heat in the microwave and read the note Robert had left on the table. He would be at work until noon.

Coward. He probably called an emergency meeting with Professor Harlot to be sure they got their stories straight.

Ugly had returned. I shut my eyes. "So how does this work when the real me shows up again, Lord?"

One word popped into my mind. Forgiveness.

Good grief. Had God totally missed the office scene?

I knew I needed to hear Robert out and was eager to put the Kathy Harmin talk behind us. Robert would confess, I would forgive and God would heal our marriage.

Determined to set a pleasant tone for our talk, I ordered Chinese take-out. When our order arrived, I popped it into the oven to keep it warm.

Robert walked in right at noon, his shoulders slumped. He held my gaze, his unspoken question clear. Can we talk?

How could his weathered face still stir up warm fuzzies even as the picture of him alone with another woman froze me to the core?

I turned away. "Go wash up. I'll put lunch on the table."

Robert reached for my hand as we sat down. But as his fingers grazed mine, I recoiled. Not only did I not want to listen to Robert, I could barely tolerate being in the same room with him. Help me, Lord.

Robert released my hand and finished his prayer. We ate in silence for several minutes before he spoke. "Skipping the rice?"

"Mm-hmm." I tossed a second helping of salad on my plate. "Trying to cut down where I can."

Robert toyed with the stem of his fork. "Biz, I'm sorry about yesterday. I never should have allowed a female to shut the door to my office. I know better. I'm not sure—"

"Not just any female, dear. We're talking Kathy Harmin—a full-blown woman in hot pursuit."

"Could you, just once, let me finish what I'm saying?"

Shame on me. I stared at a stray grain of rice on my plate. "Fine. I will listen . . . So you were in your office with a female-in-heat and . . ."

"Kathy proposed this outlandish idea about convincing the faculty to travel to Hawaii together next year over Christmas break. I thought the idea was ridiculous, but I didn't want to be entirely rude."

"Of course not."

"Biz, I know you've got the whole scenario settled in your mind. I'm not going to convince you otherwise, am I?"

"I'm trying to listen. But I don't think you can fault me for expressing a bit of emotion after finding a mature woman making advances to you in your office with the door closed."

Robert pinched his chin and sighed. "Honey, when did I ever give you reason to believe I would even be interested in another woman?"

"Uh . . . when Kathy Harmin pressed her fat lips to your face?"

"I've apologized for letting that happen."

And that should be enough, right? I pressed my palms into the lip of the table with as much force as I could muster. The sharp edge cut into my palms. I pushed harder—the pain a welcome distraction as I waited for the seething energy inside of me to boil down. Finally, I trusted myself to speak. "I want to believe you, Robert. I really do. But how can you not see what is happening?"

Robert shrugged. "I guess I'll just have to prove my innocence. But I'm not sure whatever happened to innocent until proven guilty."

What did the guy want for proof?

"Biz."

I looked up.

"That was good communication. Even in terrible circumstances. Thanks for that." He reached for my hand with question in his eyes.

My heart beat with fear. Please, Lord. I nodded.

Robert barely grazed the tips of my fingers with his and prayed. "God, thank you for this new beginning. Help us sort this out so we can learn to love each other in the way you intend." He pulled his hand away and stood. "You've given me hope, honey. The first in a long time."

Good grief. I would never understand this man.

I woke from my nap around four and did a double-take when I passed Robert's office. His messy desk was immaculate. I could hear him whistling in the garage.

"Biz?"

"Coming." My jaw dropped as I stepped through the doorway. Robert's workbench and the wall-mounted pegboard had been stripped of tools and supplies. Cabinet doors hung open revealing empty shelves. Plastic tubs, neatly labeled, lined the garage walls.

Then I saw something that blew all current thoughts from my mind. An antique oak trunk with tarnished hinges. "Where did you find that?"

Robert grinned. "I stuck it in the attic ten years ago when your parents sold their place. Your dad thought you might want it someday."

I remembered the move. I adamantly refused to keep any of my parent's belongings, though Robert insisted I would later regret my decision. He was wrong.

Robert started his thumb thing. "I figured now might be as good a time as any, since the folks have been gone for several years, and you're cleaning things out."

What would my father think important enough for me to keep? Chills crawled up my spine, seeping deep into the marrow until I shivered. "Any idea what's inside?"

"Nope. Didn't figure it was mine to nose around in."

Good.

Robert touched my shoulder and allowed his hand to remain for a moment. "Tough to think about, isn't it?"

I nodded. Was it possible that Robert wanted to share my past?

He pushed the trunk under the workbench. "Take your time. It's not going anywhere."

I nodded, wondering if Robert really dismissed our Kathy Harmin arguments so quickly. Or did he, in reality, detest me as much as I detested myself?

As we drove to Casey's for dinner, Robert drummed his fingers on the steering wheel. "I've been thinking about what you said the other day. About it being time for us to move."

I grabbed the armrest. "What?"

Robert grinned like a truck driver driving a just-paid-off rig. "Turns out the house you want belongs to Joe Carleton, one of our history professors. He's retiring and moving to Colorado to live closer to his kids. I went to the office to talk to him this morning."

"But last night you said you wanted to see where our marriage was headed first."

"Yes, I did. Then I thought about the way you handled yourself when we discussed what you saw at the office. Biz, I've never seen this side of you. It was like you switched off the ugly button and honestly tried to talk about the issue at hand."

"But . . . I laughed . . . and you left. You were so angry."

"Angry at myself. I realized you were beside yourself. Emotionally exhausted. Who was I to judge your reaction?"

Was he serious?

"Then you offered to make me a snack. That was big, honey. You could have gone on for days without speaking to me. God knows, we've done that before. But it was like you wanted to get this discussion out in the open and over."

"Yeah, that. And ask again about the house."

Robert laughed. "Well, you did make me realize how important that house is to you. I've prayed, and I believe God wants us to at least look at the house."

In shock, I grabbed hunks of hair between my fingers and yanked. "Promise me you're not kidding."

Robert shook his head. "I'm serious, but no promises. A lot will depend on the price."

Adrenaline sent chills through my body. I slid my hands between my legs to warm them. "Can we go see it?"

"Thought you might ask. Joe's going to check with his wife and give me a call. There would be a small hitch if we were to consider buying, though."

"A hitch?"

"We would have to move in six weeks."

My mind boggled at the thought. Every closet, dresser and cabinet in our house was crammed. And the basement was a Goodwill store waiting to happen. "Six weeks?"

"Yes, but please remember this is not a done deal. I haven't even checked the house out structurally. Lots of factors could change things."

I nodded, but excitement overpowered the common sense behind his words. "Will we sell or rent our house out?"

"Rent. I still want to work on the neighborhood restoration project when I retire. But the new house is on a huge track of land, and we can't afford for it to sit empty. If we aren't ready to move when Joe leaves on the first of August, we'll be forced to stay put and lease the new place out to pay the mortgage."

"No way. Our house will be ready if it kills me."

Robert laughed. "I hope it works out. Oh, and honey . . . you might want to check your hair before you go inside."

Pastor Todd and Renee were waiting in the lobby at Casey's. A waitress seated us in a back corner of the main dining room, brought our beverages and took our orders.

"So." Pastor Todd turned in my direction. "Robert says you've recently retired. Are you enjoying your extra time?"

Would lying to my pastor land me straight in hell? "It's an adjustment, but I have plenty to keep me busy."

Robert rested his arm on the back of my chair and patted my shoulder. His touch. Genuine. Welcome. "We're thinking about purchasing some land in the country. Lots of potential and—Biz has had her eye on the place for quite some time."

My steak was the best I'd had in a long time, especially with the caramelized sweet potato and buttery garlic bread.

We talked about ministries at the church over coffee.

"Renee tells me you opened the Golden Oldies meeting this week, Biz." Pastor stirred a third container of cream into his coffee. "Do you enjoy the meetings?"

I almost choked. What was with truth or dare tonight? I nodded. "The get-togethers are interesting."

"Do you know many of the ladies in the group?"

"Not really. I've been pretty busy in the past, what with the business and all. Couldn't really make daytime meetings."

He nodded as he pushed his coffee cup back, folded his hands and rested them on the table. "I don't want to put you on the spot, but I want you to consider an idea of mine."

Where was he going with this?

Pastor continued. "Olivia has led the group for years. Does a fine job but she needs a break, and Renee suggested you might be just the person to take over."

"Or not." Embarrassed at my quick reply, I tried to cover with a laugh. "I'm sure Renee was teasing. I've spent my entire life working with crotchety old men. I have no idea how to plan events for the ladies."

Pastor rumpled his nose. "I actually think your management skills might be exactly what we need. I'm fairly new at the church, but as I place key people in important positions, I'm looking for those who can take the reins and run with their programs. Not feel like they need to seek my approval every step of the way."

Did he seriously just say that?

Pastor sipped his coffee. "By the way, this is all confidential at this point. Olivia's husband, Mac, gave me a call. Seems Olivia is overcommitted but is embarrassed to back out of anything. I would prefer that the request to give up leadership come initially from her. I plan to invite her in to talk within the next couple of days."

Pastor stood and draped Renee's sweater over her shoulders. "Don't answer tonight. Just give me a call after you think about the idea."

Robert held my chair as I stood.

Pastor extended his hand. "Please tell me you'll pray about the matter."

I nodded. "I will, but I think I can already tell you what the Lord's going to say."

Pastor laughed. "I don't know about that."

Thunder rolled in the distance as Robert opened my car door. "We sure could use more rain."

"Hmmm." My thoughts were elsewhere. Lead the ladies' group? The idea scared the willies out of me, but it also intrigued me.

When we got home, Robert followed me into the living room. "Can we talk for a few minutes?"

So much for the Saturday night "Law and Order" marathon. "Sure."

"We really need to clear the air completely about the incident in my office. But first, I want to talk to you about the position Pastor mentioned. You thinking about accepting?"

"I doubt it. What do you think?"

Robert kicked his shoes off and stretched out on the sofa. "You're great at management and would do a good job, but I'm not sure I want you under that kind of pressure."

"How hard could setting up a meeting for a bunch of ladies be? Just a matter of delegating."

"Delegating, counseling, negotiating." Robert yawned. "You'd be working with ladies who have done things the same way for years and don't want to change. Right?"

"Yeah, I guess."

The house phone rang. Robert sprang to his feet.

I leaned back and shut my eyes, touched by the concern in Robert's voice. But as I relaxed into the possibility that God was changing our lives for the better, I felt a check in my spirit. Could we work through the Kathy Harmin issue without destroying what was left of our marriage?

I jumped as Robert walked into the room, talking on the phone.

"I'm sure I placed a copy in your box. Kathy has my original. She's supposed to be working late this evening." Robert shook his head, looking my direction. "Tell you what. I've got a key to her office. I'll be right over."

Was this prearranged? Disgust flared, but I fought the urge to hurl accusations when Robert clicked the phone off. "Problems at the office?"

"Copy services has a packet that goes out Monday and can't locate the original. We've got to meet the deadline."

I raised my recliner and walked Robert to the door. I hugged his neck and gazed into his eyes for the first time in years. I mean, really maintained focus until we connected.

Robert averted his eyes after several seconds. "What's this about?"

I couldn't explain. Or maybe I just didn't want to. Not now. I didn't want to discuss the tender changes God was making in my heart when my pleasant thoughts were garbled with suspicion and resentment. "I don't know. Just didn't realize how much I love you, I guess."

Robert swallowed hard. "Don't wait up, honey."

He picked up his keys and a bottle of water from the fridge. "The students from copy services go home in thirty minutes. I may need to run the thing myself."

So Robert and Kathy would meet again. Would the woman venture past a kiss this time?

I locked the door and attempted to deactivate my imagination. Staring into space, my mind tried to reconcile the warm feelings I felt for Robert with the cold muck of suspicion and anger that taunted my thoughts. "What do I do with that, Lord?"

Again, just the word forgiveness.

"You want me to forgive Robert? Just look the other way and drop the issue?" I sighed. "I'm sorry, Lord, but I'm just not there yet.

CHAPTER 17

Robert came to bed after midnight. I placed my hand on his arm. "Honey, I was worried about you. Can we talk?"

Robert lay for several seconds before facing me. "Biz, if I start thinking about this whole mess now, I'll never get to sleep, and I'm meeting with the building committee tomorrow morning before church. Can we wait?"

"Sure." I pulled my hand back and tried not to cry as distorted images of Kathy Harmin bombarded my mind. Then, in short, I realized Kathy Harmin was the one with an agenda. She should be the target of my attention. The thought energized me as I contemplated what I would say to her if given the chance.

I assumed Robert would join me for the service after his building committee meeting, but he didn't. Other members of the committee sat in the congregation, though.

I plopped down onto the padded wooden pew and sent Robert a text. He didn't answer so I turned my phone off and put it back in my purse. Where was he?

"Good morning." Pastor pivoted slowly to make eye contact with the people in each of the three sections of the sanctuary. "John 13:34 says, 'A new command I give you: Love one another. As I have loved you, so you must love one another.' Today I'd like to talk about how real love requires forgiveness."

Forgiveness, again? In truth, I was glad. I wanted to learn more about the fine line between forgiving and holding others accountable for genuine wrongs. My mind wandered to images of my father. I could practically feel his rage as he bellowed orders and screamed insults at my mother and me. Came at me with his belt.

I shuddered and shook the pictures from my mind, willing myself to focus on Pastor's words.

"We need to stop blaming others and examine our own lives. Pray for our enemies. Forgive them."

Pastor's words rang loud and clear from the pulpit. An uncomfortable silence settled over me.

"Think about God's command to love one another as he loves you. Can you do that without forgiveness? Can you love someone who has stolen from you? Or someone who has spread vicious lies about you? Someone who physically abused you as a child and got away with it?"

I wanted to run. Could Pastor explain just how folks went about letting go of that kind of pain in order to forgive?

"My mother died when I was seven." Pastor paused, and I watched his face work itself back to composure. "That's when my father began drinking and beating me. Mostly on the weekends. I used to purposely fall from the playground equipment so no one at school would question my cuts and bruises. But the nurse checked into my home life when she realized my falls always occurred on Mondays."

The congregation seemed to be holding their breath in unison.

"The sheriff came one night, took my father to jail and placed me in a foster home. I'll never forget the look in my father's eyes as the sheriff escorted him to the squad car. Though I expected an angry threat, I saw only sorrow and love. The daddy I knew before my mother died."

Pastor knew what he was talking about. And yet he talked about forgiving the one who'd hurt him. Had he been able to do that?

His experience hit close to home, but Pastor's father was sorry. Mine wasn't. Not the same situation in the end. I couldn't listen to any more. I pulled an old bulletin from the back of my Bible and started a grocery list.

Robert's car was in the garage when I got home, but there was no sign of him in the house. Should I drive to the office? One look at my unmade bed, and I had my answer. A nap was a much better idea.

I got up around three and had just brewed a fresh pot of coffee when Robert stepped into the kitchen.

"Biz, I'm glad you're awake."

With the giant smile on his face, my husband looked anything but guilty.

"You want a cup of coffee?"

"Nope. You want to go see your new house?"

"What?" The room swirled around me as I sat. I folded my arms on the table and rested my head. "I'm not feeling so well, Robert."

"You're hyperventilating. Breathe into this."

I lifted my head, took the brown lunch bag Robert was holding and buried my mouth and nose in the opening. I sat down and followed Robert's directions—closed my eyes, took long, deep breaths and focused on relaxing.

Robert sat across from me. "Sorry, honey. Didn't mean to surprise you quite that much."

I pointed to the bag. "How long?"

"Just until you can breathe normally again."

Robert turned the coffeemaker off and pulled a couple of water bottles from the frig. "The Carleton's said they'll be out of town for a couple of days. We can spend the afternoon exploring the house and land if you want to."

Well that was good for at least five more minutes of face-in-the-bag time.

As we turned off the highway and rattled down the gravel road, I wondered about the wisdom of buying the house. What if we moved and nothing changed with our marriage? Hadn't life taught me dreams were meant to be shattered?

Robert stopped at a four-way intersection, corn sprouting on every side. "Sorry if I gave you a scare earlier. This morning was the only time I could meet the home inspection team to go over the house, and until I confirmed that the place was structurally sound, I didn't want to get your hopes up. That's why I didn't answer your text."

Twenty minutes later, we pulled off the gravel road, crossed the bridge and followed the curves to the top of a hill where the stately white house with black shutters and blue-gray trim sat nestled in the shade of a dozen or so mature oak trees. The lane circled to the back. Robert parked next to the large red barn, then turned and touched my arm. "We need to talk before we go inside, Biz."

Robert lowered the windows. "Before we go inside, you need to understand the financial aspects of this decision."

Whoo! This wasn't about Kathy Harmin. I relaxed my body and removed my seat belt.

"We're going to be pretty tight until I can pay off the house in town. But with the stock market so unpredictable, I checked into the wisdom of reinvesting my retirement funds in land and I believe we're making a sound investment."

"You'll use your retirement funds?"

"Yes. That's why I need to make sure we're clear on something. If I sign this contract, we'll need to designate your savings as a backup fund for emergencies. That means putting the account in both of our names. Are you going to be okay with that?"

Uh, no. I shut my eyes to think. I was getting the home of my dreams. A second chance for happiness in life. Robert was willing to put his money on the line. Why shouldn't I do the same?

But the bank account was all I had left of what my father had given me. My stomach twisted at the thought. Life was no longer about impressing Daddy. I needed to give up that childish goal and move forward. Let go, so my hands would be free to embrace God's future blessings.

Robert's eyes were closed. I rested my hand on his knee. "I'll be fine with a joint account."

He opened his eyes and grinned. "You had me sweating."

Yeah, me, too. I needed to get out of the car before the magnitude of what I'd just done overpowered me. "Can we go inside now?"

"In a minute. We also need to discuss this notion you have that I'm interested in Kathy Harmin. That just isn't true, Biz, and you have to stop allowing your mind to go there. We can't enter into a venture this big if we don't trust each other."

"Robert, I never implied you were interested in her. I believe she is interested in you, and that scares me to death."

"So you've said. Well, you need to let that idea go, Biz. If not, we'd be wiser to invest this money in marriage counseling."

I called Lettie when we got home. As I waited for her to answer, I started sorting through the kitchen junk drawer. After all, I couldn't afford to waste time now that I had a definite deadline to meet.

"Hola, mi amiga."

"Girl, you're not going to believe where Robert took me this afternoon."

Lettie giggled. "You liked the surprise?"

"What? You were in on it?"

"Sí. José went with Robert this morning and gave him info about the county taxes and road maintenance."

Sounded like Robert. So militantly careful, he made me nuts. "I took tons of pictures. You ever been inside, Lettie?"

"No, but I'm sure I'm going to be sick with jealousy."

I laughed as I fished colored rubber bands from every corner of the drawer and wrapped them around the end of an old wooden screwdriver. "Serves you right. I've been jealous of your house for years."

"Hey, how did dinner with Pastor and Renee go last night? You have a good time?"

"Uh, yes and no. Food was great."

"Oh, Biz. What happened?"

I sat down at the table. "You're not going to believe this, Lettie. Pastor told us that Olivia might resign from leading the Golden Oldies, and he asked me to consider taking over."

Lettie gasped. "That's wonderful."

My skin prickled. "That didn't sound so honest."

"Well, you know we've talked about how you deal with people. You'd really have to work hard to get along with everyone."

I pushed my hair behind my ears as I searched for an answer. "Yes, I do have a problem with my mouth. Maybe I'm not such a good choice after all."

"No, I didn't say that, Biz. I just don't want you to go into this—"

"Sorry, Lettie. I need to go. Nature's calling."

I hung up the phone. Nature was calling. I was about to throw up. I ducked my head between my legs and waited for my nerves to calm—the panic no surprise. First, I receive a leadership offer I want to take but have no business even considering. And now I'm offered the home of my dreams if I can meet an impossible deadline.

Glancing around at the mess I'd already made of my kitchen, I decided to worry about leading the ladies group later. I changed into cutoff sweat pants and a T-shirt, filled a two-quart thermal jug with iced tea and headed to the basement. "Please, help me, Lord. There's so much to do."

In order for us to move in six weeks, the house would have to be ready to show to potential renters in at least four weeks. Twenty-seven days.

No problem. I could do this. After replacing the fifty-watt bulbs with brighter ones, I pulled out two heavy-duty 45-gallon yard/leaf bags, determined to dispose as much as possible. I'd seen this done on television. One pile to give away. One to keep, and the last for the trash man.

I started with the most dilapidated boxes. The baby clothes in the third box caught me off guard. I'd loved those baby days. I wasn't working, and Robert barely made enough to cover our house payment, but we were so happy in our cozy little home.

I saved a couple of outfits each for Robby and Morgan and tossed the rest. Memories rushed through my mind of another baby I'd loved, but I mentally slammed that door shut.

Clothes, toys, books, dishes. All kinds of junk. I wiped my hands on a rag and looked around. This was my life. My past. Almost nothing of value. But I had a future if I was willing to work. A new beginning.

"Don't drag the old into the new."

I jumped slightly and looked around. I hadn't heard an audible voice or anything, but I knew in my spirit that God had sent the thought. The strange command niggled at my mind as I continued emptying the contents of each box into trash bags. Surely the Lord wasn't concerned about all this junk. What was he really saying to me?

Suddenly, the words made sense. You're talking about what is in my heart, aren't you, Lord? My childhood. The rape. My business. My marriage.

My face grew warm so I took a swig of iced tea. Surely the Lord wasn't asking me to dredge up all of that ugliness now, when I had so much to do. I'd emptied most of the containers when Robert stuck his head in the doorway. "Biz? You still down here?"

I arched my back gently and rolled my shoulders. "Be up in a few minutes."

The ceiling creaked as Robert plodded through the house to the bedroom and back again. He appeared in work clothes as I finished the last container.

"Whoa, you got a lot done! Why don't you go clean up while I carry these bags to the garage? Rest a bit while I put some chicken on the grill."

I dusted my hands off onto my pants. "I'll just tie up the rest of these bags and stack the stuff to give away in the boxes over there in the corner. You can carry those up, too."

Robert headed up the stairs with a couple of bags in each hand. "Stop for now, Biz. You don't need to be lifting boxes or bags."

"We used to work well together, Robert. Do you remember?"

"Yeah, but I doubt we'd manage for long these days. We see things far too differently."

So much for hope.

I soaked in the tub until my fingers resembled Ruffles potato chips. Bath beads soothed my tired muscles, but nothing could relieve the anxiety in my gut.

The tantalizing aroma of grilled chicken pulled me from the tub.

"Everything's ready." Robert lifted baked potatoes from the oven with a pair of mitts. "There's a refreshing breeze, too. We may even get chased inside by rain."

"Lord, bless this food," Robert prayed. "Bless our evening, and help us to glorify you with everything we think, say and do."

"That's a pretty big order."

Robert piled a helping of broccoli onto his plate. "All we can do is try. We do need to talk about a few things."

"Where should we start?"

Robert slathered his baked potato with butter.

Oooh. I wanted butter and sour cream and cheese.

"What's this?" Robert picked up the bottle of substitute and read the label.

"That's my wanna-be butter. It's not bad. I put some on popcorn last night."

He smiled. "I'm proud of you."

My cheeks went hot as I sprinkled Molly onto my potato and crisscrossed it in with my fork. I could feel God working on our marriage . . . or helping us do so.

But as heavy clouds shifted above us, darkness invaded my spirit. You saw the woman preying on your husband, and you know how late he stayed out last night.

Robert broke the silence. "I won't be home until late the next few nights."

Fingers of apprehension crept up my neck. "Heavy workload?"

He shook his head. "A sociology professor from the Air Force Academy who specializes in Post-Traumatic Stress Syndrome is attending a conference in town. He agreed to join a few of us for dinner for a few nights. His insight will be invaluable to those of us at the university who work with returning soldiers."

I relaxed. "Sounds like an amazing opportunity."

"You can come if you want to."

"No, that's okay. Too much work to do."

Robert laughed. "Yes, you do have your work cut out for you."

His smile faded, and my apprehension returned.

"I really hate to bring this up in the middle of everything, Biz, but I talked to Robby today about your visit last week when I was gone. He regrets reacting so harshly and is worried about you."

I could have steamed another pot of broccoli with one breath. "Worried? He has a funny way of showing it. Did he tell you he ordered me to stay away from the family?"

Robert nodded. "He also told me what you said about Stephanie's feelings for her family." Robert's voice remained controlled. "Where did you get that information?"

Did I really want to tell him? I took a deep breath and reminded myself not to get ugly. "Stephanie left her diary here when she spent the night, and I read it. The poor child is hurting so badly, Robert."

Robert sat up straighter. "We need to return the diary and let Robby and Vickie help her. Where is the thing? I'll drive it over tonight."

"No way! Stephanie's got some rights here, too, you know, and I'm quite sure she wouldn't want them to read it."

"But she gave you permission?"

"No. I was wrong. But now that I know Stephanie's secrets, I'm obligated to protect her."

Robert closed his eyes and rubbed small circles into his temples.

Counting to ten, I suppose. Not that I cared. He could count to a million and back. "I'm not giving up the diary, Robert. Would you like to hear what Stephanie wrote? Then you might understand why I believe it's so important to help her."

Robert balled his fingers into fists. "I do not want to know what is in that diary unless Stephanie decides to tell me. Honestly, Biz, can't you see the problems this is causing? Why won't you listen to me?"

I crossed my arms and leaned forward. "You assume I'm not listening just because I don't agree with you?"

Robert stood and shoved his chair across the patio. "Biz McNeely, you are the most hard-headed woman I've ever known, and—"

"And . . .?"

With a straight face, he walked over and pulled me out of my chair and into his arms. "And this has been a wonderful day. We bought a house in the country and have a hopeful future ahead. Let's not ruin the night. Can we just agree to disagree on this diary issue?"

I laughed and slapped his arm. "You're the boss, right?"

CHAPTER 18

Robert offered to clear the dishes so I could return to the basement. Soft rain tapped a delightful rhythm on the aluminum lawn guards outside the windows. I pushed the panes open, and the sweet fragrance of flowers and wet earth filled the room.

I slipped a sweater out of a zippered garment bag and smiled, thinking back to my high school days. I faithfully attended basketball games, sitting in the cheerleading block where I pretended to fit in with all the other girls dressed in purple sweaters and yellow gloves. And for a couple of hours every weekend, I had almost been able to forget what went on at home behind closed doors.

One more thing in the box. My high school yearbook. I flipped through the pages. Oh my. Did we honestly pile our hair that high? I read some notes on the inside cover.

Biz – to the only girl brave enough to take shop class. Thanks for sharing your tools!

Then, Biz – I'll never forget how you kicked butt in Olson's history class. Long live the class of 80!

And from Lettie: Biz – my best friend in every way! Can't wait to be an upper classman!

My breath quickened when I turned to the back cover. Danny Cooke had gotten hold of my yearbook at the signature hop. I'd crossed his entry out years ago with a black Marks-a-Lot, but I could still read the message. *Biz – what we had together can never be shared with others. You were fantastic.*

Made me want to buy a gun and go after the jerk. Shrivel up and hide from the world. Danny Cooke had gotten away with the worst. And the saddest part was that my dad was the one who let Danny off the hook.

Twenty-six days. With list in hand, I sat down at the kitchen table Monday morning to organize and prioritize the tasks. The rest of the day would be spent with regular housecleaning, laundry and grocery shopping. After supper, I would sort out the linen closet and lay new shelf paper. The trunk came to mind, but I shook it off—not even sure I wanted to know what was inside the lousy thing.

I dragged the vacuum from the closet and started on the carpet. I'd just finished when the doorbell rang.

Lettie stood on the front step with a giant grin on her face. "Come see what my José just bought me."

In the driveway sat a brand, new Honda CRV. We hurried across the grass to take a closer look. Lettie pulled the doors open. "Stick your head inside, Biz. It smells so new."

I complied.

"Let's go for a ride."

We got in the car and backed out of the drive. "How'd you talk José into this?"

"I didn't. José, he just went out and surprised me. Said I will need it when I deliver wedding cakes. Said he wants my dream to come true."

"I am so happy for you."

"Hey, you want to go for some frozen yogurt? My daughter says we can eat a kiddie cup of the fat-free kind for only two points. She's doing Weight Watchers online."

My tummy rumbled as if to answer Lettie's question. "Sounds perfect."

Lettie led us to an outside table with an umbrella. "You hung up on me yesterday, Biz. We still friends?"

I smiled. "Always. But if that's what honesty feels like, I'm not sure I want to go there. I'm telling you, Lettie, I was super excited until you said what you did."

"And . . .?"

I bit a hangnail from my index finger. "And now I'm not sure. It's like I have so many ideas for the group, but I know what a mess I can make of things. Especially relationships."

Lettie wiped her mouth. "God will show you what he wants you to do. I'll be praying."

"Thanks." I finished my cone and stood. "Meanwhile, I've got a lot of housecleaning to do."

"Speaking of houses, I have some exciting news. José spoke to Walter Vic on the phone last night about buying Hazel's house."

"What? You'd move to our neighborhood? Right when I'm ready to move to the country?"

"No. José wants to fix the house up as a rental. Probably for one of our kids. He and Robert have been talking about the neighborhood restoration idea."

I rolled my eyes. "Those two are like little boys when they get together."

"Si. Walter asked me to tell you that Sandy and Hazel mention you constantly. We should go visit them sometime."

"That sounds fun. And since I don't have to be at work every day—"

Lettie grinned. "You starting to enjoy retirement?"

"Whatever. Yeah, I guess so. But I have so much work to finish."

"Have you arranged for painters?"

"Oh, my. I didn't even think of that."

"My son just had his game room painted. He had to schedule it a few months in advance. That's what made me think to ask you." Lettie picked up her car keys. "Let's go. I'm supposed to pick up Victoria's kids in about twenty minutes to take them to their swimming lessons."

Some things would probably never change . . . and maybe that was okay.

I carried my old radio to the basement and turned on the oldies. The basement was already looking better. I filled the washtub with hot sudsy water, dipped my cloth in and started washing shelves and walls. Window sills and light fixtures. All that remained was the floor and a cement ledge that circled the room about two feet below the ceiling. I climbed on a chair and had just started scrubbing the ledge when I reached behind the laundry chute and discovered a shoebox.

My hands shook as I carried it upstairs. I yearned to touch the precious items I hadn't seen for years, but another part of me wanted to throw the box straight in the trash. Out of sight, out of mind.

I sat down at the table and held my breath as I lifted the shoebox lid. A light blue receiving blanket was neatly tucked around the contents of the box. As my fingers caressed the soft folds, I felt the outline of the Polaroid picture wrapped so carefully and with so much love. Dean Thomas Beemer. My son.

Gut-wrenching minutes passed before I lifted the blanket. Minutes spent weeping and longing for the child I'd lost.

I might have gone on for hours had the neighbor not tapped on the glass patio door. "Biz? Are you okay?"

"Sure." My head was totally messed up, and I didn't need company. Hopefully, Marissa would go away.

But she didn't. She found the sliding door open and let herself in. "Boomer dug under the fence and was playing in your backyard." She slid the door shut and took off her flip-flops. "When I came to round him up, I heard you crying. So I brought Boomer home and came back. I hope I'm not intruding."

I didn't have it in me to be polite. "Yes, I think you are."

Without a word, Marissa fixed us each a cup of coffee and sat down. She nodded to the box. "Tough memories?"

"Slightly."

"Can you tell me about them?"

Can you mind your own business and go home? I resented her intrusion, but couldn't resist the compassion in her voice. For heaven's sakes, she was a counselor, and I sure couldn't talk to anyone else about all this.

"Did you give the baby up for adoption?"

I nodded, unwrapping the blanket and gently outlining my baby's angelic face with my pinkie finger. I handed the picture to Marissa. "I loved him so much."

"Too young to raise a baby, but not too young to bond with him, right?"

"I was fifteen."

Vivid pictures raced through my mind. The birth. The baby. The Asian nurse who lifted him from my arms and carried him out of the room. Out of my life. The doctor who explained that my father had arranged everything. I willed the images away and returned to the moment.

"My father sent me away so no one would know I was pregnant. I stayed with a great-aunt in Chicago . . . thought she would help me raise my baby, but . . ."

"Tell me about your baby, Biz." Marissa set the black-and-white photo in front of me. "Did he have your beautiful big eyes and fair skin?"

No one had ever asked me about the baby. Not even my mother. In thirty-nine years, I'd never once spoken his name in conversation. But oh, how my soul longed to remember him. "He was so tiny. Blue eyes and a tiny tuft of my grandpa's red hair. Gorgeous long eyelashes and the sweetest little mouth I've ever seen."

"Did you get to spend much time with him?"

"Nope. Just a few seconds before the nurse took him away." My lip quivered. "I thought the nurse was going to clean the baby up. I had no idea I would never see him again."

"Do you want to talk about the baby's father?"

My body stiffened as a strap of fury slapped me off guard. "No."

I stared at the table. "You know, Marissa. I'm just going to be honest because I don't have the strength to be anything else right now." I picked up the baby blanket and flexed my fingers around it as I spoke. "You see, I've been a Christian since I was a child, and I know I'm supposed to be full of peace and love. You know, the feel-good stuff."

I looked down at my reddened hands. Too many dips in tubs of cleaning solution lately. I needed to get some rubber gloves. Oh, God. Why couldn't I focus? I had no idea where I was going with the conversation.

"So you're not the Christian you think you should be?" Marissa put her hands over mine. "It's okay, Biz. I'm here to listen. Not to judge."

I nodded. "I've never been able to forgive the one who did this to me. I've tried for so many years, but I still hate the guy."

"Understandable."

Marissa's presence was reassuring. "What can I do, Marissa?"

"You've got to face the past."

I told her about the trunk. "I don't think I can go through the thing by myself. Any chance you can stick around to help me?"

She linked arms. "Let's do it together, friend."

I unclasped the latch before I lost my nerve. It took both hands. Like one refused to do it without the other.

A red plaid Indian blanket, a gift from my grandpa on my eighth birthday, lay across the top. I remembered throwing the blanket over my horse's back in place of a saddle. Spreading it over the tall grass at the back of our property when I needed to hide. Nailing it over my bedroom window when I returned home without my infant son.

Next I found photos, a large white box and two manila envelopes. Curiosity upstaged dread as I picked up one of the bulging envelopes, shut the trunk and returned to the kitchen.

Memories flooded my mind when I lifted the flap and discovered my grandpa's Bible. I was there, in church, sitting beside Grandpa, flipping through these delicate pages beneath the worn leather cover. Grandpa's tobacco-stained fingers tracing the words in a passage being read from the pulpit.

Grandpa's scraggly handwriting stirred up a whirlwind of affection and grief. I shut my eyes and savored the precious memories. "How I wish God could have left Grandpa here on earth for a few more years."

Marissa stood and touched my shoulder. "Difficult to figure God out sometimes, isn't it?"

I glanced up. "You making fun of me?"

"No way." Marissa stepped back. "I used to ask a lot of questions about God, but never got any answers. I guess he must like the whole mystery thing about his decisions. Sort of keeps him above us, don't you think?"

"In a King of the Mountain sort of way?"

Marissa shook her head. "No, I definitely didn't mean that. From the little I know, God isn't about showing off his power. He's about seeing the big picture and asking us to trust he has everything in control."

"I guess."

"You know, I'm kind of glad no one can fully understand God. Look at the mess we make of our lives. Wouldn't it be sad if there was no higher power? No one we could turn to?"

My mind refused to wrap around the idea that Marissa was trying to teach me about God. How spiritually ignorant was I?

"Listen, Biz. I wish you'd take time to do some writing about your God questions. I'm off on Thursday. We could talk again then."

"I don't know. I'm not sure if I should tell you more. You probably think I'm a—"

"Hypocrite?"

I laughed. "Well, I wasn't going to be that hard on myself."

"Hey, face the facts. You're a human being trying to pose as a sinless Christian, right? Trying to impress others by pretending to be something you're not?"

She was right.

Marissa didn't wait for an answer. Instead, she wrapped me in a hug, then walked toward the door. "I'm proud of you, Biz."

By nine o-clock that evening, my body ached. I soaked in the tub and hit the bed at ten, not sure what time Robert might roll in.

Robert woke me with a kiss on the cheek some time before dawn Tuesday morning. "I've got to go in early, honey," he said. "Have a good day."

I fell back to sleep and woke with the sun shining in my eyes just before noon. After scarfing down a two-point granola bar, I poured a cup of coffee and headed for the basement, determined to finish the first room on my list.

The clean, warm water felt good as I wiped the ledge. Comforting, in a way. Something I could control. But as I cleaned the floor, dipping the mop in and out of the bucket, the shiny suds quickly turned to flat, gray water. I dumped the mess down the drain, rinsed the bucket and refilled it with fresh hot water and a splash of Pine-Sol. Ready to start again.

I shoved my mop across the filthy basement floor, muck from the past climbing higher in my mind. Grandpa insisted God loved me, but if so, why would he allow me to experience such horrific pain? Why didn't he intervene?

The return of the questions frustrated me. I was so sure I'd given them up when I committed to trusting in God's love instead of trying to understand. When I vowed to give up my childish views of God.

I worked my way back to the staircase and sat down on the steps. Thankfully, the questions no longer threatened to crush my heart or cripple my faith. They just remained unanswered. I could live with that.

As I scanned the clean basement floor, a new thought came to mind. This time I recognized it as the Holy Spirit. Though I knew the voice couldn't be heard outside my head, it was as if someone whispered in my ear. Close, and personal. "Start at the bottom. If the foundation is unclean, dirt will continue to work its way to the top, soiling everything in its path."

And like the tine of a fork working a knot out of a child's shoelace, a finger of grace loosened the tangled grip of despair that held me captive for so many years.

God was confirming what he said. He wanted me to uncover, examine and dispose of childhood debris. And he had sent Marissa to help me do it.

Climbing the steps with renewed passion, I smiled. God was with me. I still didn't understand why bad things had to happen, but I knew for sure that God cared.

Were other ladies in our group hiding a past? Carrying pain from childhood and pretending to be happy Christians? The thought shook me. Maybe God was calling me to lead the group. Perhaps he wanted someone who wasn't yet the model Christian. Someone who was brave enough to wear a God's-still-working-on-me sign and encourage other ladies to be real about their pain and shortcomings.

I shook my head as I washed my hands at the kitchen sink. Some scary thoughts, those.

My cell phone buzzed. It was Lettie.

"Hey, Biz. Can you do me a huge favor, por favor?"

"Anything but babysit your bambinos. What do you need?"

"Cocoa. I'm in the middle of baking a cake for my neighbor's anniversary party, and I just realized I don't have enough cocoa for the icing."

I stifled a groan. My body begged me not to skip my nap for a second day in a row. "Can't you borrow some from the neighbor?"

"No. She's not supposed to know anything about the party. Her kids are throwing it. Come on, Biz. You know I'd do it for you."

For sure. "Just one box?" I wrote down the type of cocoa Lettie needed. "Be there in about thirty minutes."

A sudden shower made today's trip to the country enjoyable. When Lettie's weather-worn log cabin came into view, I rolled my window down and savored the sweet smells.

Cheery petunias lined the walk to the house. Sparkling raindrops still clung to the velvety petals of red, pink and purple azaleas planted in an antique wooden wheelbarrow beside the front door.

Everything was clean and in order. So unlike my life. Suddenly a swig of reality left me stumbling. Who was I to even think my life could ever look like Lettie's?

"Hey, Biz." Lettie swung the screen door open. "Come on in." She led the way, dodging Tonka trucks, baby dolls and puzzle pieces. "Sorry about the mess."

"No problem." I shooed away my gloom and put on a happy face. "Does look like a Toys"R"Us tornado hit. Your grandkids must love it." I followed Lettie into the kitchen where the trail of toys stopped. "Kids not allowed in here?"

"Not with toys, they're not."

Ah, so there were boundaries with Lettie. I was impressed. And embarrassed to discover another side of a friend I thought I knew inside and out.

Round chocolate cake layers cooled on dishtowels on the counter, the delicious aroma filling the room. "Good thing those cakes are already spoken for."

"Si." Lettie poured us some peach tea and sat down at her oversized pine picnic table. Sunlight spilled through the picture window behind her, the beveled glass splitting the rays into a kaleidoscope of colors that frolicked across Lettie's arms. "Thanks so much for bringing me the cocoa."

Tears lined her eyes.

"What's the matter, Lettie?"

She shook her head. "None of my kids had time to help me out. And Angelica's so upset about my catering plans that she refused to come to dinner with the family this weekend."

That made me mad. Words came to mind, but this wasn't the time. My friend was hurting. Besides, it wasn't like I didn't have my own family issues. "I'm sorry, Lettie. That really stinks."

Lettie burst into laughter. "You're a mess, Biz."

"What?"

"Oh, nothing. I just expected a snarky reply . . . and kind of missed it." Lettie winked as she picked up the cocoa box and stood. "I've got to get busy and get this cake done. Thanks, again, mi amiga."

I stood. "Right. I'll see myself out, then."

CHAPTER 19

Of course, I drove by my new house on my way home. Joy bubbled in my spirit as I realized I hadn't had to force myself to hold back ugly words. As I monitored my thoughts, Lettie became more important than my irritation, and I didn't want to say anything that would cause her pain. Whoohoo!

Energy buzzed through me, and I attacked the linen closet I'd neglected the day before, tossing paper-thin sheets and ragged towels into a trash bag. Wasn't like I didn't have stacks of new ones the kids had given us for gifts over the years. Just never felt worthy enough to use something special.

So why was I willing to change now? I didn't know except that I was tired of the old and ready for something new. Sheets, towels and . . . life.

I climbed on a stool to pull down the new linens and towels from the top shelf, removed the packaging and took them downstairs to throw them in the washer. I found my notebook in the living room and checked off the linen closet.

The notebook reminded me of Marissa's encouragement to write about my past. Her words ran through my mind. Was I really trying to pose as a sinless Christian?

Would journaling about my childhood really help?

I prayed for peace and inner healing as I showered.

Robert would be eating dinner with the visiting professor again and wouldn't be home until late, so I didn't fuss much with my hair before I stepped into my muumuu, grabbed a Diet Coke and my notepad and sat down at the kitchen table.

Strange. Though I realized the process would hurt, I was anxious to get the memories out in the open.

I ran my finger over the smooth paper. A clean, innocent page with so much potential. But Marissa wanted me to fill it with rotten garbage. Words of guilt and shame that pointed a finger in so many directions. Words unfit for anyone to read.

"Is this okay, Lord? Wouldn't it be better to forgive and forget?"

"Have you been able to do that?" The question was so real in my mind. Was God conversing with me? The possibility energized my mind. I jotted the question in the margin and wrote my answer beside it.

You're right. I've never stopped thinking about the whole mess. The lullaby. The trail of Estee Lauder perfume that lingered after the nurse disappeared with my baby. His birthday.

The words flowed out of me with ease. Almost like I'd been transported directly into the presence of God—like he was sitting with me, listening and sharing.

I continued to write, filling page after page with tight, furious scrawl. Forgotten details surfaced. I was there.

The scratchy straw. The contrast of an innocent kitten in one corner purring contentedly, while ten feet away a young child . . . That's what I was then, just a child.

I fought back until Danny pinned me beneath himself in an empty stall, our bodies burrowed deeper and deeper in the straw with each thrust of his body. Heavy winds whistled and pushed the wooden barn doors open and shut along their track. Rain pelted the barn roof and blew sideways through the open window above us, sprinkling my face and dripping from Danny's sweaty body onto my exposed chest. The rough cement floor scraped my back. I wondered why he would do this. We were friends.

The side door to the barn banged open, and I heard rustling hay in the adjoining stall—my father. Somehow, I'd known not to entertain hope that my father had come to rescue me. No, once Danny left, my father beat the living daylights out of me.

"Oh, God, help me!" I screamed the words. Crossed my arms on the table and lowered my face as horrifying, guttural groans escaped from deep within. I grasped for words, but there were none dark enough to express my anguish—that of a fifteen-year-old girl, trapped for years in a body that continued to age without her.

Eventually, the shroud lifted, and I went to bed. Exhausted, but strangely at peace. Almost like one feels after vomiting. There's the fever, stomach pain and nausea, and then one finally retches and empties the stomach of offensive contents. Maybe that's what I'd done. Maybe, in some bizarre way, I'd puked up a sizeable chunk of the garbage inside me that had soured my life for so many years. I enjoyed the thought. Then seriously considered getting up to brush my teeth one more time.

I fixed Robert a big breakfast the next morning. Good grief, we'd barely seen each other for two days. "So, you're learning a lot from your guest?"

Robert smiled around a forkful of scrambled eggs and set his fork down. "This guy really gets the military mindset. It's sad on so many levels. The troops come home from places like Afghanistan scarred for life. Some may not have received physical wounds but the emotional trauma they endure is unbelievable."

"I can't imagine."

"Listening to this guy has definitely opened my eyes. I pray this new understanding will help me be a safe friend to military students who come through my office."

Amazing Grace. I hummed the tune later that morning as I fixed a cup of coffee and sat down with Grandpa's Bible. As I flipped through the pages, the story of Joseph caught my eye. Grandpa had underlined several of the verses and written comments in the margins.

I knew the story. Basically, Joseph's brothers were jealous and plotted to kill him. But given the opportunity, they sold him as a slave to some merchants traveling through the area, instead. Eventually, Joseph was sold to Potiphar, one of Pharaoh's officials.

Not a bad life. I pushed my empty plate aside, wiped the table with my napkin and pulled the Bible closer. So, Joseph went from favored son to a dark pit, the duties of a slave, a grueling life in prison and finally, to a place of honor—in command over the land of Egypt, second only to Pharaoh.

I tried to imagine Joseph's feelings along the journey. He must have had some pretty pressing questions for God. Like why God would allow all of that pain when Joseph tried so hard to be loyal to him. I skimmed the passages again and realized how Joseph and I were different. No matter where Joseph was in life, he pressed on. He didn't get bogged down with bitterness about his circumstances.

Grandpa had written a note in red. Concentrate on what God puts in your hand today. Be thankful and praise his name.

Life couldn't come with clearer instructions than that. I committed them to memory as I rinsed my dishes and loaded the dishwasher. Then, with a tiny leap of joy, I crossed the basement off my to-do list. Whoopee!

As I ran my errands, I thought more about Joseph. His journey wasn't always easy, but in the end, Joseph accomplished amazing things for God. Even when he had no idea what God had planned, Joseph chose to trust that God had his best interest in mind.

I could do that. I sighed, a deep, final knowing settling in my soul. With God's help, I would agree to lead the Golden Oldies.

I gathered all the curtains and threw them in the washer. The living room and bedroom drapes would have to be dry-cleaned. Noticing the dingy walls, I remembered I hadn't called the painters. I scanned the yellow pages and dialed one number after another. No one available. Seriously? Who hired painters when their kids were out of school for the summer?

One number left. Hispanic name. Great. What if they didn't speak English?

I dialed, praying God would work this out. The woman who answered spoke perfect English. "I have a cancellation for the first week in July. I can send the team to your house to give you an estimate this evening at seven, if you like."

"Yes, please, and . . . Gracias."

Robert called later. Several other colleagues had invited their spouses to join them for dinner with the Army general. Did I want to come?

Does a trucker wear pink?

I trekked to the basement to throw the load of curtains into the dryer and groaned when I discovered there was nothing left of them but patches of fabric entangled in a matted mess of raveled threads.

The doorbell rang right at seven. A short, dark-skinned fellow introduced himself as Armando Juarez. I glanced past him to verify the name of his company on his vehicle. Armando wore a white starched cotton shirt sporting a patch with the same logo, so I let him in. Another man and two women followed, all of them Hispanic. They nodded, and I assumed they didn't speak English.

After I explained that I needed the outside and inside of the house painted, including closets and ceilings, Armando headed for the basement. The other three disappeared into my bedroom with clipboards and measuring tapes.

Armando returned to the kitchen. "You try washing old curtains?"

You try minding your own business? His smile spoke of genuine humor though, not ridicule. "Ended up with a mess, didn't I?"

"Sí. My wife, she can sew new ones if you like. I measure. You pick fabric. You like I bring in the swatches?"

Hmmm. Walmart would be cheaper.

Armando must have read my mind. "You want to shop first? I measure and give you estimate. Then you have measurements ready if you decide to buy fabric or curtains at store. No difference to me."

Okay. I liked this guy, and I'd learned to read people pretty well over the years. Took a new read on myself, too, and discovered a touch of prejudice. That needed to go. "Thanks, Armando. I appreciate your help. I'll call your office to schedule the job."

The ten o'clock news had just ended when Sandy texted. Can you call me?

My fingers went cold. I set the phone down and stepped away from it. No. I did not want to call. But even as my mind, abuzz with dreadful scenarios, refused to act, propriety kicked in. I reopened Sandy's message, clicked on her name at the top of the screen, and connected the call.

"Mrs. McNeely?"

"Hi, Sandy. How are you?"

"Mrs. McNeely?"

"Yes, Sandy. I'm here. Are you okay?"

"Can you help me? I've done something very bad. I thought I could stop, but I didn't."

Her words sounded slurred, her tone more ashamed than afraid. "Have you been drinking?"

Silence. Sobs. "Uncle Walter trusted me. Now he'll kick me out, for sure."

What could I say? She didn't need a lecture—probably wouldn't remember it, anyway. As I searched for words, I remembered something I'd learn at an AA meeting I'd attended as a child with my mother. "Sandy, are you safe at home? At your uncle's house?"

"Yes. I have a key. No one heard me come in. But I hate myself, Mrs. McNeely. I've made such a mess, and —"

"I know, but we need to wait until you're sober to talk about it. Go to bed, and we'll face the music tomorrow. That sound okay?"

"Yes, I'll do that. Goodbye, Mrs. McNeely."

"Goodbye, sweetheart."

I put the phone aside and regretted not asking about Hazel. Had something happened? Is that what drove Sandy to drink?

Could I call Walter the next morning without betraying Sandy? Was betrayal okay in this situation, more of an intervention?

My mind continued to whirl with questions as I tried to sleep. *In all your ways submit to him, and he will make your paths straight.* Ah, Hazel's trust-in-the-Lord verse. I whispered a prayer. "I give Sandy to you, Lord. And the decision about how to help her. Please show me what to do."

Lettie called at eight o'clock Thursday morning. "Girl, don't you remember I'm a retired woman now?"

"Get up. I'm picking you up for the Golden Oldies meeting."

"Oh, Lettie. You have no idea how I dread facing Olivia after what happened last week. The woman doesn't like me."

"Wrong. You have no idea what Olivia thinks about you, good or bad. You do that a lot, Biz—make assumptions about what others are thinking. Robert, your kids . . . even me."

I threw my head back on the pillow and blew a puff of air out my lips. "What's with everyone trying to fix Biz, lately? Enough, already."

"Okay, okay." Lettie laughed. "It's just because we have so much more time to spend with you. Now get up and get ready. I'll be there in an hour or so."

The phone rang again minutes later. This time it was Walter. I had to smile. Guess God knew I needed to talk to him. "Hi, Walter."

Walter first reassured me that Hazel was fine. Then he explained that Sandy's mother had initiated legal proceedings to force Sandy to move back with her. "Sandy totally fell apart. I should have watched her more closely last night. She went out after I'd already gone to bed."

"You can't watch her every minute of the day."

"I know, and I'm so proud that she came to me first thing this morning to own up to what she'd done."

"She's a good kid. So, she'll definitely have to move back with her mother?"

"No. Sandy wants to join Teen Challenge here in Detroit and her mom agreed."

I hung up the phone and breathed a sigh of relief that Sandy was in good hands, or more importantly, in God's hands.

Today's schedule included my bedroom closet and the bookshelves in the living room. Might as well try to knock one of them out before the meeting.

I rummaged through Robert's clothes, dresser drawers and even the pages of his Bible. Nothing. I wasn't sure what I was looking for or whether I even wanted to find something. I just needed to prove to myself that I wasn't imagining the whole Kathy Harmin situation.

An hour or so later, I had nothing but a mess on my hands. I headed to the kitchen for a water refill, startled when the doorbell rang. Drats. I completely forgot Lettie was coming. Where was my head lately?

Olivia was in performance mode when we arrived. All about Mary and Martha.

Sometimes this story flattens my tires. Did Jesus think the fine meal he shared with his friends would cook itself?

"No." Olivia spoke as if she could read my thoughts. "Jesus wasn't saying Martha was wrong for working in the kitchen. He was saying spending time with him was more important."

I thought of Pastor's words. "Seems Olivia is overcommitted but is embarrassed to back out of anything." Was this what brought her to speak on this topic?

Olivia picked up a cloth bag from the floor by her chair. "Do you ever wish you could sit down with Jesus by yourself for a while? Just to hear what he has to say to you?"

The thought intrigued me. There were so many things about life that confused me. I'd love to have time to ask Jesus about them. My shoulders and neck ached. I squirmed to find a more comfortable position. Surely Olivia would finish soon.

Next thing I knew she was handing out journals. "The Lord gave me specific verses to write inside the covers of these." She made her way around the circle. "I've prayed that each of you will receive the verse God intends for you."

Was this Olivia's way of leaving a bit of herself behind when she stepped down? I forced myself to make eye contact when Olivia handed me a journal. Her smile was warm and genuine, her eyes slightly damp. "I've been praying God will reveal himself to you in a new and fresh way, Elizabeth."

We stayed for lunch.

Lettie pulled me aside on the way to the tables. "What changed your mind?"

I shrugged. How could I tell Lettie in thirty words or less God had just filled me with a love for Olivia that I didn't understand. I mean, I still didn't really like the woman. But she said she had prayed for me. For me.

CHAPTER 20

Still amazed I hadn't found the slightest shred of incriminating evidence in Robert's things, I attacked the mess I'd made in our bedroom when I got home from the meeting. As I stuffed old underwear and socks into a trash bag already bulging with yellowed Reader's Digest magazines and linens from the master bath, I rehearsed the scene at Robert's office. Had I misread the cues?

I opened the drawer to Robert's nightstand and snickered when I discovered a box of condoms stashed toward the back. How long had it been?

Not that I cared. I needed that about as much as I needed my toenails painted.

The phone rang. Robert was going to miss dinner again. Something about taking his car in for a new set of tires. Was the man purposely looking for reasons to be late?

Fine with me. I was ready to shower and crash.

But my plans changed when I dragged the trash bags to the street for pickup. The trunk screamed my name. Should I open the white box or the other envelope?

Gritting my teeth, I collected the stack of picture frames and remaining manila envelope and returned to the kitchen.

I felt nothing as I rummaged through the pictures. What had I expected? A treasured memento? A letter from Grandpa? I wasn't sure. I just knew I felt emptier than . . . I couldn't find the words . . . The void was all consuming, sucking life, itself, from my soul.

My cell phone buzzed. A text from Lettie. *I'm on my way. Let's have dinner since the guys have a board meeting at church. See you in five.*

Robert had a board meeting? He said he was getting the tires changed. Eager to finish my task before Lettie arrived, I pushed thoughts of Robert away, pried open the flap on the manila envelope and removed the first sheet of paper. The handwriting was my father's.

> *Elizabeth,*
>
> *We've never been close, and I can't change that at this point in life. But I do want to clear up a matter for which I fear you have judged me wrongly. I'm not writing this to make you feel bad or make myself look good, but simply to set things straight and perhaps teach you not to evaluate everything in life by mere appearance.*
>
> *You will probably destroy the attached document. That's your choice. It no longer matters. Once you know the truth, you won't be able to turn your back on it. What you believe I did for selfish purposes, I did for someone you loved with all your heart.*
>
> *You may wonder why I didn't share this before. I couldn't. The grave consequence of my decision was more than I could own up to. I'm now facing*

Alzheimer's and will hopefully escape the pain and regret once and for all.

Forgive me or not. I will never know. But I pray that for your sake, you will. I'm a bitter, angry old man, and I've spoiled the lives of so many people who crossed my path over the years. Including you and your mother. I apologize for that and pray God will somehow see fit to take pity and forgive me, too.

Your Father

I loathed the man. He said he'd done what he did for someone I loved. My baby? Had he assumed I would be such a horrible mother that he intervened on the baby's behalf?

The doorbell rang and I opened the door. "Come on in, Lettie. I'm glad you're here."

She followed me to the kitchen and glanced at the pictures. "Where did you find all of these?"

"My parents left me a trunk when they moved into assisted living. Robert found it in the attic the other day."

"Oh, Biz. They must bring back some tough memories."

I picked up the envelope and handed her the first page. "From my father. There's a lot you don't know, Lettie."

Lettie read the letter. "What does this mean?"

"I was raped when I was fifteen. Danny Cooke."

Lettie gasped. "And you never told me?"

I pulled a package of cheese from the refrigerator. "You want a grilled cheese sandwich?"

"No, thanks. Why didn't you tell me?"

Melting a pat of butter in the skillet, I lied. "I didn't want to bother you. You'd just met José."

"I don't believe you. We told each other everything."

I browned both sides of my sandwich, sliced it in half and carried it to the table. How could I tell Lettie the real reason I hadn't confided in her?

"The guys won't be home for at least an hour, Biz. We have time to talk."

I kept my head down and ate my sandwich.

Lettie poured us some coffee. "I think I remember the time. You went away for six months. Your parents said you were staying with an elderly aunt who was dying, right?"

"She wasn't dying."

"And when you came back, you hid in your room for the rest of the summer. I always thought you were upset that I was spending so much time with José."

A smile surfaced. "Well, there was that, too."

Lettie crossed her eyes. "Ay-ay-ay. So, did your father force you to have an abortion?"

I shook my head. "He arranged for a closed adoption without my knowledge."

"No wonder you didn't want to see anyone. But didn't you know I'd try to help?"

"You know how my father treated me behind closed doors."

Lettie winced. "Si, I remember. And the time I reported it, your father beat you even worse after the authorities left."

I lowered my head and allowed raw grief to pour from my soul. "I wanted nothing to do with you, Lettie. I hated you so much for your perfect family and your relationship with José. You were so lucky, and I was so cursed."

Lettie moved to my side of the table and put her arm around me. "I'm so sorry you had to go through all that alone, Biz. But I'm here now."

I lifted my head and wiped my eyes and nose. I looked into Lettie's eyes and realized how much I loved her. Wrapped my arms around her neck, relaxed into her embrace and cried on her shoulder. Allowed her to be strong for me.

"Thanks, Biz," she whispered. "Thanks for trusting me enough to tell me the truth. I love you."

I removed my arms. "Wow. That was awkward."

Lettie giggled. "But not so bad, right?"

"No." I dried my eyes and massaged my forehead and temples. "And moving on—" I removed the second page from the envelope and turned it so Lettie and I could read it together—a notarized legal contract, signed by a team of lawyers, my father and Danny Cooke.

My eyes caught the dollar amount—fifty thousand dollars. My stomach heaved. I gripped the edge of the table as I shut my eyes and breathed deeply until I regained my equilibrium. "I knew my father made money on the deal. I just never dreamed it was so much."

I stared at the paper, my eyes swimming in tears. "He was so precious, Lettie. Baby Dean. The pinkest little cheeks, puffy like a squirrel with a mouthful of nuts. Blue eyes like mine and a tiny tuft of reddish-blonde hair."

I waved Lettie off the bench so I could get out. Went to the bedroom closet and returned with the shoebox I'd found in the basement. Pushed it toward Lettie who was reseated on the other side of the table. "Have a look."

Lettie stroked the baby blanket and kissed the picture. "He's so beautiful, Biz. A little angel."

I nodded and picked up the contract by the edge. "Not sure I want to finish this."

Lettie placed her hand on my arm. "There's no hurry."

I flipped the paper over. "Let's get this done."

My father had agreed not to prosecute Danny if he deposited fifty thousand dollars into a private account at Saint Phillip's Community Hospital.

I'd never heard of the place. Was my baby born in this hospital? Had Danny Cooke been told he fathered a child and been willing to pay for the delivery, give his child up and simply walk away?

My stomach twisted as I tried to make sense of the words I'd just read.

"I found the hospital." Lettie showed me her cell phone. "It's located in Knorrsville, Indiana, about an hour away."

"Grandpa—he lived and died in Knorrsville . . . Oh, God." I hurried from the table and ran to the bathroom to empty my stomach.

When I returned, Lettie had put the facts together. "So the money didn't go into your father's business?"

"No. It must have paid Grandpa's hospital bill. Now my father's gone and I can't make things right between us."

"Don't beat yourself up, Biz." Lettie hesitated. "Your father may have used the money in a charitable way, but he still put a price on your baby's head and took money from the man who raped you."

Lettie handed me the shoebox. "Does Robert know?"

I shook my head. "Would you mind if I asked you to leave, Lettie? I really need some time alone to sort this all out in my head."

Lettie picked up her purse. "You'll call if you need me?"

"Sure. Tomorrow's Friday. We still on for Chester's?"

Lettie nodded and left.

I folded the pages and slipped them into the lining of Grandpa's Bible. "Oh, God. How can I forgive and move on when the pain is so real?"

It was almost midnight and Robert hadn't even called. I parked myself at the kitchen table with a Diet Coke and a bowl of popcorn and fished through my purse for a pen and the journal Olivia gave me. Truth was, I didn't really want to be alone. I wanted to talk to God. I desperately needed to feel his strength and presence again tonight. Maybe hear his voice.

Curious to see what verse Olivia had written inside, I opened the cover and read her flowery handwriting.

"Do not be anxious about anything, but in everything, by prayer and petition, with thanksgiving, present your requests to God. And the peace of God, which transcends all understanding, will guard your hearts and your minds in Christ Jesus" Philippians 4:6-7.

I laughed. Out. Loud. Do not be anxious about anything? That was the best God could do?

Lord,

Not so sure about this not being anxious suggestion after what I just learned—this new piece from my past. I want to give up the bitterness, but how is that possible? What is this peace you offer that goes beyond what I can understand? How do I find it?

I opened Grandpa's Bible to read what came after Olivia's verses.

"Finally, brothers and sisters, whatever is true, whatever is noble, whatever is right, whatever is pure, whatever is lovely, whatever is admirable—if anything is excellent or praiseworthy—think about such things. Whatever you have learned or received or heard from me, or seen in me—put it into practice. And the God of peace will be with you."

Oh, my. I had to come up for air. This was a daunting checklist. I could never achieve this kind of control over my thoughts. I returned to my journal.

Okay, Lord. Now I'm feeling anxious about your required thought list. This was supposed to be a verse on peace. Something has to be wrong here.

I read the verses again, aloud. Ah . . . I was supposed to pray when I was anxious. Seemed there were two conditions to finding God's peace. I needed to guard my thoughts and pray instead of worrying. That made sense. Somehow, I needed to give my thoughts and worries to God.

I bring my thoughts to you, Lord. Please remind me when I stray away from this list. I also bring Robert to you. Please stay with him and show him the danger he doesn't see. Remind him of your presence and your love. And please remind me to pray when I begin to worry or become angry. I know I'm powerless to change any of this, but you can do all things.

I shut the journal. Now all I needed to do was make some lists of those recommended thoughts and post them all over my silly house and car. I sensed a trickle of peace. My problems were in God's hands instead of mine. If only I could leave them there.

CHAPTER 21

The garage door woke me the next morning and I glanced at the clock. Five-thirty. Why was Robert leaving so early? He hadn't gotten home until well after midnight.

My gut tightened. Something was going on. It wasn't like him to be gone so many nights in a row. Was he purposely avoiding me?

Lettie called as I climbed out of bed later that morning.

"Don't get mad, Biz, but I need to cancel this morning. Angelica has a bad toothache and needs to go to the dentist. I'm going to pick up the twins."

I said nothing, which was 100 percent better than what I wanted to say.

"Want to do lunch later?"

"Can't. Gotta stick to my diet."

"They serve salads and baked chicken at Chester's."

"Yeah, and fat, juicy hamburgers and onion rings. Sorry, girl, I don't think I have the willpower for Chester's."

Lettie laughed. "How about a salad at Chick-Fil-A? I'll pick you up at twelve."

I checked my schedule. I was supposed to change the sheets and scrub mildew and lime deposits from the bathroom tiles in the hall bath. Anything trumped that.

After a mini-meal of three silver dollar pancakes and half a grapefruit, I tackled the bathtub and scrubbed until it looked almost new. I would wash the bedclothes later. Right now I needed to get cleaned up before Lettie arrived.

I timed things perfectly. Stuffed a banana into my purse and disconnected my cell phone from the charger just as Lettie pulled into the drive.

"I'll find us a booth while you order our salads. I'm not sure I can resist those waffle fries."

"Like I'm eating a salad, too?"

"Ha, ha." I found us a seat near the soda machine. I would fill up on Diet Coke. Should be water, but I decided to give myself a break, being I was exercising such tremendous self-control over the food. About the only exercise I'd be caught doing.

Lettie set our tray on the table. "You sleep okay last night?"

I shook my head. "Too much on my mind . . . Rather not get my head into it again right now, though. That okay?"

"Sure."

I poured a puddle of salad dressing on the side and barely dipped each forkful of lettuce into it as I ate. That had to kill at least a hundred calories. Maybe I could afford dessert. Or not.

"You thought any more about leading the Golden Oldies?"

"What do you think about Latter-day Saints? For a new name, I mean."

Lettie laughed. "Olivia might struggle with that one. Not to mention Pastor."

"So, I think I might agree to lead the ladies. I know I struggle with my mouth and relationships, but I think God's showing me that if I'm real with the ladies, they might feel more comfortable talking about the struggles in their Christian walks. And we could help each other as we work to improve."

Lettie raised her eyebrows. "That's pretty good, Biz."

I could always tell when Lettie wasn't finished. "But . . ."

"But are you sure you're ready to be that real with others? Aren't you a little bit afraid that when you feel intimidated you might get snippety?"

"You bet I'm afraid. But I was thinking that if I tell the ladies right up front that that might happen, they can flip me some signal to show me when to back off."

Lettie laughed. "Flip you a signal? Like . . ."

"No, Lettie! Not that kind of signal. More like poking their fingers in their ears or something." I sipped on my Diet Coke. "I do have one good idea to share with you."

"Sí?"

"We need to put a bit of life in the meetings. I know prayer is necessary, but those ladies go on about their woes forever. Wouldn't it be better just to actually pray about our needs rather than sharing them first? We could still agree in prayer, couldn't we?"

"Sí. Buena idea. That would save time, too."

I peered closely at Lettie to be sure she wasn't ridiculing me. Not like she did that on a regular basis or anything. But I'd never agreed to anything like this before and wouldn't be surprised if Lettie thought I was way out of my league. "Like I mentioned the other day, the ladies focus on all the bad in their lives. They need something to look forward to. We could plan get-togethers just for fun—like one of those scrapbooking parties you go to or bowling or just dinner. What do you think?"

"I don't know."

Lettie broke into a third package of buttery crackers. Did she know how many fat grams were in each one of those things?

"I'm not sure, Biz. I think Olivia wants the group to be more prayer and project oriented."

"And I think Olivia will no longer be in leadership. Don't tell me you're going to give me a headache about changing things."

Lettie shook her head. "Just don't know if you are wise to—how you say—shake the ship so soon."

"Boat. It's rock the boat, and why wait? The whole idea is to improve the meetings, right?"

"If you say so."

"Wait a minute, girlfriend. I'm not doing this thing without you."

Lettie tipped her head to the side and just a bit forward like a mother warning her kid for the last time. "I'm with you, Biz, but I'm not going to agree with you on everything that comes up just to make you feel good."

"Fair enough. So, I still think we need to move from the church basement to someone's home for the meetings. Way more intimate."

Lettie laughed. "Like my home, right?"

I rolled my eyes and waited for her response.

"Okay, but I need to give my kids at least a week's warning that I won't be available for babysitting that day."

"That'll work." I wasn't even tempted to offer a snarky reply.

Lettie picked up our tray and stepped away, but not before I saw the grin. She noticed.

Oh, my. God did that. For me . . . in me.

Robert came home before noon. "I'm taking Christopher and Kyle to play miniature golf and ride the paddle boats. We're going to a Fish Fry. Then Christopher has a softball game at the Community Center. Want to come along?"

"Sounds fun, but I don't think so. I really need to stick to my schedule."

I sighed with relief as he pulled out of the drive. Now the evenings made sense. Robert never liked to take time off without making up the hours in advance. Silly me. Always looking for trouble.

I stripped our bed and started the sheets in the washer. Back upstairs, I popped my head outside to check the mailbox. Marissa stood in her driveway with Boomer on a leash. "Hey, Biz. How are you?"

"Fine. Just have a lot to do." I tried to duck back inside, but the determined woman ambled across the grass and up my front walk.

"So, Biz, I'm just going to be nosy. On Tuesday, I noticed most of your curtains disappeared from the windows. This morning, I noticed a mountain of trash bags by the street for the garbage truck. You moving or just cleaning house?"

"And this is your business because . . ."

Marissa laughed. She looped Boomer's leash around the porch railing and sat on the rocker. "It's my business because I don't want to lose the neighbor I'm just getting to know."

"Right." I sat beside her. "Robert signed a contract last Sunday on a house in the country. It's one I've always dreamed of owning."

Marissa's face glowed. "I am happy for you but sad to see you go."

"Yeah, kind of bittersweet."

We rocked in silence for a few moments. "Marissa, can I ask you a question?"

"Sure. Anything but my age."

"You know the other day when we talked about my childhood?"

"Mm-hmm."

"Well, after I lost my baby, I used to babysit at this house in the country and—"

"The one Robert bought?"

I nodded. "The couple I babysat for . . . they were there for me. I couldn't tell them anything, but I think they knew life wasn't so nice for me. They treated me like their own kid and bought me presents and invited me over on Sundays to spend the afternoons. They taught me to ride a horse . . . and . . ." I couldn't go any further.

"Oh, Biz. What a dear, dear memory. And the idea that you're going to get to live in their house. That's so precious."

"Yes, but my question. I've always wanted to provide a home for girls like me. Abused or mistreated. Maybe pregnant and alone. But do you think I could ever do that? Maybe offer equestrian therapy?"

"Why not?"

"I mean, I'm still so messed up by my past. How could I ever hope to help others?"

Marissa slowed the swing and stood. "You tell me."

I just looked at her. Like she'd played me for a fool. Endeared herself to me until I opened up, and then slammed me to the floor. I stood and opened the door to the house. "I've got stuff to do."

She touched my arm. "I'm sorry, Biz. Just doing what I'm trained to do. Helping you figure out your own path in life. Please think about your question and any possible answers. Have you had a chance to journal yet?"

"Yes, but I'm not convinced it's helping."

"Hard to see at first. Stick with it, though."

I crossed my eyes and retreated inside as Marissa headed down the sidewalk with her pooch. So maybe I would journal again. Tomorrow.

Sometime before daylight on Saturday morning, I heard a car door shut in the driveway. I padded to the window to peek behind the drapes and gasped. Robert was loading suitcases into his car.

I popped into the bathroom to pee. Nothing took precedence over that task. Not even my husband sneaking out in the dark to—

My hands shook as I washed them with honeysuckle soap foam and dried them on the orange flowered hand towel I'd gotten free in a box of laundry detergent years ago. Was it in the Tide or the Cheer? For the life of me, I couldn't remember. I shut my eyes, willing my brain to focus on the present. No! it screamed. I don't want to think about this.

But a clattering in the kitchen jarred me to attention. I hurried down the hall to find Robert packing an assortment of dishes and cookware into a large box. "Mind if I take the recipe file?"

I shook my head.

"Is that a 'No, don't take it' or 'No, I don't care'?"

"You can take it. But where are you going, Robert?"

He just kept shoving stuff in the box.

My knees buckled, and I slid to a seat. "Why are you doing this? Are you moving in with Kathy Harmin?"

Robert folded the flaps on the box and looked up. "The university needs a counselor at the satellite location near Chicago. I took the position for now. That's where I was the other night—filling out transfer forms and packing up my office."

"So you're leaving—just like that? You didn't even think to discuss this—" I swallowed my words. He had tried to talk. Several times. But I'd put him off. "Oh, God." I dropped my head into my arms. "Has it come to this?"

Robert stopped tapping his key on the table. "I think some space will do us good, Biz. Our marriage is struggling, to say the least. We both need to do some soul-searching and decide how much we are willing to sacrifice to make it work."

"And the new house?"

"Nothing has changed there. Look Biz. I believe we've needed this separation for a long time. Hopefully, the time apart will give us a chance to reflect and set goals for our part in the marriage." He stood. "I'll call you in a few days."

And just like that, he was gone. I stared at my hands as I listened to him start his engine and drive away. I thought about the day ahead, but my plans made no sense. Why make potato salad and pick up ribs at the Piggly Wiggly if Robert wouldn't be home to grill them?

My head pounded. I popped a couple of Advil and stretched out on the sofa. How would I tell the kids? Or did they already know?

The doorbell rang just as I settled back into the cushions. I let it ring, definitely not in the mood for conversation. A few seconds later, however, I heard a key turn in the lock. Had Robert reconsidered?

"Biz?"

"Come on in, Lettie."

"Why didn't you answer the door?"

"I don't know. Why are you here?"

"I got a text from Robert asking me to stop by as soon as possible. I texted back, but he didn't answer." Lettie sat beside me. "You're not having another dizzy spell, are you?"

"Robert. He . . ." My ears started ringing. The ceiling spiraled around me. "I'm so tired." I pushed back into the cushions, and as I did, everything went black.

The next thing I knew, Lettie was holding a glass of water to my lips. "Drink this."

The cool water revived me, but reality returned. I leaned my heavy head back. "Robert said . . ." Tears welled in my eyes.

Lettie looked toward the bedroom. "Is Robert here?"

I shook my head. "He's gone. He left me."

"He did what?" Lettie set the glass of water aside and took my hand. "You can't mean that."

I gazed into Lettie's loving eyes. "He tried to tell me several times, but I wouldn't listen. He's taken a temporary position at the university's satellite campus up north."

"Oh, thank goodness. So, this is about his job?"

"I wish." I tried to stand but sat back down when my knees buckled. "Robert said we need some space to think about our marriage."

Lettie sat in the rocker, wrapped a throw across her legs and fiddled with the frayed edges. "Biz, your marriage has been less than perfect for years. Why now?"

"There's another woman in the picture."

"What? Biz, are you sure?"

"Yes." I ducked my head with a sudden bout of nausea. "I found them together four days ago." I swallowed a belch, thankful it was just air. "Oh, I feel so light-headed."

"Get your purse, Biz. I'm taking you home with me. You're not well."

"I'm fine. Everyone would be better off if I konked out for good, anyway."

"Biz." Lettie sat beside me and put her arm around me. "Don't say such a thing. I love you. Your family loves—"

"Oh, no, no, no. You're totally wrong, there." I stiffened and chuckled. A low, sarcastic laugh that resonated through the room.

Somewhere, deep inside me, a fragile, trembling child of fifteen crumpled. Lying against the prickly hay, my panties tossed to the side, my vagina ripped and bleeding, I couldn't move. I was too friendly. I gave him the impression that I wanted it. Mistakes were always my fault.

Lettie touched my arm. "Biz."

I turned to the back of the sofa and lost control. Emotional vomit. Lettie shoved tissues into my hand and whispered the name of Jesus over and over until I calmed.

I felt more tired than I'd been in years. "What am I going to do, Lettie?"

CHAPTER 22

The church service was half over by the time I got out of bed the next morning. No worries. I had absolutely no intention of going to church two weeks in a row without Robert. What would I tell the Golden Oldies ladies?

Surely Robert would reconsider and come home before any explanation became necessary. Good grief, if he needed space, why didn't he just tell me? I would gladly have moved to the guest room and refrained from speaking to him when we passed in the halls.

Something in my gut told me life was going to get worse before it got better. Robert was gone. I would accept some blame, but what about Professor Harlot? And Robert? Sure, he had pushed away from Kathy Harmin, but he could have done more. He could have opened the door and asked her to leave.

I was hungry, but there was nothing decent to eat in the house. I reached for my purse and keys. Forget the diet. I discovered my husband with another woman, and he up and decided to move three hundred miles away with no accountability whatsoever. And I was supposed to trust that he would remain faithful?

My cell phone rang as I pulled out of the driveway.

"Mom?"

"Yes, Robby?"

"No one answered at home. Where's Dad?"

Hmmm. Why should I explain? I didn't leave my spouse after thirty-four years of marriage. "Not sure. Why don't you give him a call?"

"Why? What's going on?"

"Look, Robby. I've got to go, I'm in the middle of something." It wasn't exactly a lie. I was right in the middle of the drive-through lane at Krispy Kreme.

The line moved, and I dug a twenty from the bottom of my purse to pay for my sin—three Napoleon cream donuts and a Caramel Latte. I pulled to the curb to wait for my order. Rosie Carter, one of Robert's colleagues, stepped out the side door of the store and walked over to my truck.

"Hey, Biz. You picking up a going away breakfast for Robert?"

She caught me off guard. I simply smiled. No words came to mind. No acceptable ones, anyway.

Rosie didn't seem to notice, turning to wave to someone further back in the pickup lane. She shielded her eyes from the sun and faced me. "I just had breakfast with Kathy Harmin. She's about to leave on her way out of town, too. We could have had an office party here."

Fortunately, the clerk arrived with my order, and a dark blue minivan honked at me for blocking the drive.

"Gotta go, Rosie. Good to see you."

My imagination kicked in and squelched my appetite before the first drop of chocolate icing even melted on my tongue. I tossed the bakery bag to the floor of the truck. Had

I heard Rosie correctly? Kathy Harmin was leaving town the day after Robert? Were they both moving to Chicago?

My hands shook. Probably just the thought of sugar. Or maybe it was the discovery that my husband had left me for another woman after leading me to believe he was completely naive and innocent.

On impulse, I wheeled around to the back of the Krispy Kreme and parked where I could view the exit door. Sure enough, within minutes, Kathy Harmin stepped out of the building in a flared denim skirt, red top and jacket with wide, colorful stripes. She removed the jacket and untucked her top before climbing into her silver Lexus. Alone.

I noticed a rack of hang-up clothes across the back seat as she pulled out of the parking lot. I kept my distance. She travelled north onto Interstate 65, a direct route to Chicago. I stayed with her for nearly ten miles before I admitted that what I was doing was absurd and headed home.

Robby's truck was parked in Robert's place. I entered the kitchen through the garage door. Robby was pouring himself a glass of juice.

"Want some?"

"No." I dropped my purse on the counter on my way out of the kitchen. "I don't feel like company right now, either."

Robby hooked my arm and held tight.

"Let go. This is my business, not yours. I don't care what your father told you to win you over to his side."

"His side?" Robby let go and followed me to the living room. "I'm not on any side, Mom. I just want you and Dad to get back together."

I didn't have the energy to fight. I dropped to the sofa and pulled a throw pillow over my eyes. "Please go home to your family."

"Are you okay, Mom?"

Robby's boney knees bumped my hip as he sat down on the coffee table and wrapped his fingers around my wrist.

"I will be, and don't you dare tell anyone at the office or at church about this."

"They're bound to find out."

I ripped the pillow from my eyes. "I'm telling you, as your mother, Robby. Don't tell anyone. Understand?"

He nodded, and I relaxed, replacing the pillow. Robby would keep his word. "I don't see how your father could do this to me. Surely I'm not that impossible to live with."

"Don't give up, Mom. Dad wants to work things out. He wants you to go for counseling."

"He what?" I fired the pillow to the floor and sat up.

Robby's eyes bulged. He jumped to his feet and stepped back. "You really don't get it, do you, Mom? You chase away everyone you love. You make life so difficult that no one wants to be around you. Can you really blame Dad for wanting a break?"

Unable to control my emotions for a second longer, I ran for the bedroom and locked the door behind me. "Go home, Robby! I'm sorry you got stuck with such a terrible mother. Just go home and don't come back!"

I heard the front door shut as I threw myself across the bed and wept until my throat burned. At times, I shouted obscenities into the air. I hated them all. Robert. Kathy Harmin. My parents. And the filthy neighbor who raped me and left me emotionally mutilated and stripped of dignity and self-respect for the rest of my life.

The sun had deserted the sky by the time I woke. My cell phone rang. I didn't want to talk to anyone.

I dragged myself to the bathroom to wash my face. The woman I saw in the mirror was not me. Sagging cheeks. Deep, dark bulges beneath lifeless eyes. I felt like a stranger and couldn't find a way to connect. This woman was more than angry. She was volatile and ready to give up on life.

I turned the bolt lock on all three doors and closed the drapes in the living room. Rummaging through the freezer, I found a bag of Tater Tots, dumped every one of them onto a cookie sheet and stuck it in the oven. Forget the diet. I'd rather die of obesity. No one cared anyway.

My cell rang again. "Okay, already." I picked up on the third set of rings.

"Biz, are you okay? Why didn't you answer?"

"I don't feel like talking, Lettie. Robby call you?"

"Sí. He's worried about you. Wants me to stay with you for a couple of days."

I took a plate from the cabinet and squirted a glob of ketchup onto it. "Girl, don't you even think about coming over here. I'm wearing my big-girl panties, and I've got plenty to do to keep me busy. You know I'll call if I need anything."

"Promise?"

"Cross my heart. Gotta go. My supper's calling."

Ninety-two tater tots in a bag. I counted. But I didn't eat them all. As I dragged a few potatoes through ketchup, I kept picturing Robert with his car keys in hand. Would he call?

"Oh, God," I moaned. "What can I do? How am I ever going to change? I can't even stick to a stinkin' diet."

I was sick of tater tots, sick of crying . . . and sick of myself.

Probably would have slept Monday away if Lettie hadn't rung my phone a gazillion times. "You doing okay?"

"I was."

"You want company?"

"Nope. I'll be fine. Besides, aren't you taking care of the twins today?"

"Yes, but—"

"Double nope, I promise. I'll call you if I need you, okay?"

I wandered through the house. Nothing had changed. The air vent in the hallway outside the bathroom still rattled each time the air kicked on. The icemaker in the kitchen whined as it dropped its load, and the sun poured through the patio doors like a giant spotlight ready to expose anything shady.

What right had life to continue when my entire world had screeched to a halt? My stomach growled for breakfast and I remembered the sack of donuts on the floorboard of the truck. Not the most nutritious breakfast in the world, but I needed some energy. Besides, eating donuts would make my heart happy and a happy heart has to be a healthy heart.

I stuffed the yeasty treats in my mouth and looked at pictures of the new house on my cell phone. Had Robert known about his plans to relocate when he agreed to buy the house?

Things made sense now. Robert leaving work early to take the kids to the park. Cleaning the garage and his home office.

Flipping the phone shut, I caught my reflection on the cover. Faint, but clear enough. I shoved the rest of the donuts into the trash. I'd worked hard to lose weight. Too hard to stop now.

A tiny spark of fight ignited my soul. I would move to my new house—with or without Robert. My entire life had been ruined by men, and I certainly didn't intend to sit around on my rear and let it happen again.

I climbed back in bed and pulled the covers to my chin.

"Lord, please show me what to do about Robert. I'm scared to death and I'll do anything you say to get my husband back. Just show me what to do."

I slept until six in the evening. Maybe I would call Robert. Would he even have his phone on? Four rings. No answer.

I waited for the beep. "It's me. Thought you might want to talk . . . Guess not."

Monday night. Robert was most likely watching a game. Probably picked up a pizza or chicken wings. Kathy Harmin might even be with him. Why would he want to talk to me?

The phone rang twice before I could get to it. "Robert?"

"No, it's Marissa. You okay?"

"Yeah, other than wondering why the man I married almost four decades ago decided to up and leave me. But, hey, less laundry, right? One less bell to answer."

"You were waiting on his call?"

"Hmph. Waiting, but not really expecting it."

"Have you eaten?"

"No, but I'm not hungry."

"Can I come over? I just heated a chicken casserole and baked some chocolate chip cookies. Plenty for both of us."

Only a complete idiot would turn down chocolate chip cookies. "Sure. I'm not in a very friendly mood, though."

Moments later, Marissa and I planted ourselves on the sofa with plates of casserole. Marissa kicked off her Crocs and propped her feet up on the coffee table. Okay. My own kids wouldn't dare do that. I liked Marissa's tenacity, though. The heck with it . . . I pulled my end of the table closer and propped my own slippered feet.

"So, I let Boomer out to pee yesterday morning, and I saw Robert packing his car. You didn't come out to wish him off or anything, so I sort of figured things might not be going too well. Right, so far?"

"Does the Pope wear red shoes?"

Marissa smiled. "I believe that was a former Pope, but yes, he did when he could find them in his size. What about you, Biz? Ever wear red shoes?"

Where was this going? "No. Black or navy."

"What about just for fun?"

"Me?" I laughed. "I do remember a pair of shiny red shoes Mother bought me when I was tiny. Only let me wear them one time for a Fourth of July service at church. I could practically see myself in them. Felt so fancy and important."

"Why just once?"

Hatred surfaced. "Mother gave them to the girl down the street. Said they made me too sassy."

Marissa reached for a cookie, drawing me back to the moment.

"Mother never liked it when I smiled and danced around. She said we didn't have time for horseplay. I didn't understand. Maybe if I hadn't been so bad, I could have kept my shoes."

"Did you buy your daughter red shoes?"

I laughed. "You bet. Any color she wanted. She was the happiest little princess ever. Used to prance around the house in a tutu, waving her magic wand. Her daddy would pretend to fall under her trance and do anything she commanded."

"You didn't join in?"

My chest burned. "I wasn't invited. Besides, someone had to stay in control. That girl was the classic strong-willed child."

Marissa nodded.

I shifted my weight and placed my feet on the floor. "I know you're thinking I became mean and controlling like my own mother. Probably why Robert left and neither of my kids will speak to me right now."

I chuckled, trying to shake the gravity of the truth as it hit home. Wiggling two-finger-quotation marks in the air, I chanted, "Wicked old witch finally burns as family trots happily off down the yellow brick road without her."

Marissa popped up and carried our cups and the cookie plate to the kitchen. She returned and slipped into her Crocs. "Let's go for a walk. It's so much cooler since it rained."

"I don't think so."

"Come on, you need the fresh air. You've been in this house too long."

Right. I stood, but only to walk Marissa to the door. "Tomorrow. Okay?"

"Nope." Marissa pointed to my shoes. "Hurry up. It's getting late, and I need to get up early for work tomorrow. Let's go work off this caffeine."

Did the woman wave her own invisible wand? Before I could think of a reasonable argument, we were stepping over the cracked cement in the driveway and headed around the block.

The neighborhood was surprisingly quiet. As we walked, we talked more about Morgan's childhood and how it compared to mine. Choked me up at one point when I admitted how much it had pained me to watch my sweet little girl sitting on her daddy's lap, soaking up his love and attention. "I honestly don't think I was looking for a husband when I married Robert. I just wanted to be loved with a daddy's love. And then Morgan stole that."

By the time we got home, I was exhausted, but felt strangely free. From what, I wasn't sure. We said goodnight, and Marissa promised to be back after supper the next night. "In fact," she said, "why don't we eat supper together again?"

I guess I'd slept too much in the afternoon because I couldn't fall asleep that night. Unwilling to be alone with my thoughts, I flipped on the television. Thank goodness for "Law and Order." Reruns, but I didn't care. Just comforting to hear familiar voices in the room.

Had I really made it through three days without Robert? Seemed more like three weeks. My thoughts turned to prayer. "It's been a couple of tough days, Lord, and I've definitely regressed."

The enemy verses came to mind. "Bless Robert?" I laughed. "Lord, I so don't want you to bless him. Should I pray this even when I don't feel it?"

The answer was clear. I'd lived long enough on my feelings and gone nowhere but downhill. So, I forced myself to think through the bless-your-enemies-prayer. "Give Robert good weather in Chicago, Lord. Help him as he settles into his new routine."

I felt so fake. Surely, this isn't what God wanted. I waited and in a few minutes a fresh idea came.

"Lord, protect Robert and help him sort out the issues in his life. Give him wisdom and guidance. Give him opportunities to tell others about you while he is there. Help him find a church that will strengthen and encourage him. And Lord, please bring him home when the time is right."

My body trembled as I experienced the power of God praying through me. It had to have been him. I hadn't pre-thought one of those requests. "Thank you, Lord."

CHAPTER 23

Tuesday morning. I grabbed my notebook and sat down to work on a grocery list. Wouldn't need the V8s or Fig Newtons. Truth was, I couldn't think of anything that sounded good to eat.

I tore the page off, shoved it into my purse and headed for the car. If I didn't get out of the house, I was going to climb back into bed. When my head hit the pillow, life—ugly as it was—came to a roaring halt, and pain was forced to wait.

Today I had a plan and was determined to stay on top of my feelings. I'd shop for groceries, put them away and tackle the kitchen cabinets and drawers.

Shopping done. Groceries put away. I felt good.

After dropping a bag of butter-free, salt-free, practically taste-free popcorn into the microwave, I turned on the oven for the pie, set the lasagna out to thaw and crammed the ice cream into the freezer.

Sipping on a tall glass of ice water as I worked, I slit the piecrust, slipped it into the oven and set the timer. Ten after four. Just enough time to shut my eyes for a few minutes. Unfortunately, the phone rang."

"You home, Biz?"

"Oh, hey, Marissa."

"Got off early. Want to go for a walk before dinner?"

I rolled my eyes. My body was screaming for the bed. "Right. How'd you know what I was thinking?"

"Seriously?"

"Not quite. I've been out running errands, and I have a lot to do around here. I was thinking we could eat around six. Sound okay?"

"Sounds yummy. Can I come now and help? I need to be back at the hospital by seven-thirty for a conference call."

You'd think a woman brash enough to invite herself over for dinner would at least pick a night she was free.

"You there?"

So much for the nap. I crossed my fingers. "Yeah, just lost you for a minute. Cell phone's about to die."

"I called the house phone, Biz."

"Whatever. Come on over whenever you want."

Marissa brought some leftover Olive Garden Caesar salad and breadsticks. "Come on, Biz. Walk around the block with me. Then you can enjoy a taste of pie without guilt."

"It will be done in thirty minutes. We can't let it burn."

"You're right, there." Marissa asked about Robert as soon as we hit the pavement. Guess she was used to making the most of her time with patients.

"You don't want to talk about him?"

"Oh, I don't mind. Not much to say, though. He hasn't even called since he left."

"How long since you and Robert had a real heart-to-heart?"

"Hard to say. We used to be able to finish each other's sentences. Enjoyed spending time together."

Regret punched me in the gut. Truth was, Robert use to fuss over me like his precious flowers. But I'd put a stop to it. I was so afraid he would cross the line into control territory.

"So, Robert seemed to care about you back then?"

I nodded. "We were different before the kids came. Then my dad left me the business. Robert was finishing up his degree. There wasn't any time to spend together, and our relationship went downhill."

"Ever consider getting help?"

"You mean seeing a shrink?" I did not just say that. "Marissa, I'm sorry. It's not like all counselors are shrinks—"

"Stop, before you wade in any deeper." Marissa took a drink of water and stretched her calves. "Could your problems with Robert be related to your childhood?"

The red shoes again. "Don't go all touchy-feely on me."

She didn't even smile. Just kept walking.

A breeze cooled the air. We sat on the patio with iced tea while the lasagna baked, neither of us saying anything. Strangely comfortable. Who was this woman and why did she exert such a positive effect on me? Why did she care?

I jiggled my glass to mix in the sweetener that had settled at the bottom. "I think things initially fell apart when I started taking my dad's side over Robert's about the business, finances the kids . . . everything, really. We argued a lot until Robert decided to back off and let me run things my way."

"Yet you claim he has no backbone?"

"I know you think I'm terrible."

Marissa shook her head. "You can't know what I'm thinking unless I tell you. Remember what I said about not censoring yourself. I'm not here to judge—only listen."

I shifted in my seat. "At least we stayed together."

"For the kids?"

"I guess, partly. We don't believe in divorce. The Bible's pretty clear about this issue. Sounds ironic with our current arrangement, doesn't it?"

"I know the verses." Marissa drained her glass and stood. "What do you suppose God's view is on emotional divorce?"

I shivered as her words hit home. "I don't think the Bible actually says anything about emotional divorce."

Marissa smiled. "You sure?"

Turns out, private counseling is effective for losing weight. By the time we got to the main course, I wasn't even hungry. Marissa convinced me to eat a small portion of everything, talking all the time about balance in our lives. Naa, naa, naa. The woman could be a doggone motor mouth.

She was also a skilled listener, though, and I had to admit that talking helped. Stuff that had been rolling around in my head since the day Robert left started to make a bit of sense.

Marissa served me a small slice of pie, and I practically inhaled it. I pushed the journal Olivia had given to me to Marissa. "I've been journaling."

"Oh, good." Marissa turned to a new page and jotted some notes.

"I think it's helping some."

Marissa nodded without looking up. "Yes. Left alone, your mind muddles everything together, and you always end up the bad guy." She returned the journal to me. "I wrote down your next assignment. In the next few days, I want you to consider your role as a wife and mother. See if you can make any connections between your childhood, your marriage and how you raised your children."

I stood and cleared the dishes. "I'm not sure. Might be too hard to go back there. There's so much to do with the house, and I'm exhausted all the time. Do I seriously need to get my head into all this right now?"

"I think so. Your energy will improve as well as your relationships. Do you genuinely want life to improve? Enough to work on your own issues?"

"My issues? Robert's the one who left. Not me."

"I know, but years ago I read where a wise counselor asked someone the same question, and the thought made sense to me. Kind of an essential foundation block for any goal of self-improvement."

"Good, grief, Marissa." I stopped rinsing the dishes and faced her. "Why wouldn't someone want to get better? I mean . . . why go to the counselor in the first place?"

My friend simply raised her eyebrows.

"What? You talking about me? Because I sure never asked for your counsel. You can take it right out the door if judgment is all you're offering."

To my surprise, she did just that. But before she left, she grabbed the leftover pie and ice cream and gave me a quick hug. "Only you can decide whether you want to wallow in self-pity or let this mess motivate you to change."

Enough of this counseling stuff. I had a house to clean, and I needed to stick to my schedule and start on the kitchen. I turned on the oldies, upped the volume and emptied one cabinet after another onto the counters and table.

Marissa was probably right. I opened a trash bag and dumped in jumbo-sized Hardees cups, chewed-up Popsicle molds and blackened cookie sheets. Maybe my childhood did affect what kind of a mom I had become. God knew my own mother was about as nurturing as a mechanical teat.

I so remembered the day my father told me my mother regretted not aborting me. When he looked to her for affirmation, she nodded. That was the day I shut down completely. Vowed I would never again let myself need anyone in my life—especially not family.

My knees ached when I woke around noon the next day, and the kitchen looked like Black Friday aftermath. I opened the patio door to let in some fresh air, started a pot of coffee and flipped on the answering machine.

"Hey, Biz." Marissa's voice boomed from the machine. "I found a family to rent your house. They need to take possession in a month, though. Will yours be available then?"

I laughed out loud when I glanced around. Place resembled a crazy hoarder's house. Garbage bags thrown near the front door for the Salvation Army. Desk drawers emptied onto the floor so I could sort them as I watched television. Clothes draped over the chairs because—well, just because.

"I told them they could come by to see the house around one o'clock. Be sure to give me a call if the time won't work for you. Otherwise, good luck!"

The doorbell rang as the message finished.

No way! People were actually standing on the other side of my front door.

"Let's peek in the windows," a kid said. I dived behind the corner sofa and curled up into the smallest ball possible, which actually wasn't very small.

"The back door's open," the kid called. "Can we go in?"

Can a dump truck go through the drive-up lane at Burger King?

"Better not, son. Could be someone home. In the shower or something. We'll come back later."

Ya think?

"Oh my. Check out this mess." Sounded like that comment came from the woman of the house. Of course, after today, I doubted she'd ever be the woman of my house. "I love the backyard, but I'm concerned about all the junk inside. People who live like this are bound to have rodents and bugs. Some even find rotten food in the walls and maggots beneath floorboards."

Now, that made me mad. No one was going to find maggots under floorboards in my house. Wasn't anything under the cheap carpeting but a cement slab. As for food in the wall—that was just gross.

The voices faded, and a car started in the driveway. I crept to the window and pulled a drape away from the wall to confirm the intruders' departure.

All hope of renting the house followed them down the street. Who was I kidding? Why would anyone want to rent a house in this run-down neighborhood? I probably just blew my one and only chance to unload the place.

Might as well kiss my country home goodbye for good. Or . . . Nope. Whether this house rented or not, it was going to get cleaned. I was sick of the clutter and desperate for a fresh start. Besides, I couldn't give up. Why would God caution me not to drag my past into my new home if he didn't intend to make it happen?

All sorts of arguments followed that thought, but I pushed them aside. I would do like Joseph—trust that God's plan was good even though, for the life of me, I couldn't imagine how God could bring good from this situation. And what was it Grandpa had written in the margins? Concentrate on what God puts in your hand today. Yes, I had plenty to concentrate on.

I arranged for a Salvation Army pickup and attacked the kitchen like Mr. Clean himself. This clutter was history.

The house looked good when I finished. Could a person eat off my kitchen floor? Sure. A little dirt helped develop a healthy immune system.

I fixed myself a couple of grilled cheese sandwiches and studied my to-do list. I needed to let Pastor know my decision about leading the Golden Oldies. Remembering one of Olivia's suggestions, I tried to imagine God sitting across from me at the table. "If you really want me to take this group, Lord, could you show me one more time? Would you cause Olivia to ask me herself?"

The phone rang.

"Hi, Granny."

"Stephanie. I can barely hear you, honey."

"I need to hurry so my parents won't catch me. Did you read my diary and talk to my dad?"

"Your diary? What are you talking about?"

"I left it under the bed in the guest room the other night. Can you check to see if it's still there?"

"Sure." I walked to the guest room and touched the floor near the bed—had to make sure my timing was accurate. "Here it is."

Tiny sniffles came across the telephone line.

"You okay, baby?"

"Yeah. My dad just said something last night that . . . Gotta go. They're coming."

The line went dead.

What had I done? Stephanie trusted me. I hadn't actually said anything false, anything that could be classified as a real lie, and I would tell Stephanie the truth when I had sufficient time to explain. So why did I feel like such a louse?

CHAPTER 24

I'd just carried one of the desk drawers to my recliner when the phone rang.

"Hi, Elizabeth. This is Olivia. I hope I'm not catching you at a bad time."

"Not at all."

"I wonder if you could possibly take the Golden Oldies meeting tomorrow. Mac's mother has been waiting to see a foot specialist for months, and an appointment just opened up for tomorrow."

My skin burst into goose bumps. "Will you be coming to the meeting at all?"

"No, I'm afraid not."

I'd made a deal with God. I crossed my ankles. "Sure, I'll be glad to take the meeting."

Then another thought came to mind. One I would have liked to have drop-kicked to another time zone. But I knew God was in it, so I took a deep breath and continued.

"Olivia, I would like to thank you for praying for me. That really means a lot."

"Oh, you are so welcome. I pray for all of our ladies almost every day."

The phone practically rattled in my hand. "Well, I'll start praying for you, too. And thanks for the journal. God has been speaking to me . . . giving me peace like the verse said."

"Thanks, Elizabeth. That blesses me."

I clicked the phone off. Okay, so, glad to take the meeting may have been a stretch. But I was willing. Now all I needed to do was come up with an agenda and a devotional.

First things first. I needed to finish organizing the desk. Then I would plan for the meeting. I examined each piece of paper, eventually realizing the drawers contained nothing but newspaper clippings, coupons and magazines I'd lifted from the beauty shop. The job instantly got easier.

Without hesitation, I dumped the whole lot into a garbage bag and set the empty drawer on the floor. As I tied the bag shut, a folded article from the Summerset News caught my attention. *Daniel Cooke, Local Attorney, Voted Governor of Indiana.*

I remembered the day. Danny, standing on that platform with his skinny little wife, all smiles. The picture of perfection. Innocence. A pledge of honesty and loyalty.

Not the Danny Cooke I recalled from my teen years. Oh, sure, he fooled the teachers—the all-American kid who excelled at everything. School. Sports. Even received the Rotary College Scholarship for his essay on "The Role of Ethical Values in a Changing Community."

The doorbell rang.

I held my breath, thankful the drapes were closed.

Marissa's muffled voiced filtered through the front door. "You home, Biz?"

Were her friends with her? I set the newspaper clipping down and stood to peek out from behind the drapes.

Unfortunately, I forgot about the desk drawer at my feet, tripped and fell with a thud. "Ooh-h-h-h!"

Marissa pounded on the door until I thought she would put a hole in it. "Biz? What's going on? Are you okay?"

Definitely not. My ankle throbbed as I tried to lift it.

"Biz, tell me you're okay, or I'm calling 911. I know you're in there. I can see your shadow moving around."

"I'm coming."

I rolled onto my stomach and to a kneeling position. With the support of the chair, I stood and hobbled across the room to open the door. I practically fell into Marissa's arms when she burst inside like a doggone one-man-SWAT team.

Before I knew it, I was lying flat on my back on the sofa. My foot was propped on a pillow under a plastic bag of ice.

Marissa brought me a couple of Advil with a glass of water and rotated my foot gently to check for broken bones. "I think you've just sprained it."

She replaced the ice bag. "I've got a pair of crutches you can borrow. But if the pain gets worse or the swelling doesn't go down, you need to be evaluated by a specialist."

I shut my eyes, hoping the Advil would take effect soon.

Marissa woke me some time later, helped me sit up and handed me a bowl of steaming Spaghetti-O's. "I made fresh coffee, too. Would you like a cup?"

"Smells good, but you don't have to wait on me." I started to get up, but Marissa pushed me back and propped my swollen foot onto the coffee table.

"Don't even think about going anywhere without help."

She disappeared into the kitchen and returned with two cups of coffee. "Feel like talking for a while?"

"Feel like going home?" I scooped some noodles into my spoon. "Not sure I trust myself. This medicine has me pretty relaxed."

Marissa laughed. "Don't worry, I won't lead you astray. I just thought while you're down the next few days, maybe we might talk through some things."

Uh . . . no. One pain at a time. "Like therapy?"

She smiled.

"Right."

Marissa played on her cell phone while I finished my meal. Didn't look like my friend planned to go anywhere soon. Might as well roll up my pants legs and wade through it, though it might be deeper than Marissa expected. I pointed to the newspaper clipping. "Check that out."

Marissa scanned the article. "The governor who retired several years ago. Good guy. Did you know him?"

"We grew up on adjoining farms."

"Oh. Were you interested in each other?"

"I thought I liked him at one point, but he was three years older than me. Told me he was headed for Harvard and shared his political dreams. This went on for a couple of weeks until my dad caught us sitting up in the hay mow playing cards and talking. Practically threw the boy to the ground, calling him every name in the book and swearing I was a no-good little tease."

Marissa's eyes grew round. "Is this . . .?"

I nodded. "Danny was just a friend. He had a girlfriend—a senior like him. They'd already announced marriage plans. I just figured he was bored in the evenings and came over to kill time."

Marissa's cell phone beeped. "Sorry, Biz. I need to take this. It's the hospital."

Strange—the emotions that washed over me when Marissa disappeared into the kitchen. Why wasn't I relieved? Here was my chance to stuff the story and maybe even convince Marissa to go home.

Instead, a profound sorrow overshadowed me. The sorrow of someone brutally raped by a young man she considered a friend. She'd accepted the fact he loved another girl, and she'd been so careful not to expect too much. She didn't need romance. No, what she treasured most was spending time with someone who actually listened.

As I relived the emotions, a fresh layer of sorrow iced the old, this belonging to a fifty-four-year-old woman who wanted, more than anything in the world, to rid herself of the secret that had influenced her life for too long. She'd finally opened the spigot and allowed the story to pour forth to someone she trusted. Someone trained to slay this kind of demon once and for all.

My neck stiffened. Deliverance couldn't be this simple. Not for me. Marissa would leave to help someone who needed her more than I did.

Marissa stood in the doorway. "I'm sorry, Biz, but I need to go."

Fine with me. I needed a bathroom break anyway. My body trembled. Not sure if I needed more caffeine or just to close the door on the past. Didn't much matter. Both were about to happen soon. I eased to my feet. "I'll just lock the door behind you. Thanks for checking on me."

Marissa laughed. "Hey, I'll only be gone for a minute. I just realized I never let Boomer out to pee after work. Came straight over here instead."

Squeezing my thighs discreetly, I sympathized with poor Boomer. "But the hospital called. Don't you need to go?"

Marissa gave me a gentle hug, making solid eye contact. "There's no way I'm going to leave you in the middle of your painful story. Told them to find someone else."

The phone rang when I returned from the bathroom. I looked at the screen, and my pulse quickened. "Hi, Robert."

"Biz. Are you doing okay?"

"Without you, you mean?"

"I still care, you know."

"That's why you left?"

Robert sighed so deeply I regretted my harsh tone.

I leaned back on the sofa and propped my foot on the coffee table. "I'm sorry, Robert. Thanks for checking."

"Biz, have you thought any more about returning the diary?"

O-o-okay. Let's skip the small talk. "Thought we agreed to disagree about that."

"I know, but I can't stop worrying."

"Yeah, well, I agree something needs to be done. But I don't want Stephanie to pay for what she wrote in private."

"Why do you insist on expecting the worst?"

The door opened, and Marissa walked in carrying a Piggly Wiggly shopping bag and a pair of crutches. "Look what I brought."

"You've got company?"

"Marissa is here."

"Can you tell her you're busy? We need to talk."

"I know, but this isn't a good time. I fell a little while ago, and my back's killing me."

"Please don't put me off again, Biz."

"I'm not. I promise. Call tomorrow night, and we'll talk through everything."

Marissa kicked her shoes off by the door, pulled a box of Wheat Thins and a dish of sliced cheese and apples from the bag and set them on the coffee table. "I'll grab us some ice water." She headed for the kitchen. "That Robert?"

"Mm-hmm. I cut him off a little sharply, but I couldn't deal with him and the stuff I'm telling you. Not in one night."

Marissa returned with water and a couple of napkins and sat down on the other end of the sofa. "I guess you can explain why you were so short when he calls tomorrow."

"Yeah, like when God sends an ice storm to Africa."

Marissa laughed. "You know, Biz. I like your sense of humor."

We relaxed into the cushions and munched on snacks. My ankle started to throb. "Time for meds yet?"

"Another hour. Can you make it?"

I nodded, shutting my eyes against the pain.

"We won't talk for long. I just didn't want to leave you in the middle of what you were telling me." As she spoke, she pulled an elastic bandage from her Piggly Wiggly sack and wrapped my ankle. "You said you weren't interested in Danny Cooke in a romantic way?"

Whoosh—and we were back on Memory Lane. Was it seriously that easy? "He was just a good friend. Like an older brother, actually."

"What happened to change things?"

"Danny came back the day after my dad caught us in the hay mow. Said he saw Dad's truck heading toward town. Knew I'd be alone."

Marissa nodded.

"Danny was furious about the way my dad had handled him and even more so that Dad accused him of wrong intentions. At first, Danny just vented his frustration. Then he snapped. Like this whole different person took over."

Fractured, distorted images appeared, one blurring into the next. Danny raising a pitchfork when I refused to undress. Marmey, our old cat, purring contentedly just feet away with her babies. The stench of soiled hay and the spicy scent of Danny's aftershave as his body awkwardly found its way inside of mine.

Piece by piece, I shared the experience with Marissa. Pain shot through my chest as I relived the horror, memories held in darkness for nearly forty years.

I picked up a sofa pillow and hugged it to my body as I moaned. The physical pain was there. As real as the memory. Danny moaned as he came to fullness within me. I whimpered inside, but never uttered a sound. "Oh, God," I screamed. "He was my friend. Why did he do that to me?"

I cried until my head hurt. Slobbered all over the pillow. Called out to Jesus for strength to go on as filthy, biting words of shame and hatred passed through my lips.

Eventually, the tears slowed.

Marissa handed me a wad of tissues—for the tenth time, I think. Her long, dark eyelashes glistened with wetness. She didn't profess to be a Christian, but I sensed more love and concern from her than I'd ever felt from anyone at church. "No one ever found out?"

I shook my head. "Danny Cooke's father was the county sheriff and his grandfather a senator in the United States Congress. Family blood didn't come any purer. Or more influential. My father . . ."

I laced my fingers together tightly in an effort to control the rage forcing its way from my heart to my mouth. Jagged pain pricked my rib cage. "This is the hardest part."

Marissa placed her fingers on mine.

Her gentle touch calmed the storm within and I found courage to continue. "My father accepted thousands of dollars to keep the matter quiet. I always assumed he put it into the business to avoid going bankrupt. Only discovered my error a few days ago."

The air conditioning kicked on, and Marissa wrapped an afghan around her lap. "Something you found in the trunk?"

"Mm-hmm. A letter from my father. Turns out the money he received actually went to the hospital where my grandpa died."

"Why do you think your father never explained that?"

I shrugged. "During the weeks after the rape, he ranted constantly about a bad turn of the stock market. But the night I announced I had missed my third period, the ranting stopped. Easy to see why I misunderstood."

"How'd he handle the news of your pregnancy?"

"Called me things you don't want to hear. Asked me if I'd thought about what it meant to be saddled with a kid. Told me I'd ruined my life—that I would never amount to anything."

"He just assumed your pregnancy was by choice?"

I nodded. "He had it all figured out in his head. Knew the father was Danny Cooke. Swore we'd been sleeping together for weeks—that I had teased the boy into giving me what I wanted."

"Your mother?"

Acid burned my throat. I drained my glass of water.

Names came to mind, but I held my tongue. "My mother just sat there like a heartless mute and let him trash me."

"I'm sorry."

As I nodded and blew my nose, a massive surge of grief overcame me. I turned my face into the sofa and sobbed. Groaned. Pounded the cushions with my fist. No thoughts. Just a tsunami of unfiltered pain being flushed from my body.

Finally, the current slowed to a drizzle. Then a full stop. I sat, in a daze, wondering what came next in this process called therapy. I looked over to Marissa and smiled. "Can I tell you something, Marissa?"

"Please."

"The other day you asked if I wanted to get better. Made me mad that you'd even ask. But I think I get it now. When I told you about my relationship with Danny Cooke, I felt my reserve crack, and I knew God had sent you to help me.

"I couldn't understand why I trusted you. But then . . . when . . ." I pulled a tissue to my nose and waited for spasms of bottomless sorrow to ease. "When you got a phone call, I thought you were going to leave me to go to someone else, and . . . and the whole rejection, you're-not-worthy thing hit me again. And . . . I realized how very badly I want to get better. And how much I need someone I can trust to talk to. And I'm so thankful God sent you to me."

Marissa scooted closer, stretched her arm around my neck and patted my shoulder. "You're awesome, Biz."

I giggled. "Maybe God had to literally knock me off my feet, so I would take a step in this direction."

"Could be."

"Now, is it time for a pain pill?"

Marissa left around midnight. I still needed to plan for Golden Oldies, but I was whipped. Besides, it was only a thirty-to-forty-minute meeting? I hobbled to bed and set my alarm for seven.

CHAPTER 25

I waited for the Golden Oldies to quiet. "Good morning. Olivia asked me to take the meeting, today. Seems she had more important things to do. Fortunately, I was available to be used by God."

My head swelled with an exhilarating sense of significance as the ladies murmured among themselves. "Let's not judge, my dear sisters. We will do as the Bible says and pray for our enemies."

Blue and white heads nodded in agreement, an understanding look of mercy on each face.

The meeting was going well. What had I worried about? Opening my Bible, I prepared to share the message God had given me.

But before I could say a word, Olivia burst through the back door. "Don't be duped. She's an impostor. A hypocrite of the worst kind!"

I groped for words. But my tongue stuck to the top of my mouth like a wad of bubblegum to the underside of a picnic table. Why would God allow Olivia to do this? Surely, he didn't want the ladies to discover the real me. He would never be able to use me if that happened.

"This is your fault, God!" I screamed, startling myself out of a heavy, muscle-relaxer-induced sleep. My breath came in spurts, my body shook, and I needed to use the bathroom. All very good reasons to turn on the light and get out of bed—regardless of the fact that it was still pitch dark outside.

Thankful for the crutches, I took care of business and started a pot of coffee. I was not going back to sleep until I got this meeting planned, even if it was only four o'clock in the morning. But all I could think about was the horrible, bigger-than-life dream. "Seriously, God. How am I supposed to hear your plan in the middle of this nonsense?"

Then it hit me. Maybe the nonsense was God's voice.

I panicked when the phone rang around nine the next morning, sure I'd set the alarm clock for seven.

"How's the ankle?" Marissa asked.

"Stiff, but not any worse than last night. I managed to hop to the bathroom when I needed to."

"Using the crutches, right?"

"Yes. I've got to hurry and get dressed. Lettie is going to pick me up for the Golden Oldies meeting in about thirty minutes."

"Okay, but I wanted to tell you I talked to the people who stopped by your house yesterday."

I braced myself for the worst.

"They want to come back Saturday. Think you'll be up to company by then?"

"Sure. If not, I'll just hide behind the sofa again."

I checked my alarm clock. Set for seven—in the evening. After a hot shower, I dressed in a large T-shirt and my black slacks. My back twinged as I twisted to fasten my bra. I made a mental note to let an Advil kick in before dressing the next day.

Frieda approached me first as I hopped into the church fellowship hall on my crutches. "Biz, what on earth happened?"

"You don't even want to know."

The other ladies crowded around as well, so I relented and described my fall.

"Will Robert be able to take a few days off to baby you?" Frieda asked.

Lettie touched my elbow, and I mustered a tad of strength.

"Unfortunately, Robert was assigned to a satellite university in Chicago for a few weeks to lead some training classes. He left Saturday."

I explained Olivia's absence, being sure to relay her sincere apologies.

I'm not going to say several ladies' eyes didn't light up when I mentioned I would be taking the lead for the day, because they did. I squashed the inclination to take credit, though. One thing I realized in the wee hours of the morning was that I had absolutely nothing to offer these ladies. They needed God, not me.

"Let's go ahead and start." I led the way to the circle of chairs and took a seat.

Renee placed a chair in front of me. "You should keep your foot up, Biz. That's what the doctor said when Lindsey twisted her ankle in volleyball last year."

I nodded my thanks, touched by her thoughtfulness. "Let's begin with prayer."

Little Sister waved her thin arm in the air. "Could we pray for my cousin's grandson's wife? She was raised in a Christian home, but hasn't been—"

I interrupted. "I'm sorry, dear, but I forgot to explain that I'd like to do our prayer time a bit differently today. Rather than sharing our requests, we're simply going to pray over our own needs. As each one does so, the rest of us can agree silently. I will begin. Will you close when we're finished, Lettie?"

A stillness settled over the room as Lettie nodded. Reverence, I figured. I bowed my head, but words left me. I remembered how eloquently Olivia prayed. Me? I'd never prayed in front of a group in my life. What if I used the wrong words?

Lettie must have sensed my discomfort because she began to pray. Nothing fancy. Just talking to her Father in heaven.

When she finished, I blurted out a prayer of my own. "Father, you are right here with us. Help me trust you instead of being afraid. Lead us in your perfect will as we learn to stop talking and listen to your voice."

Frieda prayed for a patient waiting for news from her oncologist.

Corrine asked God to intervene with an unspoken family situation.

Renee prayed for Lindsey and the other youth in our church as they struggled to maintain their Christian witnesses in school. She also asked God to bless the pastors and staff of the church.

That was it. We waited in silence for what seemed like fifteen minutes. Actually, I squinted my eyes to check the time. Two full minutes passed before Lettie closed the prayer.

What happened? Prayer time took up practically half the meeting when Olivia led. What was I going to do with the extra minutes? Whatever, I needed to get started because when I opened my eyes, the others were looking to me for direction.

Except for Little Sister. She kept her head down. What happened to her prayer request? I knew she wasn't afraid to pray aloud. Did I embarrass her?

Lettie smiled. She would help me sort things out after the meeting. I swallowed a gulp of air and began. First, I shared my horrible dream. Their eyes popped open wide and stayed that way until I finished. Oh, and did I mention that almost every one of them froze in place, right hands covering their gaping mouths? Felt like delivering a speech to a Ripley's Believe-It-or-Not.

Little Sister kept her head bowed.

I paused for a moment, giving the ladies time to catch their breath—and to whisper a prayer for strength as I readied myself to share the toughest part.

"Okay." I looked around the circle to make eye contact. Little Sister glanced up and winked—the sparkle back in her eyes.

"I'm not sure what you think of me now. Truth be told, I'm scared to death you are as disgusted with me as I am with myself."

My knees shook, but I pressed on. I'd promised God. "When I woke this morning, God and I engaged in a major talk about my life."

I straightened my shoulders. "I realized how hypocritical my life has been. Always a competition. I fight for control and put others down in order to feel better about myself. But in reality, I don't like anything about myself."

That was it. I'd completely exposed my tattered underwear for the ladies to see. Problem was, I hadn't considered where to go next.

No one moved. Except for Little Sister. She stood and stepped outside the circle, stopping behind my chair to place her hands on my shoulders.

"Our loving Father," she began, "wrap your arms around your dear child. Show her how much you love her—just like she is."

The last four words broke the dam.

We were finishing lunch when Pastor came into the fellowship hall and asked to see me for a few minutes. I needed to empty my bladder but decided not to keep Pastor waiting. Bad decision. Hopping on crutches while squeezing my thighs together was quite a feat.

"Have a seat." Pastor shut the door to his office and pulled a chair from a corner table across the room for me to prop my foot on. "Sorry to hear about your accident."

"Oh, thanks. Quite clumsy of me, actually."

"I wanted to connect with you about leading the Golden Oldies."

My face dropped before I had a chance to stop it.

"Oh, no, Biz. Nothing negative. I'm still very interested in having you take the position. Have you prayed about it enough to come to any conclusion?"

"Actually, I believe God does want me to take the position. But you need to know that I'm not the perfect role-model for these ladies."

"Well . . . I've got to admit something. I hid in the kitchen to listen when you shared with the ladies this morning. And I liked what I heard. Transparent honesty. That's exactly what I want for our church body. That's what Jesus was all about."

"*Is* all about."

Pastor laughed out loud. "Yes, you're so right."

"Pastor, I'm sorry. I didn't mean to correct you. That just came out before I thought about it. But I want you to know that I've been going through some rough times lately, and Jesus is showing himself very real to me in so many ways."

Pastor's eyes softened. "You doing okay? You want to schedule a time to talk with Renee and me?"

I shook my head. "Not right now. But I want you to know something special God showed me. I was reading the story of Joseph, and I realized that God might have allowed all the suffering in my childhood for just this time in my life. Scares the daylights out of me, but I'm thinking maybe God wants the ladies to see someone who's far from perfect, but who is willing to allow God to change her. Maybe that will help them take a chance on trusting God with their fears and troubles."

"That sure sounds like a God-plan to me."

I swallowed the lump in my throat and forced myself to say the next few words. "I'm going to make mistakes, Pastor. I'm so far from perfect."

"That's just fine, Biz. I'm right there with you." He handed me a tissue. "I haven't been able to meet with Olivia yet, so we'll keep this discussion under wraps for now. I just thought we should touch base."

"I'm glad we did."

"Me, too."

Robby had been leaving messages on the answering machine for three days, so I wasn't surprised when he and

Vickie showed up at the house. I moved to the side of the doorway. "Hey, guys."

Vickie nodded and headed for the sofa. Robby attempted a hug, but dropped his arms when I failed to respond. Not that I wasn't willing to return his affection. Actually, I was just so shocked by his move that I froze in place, and at that point . . . well, who would want to embrace an iced orca?

I limped across the room and lowered my body into the recliner.

"How did you hurt yourself, Mom?" Robby asked. "You look miserable."

"Thanks a lot. I fell yesterday and sprained my ankle."

"I'm sorry. Do you need anything?"

I shook my head.

Robby sat next to Vickie. "Mom, we are desperate to clear the air. We can't stand this rift between us."

He slid the palm of his right hand along his pants leg, pinching the fabric between his thumb and forefinger. "I talked to Dad last night. He told me about the diary and your reasons for not wanting to give it to Vickie and me."

"We just want a chance to talk," Vickie said.

Ugh. Could life get any worse?

"We hope we can convince you we want what is best for Stephanie." Mascara dripped into the pockets beneath Vickie's eyes. Made me think of those 300-pound quarterbacks Robert watched on Monday night football. But Vickie was anything but tough.

I dropped my eyes and sat forward in my chair. "I'm not sure what to say."

In truth, I knew what I wanted to say, but what if they used it against me? What if I admitted how wrong I'd been, and they chose never to listen to me again? What if they used my words to turn Stephanie against me?

Robby cleared his throat. "We're aware of how unhappy Stephanie is, Mom. She came clean the other night and told us everything she'd written in the diary."

Vickie walked across the room and sat at my feet, looking up into my eyes. "I want to apologize for all the times I assumed the worst about you. I kept my distance, unwilling to allow any sort of relationship to develop between us, and I was wrong. Will you forgive me?"

Okay, this was downright uncomfortable. But I sensed the kindness in her words. With a slight smile, I waved her words away. "Of course, I'll forgive you, although I don't think your apology is necessary. You've always been a dear, and I know you do your best."

"How do you ever expect to serve me when you continue to be so blatantly dishonest?"

Oooh. I definitely recognized that voice. Should I just out and out admit what I thought about Vickie? Apologize when I wasn't sorry?

"Mom?"

Robby's voice broke through my reverie. Vickie still sat at my feet. As it should be. I enjoyed a silent giggle. Until the truth slapped me to my senses. This wasn't funny. I had made myself a god, never happy unless others walked according to my word—control, Control, CONTROL.

Instantly, I knew precisely what I needed to say, changes I needed to make. I'm sure I'd known all along, but at that moment, I could no longer deny the urgency.

"Vickie, I'm sorry, too. Sorry I pointed out all your mistakes in the office. I really should have considered your education. Beauty school hardly prepares you for the real world of finance and management."

Vickie's eyes grew rounder with every word. She stood to her feet and glared down at me with a force capable of pushing the entire army of Israel back to Egypt. With one hand on her hip, she pointed a finger in my direction as if I might miss the fact that she was speaking to me. "Look here, Biz. I'm not sure who you think placed you on the throne, but if you ever intend to enjoy this family, you seriously need to rethink your position.

"You want to be brutally honest? I should apologize for all the times I muttered your name in disgust as I worked through the maze of outdated files at the office. And I probably should pity you for that bitter chip on your shoulder, too.

"Will I forgive you as you asked? Yes, but I will not stick around to be beaten to the ground with your rod of superiority. Maybe you should turn it on yourself for once." And with that, Vickie marched her combat boots right out my front door—her battle buddy only steps behind her.

So, Vickie Mouse had a bit of stinky cheese inside, too.

CHAPTER 26

I found it odd the kids didn't start their car and leave. Boy-howdy, what I would have given to be one of those dice dangling from their rearview mirror.

Shame washed over me as I replayed the words Vickie and I had shared. The girl had been spot on with the throne talk. Hadn't Robert basically said the same thing to me many times? Morgan and Lettie, too. Why hadn't I listened?

Don't drag this into your new house.

I wanted to order the thought to a land where the sun doesn't shine, but I knew exactly where the thought originated. So I allowed the words to etch themselves permanently in my memory. Get rid of the past—repent, receive forgiveness and make a change. That's all God asked.

I'd tried but failed when the water got too hot.

And speaking of pain, I needed a pain pill. Inching forward in the recliner, I pushed down on the armrests to propel myself to a standing position, grabbed my crutches and headed for the bathroom.

Robby walked in the front door as I returned.

"Where's Vickie?"

"She went to pick up some chicken for dinner. I wanted to talk to you alone for a few minutes, Mom."

Fried chicken? Why didn't he just stick the knife in and turn it full circle? I hobbled toward the kitchen. "I can't eat fried foods. I'm on Weight Watchers."

"Dad told us. Vickie's getting grilled chicken salads."

"That was thoughtful. I'll fix some iced tea."

Robby touched my arm from behind and pointed to the kitchen table. "Sit down, Mom. Put your foot up. I have a few things I want to say."

I sat. "You don't think we've said enough for one day?"

Robby stepped across the kitchen to fill a couple of glasses with water and returned to the table to sit in his father's place.

"First, I won't tolerate another verbal attack on Vickie, Mom. We need to talk without putting one another down."

"You're right." My mind reeled with excuses, but I didn't want to go there. "Can I just be honest with you, Robby?"

"I hope you will be."

"God is working in my heart, son. I'm seriously trying to sort out all the ugly inside me so I can be a better person." I lifted my eyebrows. "And . . . right now, my discomfort factor is way off the charts."

"You're doing great, Mom."

"Okay. So, Lettie talked to me about trying to be more honest with others. That's what I was going for, but definitely not in the right way. I do think it's good that we finally got our grievances on the table, though. I'm frankly glad Vickie said all she did because I had no clue that—"

Robby held up the stop-sign hand. "Let's don't rehash all that. Vickie feels bad about blowing her lid. Obviously, both of you have harbored ill feelings for too long. That's why we need to continue talking, and hopefully end on a better note."

"I really don't want to get into it all again, Robby."

His eyes searched mine, and I felt the connection. "Sorry. I'm not going to let it go, even if you don't appreciate my loyalty and persistence. Those are good qualities, Mom. I learned them from you."

Affirmation. His words filled me with unexpected joy.

Robby reached across the table and took my hands. "We'll keep this short. We can't ignore what's happened in the past. Let's face it so we can move beyond it."

The chicken smelled delicious, but I pushed the container away when Vickie set it on the table. "I want to enjoy this. Let's finish this talk first."

Robby propped his elbows on the table and rested his chin on folded hands. "First of all, let's catch up about what's going on at the office. I was wrong to shut you out of everything, Mom, and I'm sorry."

My eyes popped open.

Robby unfolded his arms. "Relax, Mom. You may not be the fastest-firing spark plug in the engine when it comes to technology, but I can't tell you how much I've missed your wisdom and experience. Especially with those crazy truckers."

I sipped from my glass of water to stay busy . . . and to keep from crying. Was this really happening?

Vickie handed me the box of tissues from the counter.

Robby pulled one out and wiped his eyes. "I'm really sorry, Mom. You came to the office with something on your mind the other day, and I laughed it off. I was so afraid I wouldn't know what to say if you broke down and admitted how painful giving up the business really is for you."

I smiled through tears and nodded. Robby waited patiently while I fought to find my voice. "I just wanted to remind you not to throw out the baby with the bathwater."

"Meaning . . .?"

"Meaning that, while I lack technological knowledge and skills, you don't have to throw me out completely. I have years of experience and could serve you and the company well as a consultant. You know, maybe be in on the discussion side of your decisions."

Robby sat up taller. "And you'd be willing to stop there? Because that's exactly what we need. What I need."

I laughed at his amazement. "Never been much an example of submission, have I? I guess I can see why my offer comes as such a shock to you. But I'm dead serious. I love this company, Robby, for more reasons than you can ever imagine."

Determined to do the right thing, I ignored my jitters and faced my daughter-in-law. "Vickie, you were spot on about my control problem. The Lord has been asking me to make a lot of changes in my life lately. So, I want to be honest, but hopefully, not ugly. As you probably know, this is all new for me—thinking of others before I speak."

Vickie swiped the tip of her pinkie finger beneath each of her eyes and sniffed.

This was getting tough. "First of all, I'm sorry for my words earlier. True, they honestly depicted my thoughts. But my thoughts were way off base.

"When Stephanie's mom abandoned her, the child and I grew very close. It just about killed me when you entered the picture and Stephanie began turning to you instead of me. I guess I've been jealous for a very long time."

Did I say Vickie had now gone through almost half the box of tissues? She was no longer looking at me, but had her face buried in her hands. I got that.

I went on because I was afraid that if I stopped, I'd never start again. "I've given up precious years with the grandkids because I didn't want to be around you. I was so afraid you bad-mouthed me and turned Christopher and Kyle against me." I cried openly. "And afraid you would do the same with Stephanie. "Vickie, I want you to look at me now."

She obliged.

"I am so sorry for the pain I've caused you over the years, and I beg you to forgive me and give me another chance. I'm working on the control thing and give you permission to remind me any time I step back into my old ways.

"And Robby." I reached across the table and took the hands of both kids. "The business is yours and Vickie's. Completely. I want to help in any way I can, but I will try my best not to fight you for control. And that goes for the kids, too."

There. I'd done it. I sucked up my sniffles and waited for a response.

Robby and Vickie smiled at each other. Robby rolled his eyes and grinned. "I think we're good, Mom."

"Okay, then." I pushed myself onto my good foot and leaned into the crutches. Time to hit the bathroom . . . and to end this uncomfortable discussion. I could only handle so much truth at one time. But before I could take a single hop, Robby wrapped me in a long, tight hug. "I love you, Mom."

I gave in. Resisted the urge to shove my feelings down and run from the moment. Instead, I studied my son's sweet eyes. "I love you, too, Robby."

And then Vickie was in on the hug, too. And maybe that was okay.

Vickie cleared the table. "Would you be interested in helping with some mail outs?"

"Sorry. I'm under a real deadline to finish this house."

"Yeah, I saw how organized the cabinets were. Did you do all this yourself?"

All kinds of flippant remarks came to mind, but I refused to go there.

Robby stepped inside from the garage. "Wow—that's a truckload of garbage bags out there. You're not throwing away anything valuable, are you?"

Was he making fun of my pointless life? "Ha-ha."

He squinted his eyes in confusion. "You didn't give away my old train set and wood burning kit, did you?"

Not to worry, just my little Robby in a big man's body. I simply had to stop making assumptions. "There are a couple of tubs of stuff in the basement for you and Morgan."

"Oh, good. By the way, Mom, do you think Stephanie could spend Saturday night with you? She's scheduled to march with her high school band in the parade. Vickie and I thought we'd take the boys to the lake for the weekend."

You couldn't find anyone safer to keep her? I steadied my voice. "Sure. Sounds fun."

The ugly feelings terrified me. Robby and Vickie had apologized. We'd prayed together. Would I ever be able to rid myself of such poisonous reactions? For good?

The Salvation Army truck pulled into the driveway promptly at three o'clock, just as Robby and Vickie were leaving. "I'm exhausted, and my ankle is killing me. Robby, will you tell them I'd like to reschedule?"

"Go, Mom. Vickie and I will stick around."

After quick and gentle hugs, I grabbed a fresh ice bag and withdrew to my bedroom. As my body relaxed into the mattress, I prayed for wisdom and drifted off into dreams of battle gear, making Christmas chains out of shredded files and gorging on humble pie slathered in chocolate.

When I woke, the most delicious aroma filled the air. Apple pie. Who was baking in my kitchen? Was I dreaming, or had Robert returned while I slept?

Almost unable to contain my excitement, I steadied myself with the crutches and hurried as quickly as possible to the kitchen. My nose hadn't failed me. A pie bubbled and browned in the oven. But Robert was nowhere around.

I heard voices outside the patio door and found Stephanie—complete with original blonde-colored hair—and Marissa washing the basement windows. "What on earth?"

Stephanie laughed and ran to give me a hug.

Marissa joined us. "Robby and Vickie are in the basement with Christopher and Kyle, working on the inside windows."

"What? How did you . . . Why?"

Marissa smiled. "Vickie noticed your list on the table and came up with the idea. We're here all evening, and tomorrow as well."

I sat on the glider and patted the cushion for Stephanie to join me. "You guys are blowing me away."

"Look, Granny." Stephanie pointed to a basement window where her brothers were grinning and waving.

I blew them a kiss. If only Robert could have been there. The void in my heart threatened to swallow up the delightfulness of the moment. "You are wonderful, but I can't let you—"

I stopped, my words interrupted by the doorbell.

"I'll answer it," Stephanie called with a gleam in her eyes.

No, it couldn't be. Oh, God, did you bring my husband home to me?

Vickie ran up the basement stairs as I stepped into the house. Giving me a wink, she hurried across the kitchen to pull the pie from the oven. "You go sit in the living room. I'll bring you some iced tea."

What was she saying? Was this part of her surprise?

I did as she suggested. Stephanie was on the front porch talking in low voices. "Who's there, Steph?"

"Just me." The front door opened, and Morgan stepped inside. I smiled and kept my eyes glued to the door, waiting for Robert's arrival. But only Stephanie followed.

I broke. Despair poured from deep within, and before I knew it, Robby and Morgan were kneeling beside me, alternately holding me in their arms. "I can't go on without Dad. I know I don't deserve him, but I miss him so much."

Morgan pushed my hair from my face and kissed my cheek. "It will work out, Mom."

I shook my head. "There's so much I need to say to you, Morgan. I'm sorry for so many things."

She put a finger to her lips. "Shhh. Robby talked to me. Don't worry, I forgive you for everything." She hugged my neck. "I missed you, Mom."

"When I smelled the pie, I thought maybe Dad had come home. Then the doorbell rang and . . . ."

Understanding registered on the kids' faces. Morgan stroked my hand. Robby stood and walked across the room. With his head in his hands, he leaned against the door and cried.

CHAPTER 27

Vickie and Stephanie stayed the night, refusing to let me lift a finger. As if I hadn't been humbled enough today. The swelling around my ankle was practically gone when I woke the next morning around ten. I tried a bit of pressure and decided I could forego the crutches.

Stephanie sat on the kitchen floor cutting strips of shelf paper. "Morning, Steph."

"Hi, Granny. How's your ankle?"

"Much better." I removed a small carton of yogurt from the refrigerator, grabbed a spoon and sat at the table. "Looks like you've been busy for a while."

Stephanie turned and grinned. "Mom and I worked until about three in the morning."

I laughed. "And you're already out of bed this morning?"

"Mom's idea."

I retrieved a hidden Hershey bar from the pantry and handed it to Stephanie. "Thanks for helping, honey."

She looked up. "Love ya, Granny."

Vickie stepped in from the garage with empty boxes and a Walmart bag. "Morning, Biz. How's your ankle?"

"I think I'm going to make it. The swelling is down and I'm doing fine without the crutches."

"Great. Now go back to bed and stay off the foot. Holler if you need anything." Vickie disappeared into Robert's office with the boxes. I felt guilty not helping, but I couldn't stand the thought of seeing and touching Robert's things. Maybe I should call him.

I practiced putting more weight on my ankle as I walked to the bedroom. It felt stiff, but it no longer ached. I climbed into bed and tapped Robert's number into my phone.

"Hi, Biz. Why are you calling in the middle of the day? Are you okay?"

"You didn't call last night."

"Yeah, sorry about that. Listen, can I call you back a little later? I need to get upstairs for a meeting."

"Sure." I clicked off without a goodbye and dropped the phone into my purse.

Vickie poked her head in the door. "Forgot to tell you that Lettie called. Said you were supposed to meet her for breakfast?"

"Ooh, I forgot. What did you tell her?"

"That you'd been up late and were sleeping in today. She was fine. Said she had errands to run, anyway."

I smoothed the covers on Robert's side of the bed to make a place for Vickie to sit.

She dropped to the mattress and yawned as she propped several pillows behind her head. "Sorry. Guess I stayed up a bit too late."

Her fatigue touched me, the idea that she would do so much for me after the way I'd treated her. My hand spontaneously covered hers—a heartfelt, yet extremely unnatural move on my part. "Thank you for all your help."

Vickie flipped her wrist and wrapped her fingers around mine. "I'm just glad we're finally talking."

Stab. Twist. Kill. I flinched, wanting to strike back. The old me fought for control, filling my mind with vindictive words. After all, hadn't Vickie always—

Vickie released my hand, sat upright in the bed and crossed her legs in front of her. "Robby and I have a wonderful idea."

Should I be excited? I stretched my eyelids in question.

Vickie did a bounce thing on the bed like a giddy cheerleader. "We think you should fly to Chicago next weekend. Robby checked out the prices and we want to buy the ticket if you'll say yes."

What I wanted to say was that their idea stunk like a trapped rat decomposing in an unknown location between the walls.

Vickie bounced a couple more times. "Come on, Biz. Do you like the idea?"

"I hate to disappoint you, but Robby knows I'm afraid to fly."

Instantly, I witnessed a new strength in my daughter-in-law. She pouted and reasoned and fussed until I finally agreed to the trip. Truth be told, I would have done anything to convince the determined woman to leave my bedroom.

My cell phone rang, but by the time I found the thing, I'd missed the call and spilled half the contents of my purse onto the bed. I recognized Robert's number.

"I'll return the call later." I looked up . . . and wished I hadn't. There stood Vickie with the little black cosmetic bag in her hot little hands, going through it like a kid at Christmas. So, life could get worse.

"Biz, where did this come from?"

Oh, just from some harlot your revered father-in-law is currently involved with.

"Biz? You're staring at me like I'm holding a bomb here. Seriously, I've been looking all over for this. Where did you find it?"

The bag belonged to Vickie? "I found it under the seat in Dad's car."

"Oh-h-h, yeah." Her face brightened like a super-watt light bulb. "He gave me a ride home from the tire shop. I guess I dropped it when I was digging for my keys."

Life lesson. Never ask God if life can get worse.

Thankfully, Vickie missed the significance of the moment. Either that, or she was immortally gracious enough to change the subject. "So, I hear Pastor asked you to consider leading the Golden Oldies."

"I was under the impression the whole thing was confidential."

Vickie nodded. "Dad told Robby not to say anything to anyone else. He's worried about you."

I laughed out loud. "Dad or Robby?"

"Dad." Vickie waited an appropriate time before continuing. Must have realized I didn't need her opinion or advice. The girl was starting to impress me.

"Are you going to take the position?"

Did she care, or was she simply fishing for information? "Praying about it."

I wanted to tell Vickie about God speaking to me through a dream and that I'd actually agreed to lead the group, but I couldn't bring myself to do so. How do you admit to your kids you've failed at life when you've spent your life trying to convince them you know it all?

Vickie turned my direction and held my gaze. "I think you'd make an awesome leader. I love the new tenderness I see in you. And you really are wise. I think that with God's help you'd make an amazing impact on the ladies."

Okay, just try not to cry when your archenemy dumps a bucket of that kind of stuff all over you. But there wasn't time for tears because my potential renters showed up a full hour early.

"It's fine," Vickie assured me. "Everything is ready."

After welcoming the family inside, I answered their questions about the rent and suggested they take their time browsing through the house. Stephanie and I sat on the sofa, Vickie in my recliner.

"I'll replace the curtains soon." I crossed my ankles as the family headed for the guest bedroom. "I wanted to buy something fresh for my future tenants. I can order new drapes in the master bedroom, too, if the color isn't right."

Stephanie nudged me with her knee. "Back off, Granny—you'll scare them away."

Marissa showed up as the family gathered back in the living room.

"Hey, Rissa." The father wrapped his arms around my neighbor.

Uh, excuse me, was there something she hadn't told me?

Marissa burst into giggles. "Oh, Biz, I totally forgot to tell you Justin is my cousin. He and his family live about thirty minutes south of town, and he's tired of the commute."

Marissa hugged Justin's wife and kids. "So, what did you think of the house?"

"We love it." Mrs. Justin turned to face me. "We are considering another house a couple blocks over. Any idea when yours will be ready? Our current lease runs out on July 20."

Less than three weeks . . . to be completely moved out of the house? Thank God for thirty years of backroom poker games at the trucking office on slow days. The time I spent developing my face was about to pay off big-time. "I'm sure we can make that happen. Are you ready to commit, then?"

Mrs. Justin smiled. Mr. Justin shrugged. So, it was up to the wife. Should I bring up the curtain colors again?

The phone rang. "The message machine will get that." I didn't want to lose the couple's attention. "Do you have any other questions about the house?"

"Mrs. McNeely, this is Armando, the painter. We have a problem."

Drats! The volume on the answering machine was on high.

"It's my father. He's old. He had a stroke last night, so I must travel to Florida for a few weeks."

Vickie followed me to the kitchen. I picked up the receiver and answered with my tiniest voice. "Hello, Armando. I'm so sorry about your father. What about your crew? Could they do the job?"

"I'm sorry, but they no paint without me. My rules, you know."

"And the curtains?"

"I'm sorry. My wife, she go with me, and I have no idea how long we stay."

Armando assured me he would call as soon as he returned. Unfortunately, that would be too late for these renters.

Vickie's face drooped with empathy as I relayed the information. "Maybe Robby could take some time—"

I shook my head, not willing to expose the true extent of my discouragement. "He's too busy. I'll figure something out."

I'm not sure how Marissa convinced me to meet her at IHOP later for dinner. The thought of going to one of my favorite restaurants without tasting those melt-in-the-mouth buttermilk pancakes was enough to make me crazy. But Marissa insisted there were selections for dieters.

I bought a newspaper from the rack outside the restaurant in case Marissa ran late. I definitely couldn't sit in IHOP with nothing to eat and nothing to do.

Fortunately, Marissa was right on time. "No crutches?"

"Nope. The ankle's a little stiff, but I haven't needed a pain pill all afternoon."

The waitress brought our drinks, and I ordered the Simple-and-Fit dinner.

Marissa handed the waitress the menus. "I'll take the same."

"You don't need to do that. I'm a big girl, you know."

That wasn't meant to be funny, but Marissa obviously thought otherwise because a second later she was coughing and spurting. "Sorry, Biz."

I rolled my eyes and did my best to appear offended.

Marissa seemed to pace herself, eating exactly what I ate. Like she was purposely trying to finish her food about the same time I did. "You really could have ordered anything, but thanks."

She returned a nod, with a slight curve to her lips. "Want to talk or just chat?"

I knew exactly what she meant. I loved this lady. "Talk."

"Okay. The other day you asked me how you could ever help others when your own past still controls you. Have you thought anymore about that?"

"The obvious answer is to work through my past first. Put it behind me. Then reach out to others. Am I close?"

Marissa winked. "Partially. But your past has colored your life and made you who you are. You'll never be able to totally walk away from that. And you wouldn't want to because it could be that very past that will bond you to the hurting young women. Open doors for ministry that only you can provide because you understand where others are coming from."

"Thanks. But I still wonder how I will do that when my pain is still so real."

"When you first talked to me about your baby, you almost couldn't speak for your tears. Do you remember that?"

I nodded. "But now that I've told you, I'm able to talk about it without becoming so emotional."

"Right. You're able to look at the situation with a slightly different perspective. Through eyes of logic and discernment."

Marissa was starting to make sense. I sipped my iced tea. "So let me see if I have this right. In order to minister to others, I'll need to stay emotionally neutral about my own pain. Deal with my pain privately and concentrate on their needs when I'm with them?"

"Good job, Biz. Now you've answered your own question."

Marissa stacked empty dishes and moved them to the edge of the table. "By the way, my cousins really liked your house."

"Yeah, too bad. I can't get another painter for a month or two. Guess your cousins will be forced to take the other house."

"Probably so. I'm not sure who's more disappointed, you or me."

"So, you're close to them?"

"Not in the past. But there are other circumstances to consider. I'll tell you sometime."

"Now's as good a time as any."

Marissa nodded. "It's a long story. A few years ago—"

She paused when the waitress returned for our empty dishes. "Coffee?"

Marissa's beeper sounded. She slipped out of the booth. "Black for me. Be right back."

But she wasn't. I watched her through the window, embellishing her conversation with hand motions. No problem. I checked my messages—one from Robert.

"Biz, we'll close on the new house on July 16 at six o'clock in the evening. Let me know if the date doesn't work for you."

My birthday. Did he purposely choose that date? I shook the sappy sentiment away, refusing to be disillusioned. Why had Robert agreed to buy the house if he wasn't sure our marriage would last?

But then, he still insisted I was imagining the whole affair. Was I wrong? I ran through my mental list. The phone calls in his office. Kathy's voicemail suggesting she and Robert sneak away. The office scene. The late nights before Robert left town. Kathy leaving town a day after Robert did.

No. There was just too much evidence. And Robert would have to answer for his actions—after I had the keys to the new house.

I opened the newspaper and fought to catch my breath. Danny Cooke's face was plastered across the front page. "Former Indiana Governor Dies in Plane Crash."

Staring at the text, I tried to glean details, but my brain wouldn't cooperate.

Marissa slid into the booth. "You okay? You look like you just saw a ghost."

I pointed to the paper. "Of yesterday past."

Marissa flipped the paper her direction and read aloud. "The late governor's son, Daniel Graham Cooke, Jr., was flying the plane. He is listed in critical condition with extensive burns and several broken limbs. Paul Schnipper, of Noblesville, Indiana, witnessed the crash, saying, 'The plane had just taken off when I heard an explosion and saw a giant fireball twirling through the air as it plummeted to the ground a few miles from the airport. I can't believe anyone survived.'"

I felt so sorry for Danny's son. As excruciating as the burns must be, the physical pain couldn't possibly come close to the torture of realizing he might have been responsible for the death of his parents.

"Were you aware Danny had a son?"

"I knew he had a child. Marjorie was pregnant at graduation. They got married the day after and moved to Massachusetts where Danny attended Harvard on a full scholarship. Danny's parents followed him east a few years later. I didn't hear much after that."

Marissa fanned through the newspaper. "His career is listed here. Pretty impressive."

My fingers shook as I tipped my coffee to my lips.

Marissa folded the paper in half and set it in front of me. "Didn't you say your son had red hair and was born on the 4th of July?"

Muscles squeezed my neck like a vice, possibilities of what might lie ahead wrenching its handle, winding tighter and tighter until I feared losing the capacity to breathe altogether. "What are you saying?"

Marissa pointed to a colored picture of Danny, Marjorie, and their son. The caption read: "Daniel Graham Cooke, Jr. is listed in critical condition at Indiana University Medical Center from injuries sustained when the plane he piloted crashed and took the lives of both his parents. The late governor and his wife were visiting their son for the 4th of July holiday weekend, which also happens to be the younger Cooke's thirty-ninth birthday."

I pressed my palms against the edge of the table for support. I had given birth to a son thirty-nine years ago on the 4th of July. "But this man has green eyes. My son had blue eyes."

"Most babies are born with blue eyes, but the color often changes after a few weeks. Did anyone else in your family have green eyes?"

"Grandpa." The room swirled around me in a funnel of disbelief and unwanted hope. Noblesville—only thirty minutes away. Could my son really live that close to me? "Oh, God. This can't be happening."

Distorted nursery songs plagued my sleep when I finally dozed. Melodies I had sung to the child in my womb.

Over and over, the Asian nurse marched into my hospital room, pressed her face to mine and ordered me to hand my baby over. "You're not old enough. This child needs a real mama."

I lay in bed for hours the next morning, replaying the words from Stephanie's diary. Where are you, Mommy? Do you ever think about me? Do you miss me?

Would baby Dean want to meet his birth mother at such a vulnerable time in his life?

I'd sworn Marissa to secrecy, but the thought of my family somehow discovering the truth about my past terrified me.

If I didn't want them to become suspicious, I had to continue as if nothing had changed. And that meant following through with plans for Stephanie to spend the next day and night with me while the rest of her family took off for the lake.

CHAPTER 28

"If you'll take down the drapes in the living room and my bedroom, we can drop them off at the drycleaners while we're out. The stepladder's in the linen closet."

"Sure, Granny. Anything before a shopping trip with Granny's wallet!"

"Right."

We hit a donut shop for breakfast. Glad I'd stuck a protein bar in my purse, I ordered a large coffee for myself, mentally patting myself on the back for not getting my favorite cream-filled, chocolate-iced Long John.

As we finished our food, Stephanie pulled up something on her cell phone and handed it to me. "We've just got to go to The Home Shop. It has everything."

She was right. The upscale home décor store was located in an exclusive area of town. Room after room of color coordinated merchandise. We walked out an hour after we arrived with a carload of sofa pillows, ocean-themed bathroom accessories, quilt and sham sets and lamps for the living room. My granddaughter thought I was made of money, and I wasn't about to disappoint her.

For lunch, we went to Jennie's Place, a quaint tearoom tucked behind a strand of tiny cottages selling anything from stained-glass window hangings to homemade fudge.

She narrowed her eyes as we parked. "How long since you went shopping, Granny? Everyone's been to this place."

I laughed. "Too long, I guess."

The thrill of spending time with Stephanie was bittersweet. With her mindless babble and joking, all appeared to be fine between us. But eventually, I needed to admit I had lied about the diary. I prayed God would give me the right words.

I ordered a chicken salad sandwich minus the croissant, a slice of melon and a Diet Coke. When the waitress walked away, I summoned my courage, determined to say what I had to say before the food arrived.

Stephanie beat me to it. "Granny, you're fidgeting like a kindergartener in line for the bathroom. Is it about the diary?"

I searched my granddaughter's eyes, expecting anger but finding only sweetness.

"Dad told me how it all happened."

"I'm so sorry, Stephanie. I acted without thinking. But I lied, and that wasn't right."

"It's okay. Really. Mom said you probably just didn't want to explain what was going on over the phone because I was upset and in a hurry."

Vickie took my side? I nodded, a bundle of nerves stuck in my throat like a doggone beaver's dam. My precious granddaughter was growing up. "I love you, honey."

She smiled. "I love you too, Granny."

Stephanie told me all about summer school and her cheerleading and band camps as we ate. "Oh, by the way,

Lindsey texted me earlier to say the band director wants us to arrive early to warm up. Five o'clock."

"Fine with me. Just tell me when you're ready to leave."

"Lindsey's going to pick me up and bring me home by ten. Is that okay?"

Something felt wrong. Stephanie seemed way too eager to please. "I didn't know Lindsey played in the band."

Stephanie squirmed in her seat. Just slightly, but definitely enough for me to notice.

"Lindsey's not in the band, but she wants to go to the carnival with us after the parade. By the way, did I tell you Olivia's daughter Kelly went to cheerleading camp with me? She said you and her mom were friends. Her mom seems sort of weird, like way too strict."

"Like more than your parents?"

Stephanie laughed. "Good one, Granny. My parents are okay. I'll admit I'm a challenge. Kind of like you, right?"

My turn to shift gears. "Doesn't Olivia have an older son, too? I think I've seen them on the worship team at church."

"Yep. They look a lot alike." Stephanie picked at the last few shreds of ham left on her plate. "Their other brother is nothing like them, though. Way older. He spends like every day hunting and only comes to church for Christmas and Easter. Kelly says he's on drugs and stuff."

No way. I purposed not to let shock register on my face but couldn't stop the questions from pummeling my mind. Why did Olivia only mention two kids when she talked about her family at the Golden Oldies meeting?

Stephanie rattled her glass of ice. "Earth to Granny. Ready to go?"

I sighed as I pulled in the drive and glanced at the front lawn. Overgrown grass and weeds crowded into the flower beds and along the sidewalk. Robert would have died. Not a bad thought. I could collect life insurance and move out of this rotten neighborhood.

Okay. I didn't really want Robert to die, but how could he just up and leave without arranging for the work to be done? Not like I didn't have enough responsibilities of my own. "Remind me to call someone to cut this grass, okay, Steph?"

Stephanie nodded, yawning. "You wore me out, Granny."

I laughed. "How about we leave all this stuff in the truck until after a nap? Might be more fun to mess with later."

"Sounds good to me."

Stephanie disappeared into the guest room as I headed for my room. After a long shower, I turned on the fan and climbed into bed. But I couldn't sleep. Why was I so uncomfortable with the idea of Lindsey picking Stephanie up for the parade? And if Lindsey wasn't in the band, why was she the one who texted Stephanie about the change in time?

I finally gave up on the nap and decided to put on a pot of coffee and journal while Stephanie rested. But when I stepped into the kitchen, my plans vanished.

Stephanie stood at the counter with her back to me, talking on her cell phone. "Granny fell for the whole line, Lindsey. I'm not kidding. I already left my band director a text saying I'm sick. Girl, this party is going to totally rock."

Pause.

"Okay—my lips are sealed. I'll be ready at five. Don't be late." Stephanie punched her fist into the air and whispered, "Yes!" as she swiveled around.

Our eyes met. "Granny? I thought you were taking a nap."

I'll admit that I was speechless for a split second, after which an explosion of words battled to be the first to tumble from my mouth. Questions. Accusations. Threats.

By the grace of God, I managed to hold my tongue, taking in deep swigs of air as I sat down at the table. The silence proved effective. Stephanie broke into tears.

When Robby and Vickie told me about her misbehavior, I figured they were exaggerating. But here it was. Stephanie had blatantly deceived me. "Stop the crying. We need to talk."

Stephanie quieted. "Granny, I'm sorry. I just wanted to have a good time. Mom and Dad never let me go anywhere fun, and I hate the stupid band. Why should I be forced to march around in that ridiculous uniform for a bunch of bratty kids who want candy and senior citizens who refuse to move past memory lane? My friends get to party every weekend. It's not like I'm still eight years old."

Nice cast, but no nibbles. This situation was too big for me. Where were all the I-would-have-done-so-and-so ideas I'd mumbled to myself in the past?

"Tell you what, Stephanie. I'm not sure how to handle this, but I know one thing for sure. You're not going anywhere this evening."

"What? You can't do that, Granny. Can't I at least go to the parade?"

"Nope. What you can do is get your tail outside and mow the grass. Use the time to think about what you've done and how you're going to explain it to your parents tomorrow."

"But, Granny—"

"Get going. And hand me the phone. You won't need it."

"But what about Lindsey?"

I shook my head and pointed to the patio door. "I'll take care of that. The mower is in the shed."

Stephanie stomped across the kitchen. "This is so lame! My parents are going to be furious with you!"

"I'll take that risk."

I called Renee. Crazy woman brushed it off with a shaky laugh. "We all did things like that when we were kids, right?"

Bothered me. Renee wasn't doing Lindsey any favors by ignoring her behavior.

I brought Stephanie her phone and instructed her to call her band director to say she would be marching in the parade after all. I balked when she said she felt better. I was quite sure she actually felt much, much worse, but I decided not to go there.

Where I did go was to the wretched 4th of July parade. About cooked my goose sitting in the truck for over an hour while the marching band made the circuit, but I wasn't about to let Stephanie out of my sight. I walked her from the parking lot to the starting line and picked her up at the finish. One fat, granny escort for the entire evening.

We stopped for supper at Dairy Queen. Stephanie ate her chicken nuggets and fries without a word but broke into a smile when I offered to buy dessert. "Okay, Granny. You totally earn the Granny-of-the Year award."

I covered a grin with my hand.

"The whole escort thing. Embarrassed me to death."

I dropped the smile. "What you did is a serious matter, Steph—telling lies. You realize I have to tell your parents about this when they return, right?"

She lowered her gaze. "Yeah, I guess."

Watching her down a Butterfinger Blizzard while I slurped on a fat-free fudge bar was no easy task. Especially when she claimed she was full before the cup was even half empty. One of the things I can't stand about skinny people. Makes me want to shove a pound of lard down their stringy throats.

Stephanie wrapped her straw wrapper around her finger. "When's Grandpa coming home?"

"Not sure how long his job in Chicago will last."

Stephanie twirled her red plastic spoon through the melting ice cream. "Probably not until you guys figure out how to get along, right?"

Heat rushed to my face. Another 500 calories worth, I'm sure. "What makes you say that?"

Stephanie looked me dead in the eye. "Can I be honest, Granny?"

Or just shut up? "Of course."

"Do you realize how mean you are sometimes?"

No way. She did not just say that. My silence obviously didn't faze her because she continued. "Like when you constantly argue and say he's doing something wrong. That's embarrassing, Granny."

"Grandpa's never said anything."

Stephanie rolled her eyes. "Of course not. He's Grandpa. I feel sorry for him, though. It's like he can never please you."

Tears leaked from my eyes. The child was right.

"I'm sorry, Granny, but I miss Grandpa. If you would treat him as special as you treat me, he might come home."

Thankfully, Stephanie dropped the subject and stared out her window on the way home. After helping me carry our shopping bags inside, she locked herself away in the bathroom to shower.

I barely heard the doorbell ring over the music blaring from under the bathroom door. "Hey, Marissa." I stepped outside and pointed to the porch swing. "Want to sit awhile?"

"Sure. I just wanted to be sure you were okay after last night's shock."

"Baby Dean . . . or . . . Daniel Cooke, Jr." I shook my head. "Honestly, the day has been so full I haven't even had a chance to process that."

"I noticed the yard looks better. You had some help?"

"Hmph. Not a willing volunteer, I can assure you."

I kept an eye on the bathroom door through the front window as I described Stephanie's devious little plot. Before I could blink, we were hot and heavy into a discussion that led all the way from what I read in Stephanie's diary to Vickie's role as stepmom to my role as grandmother.

Talk about interference. I hadn't been looking for counsel. Just sharing, the way neighbors do on their front porches. But Marissa did make some good points about setting boundaries and such. Guess this was my night to be put in my place. If only I could figure out how to stay there.

After getting up at least five times during the night to check on Stephanie, I was in no mood to be messed with the next morning. I banged on the guest room door for the third time in an hour. "Young lady, you have exactly five minutes to get your sorry behind dressed so we can leave for church."

"Aw, come on, Granny. It's not like Mom and Dad will care whether we go or not. After all, they're skipping, too."

So this was the Stephanie who lived with Robby and Vickie. The one I swore in my mind did not exist. How could I have been so wrong?

Stephanie didn't open the door until her parents arrived.

Didn't stay open for long, either. After sending the boys to the backyard, Robby and Vickie disappeared into the guest room and shut the door.

She's all yours. My eyes had been opened. That said, I did stand to the side of the door to listen. After all, this was my house.

Robby didn't yell. He just calmly explained to Stephanie that life as she knew it was over. No more cell phone or hanging out with friends at the mall. From here on out, she would be accountable for every step she took.

To my surprise, Vickie actually defended Stephanie several times when past issues came up. And when all was said and done, the three of them cried and prayed together before they came out of the room.

Oh my. Was that how Christian parenting was done? Where did Robby learn that?

Robby and the kids trimmed the bushes and weeded the flowerbeds while Vickie ran to get groceries. I brought water bottles out, purposely saving Stephanie's for last. She worked alone in front, picking wads of grass from between the cracks in the sidewalk.

Stephanie glanced around the yard as she stood. "Where is everyone?"

She wasn't fooling me. I was well aware ugly was coming once she verified our privacy. I braced myself for the worst. "They're busy out back."

Flames screamed from the child's eyes. "I trusted you, Granny."

"I know."

"I thought you'd understand."

"Honey, deception is a lie, and a lie is wrong no matter how good the reason."

"What about when you lied to me?"

"I was wrong. Somehow, as I was growing up, I came to believe that it was okay to tell a lie to keep from hurting someone or to protect yourself. But that's wrong, and I'm still trying to change that habit. Will you please forgive me?"

Stephanie hesitated. "Still doesn't seem fair that I should be punished when you . . ."

I held up a finger. "You know, you're right. Why don't you help me down there and we'll work together to weed this stinkin' sidewalk."

Stephanie giggled and offered me her arm. "Age before beauty."

Did I say we were cast from the same mold?

The kids left after lunch. I needed a nap, but I couldn't sleep. I kept hearing Robby's firm but kind voice correcting his daughter. I kept picturing the two of them as they walked out of the bedroom, Robby's arm around his daughter's shoulder. So different than the father I'd known.

I tried desperately to hold back images of my childhood. My father telling me I would never amount to anything. I was the biggest disappointment of his life. He would rather have been childless than forced to raise such a useless daughter.

I tried so hard to make him proud of me when his heart acted up and he turned the business over to me. When he criticized every decision I made, I tried harder. I learned to hide things from him. Mistakes.

As his body failed, the business prospered. Still, he belittled my plans for the future. "You'll never be able to keep the place running. You need to sell before you end up throwing everything I've worked for to the dogs."

That was the last time I visited my father. He died six months later—reportedly, with a scowl on his face.

CHAPTER 29

I left for Olivia's house around six. She'd invited a few Golden Oldies and their families to the ranch to watch fireworks. The two-story brick house, set back on a meticulously manicured lawn, spoke of elegance. Flaming orange and yellow marigolds flourished along the cobbled walkway, and to the side, water bubbled from a fountain down a path of smooth, scattered stones, that spilled into a kidney-shaped pool.

Mac and Olivia greeted me at the door and led me to a spacious garden room with an adjoining greenhouse. Lettie, José and several others were already there, observing thriving flowers of almost every color imaginable. "Wow." I faced Olivia. "Who has the green thumb? You or Mac?"

"Actually, it's our son who loves the flowers."

I thought of Robert's prized flower beds. "Do you think he would work for hire?"

Olivia smiled—like I'd been teasing. "If you'll excuse me, I need to help Mac at the front door."

"Sure."

Corrine sat at a white wrought iron table, practically hidden by a plush lemon tree. I helped myself to a glass of iced tea and hurried over to the table. "Mind if I join you?"

"Not at all."

"You flying solo tonight?"

Corrine turned to face the greenhouse. The other guests had headed outside where fruit trees and flowers lined the backyard. "Davis and I had a bit of a tiff."

"Happens to the best of us. Glad you came on your own."

She nodded. "Yes, but I doubt I'll return to the meetings."

"Too much socializing?"

"No." Corrine took a sip, set the glass down and traced her finger in the condensation around the base. "I just don't feel like I belong. I'm struggling to deal with some childhood issues, and I'm not sure I'm emotionally ready to interact with others who have no idea where I'm coming from."

"I'd like to know."

Corrine adjusted her position. "I'm sure you don't want to hear my sob story. You probably have your own."

And you really don't want to share, do you, Corrine? Believe me, I understood. "I'd really like to hear your story, Corrine."

She dropped her hands to her lap. "I came from the hood. An uncle raped my mom when she was twelve years old. We lived with my Big Momma until she threw us out. I was six. Mom said Big Momma had enough worries of her own. A few months later, we received word she'd died in her sleep."

That hurt. Though temped to compare stories, I somehow knew that would devalue the depths of Corrine's pain. This was her time, and I would be there for her. "I'm so sorry, Corrine. Did you have a place to stay?"

"Just shelters. Or sometimes we hung out at overnight parties. Mama would put me on a blanket in the corner of a bedroom that reeked of liquor and sweat. I tried to sleep, but couples used the bed. In and out of the room, all night. I felt so alone and afraid. I just wanted Mama to snuggle with me, but she never came."

I thought of my grandpa. "Did you ever lie there and fantasize about a normal life? Dream that Big Momma came to rescue and protect you?"

Tears streamed down Corrine's cheeks. "Every night."

Corrine gazed off in the distance, absentmindedly shaking her head a couple of times. "Mom sold herself out to pay the rent. Four younger brothers—each with a different dad." She faced me again, her frigid eyes empty, her jaw set. "Not that it mattered about those men. They always disappeared when Mom announced she was pregnant."

"Have you kept in touch with your brothers?"

Corrine paused for several seconds before answering, her eyes regaining life. "I ran away the day Mom told me I needed to start earning my keep. Her way."

Oh, God in Heaven. Give me the words. "I can't imagine the journey you've taken, but you've come so far, and I'm proud of you, Corrine. We really never know what lies behind a smiling face, do we?"

"No. I try not to go there. God has blessed me with a wonderful life. But sometimes, when something triggers memories, I regress emotionally. Immediately assume others think I'm not good enough."

As fate would have it, our conversation ended when Mac and Olivia entered the room with Frieda, Pastor and Renee. Other guests returned from the back garden.

Pastor prayed over the meal and Olivia started passing the platters and bowls—barbequed pork ribs, T-bone steaks and honey-glazed grilled chicken quarters, accompanied by a garden salad, baked beans, smoked corn-on-the-cob and twice-baked potatoes.

Mac poured dressing on his salad. "Olivia tells me Robert is working in Chicago. How long will he be gone?"

Did I say I was hungry? Scratch that. The question somehow attracted everyone's attention like a stinkin' puff of expelled gas, and all eyes turned in my direction. I did my best to smile away the discomfort. "Oh, he thinks it will be for around six weeks. May be longer, though."

Fortunately, the good Lord guided a pesky wasp into the room at the perfect moment, and the crowd's focus shifted abruptly. Conversation picked up, my appetite returned and the rest of the evening actually turned out to be quite tolerable. Good to be out of the house. This was normal. Friends ate with friends. Talked about the weather and grandkids and vacation plans.

Normal. Who was I kidding? My life was anything but normal right now, and I detested pretending it was.

José nudged Lettie's arm. "We should go."

She turned to Olivia. "So sorry to eat and run, but the grandkids are waiting at home to make homemade ice cream and burn their sparklers."

Olivia pushed her chair back and set her napkin on the table. "Not to worry. I remember you mentioning that when I invited you. Thank you for coming for dinner, though."

Perfect time to slip out, myself. I made my apologies and headed for the truck. As I turned the keys, José pulled up alongside. Lettie lowered her window.

"You leaving early, too?"

"I've got a terrible headache. Just started."

Lettie winced. "I'm sorry. We wanted to invite you over. The kids would love to see you. It's been way too long."

In her opinion, maybe. I had no desire to be around people. "I think I'll just head home and hit the bed. Thanks for the offer, though. Maybe next time."

Lettie laughed. "Right."

Robert called just after I got home. He skipped the small talk. "I talked to Robby. He's upset Stephanie gave you such a hard time."

"Yeah, I sure saw a different side of her. Steph misses you, Robert. Wonders when you plan to come home."

"Hard to say."

"Stephanie says you would come sooner if I treated you as nicely as I do her."

"There's a grain of truth in that, but it works both ways, dear. I've been thinking a lot about my part in the breakdown of our marriage. God called me to lead our family, but I gave up years ago. At the time, it seemed easier, but now I realize I neglected asking for God's direction. I'm sorry for that."

"I miss you, Robert."

A long pause, punctuated with a few sniffs. "I love you, Biz. I always have and always will."

"You say that, but I don't understand how this separation is going to help resolve our issues."

"I talked to a counselor at the church here. He suggested that if we choose to work on our marriage, we should each do some serious thinking about what we want out of it."

"If we choose? You know what the Bible says about divorce."

"Don't put words in my mouth. I just want to be sure we are on the same side. With the same goals."

His side. I didn't say it, but I knew that's what he meant. Robert knew best. Would he even welcome my surprise visit at the end of the week? I sucked up and allowed my true feelings to express themselves in words. "I'm not sure I'll ever be able to measure up to your expectations, Robert. But I do want to work on our marriage, and I definitely want you to come home."

Must have taken him by surprise, because he didn't respond for several seconds. "The counselor gave me some topics to write about. You might want to write about them as well. Good place to start."

I reached for my notebook and pen. "What are they?"

"First, consider what you see, feel and think about our marriage as it is now. Then explore what you want from our marriage for yourself, for me and for the two of us together. What would it require from each of us to achieve those possible goals? And finally, what are you willing to do?"

Way beyond anything I'd imagined. "You're going to take time to do this?"

"Yes, and I hope you will, too. Then we can meet with a counselor to discuss how to move forward."

I stared at the phone after I said goodbye. Important stuff. There was still so much to do to get the house ready. But this was sort of a Mary-over-Martha kind of priority I needed to make sure happened.

By the time the ten o'clock news came on, I'd taken Tylenol, Advil and some old extra-strength Midol I found in the medicine cabinet.

Pain was one thing, but when my heart plunged deep within my chest, I got scared. Was this a heart attack? I was short of breath and sweating like a bloated weight lifter.

No one answered my calls—Robby, Morgan, Marissa or Lettie—and that was the extent of the numbers I had in my phone, except for Robert, and there was no way I was going to call him unless I knew for sure it was something serious. One choice left. I unlocked the front door, jotted a note to the kids in case I didn't make it and dialed 911.

Five minutes later, my heart stopped tripping over itself, and my breathing returned to normal. Unfortunately, there was no backing out of the 911 situation. The operator had me on the line, assuring me every few moments that help would arrive soon.

I must have fallen asleep because the siren almost scared me to death—literally. The responders made quick work of loading me onto the truck. My heart started plunging again, and I sensed myself checking out. I didn't care. Life had to be better on the other side.

Once the attendant slapped the oxygen mask over my face, I gave in to drowsiness.

"Blood pressure high," was the last thing I heard before waking up in an emergency room cubicle sectioned off with curtains made from the same fabric as Robert's boxer shorts. Guess I hadn't advanced to the heavenly realms.

A young man in green scrubs wrapped a blood pressure cuff around one of my arms while an older woman in an obnoxious Betty Boop uniform jabbed a needle into the other, taped it in place and attached rubber tubing to a bag of clear liquid overhead. "The doctor will be in shortly."

Twenty minutes later, the doctor still hadn't arrived. "Oh, bother," I muttered to myself, kicking my feet from under the blanket. "A woman could die and be thrown on the slab before ever meeting the doctor in this place."

I heard a guffaw on the other side of the curtain, and a fit, dark-haired doctor, probably somewhere in his mid-thirties, stepped into my cubicle. "Behold. I've come to rescue you from the slab."

I pulled the covers up to my chin, my internal reflexes going wacko over a faint trace of spicy aftershave.

He held out his hand. "Doctor Garrison. I'm sorry it took so long. A trauma case arrived right after you."

"I'm sorry, Doctor. I was making a joke."

Laughter rang from his half-moon-shaped eyes. "Not to worry. Now suppose you tell me what brings you in here."

This guy was drop-dead gorgeous. Suddenly, body systems I thought shorted out years ago started firing sparks right and left. I clearly needed to rip the blood pressure cuff off my arm before the guy actually examined me. No telling what kind of jolt I might register.

Three hours and a myriad of tests later, Dr. Garrison returned. "So, we've ruled out all the scary stuff and got your blood pressure under control. I'm reasonably sure your heart palpitations and the trembling in your legs were caused by the ephedrine in the extra-strength Midol you took. You said you got it from an old bottle, right?"

I nodded, terrified he would send me home without being sure I was okay. "What about my other symptoms?"

"You hyperventilated. Sometimes when we are upset or afraid, our breathing becomes shallow. This causes a shortage of oxygen in our system that leads to dizziness and shortness of breath. Once you relaxed, you breathed more deeply and the symptoms you experienced faded. That's when you fell asleep. Make sense?"

"Yes." Robert had given the same explanation weeks before, but somehow, I had more confidence in the words when they came from the mouth of a doctor. "You're sure there's nothing at all wrong with my heart?"

"You were wise to seek medical care when you became dizzy and short of breath, Mrs. McNeely. Many women don't take their symptoms seriously unless they experience more classic symptoms of a myocardial infarction."

"My—what?"

"Myocardial infarction. Heart attack. You don't need to worry, though. Your EKG and enzyme blood test results are normal." The good doctor tipped his head slightly to the side and lifted his hands, palms up. "Could there be something we didn't see?" He nodded. "There's always that chance."

I rolled my eyes. "Thanks for the reassurance."

"You'll be fine. Your blood pressure was dangerously high when you arrived. We checked it again after we gave you some drugs to help you relax. It still wasn't where it should be, so we started you on a medication designed specifically to lower blood pressure. That seemed to do the trick. We'll send some home with you tomorrow."

"Tomorrow . . . as in stay in the hospital overnight?"

He grinned. "You're a sharp one, aren't you?"

Not funny. But I smiled. After all, a person can't afford to insult their physician in a life and death situation like mine.

Dr. Garrison jotted some notes on my chart and turned to leave. "I just want to monitor your numbers. Rather err on the side of precaution, wouldn't you say?"

"Hmph." I was sick of the place and ready for my own bed. "I'd frankly rather you not err at all."

A good night's sleep I definitely did not get. The orderly wheeled me to the third floor to a bed by the window. "You don't happen to have a bed near the bathroom, do you?"

"No, I'm sorry. Every bed is full."

Fine. But my shriveled up, white-headed roommate had better not even think about complaining when I turned the light on several times throughout the night to pee.

Not to worry. The little lady had other battles to fight. Like breathing. And just before dawn, she lost the war.

Did God think it was funny to take her just as I climbed out of bed to use the bathroom? I sure wasn't going to traipse across the room, invading her family's privacy as they mourned, reassured themselves that their mother was in a better place, and assigned death duties—calling relatives, writing the obituary, buying her the prettiest yellow dress they could find. She loved yellow, they said. Everything would be yellow. The flowers, the casket lining. Even the funeral bulletins.

I guess there comes a time, at least once in every woman's life, when the brevity of life hits her full in the face. My time had come. As I lay there and listened, I realized just how badly I wanted to live. I mentally replayed my past. Regret grossly outweighed satisfaction. I cried, without a sound, and determined right then and there not to let whatever time I had left slip absentmindedly through my fingers.

CHAPTER 30

Dr. Garrison didn't get around to signing my release until after lunch. Not that I minded the meatloaf and mashed potato dinner. Even if the staff did refuse to give me any salt because I'd been placed on the heart-healthy meal plan.

"I'd like for you to follow up with Dr. Thress, an Internal Medicine physician, on Thursday." Dr. Garrison handed me an appointment slip, a discharge summary and a bottle of pills. "You'll need to buy a blood pressure cuff to check your pressure before you take your medicine each time. Keep a log of your numbers and any symptoms you experience. Dr. Thress will need this information to fine-tune your dose."

I was puzzled. "Why will I still have symptoms if I'm on the medicine?"

Dr. Garrison grinned. "It's going to take more than medicine to get you healthy and feeling well. I've also given you a consult for the hospital nutritionist. She'll be able to set you up with a diet and exercise program that will help with your health issues."

"Been there and done that since you were in diapers." I turned my head and cranked up the volume on the television.

The good doctor laughed and left the room. I picked up the phone to call a cab, but reconsidered and called Lettie. Fortunately, she was already in town. "Don't go anywhere," she said in a flustered voice. "I'll be right there."

Like I had a choice. Only place I was going was to the bathroom. The phone beside the bed was ringing when I returned.

"Mom? Are you okay?"

"I'm fine, Robby. Had a pretty major scare, though. Thought it was my heart." I told my son the whole nine yards and assured him he didn't need to come talk to the doctor, himself. "I may be old and fat, son, but I'm not brain-dead."

After dressing, I sat on a chair and watched Matlock until Lettie arrived.

"Sorry I took so long. I had to drop the kids off at the library for the Story and Craft time." She set her purse on my bedside table. "So why are you here? And why didn't you call?"

"I tried. No one answered the phone, and my heart was going wacko. I called 911 when I started having trouble breathing."

Lettie framed her face with her hands. "We must have been outside, and I didn't check my messages because the kids were all there with us. I'm so sorry you had to go through this alone. What did the doctor say?"

I filled Lettie in on the details as we drove to my house. Nothing life threatening. Needed changes. Follow-up appointment. I said nothing about my roommate. My feelings were too raw. The experience too surreal.

Once Lettie was sure I was comfortable, she left to pick up her grandchildren.

Ten minutes later, the doorbell rang. Not like Marissa needed to ring. With no drapes on the window, I couldn't miss her arrival.

"Biz, where have you been? I saw your number on my caller ID and tried to reach you all night. I was so afraid you'd fallen again."

"Nothing that exciting. Just a bit of chest pain and shortness of breath. Dizziness. You know—"

Marissa wrapped her arm around my shoulder and guided me to the sofa. "You need to sit down and tell me everything. First of all, did you see a doctor?"

I barely finished filling Marissa in on all the details when the phone rang in the kitchen.

Marissa jumped to her feet. "Want me to get it?"

I shook my head. "I'm beat. I don't want to talk to anyone."

The answering machine kicked in. It was Morgan. "Mom? Are you there? Guess not. Just returning your call from last night." Click.

"That's it?" Marissa scrunched her nose so high her cheeks followed.

"Hey, I'm on my own here. My kids have busy lives."

"Aw, poor mistreated Biz. Nobody loves me. Everybody hates me. Guess I'll go eat worms." Marissa laughed as she walked toward the kitchen.

"You enjoy making fun of me?" I shouted after her. "Make you feel superior?"

The refrigerator door shut and a soda lid popped. "Hey, what's with the ugly? You know I was just teasing, right?"

"Sorry. I guess that side shows up when I'm tired and hurting. Forgive me?"

"No problem. Shouldn't you call Morgan and let her know you're okay?"

"Lettie said she would call her."

I pushed past Marissa on my way to the bedroom. "Look, I'm exhausted. I think I'd like to hide out in my room and enjoy my worms in privacy. Who knows—I might even add some chocolate sauce if no one's watching."

Female voices woke me from my nap. I slipped into the bathroom to use the toilet and brush my teeth. When I opened the door, I peeked around the corner and saw a reflection of my guests on the dark face of the television. The sisters?

"That you, Biz?"

Hadn't thought about the reflection bouncing both ways. "What a surprise, ladies."

Proper Older Sister sat up straighter. "We saw Marissa at the Piggly Wiggly. She told us you weren't doing so well."

Little Sister grinned. "We brought you some supper. Marissa let us in."

I would have to have a word with my friend about social boundaries. "Well, this is really nice. Smells delicious."

Proper Sister disappeared, and I heard pan lids clatter and the ka-chinks of ice cubes being dropped into glasses.

The front door opened, and Marissa ushered herself in like she owned the place. She held a bag from the Piggly Wiggly. "Who'd have dreamed Biz McNeely wouldn't have vanilla ice cream in her freezer?"

So who could stay aggravated at someone delivering ice cream? Besides, Marissa was becoming special to me.

"The pot roast smells scrumptious, Gracie," Marissa said to Little Sister. "Did you cook, or Gladys?"

"Oh, we both helped some. Gladys punched the bread dough, and I rolled out the crust for the pie. Had quite a time of it, we did."

Gladys called us to the kitchen where she had the table set for four. Great. Guess they were staying for a while.

Marissa served cherry pie a la mode when we finished our meal.

"Thank you," Gladys said. "I don't believe I've seen you at church, Marissa. Do you worship elsewhere?"

Marissa didn't cross her fingers. Nor her ankles. She didn't cross anything, yet she bobbed her head confidently. The woman was telling a blatant lie. I knew for a fact her car never left the garage on a Sunday morning. She didn't even open the drapes until well after noon.

"Well, bless Jesus," Gracie said. "I told you she wasn't a heathen, Sister."

Gladys and I cringed. Marissa laughed. Gracie changed the subject.

"Biz, a couple of weeks ago Pastor told Sister and I that he asked you to consider leading the Golden Oldies group. He asked us to pray for you as you make the decision."

Was everyone in the church in on this? I wasn't about to announce my decision in front of Marissa. "I'm praying about it."

Gracie giggled. "Well, get off your knees and say yes. The meeting you led last Thursday was the most refreshing meeting I've attended in years."

That reminded me of something. "Gracie, I want to apologize for cutting you short on your prayer request at the meeting the other day. You didn't pray aloud. Was something wrong?"

The sweet little-bit-of-nothing shook her permed white head. "I sensed in my spirit something significant was about to happen, and I was praying pride wouldn't keep you from following God's direction. Brought me pure joy, you following God's lead like you did. Nothing like witnessing the good Lord doing a mighty spiritual work in one of his babies."

I loved this old woman. "Yes, God definitely spoke to me. I never had much time to pray when I was working full-time, but now that I'm retired things are different."

Gracie's wrinkles relaxed. "Can't say we ever experienced the working world, did we, Sister?"

Gladys shook her head. "Our men would have died before letting us work outside the home."

I laughed out loud. "Yeah, and my man would have died if he had tried to stop me."

Ooh, the fun of shock value. I swear, the sisters didn't take a breath in or out for a good five seconds before Gladys politely stood and began gathering dishes.

Gracie followed suit, skittering here and there, finding lids and wiping the counters. "I guess we'd better be going and let you rest now, dear."

Fine with me. Hopefully, Marissa would follow them out.

Unfortunately, my neighbor failed to pick up on my thought. After carrying the dishes to the sisters' car for them, Marissa returned. "What time do you need to take your medicine?"

"Eight o'clock."

Marissa headed for the door. "Be right back. I stopped by Walmart and picked up a blood pressure cuff for you."

Great. Like skinny-limbed Marissa would realize I needed the extra-extra-large sized cuff. I'd been so mortified when the stupid thing at the hospital popped its Velcro and the nurse had to scurry around looking for a bigger one.

To my surprise, the white vinyl cuff fit perfectly when Marissa wrapped it around my upper arm and showed me how to use the thing. She set the cuff aside and recorded the numbers in my log. "One-twenty-six over eighty-two. That's good."

"Thanks."

"You're not actually thinking of taking the church group, are you?"

Another reason to keep your hand close to your chest. Keeps everyone from getting all up into your business anytime they choose. "You don't think it's a good idea?"

"Just doesn't seem to fit your profile. You don't even like mixing with other ladies much, do you?"

How could I tell Marissa this was a God thing? "You think relationships can ever be anything more than a pain in the neck, Marissa? I mean, based on your professional experience."

"Churches are full of desperate folks looking for relationships. You realize that, right?"

Was that why Marissa didn't go to church?

She gawked at me like I was a dead kitty on the side of the road. "If you took this group, what would it look like?"

"I'm not sure. Probably not too holy. Olivia practically crams the Scriptures down our throats. It's all about Bible study and prayer. I was thinking we might incorporate some fun activities like shopping, dinner out or scrapbooking. You know . . . the stuff normal women do in their spare time."

Marissa winked as she extended her hands, palms up. "Normal women? As in . . . not holy women?"

My bladder was full, but that discomfort was nothing compared to the stuff rolling around in my head. "This what therapy looks like—making a person feel like an idiot for asking questions?"

"Nope. Just helping you shovel manure to find out what you think deep down. What do you think is more important for Christian women—fun activities or the Bible-prayer stuff?"

"What would you say?"

"Doesn't matter. Remember, I'm not judging you, so don't give me what you think I want—or need—you to say. From what I can see, you've spent your life trying to be what others think you should be. It's time for you to figure out who you want to be. What's most important to you?"

Okay, so maybe the uncomfortable stuff was called truth.

A Scripture popped into my head from somewhere. "Jesus is the truth." I mumbled the verse before I thought to stop the words. Suddenly I didn't care what Marissa thought. A light was warming my spirit. Was Jesus the same truth that caused me discomfort as I searched my heart to understand myself? Was truth the real culprit, or was it the discrepancy between the truth and the faulty thinking I'd relied on for my entire life?

I looked at Marissa, my heart so full I wanted to cry.

"Want to share?"

"I'm just trying to put it all together, Marissa. This whole thing about truth and trusting God and facing the past and deciding who I really want to be. Then there are the love verses and the thought verses I'm trying to follow."

I chewed on the side of my tongue as I searched for the next words. "Sometimes it's like a spiritual roller coaster I'm on. One minute I'm on top and God is showing me something new. Then I hit bottom when I realize I can't possibly be all God asks me to be."

Marissa leaned her head back on the sofa and yawned. "I get that, Biz. I really do. But I think it's more about total surrender to a higher power—or God, as you say—and admitting you can't fix yourself. Then you'll genuinely change as you sort through the ugly in you and understand how it has been driving your life. Replace your faulty thinking with truth. That takes time . . . and devotion. Does that make sense at all?"

"Yes, and you reminded me of a verse I read the other day that says God is more concerned with my heart than what I can or can't accomplish on my own."

"Exactly. Think about it. If you could have fixed yourself on your own, you would have done it long ago. That's why it's so important to give up and surrender to your God."

Your God. That hurt. I so wanted Marissa to know my God. The new life he was showing me. But I was still so confused, and she seemed to understand how everything worked. Who was I to consider bringing enlightenment to her?

As I mulled over Marissa's question through the night, I realized that neither the activities nor the Bible-prayer stuff was most important for the group. Jesus' life on earth was all about relationships. Even when he mixed with groups, he talked about the individual. That's where life began. First a relationship with Jesus. Then with others.

Marissa suggested I should not take the group. Sisters insisted I should. Robert had his reservations. Lettie and Vickie were convinced I would do well. Guess I couldn't please everyone.

Took me awhile to figure out which buttons to push on the blood pressure machine the next morning to avoid setting off the annoying beeps. But eventually, I managed to get it right. One-forty-six over eighty-eight. I recorded the numbers in my log and took my medicine. I'd have to start setting an alarm to take the medicine on time.

Robert called as I finished lunch and carried my dishes to the sink. He sounded out of breath. "Honey, are you okay?"

"Yes. Did Robby call you?"

"He said you went to the emergency room Sunday night. Why didn't you call?"

"My cell phone was dead, and I was only there overnight. When I got home, I decided not to worry you because it all turned out to be a false alarm."

"Heart palpitations a false alarm? I don't think so. What did the doctors say?"

Robert's concern touched me but shook my emotions. I couldn't get my sweet roommate-to-be-dressed-in-yellow out of my mind. Life was too short for all this ugliness. I just wanted Robert to come home so I could show him how much I loved him. How much I didn't want to lose him.

"You there, honey?"

"Yes. The doctor said my blood pressure was high. I need to limit my intake of salty foods and all. The doctor ran some tests and gave me some pills that are helping."

"Thank God. I love you, Biz."

"I love you, too, Robert. I really do."

I ran some errands and caught sight of the trunk when I pulled into the garage. There was only one item left inside.

As curiosity evolved into nauseating dread, finger-like muscles curled around the base of my skull, tightening their grip and edging their way down my spine.

I yearned to reconcile my past life with that of today. How could I ever find real peace if the two of me continued to war against each other? They had to find a way to come together. To accept and love each other as one.

Oh, bother. I walked past the trunk into the kitchen. Maybe after supper.

The phone rang as I popped a frozen roast beef and carrot dinner into the oven.

"Hey, girl. Frieda, here. What'ya doing?"

"Just heating up some supper."

"You talked to Corrine since the other night at Olivia's house?"

Where was this conversation headed? "No."

"But you are aware she came alone? As in . . . no Davis?"

I mentally dodged a couple of red flags waving in my path. Maybe a bit of information about Corrine would help me be a better friend to her. "Yes, I noticed."

"Well, Corrine's daughter told my daughter that Corrine had a big fight with her husband. Something about her disapproving of her stepson's fiancé."

"How do the girls know each other?"

"They work together at the mall. Hannah says when Corrine's first husband left her for a woman half her age, Corrine went ballistic. Slammed a golf club through the front window of the woman's house. Actually got hauled off to jail for the night."

"No kidding? So she has a record?"

"Yeah, I guess so. Her daughter had to bail her out. Can't you just imagine Corrine in that orange jumpsuit?"

By now there were so many red flags flapping in my face that I felt like a rodeo bull. I should not be entertaining this conversation. What kind of an example did I plan to be, anyway? "I'd better go, Frieda. My dinner's almost ready."

CHAPTER 31

I'm not sure what kind of evil spirit possessed me Wednesday morning when I agreed to shop with Morgan for my upcoming trip. Perhaps I was afraid to say no after we'd just renewed our friendship. Or maybe Morgan's enthusiasm caught me off guard.

Whatever, I almost died with shock when the first store we hit was that secret underwear place. Here we were, in broad daylight, and there didn't seem to be an embarrassed bone in Morgan's body. Well, I'll tell you what, I had plenty for both of us. "Why don't we check out Walmart? Might be cheaper."

Morgan burst into a stupid grin. "You can do this, Mom. Remember, you're flying to Chicago to impress Dad, not bore him with those old flannel rags you usually wear."

The girl irritated me, getting all up into my personal space. "I can't imagine them having anything that will fit me."

"They do, though. I checked it out yesterday. There are some sexy gowns in the back—not too outlandish, but not prudish either."

Turned out there are lots of clothes that will fit bulges if a person is willing to pay the price. Three hours later, Morgan and I left the mall with four new tops, two pairs of black slacks and two skimpy nighties I would shove in a drawer and never wear. But Morgan and I had gotten along. For three whole hours. That had been worth every bit of the discomfort.

When our tummies rumbled in unison as we walked to the car, Morgan and I agreed to a late lunch before heading home.

Morgan surprised me with a high-five when I ordered vegetable soup and half of a turkey sub, without dressing. "I'm proud of you, Mom."

Everything in me wanted her to say more. I longed to hear her tell me she loved me. That she could truly forgive me for being the world's worst mother.

Morgan crumbled two packages of crackers into her chicken noodle soup, the broth immediately soaking them up until the concoction resembled a casserole.

"I didn't know you still ate your soup that way."

She took a tiny bite. Was she, too, holding back words? Wanting to remind me that I never got to know her at all—as a child or an adult.

My appetite waned. The sandwich before me looked enormous. I lifted the bun and picked at the meat with my fork.

"This is tough, huh?"

I nodded, wiping my nose on a napkin. Was I afraid of the conversation ahead or relieved that the cards were finally on the table? Whatever, I wasn't going to waffle. I desperately longed to be the mother Morgan deserved. If she could talk about this, so could I.

"I'm proud of you, Morgan. I always have been. I just never took the time to say so, and I'm sorry."

My daughter's eyes disarmed me when she lifted her head. Tears swam around a dark clump of skepticism. Or was I simply imagining the ill feeling because I believed I deserved it? Marissa had cautioned me to stop putting thoughts in others' minds. To use words instead. "You have every right to be skeptical, honey."

"No, it's not that at all. I can see you are sincere. I just don't deserve your kind words. I've done nothing to earn them."

Where did that come from? "What are you saying? You're such a responsible adult."

Morgan's cheeks fired red, and her tears evaporated like sizzling drops of water on a hot skillet. "You influenced my life more than you think, Mom—in a positive way. Especially in my teen years. Like when I let my grades drop, you stressed the value not giving up. Took me to the shop to see what you did every day. You taught me to defend myself and nagged me to go to church every Sunday, even when you were aware I was secretly nursing a hangover."

Pride bubbled within me. Not in myself, but in the assertive young woman who sat across from me.

"Look at me now, though. Stuck in a silly sales position with no future whatsoever. I love and live with a married man who is trying to divide his time and affections three ways."

I sifted through the words percolating in my mind, weeding out condemnation. "I'm not sure how to respond. You're aware of my feelings on the live-in situation, but you're an adult. That's what I need to remember. I'm trying hard to learn to live within boundaries, honey. Not to interfere in areas where I have not earned the right to express myself."

"Thanks. I realize I'm disappointing you, but I'm not emotionally ready to make changes."

Our gazes met, my eyes searching for a hidden entrance, hoping to connect in a level beyond words. Unexpected love for my daughter burst to the surface until I feared I would faint from the force of it. Suddenly I yearned to hold my baby in my arms, to comfort her bruised spirit and protect her fragile heart.

I longed to tell her I loved her, but I couldn't. First, I had to prove myself worthy of her love.

Morgan hung my dry-cleaned drapes before she left, so I took advantage of the dark, cozy bedroom. After a well-earned nap, I popped my new tops into the washer on a gentle cycle.

Passing the garage door on my way back upstairs, I thought of the trunk in the garage. Should I open the remaining box?

I decided otherwise and rummaged through the almost-empty freezer until I found a package of chicken breasts under a bag of chipped ice. I arranged the meat on a plate, stuck it in the microwave to defrost and wiped the counter with Lysol.

I would miss this house. Good or bad, it held over thirty years of my life. The creaking basement step—second to last—that we all tried to avoid. The grapevines and the knotty oak tree in the backyard with outstretched arms just right to support a tire swing, stretch a hammock or hang a birdhouse. The chipped door frame where Robby tripped and broke his front tooth while running from his younger sister. The small notches up the pantry wall where Robert had marked the kids' growth.

Nine more days until we signed a contract on the new home. Was I ready?

The phone pulled me from my musing. "Hello?"

"Biz, this is Corrine. Can we talk?"

I sat down at the table. "Sure." Several moments of silence passed. "You okay, Corrine?"

"Yes. I just can't believe what I heard a few minutes ago."

Creepy crawlies began their descent along my spine. "Your family okay?"

More silence, followed by sniffling. "A friend who works with me called to inform me Frieda Anderson is spreading vicious gossip about me."

Uh-oh. I considered rolling up my pants. "Can you trust the word of your friend?"

"Definitely. Though I'll never trust Frieda again. The woman took my words and twisted them completely."

I'd have to play dumb. "Are you referring to things you've said at our Golden Oldies meetings?"

"That and more. My past. Things I've not shared with anyone here. I can't figure out where Frieda got her information."

"I'm sorry, Corrine. Do you want me to call Frieda and confront her?"

"No. That's not necessary. I already called her. She didn't receive my words well, either. Didn't even apologize. I know she's a new Christian, Biz, but someone needs to sit her down and teach her a few things."

Guilt soaked into my conscience as I remembered what Marissa had said weeks ago. *You're a human being trying to* pose as a sinless Christian, right? Trying to impress others by pretending to be something you're not.

I needed to tell the truth. No matter the consequences.

How much should I share? Was it my place to explain that Corrine's daughter shared information with Frieda's daughter? The web was growing. "I need to apologize, Corrine."

"You?"

"Yes. Frieda called me yesterday and told me a few things about your past. I'm ashamed of myself now, but I let myself get sucked into the conversation. I'm just as guilty as Frieda, and I'm sorry."

Silence.

"What did I ever do to you, Biz? I thought we might become friends. You were so kind at the picnic last Sunday."

"I blew it, Corrine, but I do want to be friends."

"Well, you have a funny way of showing it. I need to go, Biz. Davis just pulled in the drive."

No time for a response or goodbye. Just a slam-the-door-in-my-face click.

The microwave dinged. I pulled out the plate of chicken. Nasty. White and over-cooked around the edges. Raw on the inside.

My stomach tightened and I fought the urge to vomit. The mess so resembled my life.

On the outside, I appeared finished. But my tough shell masked the raw me on the inside where so much of my past remained unresolved and messy.

This could be Corrine. Or Frieda, or any of the other ladies I was getting to know. Weren't we all the same?

I tossed the chicken in the garbage and looked up the number for Pizza Hut. How I wanted to shed my fake shell and allow God to perfect my heart.

Could the ladies in our group do this together? Uncover our deepest beings and begin to heal from the inside out? Allow God to first do a work in us, so we might share his grace and love with the younger girls in our congregation at some point in the future?

At this very moment, I knew God was confirming that he wanted me to lead the group. Not because I was ready, but because I wasn't. Because he could use me as an example if I was willing to be transparent and honest. Willing to give up my strength and allow others to see my need of God's strength.

But first, I had to deal with the gossip issue.

Pastor called as I was changing for bed.

"Sorry to call so late, Biz, but I wondered if you would meet with me in my office about thirty minutes before the Golden Oldies meeting tomorrow."

"Of course, Pastor. Is anything wrong?"

"Nothing we need to talk about tonight. I'll see you in the morning."

Olivia sat across the desk from Pastor, her eyes red and puffy, a rumpled hankie in her hands. "Good morning, Elizabeth."

I sat beside her. "Good morning."

Pastor opened our meeting with a quick prayer. Then, "Olivia has decided to step down from leading the Golden Oldies but would like to continue providing devotions for the meetings. She holds a Master's Degree in Biblical Studies, and

I appreciate her willingness to stay involved. Would this plan work for you if you were to agree to lead the group, Biz?"

I recognized pride attempting to take over, but my Jesus-filter obviously intervened because what came out of my mouth sounded more like, "Works for me. God confirmed that I should take the group, and I am willing to do whatever you think best." I turned to Olivia. "Are you ready for this change?"

Olivia nodded slightly. "It's not something I want, but I do believe this is God's timing."

Pastor leaned back in his chair. "I'd like you to start next week, Biz. Is that feasible?"

"Definitely."

Olivia tapped her lips with a finger. "Uh, Pastor. We need to talk about the gossip situation."

Pastor turned to me. "Olivia mentioned some gossip Frieda Anderson is allegedly circulating. I'd like for you to handle that, Biz."

Color zoomed up Olivia's neck and into her cheeks. "I think I might be better prepared to do so, Pastor."

Pastor shook his head. "Thank you for offering, Olivia, but I believe your life is full enough at the moment. We'll leave this to Biz."

"But Pastor, I promised Corrine—"

He held up a hand and turned to me. "Can you clarify what happened?"

"Yes. I totally blew it and entertained Frieda's words when she called. But Corrine and I had a very intimate talk a few days before that, so I'm hopeful we'll be able to patch things up."

Pastor appeared to be waiting for more.

"God used this experience to confirm my call to lead the group. I realized we are all carrying baggage on the inside while trying to pretend all is fine on the outside. I plan to use this incident to talk to the ladies about the need to trust each other as we learn to bond as a group."

Pastor nodded with my every word. "You realize you will be held accountable at a higher level when in leadership, right? The gossip must stop completely."

I didn't like what I caught in my peripheral vision—Olivia's chin riding high. Or maybe it was just my angle of perspective.

Pastor had counseled with love—not condemnation, nor superiority—and I received his words as such.

"I obviously can't promise to be perfect. God is doing a new work in my heart, though, and I trust him to keep me on the right path."

Olivia jumped in. "But Elizabeth has absolutely no experience in working with women and has already shown she makes rash decisions before praying. Beyond that, she is full of ideas about changing things. I-I'm afraid she will undo all my hard work, and I can't—"

Pastor interrupted. "I know you're upset, Olivia, but you're talking from emotion, and I'm going to ask you to stop." He looked back and forth between us. "Are you ladies going to be able to work together?"

No. Though we likely agreed for once, neither of us dropped the bomb. I was too terrified to open my mouth, and Olivia was boo-hooing into her hankie like she'd just discovered she'd gained ten pounds or something.

Pastor stood. "Okay. Biz, you will begin next week. Now would you please excuse us? I'd like a few words with Olivia in private."

A hush spread through the Golden Oldies when Olivia entered the room and took her seat. She smiled sweetly. "Any prayer needs?"

How could the woman make me feel so stupid mad one minute and then impress me with her gentle composure the next? Was she for real?

She began her devotions with a short poem: The listener and the gossiper ought to be hung. One by the ear and one by the tongue.

Hadn't Pastor just said this was my territory? Everything in me wanted to run and tattle.

The Holy Spirit stopped me. Olivia had most likely prepared this lesson prior to our meeting with Pastor. As long as she didn't mention the situation at hand, she wasn't really trying to take control from me. I needed to calm down.

Besides, she might teach something that would give me a clue as to how to handle this situation with Corrine and Frieda because I sure didn't know what to do.

Slipping out as the others read aloud from the Bible, I headed to the kitchen for a glass of water.

Frieda popped in the side door as I turned on the tap. She gave me a warm smile and waited for me so we could return to the meeting together. As we pushed the swinging door open, though, Olivia's words stopped us cold.

"Gossip will quench the Holy Spirit faster than anything I know. God's Word commands us to forgive a gossiper, but believe me, forgiveness is not the same as trust."

She paused and the room became as still as a roomful of stuffed cats. "Trust must be earned and that process can often take time. We must be careful not to be fooled by hasty apologies but must wait to see a genuine change in lifestyle."

"Whew!" The reaction slipped right past my lips.

Frieda stepped back into the kitchen.

I didn't blame her. "I'm just as guilty as you, Frieda, and I hate to say it, but Olivia is spot on. But we're not the only sinners in the group."

"By far. If you only knew what my daughter told me last night."

I shook my head. "Let's not go there."

Frieda threw her hands in the air and headed for the exit. "I'm not going anywhere but home."

I waited for the door to shut behind her. Then I returned to my seat.

"You okay?" Lettie asked.

There was so much I wanted to say, but I wasn't sure where to draw the line. Would asking for advice be considered gossip? My stomach burned, acid bubbling into my throat. I fished through my purse for a Tums.

In closing, Olivia announced the change in leadership. Many offered Olivia their thanks for her years of service, and Olivia teared up again. "I'm not upset. I just don't do well with change."

Gracie stood, clapping her hands to get everyone's attention. "Biz, why don't you come and sit next to Olivia so we can pray for the two of you."

Not my idea of fun.

But as the ladies prayed, I felt God's presence surround us. My reserve started to crumble as I tried to put myself in Olivia's place and feel her discomfort. I knew what it meant to relinquish dreams. Purpose. And routine. How hard it was to give up control, even when you knew it was the right thing to do.

With awe, I realized that this opportunity to serve God would never have been possible if I'd refused to give up control of the company. My heart smiled as I recognized God's hand at work behind the scenes, his plan in action.

And now, I witnessed a strength in Olivia that I admired. Respected. What was it she'd said? It's not something I want, but I do believe this is God's timing.

Lord, please be with Olivia during this transition. Fill her with joy as she adjusts to the changes in her life.

God moved. As I reached for Olivia's hand, she reached for mine.

CHAPTER 32

Marissa came by that evening as I packed for my trip. "What did the doctor say this morning, Biz?"

"Oh my. I totally forgot the appointment."

I could tell from Marissa's expression that she didn't believe me. "What? Would I lie to you?"

She laughed. "Seriously, Biz. How many blood pressure pills are left?"

"Uh, that would be one."

"But you'll need more for your trip, right?"

I groaned.

"Have you kept your log?"

"Yes."

Marissa studied the entries. "Okay, I'll call in a one-week prescription. Pick it up before you leave. You'll also need to call tomorrow morning to reschedule your appointment."

"Yes, Doc . . . Thanks."

Marissa handed me the gift bag. A vanilla candle, a box of matches, a bottle of bubble bath and a bag of dried apple slices and raw almonds. "It's a survival kit for your trip. This is your weekend, Biz. Let go and enjoy yourself. I'm sure your God will take care of all the details."

"My God? I don't own squatting rights, believe me. He's available to you, too."

Marissa laughed. "Well, Biz McNeely. I believe you just witnessed to me, and I didn't mind it a bit."

"Whatever. You're nuts. I ever tell you that?"

Marissa shook her head. "Hey, good news. My cousins want to rent your house. They found someone to do the painting." She handed me a scrap of paper with a number on it. "If you can work something out, my cousins would like to sign the contract before you leave in the morning."

Absolutely unbelievable morning. A quick breakfast with Lettie. Made a new appointment with Dr. Thress, called to schedule the painters and rented the house.

Now here I was, five minutes away from boarding, and as uncomfortable as a mechanic in a lousy housedress. Would Robert be happy to see me?

Robby had arranged for me to pick up a key in the lobby.

I took a taxi to Guest Housing at Carmichael University. Robby had arranged for me to pick up a key in the lobby.

Robert wouldn't get off work for hours. Plenty of time to freshen up. My arms ached to embrace Robert's body. Feel his warm skin next to mine. Rediscover the fulfillment and ecstasy found in the union God created for man and wife.

The suite was clean and cozy. I cringed when I noticed our recipe box and cookie jar on the counter. This was not how marriage was supposed to work.

Twelve noon. Maybe I could pop in and surprise Robert for lunch. I found the building and was headed toward Robert's office when I heard a familiar voice.

"Robert. So sorry I missed you. Your secretary tells me you won't be in this afternoon. I hope you get my message."

I froze in place at Kathy Harmin's syrupy voice.

"I'm leaving a surprise in your desk drawer, Robert, but please call me before you open it. Hugs."

The door to Robert's office opened. I ducked my head at a water fountain, shielding my face with my arm, as a trail of strong perfume passed me and a cell phone beeped.

"Kathy Harmin, here . . . Yes, I'm on my way."

I dashed into Robert's office, shut the door and pulled open the bottom drawer. Bingo. I plopped the gift-wrapped box into my purse and exited as quickly as possible.

When I got back to Robert's room, I wrapped the gift in a pair of tattered undies and crammed it into the zippered compartment of my suitcase. No security worker in his right mind would probe into that package at the airport.

I'd come so close to believing in Robert's innocence. But even as I added the latest evidence to my case, I had to admit that it was one-sided. Kathy's work. Not Robert's.

Was Robert still in contact with Kathy? She obviously had his number. Did he have hers?

My fingers were wrinkled by the time I climbed out of the tub and wrapped myself in my bathrobe.

I came out of the steamy bathroom and tried to decide which outfit to change into. Robert should be getting home any time. Maybe I should just stay in the robe. Hmmm, not a bad idea . . . if he could explain why Kathy Harmin had been in his office.

I closed the suitcase and was about to go fix something cool to drink when a key turned in the lock. Goose bumps traveled inward from my fingers and toes, setting off nerves until I buzzed like a vibrator. I closed the bedroom door most of the way and peeked through the crack. The suspense would be over in a few minutes and the fun would begin . . . if Robert cooperated.

It wasn't Robert who stepped inside when the door opened, however. An attractive blonde with a so-so figure shut the door and leaned up against it, a cell phone pressed to her ear. "Hey, Robert. Where did you say you put my sweater?"

There were two women in Robert's life? My knees went weak as my breath came in staggered intervals. I backed up and sat in a nearby chair. There was a closet door across the room. Should I hide in there? No, I might miss something.

I could hear the woman poking around in the living room, opening and shutting drawers. "Oh, here it is. Thanks so much. I'll see you soon." Keys jangled, and I tiptoed over to peek into the living room. The woman draped a gorgeous crème-colored cashmere sweater over her shoulder and laughed into her phone as she turned the knob. "Oh, Robert, you're such a dear."

The front door clicked shut. I rushed into the room. Turned the bolt and slid the chain lock into place. One mystery woman a day was enough. Not that I wouldn't let the woman in if she returned. Believe me, I would hold her at knifepoint to make her talk. Yank every last blonde hair from her head if necessary.

I grabbed a bed pillow and sacked out on the living room sofa. I tried to relax, but my heart refused to cooperate, repeatedly quivering and sending a sinking sensation deep into my chest. Sharp pains shot up my back and behind my left shoulder blade. Maybe I was having a heart attack. I didn't care. I'd so counted on Robert being innocent.

I sat up with a start when the bells rang. The room was dark. I must have fallen asleep waiting for Robert. I flipped on a lamp and glanced at the time. Four thirty in the morning. Where was he?

The tiny red light on my cell phone caught my attention. The blinking stopped, and the phone lit up as it rang again. The bells. I smiled and checked the caller ID. "Marissa?"

"Biz, didn't you fly to Chicago this morning?"

"You're calling at four in the morning to check my itinerary?"

"Of course not. I just let Boomer out for a pee, and a strange car pulled up and parked in your driveway."

Atten-n-n-tion! The troops returned. Goose bump warfare. I shivered, suddenly glad I was in Chicago. "Did you call the police?"

"I was about to when—"

"About to? What are you waiting for?"

"The car had Illinois plates. It was Robert. He carried an overnight bag into the house."

"Robert? Are you sure?"

"Positive. There's still a light on in the living room. Think you should call? He might be worried."

"He'll call the kids. Go back to bed, Marissa. I'll straighten things out in the morning."

My back was cramping and my bladder about to burst. I stared in the bathroom mirror after I took care of business and unrolled a wad of toilet paper to wipe the dripping mascara from below my eyes.

Why had I bothered with any of this? I pulled a hand towel from the rod, buried my face in it and wept. I couldn't stand the sight of myself. The hair. The makeup. The perfume. Nothing but a pathetic, phony attempt to be something I wasn't. Something I really didn't even want to be.

I slipped out of the hot bathrobe and into the disgusting nightie Morgan conned me into buying. Soft black lace trimmed a slinky red satin top that barely managed to cover the girls. And the bottoms? Hmph. My upper arms wouldn't fit through those leg holes, let alone my thighs.

Without a second thought, I stepped into my comfy, white cotton, high-top underpants, popped a couple of muscle relaxers and climbed into bed, more than ready to sleep the next day right out of existence.

Sometime the next morning, I forced myself out of the bed for a trip to the bathroom. The bedroom was warm, so I lifted a window. I was pleasantly surprised with a brisk breeze. I'd forgotten Chicago was known as the windy city. Felt so good, I opened the other bedroom window as well.

My head hurt. I found some Tylenol in the medicine cabinet and took three.

Dad deserves better than this. Morgan's words reverberated through my ears as I stared into the mirror. What the hairdresser had teased now stood on end like some sort of ransacked bird nest. Smudged mascara framed my puffy eyes.

I laughed—more of a sardonic eruption, really, that had nothing to do with amusement. For I could feel, under my skin, a growing sense of hysteria and fatigue. I couldn't take much more. I set the medicine bottle back on the shelf and noticed a small detail I'd missed before. The label actually read Tylenol P.M.

So be it. I stretched out on the bed and shut my eyes, savoring the cross-breeze between the windows. I had nowhere to go.

Sometime later, I woke to use the bathroom. My body wouldn't cooperate. Groggy beyond belief, I fought to persuade myself to get up. Sleep—delicious, heavy slumber—called to me. My eyelids refused to stay open. The bathroom would have to wait until later. But alas, I woke again. This time, the urge too strong to deny.

"Oh, bother." I rolled out of bed and stumbled across the room. Opened the door and shuffled into the bathroom in a sleepy stupor, only to have the air current slam the door shut behind me.

I jumped and woke up real fast . . . not in the bathroom, but in a carpeted hallway outside Robert's suite. Must have mistaken the closet door for the bathroom door. Only the closet door actually turned out to be an exit. And worst of all, there was no exterior knob.

As the full reality of what I'd done hit me, I wanted to laugh. Call it nervous energy or something. Here I stood in a mere scrap of a gown, my wings and thighs exposed for the world to view.

On the positive side, my headache was gone. But I still needed to pee. Where were the cleaning ladies? If only they would come along with their keys and —Oh my! Their keys would do no good. I had chain locked the door. They would need to call a maintenance man. Where could I go?

Looking around, I saw what appeared to be my only salvation. An artificial ficus tree dressed in tiny white tinkling lights. Did I say tinkling? Oooh. I tightened my thigh muscles as I waddled down the hall. I meant twinkling.

The tree obviously wouldn't cover all of me, but would hopefully give onlookers a chance to look away before they saw the vast entirety. Feeling encouraged with my plan, I bent to unplug the lights, my back to the elevator. But just as I did so, the elevator doors slid open.

A woman shrieked and a couple of men chortled. I heard no one step off.

Dear Jesus, come quickly, I begged, frozen in place. I heard the doors close, and the elevator moved on. The number five above the door frame stayed lit for several seconds. They would take the stairs back down, probably with their cameras ready. I quickly punched the down button and picked up the tree.

An empty elevator returned to my floor. My tree and I quickly entered and punched the down button, and in a few seconds, the doors opened on the ground floor. Jamming my thumb against the hold button, I hollered as loudly as I could. "Pl-e-a-s-e. Someone, please help me."

Several folks wandered by, obviously trying not to gawk, but bursting into laughter once they rounded a corner. I crossed my ankles. The water show was about to begin.

Then, in the twinkling of an eye, my savior appeared.

"Robert?"

"Biz? What are you doing here . . . like this?"

"Please, get some help. I locked myself out of your suite."

He pulled out a set of keys. "No problem."

I shook my head. "The chain lock is on. I accidentally went out the bedroom door, and it slammed shut behind me."

Robert's lips quivered before giving way to an all-out-belly-laugh. "Oh, Biz." He stepped behind the tree to hug me. "I've missed you."

A long-haired hippie entered the elevator. He looked me up and down like he was picking out a crazy Christmas tree or something. "Third floor."

"Sorry, fellow." Robert motioned for the passenger to step out. "You'll need to take the stairs this time."

Robert followed the dude down the hall toward an exit door. "I'll be right back, Biz. Don't go anywhere."

Right.

My knight in shining armor returned moments later with a flat, queen-sized sheet. I gladly abandoned the ficus tree and wrapped the sheet around me.

Maintenance had gained entrance to the suite by the time we got back upstairs. I headed straight for the bathroom. After repairing my hair, I applied fresh makeup, slipped on the bathrobe and opened the bathroom door.

Robert sat on the chair taking off his tennis shoes.

"You pushed the bed in front of the exit door?"

He nodded. "Figured we didn't need to repeat that experience. Almost did the same thing myself when I first got here."

"I didn't see that your Tylenol was P.M., and I took three of them for a headache. Made me just a little groggy."

"Was that a new nightie you were wearing?"

I crossed my eyes. "Morgan thought I needed to spruce myself up a bit."

"Oh, honey." Robert stood and pulled me into his arms. He kissed my forehead and ran his finger down my chest, stopping where flesh intersected with fabric. "I love you just the way you are. In fact, I kind of missed your flannels."

He released me and straightened the covers on the bed. "I just drove five hours, twice. Want to join me for a nap?"

I hesitated.

He took my hand in his and gently squeezed my fingers. "It's okay, honey. No hurry."

My muscles relaxed, and I kissed his cheek. "I love you, Robert."

We could talk later. I still felt top heavy and needed to sleep off the effects of the Tylenol. "I'll just check out what's on television in the living room."

I shut the bedroom door and sprawled out on the sofa, burying my face in the pillow to muffle my sobs. I wanted my husband more than ever. But the fact was, I couldn't bring myself to lie down beside him until I was positive I was his only woman.

We woke around five. Robert made some coffee and sat next to me on the sofa. "So, when did you decide to come to Chicago? Do the kids know you're here?"

"You didn't call them?"

"No. I intended to on my way back from Indiana but when I looked in my bag, my cell phone wasn't there. I think I left it in my car."

"Marissa said you had a strange car at the house."

"Marissa?"

"She called when she saw someone going into the house in the middle of the night. She knew I was out of town and said the car in the drive had out-of-state tags."

Robert nodded. "My car needed some brake work, so I drove a rental from the dealership."

So Robert hadn't received Kathy Harmin's message yet. Should I show him the gift or trash it? After checking out the contents, of course.

CHAPTER 33

We freshened up before dinner. Sharing the bathroom felt good. Robert winked. "Anything particular sound good for dinner?"

"Maybe someplace with a salad bar."

Robert smiled and put his arm around my shoulder. "You've lost weight. I'm proud of you. You look good."

The electrifying touch of his fingertips on my bare arm brought back feelings I'd nearly forgotten. Overwhelming, delicious feelings. But I couldn't let myself go there. Not trusting my voice, I simply smiled and nodded.

Robert held the car door for me, and for the first time in years, I appreciated it. There was something delightful about being taken care of. Something I'd been too proud to consider in the past.

We settled on a buffet. Robert sat across from me and opened his hand on the table. "Grace?"

I nodded and slipped my hand into his. He wrapped his fingers around mine, and the flame in my soul exploded, blowing a myriad of glowing kisses my way. Oh, God. Please save our marriage.

"So, what made you decide to drive home?"

Robert gazed into my eyes. "Like I said earlier, I've missed you, Biz. I wanted to spend some time together—maybe work out a few things."

"I'm surprised you didn't call first."

He laughed. "Back at you. When did you decide to fly to Chicago, anyway? The Biz I know is terrified of planes."

And the Robert I know stopped being this kind about thirty-four years ago. The enormity of our situation clapped me in the back of the head like a giant wrecking ball. I pushed my plate away. The spark of romantic ambiance had fizzled. "I can't do this, Robert."

The man I was eating with set his silverware down and straightened his back. "Do what?"

"Pretend. I can't play the happily married woman when the truth is I'm not sure I'm the only woman in your life."

There. I'd said it. I ducked my head until the room stood still, removed my napkin from my lap and stood. "I need to get out of here."

Robert jumped to his feet. "Please, don't go, Biz."

Customers stared. I threaded my way through the tables—wishing I knew some Christian mind-your-own-business hand symbol I could flash to accompany my disingenuous smile. Robert stopped at the front to pay our bill.

We turned left out of the parking lot. "Isn't the campus the other way?"

"I have a better idea."

A better idea, indeed. Robert pulled through a Sonic drive-in, ordered large chocolate shakes, cheeseburgers, tots, onion rings and lots of ketchup. Did this man recognize the way to my heart, or what?

Unfortunately, I'd never taken the time to find the way to his.

The sack of food sat at my feet, the smell so enticing I thought I would pass out before Robert finally pulled into a sandy lakefront parking lot. I wiped sweat from my forehead. "Thank God for the breeze."

But the breeze couldn't cool the fire that burned within. Robert had no right to entertain thoughts of other women, even in friendship. Always an excuse. Well, I was tired of wondering whether my marriage was going to survive or not.

We talked about beach activity as we ate. Disposable conversation, really, in light of what was on my mind. But even as I considered walking away, hope—what was left of it—implored me not to cast it away.

Children built sand castles and splashed in the shallow water, teens chased Frisbees. Adults lounged on blankets, sat under faded umbrellas, and walked the beach—many of them, hand in hand.

Music came from every direction, but with the waves lapping the shore and a gentle breeze swirling around us, the muted noise seemed miles away. We were alone in the middle of a busy crowd, enveloped in our own bubble.

What a dichotomy.

I pulled the meat from my sandwich and left the bun, tots and onion rings. Washed it down with a few drinks from my shake. And I was full.

Robert finished the last of his tots. "Let's hit this thing head-on. Tell me why you still think there's another woman."

Okay, Best-Repressed-Actor-of the Year, you just lost your award. At this point, my fear of the unknown surpassed my fear of the truth. "There was a time in history when a woman didn't possess a key to a man's home unless—"

Robert groaned. "A blonde woman in her forties?"

"Not sure. We never made it to the introduction stage."

"The woman is leaving to visit her parents and needed to pick up her sweater. Last weekend, I—"

"Why would her sweater be in your apartment anyway?"

Robert smiled. A tired expression. "Honey, we need to listen, or we're never going to be able to communicate effectively. If you will let me explain without interrupting, I will listen to everything you say. Or you can go first."

"Go ahead."

"The woman's name is Betsy Carmichael. Her father is dying from congestive heart failure, so every weekend she and her husband visit him at a hospice center two hours away."

"I'm sorry, Robert."

"No. I think it's important that you know. They were unable to board their Persian cat last weekend because they discovered, too late in the day, that his immunization shots were not current. I kept the cat overnight for them. Betsy unintentionally left her sweater behind, and I stuck it in a drawer to avoid getting cat hair on it. Her husband picked up the cat, and I forgot to give him the sweater."

Could I sink any lower?

Robert brushed sand from the top of his shoes. "Tom called to say Betsy was going to stay at hospice through the end. Her father gave her the sweater last Christmas, and she wanted him to enjoy seeing her wear it. I contacted the housing office and asked them to issue her a spare key."

"I'm so sorry, Robert. For Betsy and her father. And for not trusting your word and your integrity."

"Or my love."

I stared across the lake. "Honey, I went to your office yesterday. When I got there, though—"

"I wasn't there."

With playful eyes, I put my finger to my lips.

Robert grinned.

"When I got there, Kathy Harmin was there."

Robert jumped to his feet. "You what? What in Heaven's name was she doing there? Biz, you have to believe me, I have no idea what she was doing there."

"She's not living here in Chicago with you?"

"Oh, God, help me! That's what you thought?" Robert wrapped his hands around the back of his head and stormed off toward the lake.

I shivered as I watched him crouch at the water's edge, his head down, his body rocking gently. I wanted to go to him. Beg him to forgive me for even implying impropriety on his part. If ever I was sure of his innocence, it was now.

He returned and sat beside me. His voice was subdued. Whipped. "The last I knew, doctors said Kathy needed a hysterectomy. She took a leave of absence and went to stay with a daughter in Ohio. I believe she was going to leave the day after I did, but I don't know for sure if that happened."

"You haven't heard from her at all?"

"No. I didn't give my new cell phone number to anyone at work when I had it changed last spring. I got tired of getting so many calls at home."

Stupid tabloid. Robert hadn't started taking his calls in secret. He'd put a stop to them.

"Oh, Robert. Can you ever forgive me?"

He took my hand and gently kissed the top of it. "Yes, I forgive you. Always."

I leaned on his shoulder, so thankful for his strength.

Robert patted my hand. "Women like Kathy Harmin are to be pitied, Biz. I didn't see it at first, and I'm sorry for being too pigheaded to listen to you."

He wrapped his arm around my shoulder and gently lifted my chin. Our eyes met. Robert lowered his head and brushed his lips across mine. An invitation for more.

I leaned into the kiss.

The winds picked up. The beach was almost empty. Sadly, as the scent of Robert's aftershave sweetened the air and the touch of his body warmed mine, anxiety lingered. How I'd longed for this strength and closeness. But what if that changed when I told Robert about the rape. What if he saw me for who I really was—a tainted woman? What if he hated me for living a lie, for not telling him sooner?

We watched the sun shrink from sight, the sky soaking up the sun's spray of orange, yellow and red, stretching the colors across the horizon until the blue of day disappeared completely.

Robert stood and stretched. "Be right back."

He returned to wrap a travel blanket around my shoulders. "Let's go for a walk."

As we ambled toward the lake, I began unveiling my soul. "There so much I need to tell you, Robert. In the last few weeks, I've begged God to change my heart, and he's helped me understand how greatly my past has influenced my life."

Robert stopped and pulled me to himself. I sobbed into his shoulder, gripping his shirt between my fingers.

He tightened his hold and kissed the side of my neck. Placing his hands on my shoulders and tipping me back just a little, his eyes met mine. "For better or worse, richer or poorer; until death do us part, I will love you."

We slipped out of our shoes and waded through the shallow water that lapped the shore.

"There are things you don't know about me." I whispered, as if afraid the wind would carry my words to the world. My secrets. My shame. "I was raped when I was fourteen."

Robert said nothing. He just stepped to dry sand and offered me his arm. I accepted, and we sat as the moon and stars appeared.

And I talked. Described my father's abuse. My mother's unwillingness to intervene. My friend, Danny Cooke, who turned on me and desecrated my body. Left me with child. My tiny son. Dean.

Robert remained mute and physically separate.

All kinds of ugly surfaced. Ugly I had yet to face. Ever. I loathed myself. My filthy, adulterated body.

I wanted to stop. To walk away and never look back. But the backwash was too strong. The sewage continued to spew from my mouth. I gritted my teeth and swallowed waves of nausea as I spoke my father's name and recounted his scheme to sell my baby to profit his business. And his letter from the trunk that revealed I'd been wrong.

I didn't stop talking until I was empty. Numb. Drained of anything that mattered to me. Anything that stood between my husband and me. And I waited for Robert to respond.

He stood. And walked in the opposite direction.

I was sure I'd lost him, but I could find no energy to process my emotions. Whatever. It was done. The truth had been told. That's all God asked of me. And if he chose not to intervene and save my marriage, so be it. It wouldn't be the first time God had disappointed me. I would deal with that later. Talk to God and ask him to help me accept his plan and trust him. But I wasn't there yet. I shut my eyes and rested my chin on my knees. Cool water sprayed my face as gentle waves slapped the shoreline.

I smelled his aftershave first—the clean, sweet scent heightened my senses until I thought I would explode with anticipation. Then I felt his touch as he took my hands and helped me to my feet. No words were necessary. The love in Robert's eyes spoke forgiveness. And acceptance. And reconciliation.

He placed a tiny stone in my palm. "It's time to give it all up, honey. Let this stone represent the memories that haunt you. The wrongs that were done to you. Name them and toss the shell into the sea of forgetfulness. Let God take your past and refuse to ever allow it to rule your life again."

The moon was full by the time we returned to the car. I was exhausted, but so relieved to have broken the chains of my past. We pulled out of the parking lot and headed home in silence.

What was Robert thinking now that he knew the truth? I searched for something significant to say but came up empty. How do you follow a conversation like the one we'd just had?

Robert patted my leg. "Now I understand why the business was so important to you. Losing the shop would be like losing precious little Dean all over again, wouldn't it?"

Precious little Dean. Robert expressed the baby's name in a tender, almost reverent voice, as if, somehow, he knew the sweet infant I once held in my arms. Love swelled within me for a husband I didn't deserve. But here he was—committed for the long haul. Thank you, Lord.

We said very little as we dressed for bed, touching fingers lightly as we passed in the hallway. I dressed in a long t-shirt I'd thrown in the suitcase at the last minute, replaying the intoxicating events of the evening I'd just shared with my husband.

Robert gave a low whistle when I came out of the bathroom. He took me into his arms. "Now this is the Biz I love . . . with my whole heart."

I kissed his neck. And his cheek. And finally, our lips touched, and our kiss became intimate. "I've missed you."

Robert took my hand and drew me into bed. Tingles ran up and down my spine at his touch. He pulled me close for another deep kiss that set me on fire. Or maybe I was experiencing a hot flash. I couldn't be sure. But here I was. We were married. And it had been so long . . .

Unfortunately, the ambience temporarily vanished when I slipped between the sheets and burst into laughter. And for once, Robert understood. Jumping out of bed, he shook his puny little booty in my direction and laughed. "Really, honey. Did you seriously think I would consider having an affair wearing pink underwear?"

We left for the airport early the next morning so we could eat breakfast on the way. Robert placed our order while I found a table.

He set the tray down. "We need to be at the airport in about an hour."

I nodded, my emotions as scrambled as the eggs on Robert's platter. Unwrapping my sausage and egg biscuit, I took a bite, but was immediately sorry. The moistened mush clogged my throat. What happened to the affectionate feelings from the night before? The confidence and security in Robert's love.

Robert didn't seem to notice. "The lawn and flowers look great back home. I guess the young guy from church is working out after all. I worried when I paid him in advance."

So, my meticulous husband had arranged for lawn care after all. Go figure. "Guy from church?"

"Are you telling me he never showed?"

I shook my head. "The lawn was a disaster until Robby and the kids took care of it on Sunday."

"I'm so sorry you were forced to put up with such a mess. I'll definitely follow up on the situation." Robert's eyes softened as he placed his hand on mine. "The house looks wonderful, too."

His touch lessened my anxiety. "You checked it out?"

"Every room, including the basement. How did you ever get the work finished in so little time?"

Was that approval? Admiration? I rewrapped the remainder of my sandwich, folding each corner of the waxed paper to a precise angle as I waited for my lips to steady. "I've never wanted anything as much as I want this home in the country."

That was wrong. As soon as I spoke, I realized what I really wanted was not the house, but the new beginning it represented. A chance to work through the past and destroy its grip on my heart and life. And to allow God's love to heal our marriage and draw our family together.

Robby picked me up at the airport, his mischievous eyes filled with amusement like some pubertal adolescent. "So, what did you do all weekend?"

Believe me, I wasn't going there with my son. Unfortunately, my face didn't catch the memo. When my lips jumped into a silly smirk, I'm sure Robby realized that his father and I had finally kicked the stick out of neutral.

Whatever. I ignored Robby's response and texted Robert to let him know I made it home okay.

CHAPTER 34

What a weekend. Taking cover behind an artificial tree in an elevator, strolling the beach and flying two ways in a metal bird with seats designed for Jack Spratt. It's no wonder my body practically refused to move when I woke Monday morning.

More rain. Appeared the drought was over. The change in air pressure brought on another headache, though. I popped a couple powders, poured a third cup of coffee and checked the phone messages I'd missed over the weekend. A total of three.

"Biz, this is Renee. I'm so embarrassed, but I think I caused some trouble for you. Pastor and I were talking about last Thursday's Golden Oldies meeting. When I mentioned Sister Gracie praying for you and Olivia, Pastor asked me if I sensed any ongoing tension between the two of you. I feel like a spy, Biz. I am so sorry."

I shook my head, second-guessing my decision to take the group. The message machine beeped and the second caller began.

"Mrs. McNeely, this is Ron Magaren—the painter friend of the folks who are going to rent your house. Unfortunately, when I spoke to you the other day, I misread the books, and I need to reschedule. My next opening is the first week of August. Give me a call to let me know if that will work for you."

I shut my eyes. This could not be happening again. Was I cursed?

Before I had time to deliberate, caller number three began.

"Mrs. McNeely, this is Donna Fester from the church office. I'm calling to remind you to e-mail your weekly Golden Oldies announcement by noon Tuesday for the Sunday bulletin. I just need a short blurb about the topic you'll be discussing as well as any upcoming events you're planning. Don't worry about the devotionals. Olivia has already submitted her plans for the rest of the month. E-mail me if you have any questions."

E-mail? Why not just write the thing out and drop it by the church? Something wrong with good old-fashioned paper and pen?

And how on earth was I going to come up with plans for more than a week ahead of time? Didn't Pastor realize some people worked better under pressure? I fully intended to plan my meetings, but probably not until the night before. Good grief, I wanted it fresh from the Lord.

The pressure scared me. Pastor hadn't mentioned this expectation. I ripped a piece of paper from my notebook and divided it into several columns. My throat tightened. I had no idea what to plan for this Thursday, let alone weeks ahead. My breathing became shallow, and my eyes swam in a swirl of movement.

Another panic attack. I grabbed a brown lunch sack from the pantry, stuck my face inside and tried to calm myself as I inhaled the recycled carbon-dioxide-saturated air.

Whatever. The process worked, and that's what mattered. Setting the bag aside, I whispered a prayer. "I'm drawing a major blank, here, Lord? Are you sure I'm the right one for the job?"

The phone rang. It was Corrine.

"Hi, Biz. Could we meet for lunch at Chester's?"

"Tomorrow be okay, say . . . noon?"

"Sure."

"Okay, then. I look forward to it."

God's calling had seemed so clear last week, but today's hurdles made me question the call again. "With so many roadblocks, Lord. I'm not sure whether this is the enemy trying to thwart your plan, or you trying to redirect me. How can I know?"

"Ask, listen and obey."

I almost laughed at the command—all three tasks were tough for Biz McNeely. I headed to the bedroom to empty my luggage. As I unzipped my suitcase, I remembered Kathy Harmin's gift. My shoulders slumped when I considered how close the woman had come to duping my husband into an affair. Did I totally believe in Robert's innocence at this point? I wanted to.

Robert had done the right thing when Kathy made advances in his office. At least the event I witnessed. The cosmetic bag had been explained. Kathy had been living in Ohio, not Chicago.

But there were still the late nights and the voicemail message.

I removed the gift from the lining pocket. Wanted to spit on it. Stomp it to smithereens.

History cautioned me to listen to logic. Weigh the facts. But, I refused.

I would stand by my man. Embrace his side of the story. The Robert I knew and loved had promised me—convinced me—I was the only woman in his life, and I was going to fight the feelings of suspicion and walk forward in that promise.

"So," I blurted out. "Time to check this thing out."

I ripped off the wrapping and opened the box. A piece of heavy blue poster board was folded twice to form a little book with a spine. The thing fell open as I removed it.

Candy was glued to the poster board, words added to complete the message:

Just wanted to say I've missed you. When you came into my life, it was like a special STARBURST in heaven. I eagerly anticipated PAYDAY each month when we sat together at staff dinners. I'm sorry we hit a SOUR PATCH and things ended the way they did for us because you put a lovely CRUNCH in my otherwise boring life. You will always be worth 100 GRAND in my book! I do hope you and Biz can work things out. P.S. Please accept just one little KISS for memory's sake.

How thoughtful of the conniving wench. Though tempted to unfasten the innocent candy and shove it all in my mouth, I slid the book back in its box and set it on a top shelf in the pantry to deal with later. One thing I knew for sure. This gift merited the perfect thank you card. Just not from Robert.

I grinned as I clicked my phone on, googled my way to a thesaurus and drafted my response. When satisfied with the results, I stuck the note in the box with the gift. Now, all I needed to do was figure out a way to get Kathy Harmin's address.

Morgan dropped by as I straggled out later in the day. I fully expected her to rant and rave about my appearance. Until I noticed hers. Disheveled hair, bags under her eyes.

"Honey, what's happened?"

She dropped to the sofa and kicked off her shoes. "I should have known better."

"Are you okay, honey?"

She turned my way. "I don't care if he is married, he promised to stay by me. I can't do this by myself."

I understood as soon as the words tripped from her tongue. My daughter was pregnant.

She should have known better. The thought surfaced, but the words never left my lips. That was a major accomplishment. "Do you want to talk about it?"

"Tony moved back home to his wife but keeps sneaking away to call me. Says he's miserable but wants to do the right thing."

"Kind of late to think about that, huh?"

That one did pop out, but Morgan didn't seem to mind. "Exactly what I told him. I just feel sorry for his little boy. The mother doesn't want anything to do with him. She works all kinds of hours and goes drinking with her friends afterward. Like the kid is a lower priority than anything else in her life."

I flinched. That ball hit a little too close to home plate. "Does she abuse him?"

Morgan shook her head. "Not that I know of, unless you count neglect as abuse."

Strike two. I squirmed to a more comfortable position, reminding myself this discussion wasn't about me. What did Morgan want—advice or just a listening ear? She'd presented her case, and I'd heard enough to render my decision. Two wrongs didn't make a right. The guy was definitely a loser in my book. "Any idea what you're going to do?"

Morgan twisted her fingers together in her lap. "Can I come home?"

What? To play alpha-woman? Survival of the fittest?

"You're hesitating. You don't want me."

"No, it's not that, honey. I just can't believe you asked. You sure we wouldn't kill each other?"

Morgan shrugged. "Might come close now and then, but"—she touched her belly—"we're going to need you."

I moved to the sofa and hugged my daughter. "Of course, you can come home. Fixing up the new house together will be fun."

Morgan lifted her head from my shoulder and drew back. "You sure?"

I nodded. "Your father will love having you home, too."

"Oh, Mom. I totally forgot to ask about your trip. So, Daddy's coming home?"

Strike three. She needed me. She wanted her father.

We talked late into the night. Around midnight, I convinced Morgan to take a walk around the block in the rain. I laughed and cried as the drizzle soaked through my clothes and into my spirit. God was birthing new life in my soul. The drought was over, and it felt so good to feel so good.

I turned the girls loose and changed into my muumuu— might as well find out from the get-go if Morgan was willing to accept me as is. She didn't react.

Morgan wanted a fresh start. So did I. I kept my eyes dug into the carpet when I told her about the rape. They scraped the ceiling when I shared about the birth of little Dean. When

I did look at my daughter, when I was finished and drained and weak, she was weeping. And she reached for me. Morgan reached for me.

She tucked her beautiful hair behind her ears. "Maybe that's why you couldn't bond with Robby and me."

I searched her eyes through a lens of remorse. "You deserved better. I'm sorry."

Morgan shook her head. "You were emotionally handicapped. Afraid you might lose us, too, if you allowed yourself to get too close."

The girl possessed the wisdom of her father. Why hadn't I seen it before? I leaned my head back and shut my eyes as an overwhelming love for my daughter bathed my entire being. A love too deep to have recently sprouted. Though held back by resentment and intimidation, this love had been growing for many years.

My mouth grew bitter as I realized how my own insecurities had built a wall between us. Morgan had captured Robert's heart at birth, and I had hated the attention and love he showered on her at any expense. As she grew, I resented her graceful figure, her charm and her ability to successfully accomplish any task set before her.

She was the young woman I had always wanted to be. And I'd hated her for that. God, forgive me.

My phone buzzed before the alarm went off. Robert sent a text. Didn't want to wake you. Call me when you get up. I'm okay, but we have a bit of an emergency.

I didn't even hear the phone ring on Robert's end before he answered. "Hi, honey."

"Robert, what's the matter? Are you sure you're okay?"

"I'm fine, honey. It's about my job . . . and the house in the country."

No. Please, God. No. "Your job there? Or here?"

"Both. My boss flew up yesterday. Biz, the university is eliminating my position there completely. I have a choice to make. I can retire early or take a part-time position here in Chicago for another year before retiring."

"What are you going to do?"

"I'm not sure, but I can't see how we can go ahead with the home in the country. We'll just have to forfeit our deposit."

Tears spurted from my eyes. "No, Robert. Please don't say that. There has to be a way."

"I'm sorry, honey. I've been awake all night trying to figure something out. I was planning on using my retirement money for a large down payment so we could afford the house payments when I retire. And I counted on my income to pay for the second mortgage payment until we can pay the house in town off."

"Couldn't we use my money for that?"

"That isn't wise. I did consider it. Maybe we can look for a smaller place in the country. One without so much land."

"No. No, no, no, no. Please don't do this, Robert."

"I'm sorry. I've got to go. I have meetings all day. I'll call this evening. I love you, Biz."

"Love you, too."

I clicked my phone off and cried until my eyes burned. "Please, God. Please work a miracle."

Corrine was waiting for me in the lobby when I arrived for lunch. We ordered salads and iced tea. "Thanks for agreeing to meet me, Biz. I want to apologize for hanging up on you the other day. I never should have called until I calmed down."

"Been there and done that."

Corrine sipped her tea, set the glass to the side and folded her hands on the table. "I don't want to waste your time, Biz."

My lips stayed locked, but I watched Corinne closely.

"I'm sure Frieda told you my ex-husband left me for a girl half his age. What Frieda probably doesn't realize is that my ex-husband desperately wanted a son. I was only able to give him one child, a daughter.

"Of course, when Clarissa was born, he said it didn't matter that she was a girl. But I guess it did." Corrine dabbed her eyes with a napkin and lifted her chin. "That wild child has given him four sons."

She spit the words out like dirty dishwater. I didn't blame her. "I'm so sorry."

Our lunch arrived. I picked at the grilled chicken and croutons, no longer hungry.

Corrine pushed her plate aside and propped her elbows on the table. "I blew it big time the other night, Biz."

I waited.

"Davis' son, Brayden, brought his girlfriend over for dinner, and they announced their engagement. The girl had earrings all the way up her ears and a loop hanging from her nose. I guess she reminded me of my ex-husband's wife because something broke inside me. Ugly, bitter rage that I had no idea still existed. I slipped away from the room to keep from saying something I would regret.

"Davis came to find me, and I thought the kids had gone home . . . They overheard me telling Davis that Brayden could do so much better than this girl."

"Oh, my. Sounds like the kind of crap I pull."

Corrine's eyelids practically disappeared into her forehead. But she rebounded quickly, relaxed her eyes, and smiled. "I like you, Biz. You just lay it right on the line, don't you?"

To say I blushed would be a gross understatement. "Pretty much. But believe me, that's not always a good thing. I'm working on that."

Corrine laughed. "Can we talk?"

CHAPTER 35

Hazel's verse came to mind as I headed home. I dreaded Robert's call, but I refused to give up on God. "This one is all yours, Lord. I don't understand what is happening. You've asked me to trust in you, and I'm trying to do that. Give me peace, Lord. Help me accept your answer . . . either way."

I would work. Whether I got my home in the country or not, I was going to finish this house. We'd rent it out and move somewhere. Aside from wanting curtains and fresh paint, the house looked amazing. I just needed to find painters.

Oh, and there was one other task that needed to be completed. Putting on a pot of coffee when I got home, I mentally chastised myself for not taking care of it sooner.

The final large box in the trunk was sealed. I slid a knife along the yellowed tape and prayed for strength to break what I hoped to be the final chain link to my past. I lifted the flaps slowly. The contents were wrapped in a black garbage bag.

I drew in my breath as I pulled out a beautiful, hand-stitched quilt, carried it to the bedroom and spread it out on the bed. An envelope fell from the folds of fabric. I carefully pulled the glued flap loose and removed a letter. My body went weak when I saw my mother's handwriting.

My sweet Biz,

I want to say so many things, but I struggle to find the words. I hope this gift will somehow speak of my love. I saved tiny patches from your clothing as you grew and pieced the blocks in the late of the night. I found healing in putting together something so beautiful, especially on those nights when your father put his fists to my face to vent his drunken anger. Please forgive the small bloodstains too stubborn to remove.

You hated me for my passivity and unwillingness to stand up to your father, but there were so many things you didn't realize, my child. Every time your father discovered my efforts to comfort or make life easier for you, he became irate and found an excuse to beat you. I couldn't continue to let that happen and chose, instead, to let you think I didn't care.

You shut us out once you left home, Biz. I'm sorry that I never met my grandchildren, but I don't blame you. Someday, I pray you will find it in your heart to forgive your father and me.

Your grandfather loved you more than life itself. So, when your father told him you were pregnant, your grandfather was greatly upset. When your father revealed that he had arranged to take your baby from you, your grandfather argued over the phone until his heart literally gave out.

Your father never told me where he got the money, but he rushed to your grandfather's side and arranged for open-heart surgery immediately. Unfortunately, your grandfather didn't make it.

Move forward in life, Bizzy. I'm sure you saw to it that your children enjoyed a better life than you did. That eases my guilt. Your Robert is such a dear. I've prayed for your future husband since the day you were born, child, and God answered by giving you the most incredible man. Take care of him. Not every woman is so blessed.

My life is coming to an end. I will spend my final days in an institution. Others are packing up my house as I write, tossing so many things in the trash. I regret wasting so much of my life. How I wish I could start over and do it differently. Unfortunately, there is no more time.

Don't make the same mistake, Biz. Allow God to heal your heart and bless you with a wonderful future.

Love, Mom

I rushed to the bathroom and threw up. The immensity of the situation zapped my heart. I lay on the floor, my face in the rug, unable to move. God hadn't taken my grandpa. My father had as much as murdered him in cold blood.

Visions of holding a gun to my father's head filled my mind. I shivered as I imagined stabbing a knife into his chest, jeering as his lifeblood spilled out.

I have no idea how long I lay in that position, crying and begging God to deliver me from the repulsion and contempt that pulsated through my thoughts.

And Danny Cooke. Didn't he share responsibility?

My head swam and my legs threatened to collapse when I finally stood to wash my face. God gave me the strength to call Marissa. To fall into her arms and allow her love to hold me together as I processed the most horrendous news I'd ever received in my life.

When the tears finally subsided and I found my voice, I showed Marissa my mother's letter. As I reread the words, snippets of childhood memories surfaced. Good times. My mother taking me in her arms when a stray cat I loved was run over by a car. Sitting by me on the sofa, reading me one story after another when my father was out drinking. Kneeling by my bed when she thought I was asleep—praying God's love and protection over me.

Had bitterness and rage blocked these memories all these years? Why were they so boldly stepping forward at this time?

"You know what, Marissa?"

"Hmmm?"

"This is like a birthday gift from my mom. The quilt, and new memories."

"Loving memories. Today's your birthday, Biz?"

"Friday. But close enough, right?"

We ordered a veggie pizza and talked about the quilt and my past. "Have you given any thought to contacting Dean?"

I nodded. "This will probably sound odd to you, but I'm praying and asking God to show me the right thing to do. For Dean and for my family."

Marissa smiled. "Never apologize for your relationship with God, Biz. Not if it's real."

Robert called a few minutes later. Marissa answered and pressed the phone against her leg. "You sure you're ready to talk?"

I nodded. "Hi, Robert. How did your day go?"

"Better than I expected. I've got some good news."

I dared not picture the country house. "I'm afraid to ask."

"I don't blame you. Well, Joe Carleton phoned me today. He'd heard about my position at the university and offered to sell me the house on contract. I'd make the large down payment and then pay what I can for six months or until I can sell the house in town. But overall, it's a plan we can work with, Biz. We're back on with your dream house."

I almost screamed in his ear. "Oh, thank you, Robert. Thank you so much."

"You're welcome, honey. I'm happy for you and for us. All those years at your company have paid off. Without your savings, we could never take such a huge leap of faith."

I wiped my eyes and nose. "There's another problem, though. These folks need to move in on the 20th. The painters they found have cancelled and can't begin until August 1st. Robert, I don't care if I have to paint the place myself. I'll call every person I know—"

"Honey, God has everything in control."

"I've heard that, but he sure can keep a person on pins and needles."

"That's to stretch our faith."

"Yeah, and our blood pressure."

Robert laughed. "Well, listen to this. Pastor called this morning to ask if I knew of anyone who needed some skilled labor done around the house. A team of men and teens are leaving for a missionary trip in a few weeks and need to raise some funds as soon as possible. I'll give them a call."

I put the phone down and whispered a prayer of thanks. So maybe God was in control, after all.

Marissa stood before me with wide eyes. "You want to share?"

Despite the fresh grief over my grandpa's unnecessary death, my heart practically burst with excitement as I dressed Thursday morning. Arrangements were completed for next week's move. The truck was coming on Monday and Tuesday and the painters on Wednesday. In five days, I would be sleeping in my new home.

I got to church early so I could have a word with the pastor about turning in my meeting topics in advance. He laughed and told me that was the previous secretary's idea. He didn't need my plans at all.

Relieved, I opened the meeting with prayer, allowing the ladies to share their needs and praise reports. When I looked at Gracie, she winked. Had I seriously thought that listening to one another was not worth the time it took?

Fact was, my view of life itself was changing, and I liked the difference. But could I sustain the change and harness the real me in order to maintain the new me?

Olivia shared a devotion on integrity. She mentioned the masks we wear, pretending to be someone we are not because we're afraid to take the risk of revealing our true selves.

Had the woman read my mail? Or had the Holy Spirit shared my personal stuff with her? That idea made me uncomfortable.

But as she continued, I realized the game I was playing. Like I had a split personality or something—the old me and the new me. Which was the real me?

"You are a new creation in Christ Jesus," Olivia said. "The old man has passed away . . ."

Right. So where had the crap word come from yesterday?

"Of course, the old nature is still there."

Stop already. You're freaking me out, Olivia.

"The apostle Paul understood. In Romans seven, he talked about how he did the things he didn't want to do and didn't do the things he wanted to do."

Made sense. The real me was both. Spirit and flesh. I found my pen and wrote the Scripture passage down on the back of my notebook to check out later. Was the apostle Paul another kindred spirit?

Olivia finished, and I talked about dreams. I shared my excitement about my new home, but held my dream for the barn close to my heart. Morgan came to mind. "God is definitely a God of second chances."

I spoke of faith and fear. God gave me the thoughts from my own experiences. I shared the struggle I'd endured to get painters and the way God had miraculously intervened. Then I turned the conversation to include the ladies. "So, what are your dreams?"

Though several others started to speak, Olivia jumped ahead of them. "I've dreamed for years of this group becoming one which could minister to the young girls in our church. Of course, you know, this is the instruction God gives us in Titus 2."

Déjà vu? Hadn't we covered this issue before? Silence reigned.

Once again, Sister Gracie saved the day. "I know we talked about this a couple of weeks ago and decided to get to know each other first, but I'm afraid if we wait too long, the girls will grow up and leave the church."

Did I say she saved the day? "I didn't plan to discuss this today, but I do have some ideas along this line. First, I'd like to commend Olivia for her work in the past and her excellent ideas for the future."

A brief applause broke out. Olivia smiled and nodded her thanks.

When eyes turned in my direction, I proceeded with what I knew might very well rub the feathers right off the bird's back. "I've been thinking that instead of trying to counsel the young girls, we might just want to plan some activities with the girls so we can get to know them a little. We could go shopping or bake cookies. Sort of earn their friendship and trust before we pounce on them with our counsel."

Heads nodded all around the circle. Well, almost all around.

Olivia turned somber. "I'm sorry I didn't think of that."

Oh, give it up. This isn't about you, Olivia. But Olivia was one of the group, and I needed to address her needs as well as those of the others. Maybe a baseball bat to the head would help . . . just kidding.

Today was the day. I thought about my new house as I lathered my hair, still unable to believe we were closing on the place this evening and moving in less than a week.

Around noon, I ran to Subway. Then I stopped at The Home Store. I wanted to buy something special for my new home. As I browsed the aisles, I prayed God would show me what to buy. I found a lovely oak quilt rack—perfect for my mom's quilt. I put it in my cart, but knew this wasn't what I had come for.

Then I saw it. A simple wrought-iron wall décor with a profound message. *The best things in life aren't things.*

Robert pulled in the drive promptly at five. I headed out to meet him to save time. He reached across to kiss my cheek. "How are you doing, honey? Excited?"

I curled my toes, determined not to reveal that I was shaking like a love-possessed schoolgirl inside. My husband's cologne had just thrown my hormones completely out of whack, and everything in me wanted to jump over the silly console and sit as close to my man as possible.

We signed a zillion or more forms, many with our birth dates printed in what appeared to be the darkest black ink I'd ever seen. So why was I the only one who saw it? Were Robert and the real estate agents totally blind? Were they purposely ignoring the fact that today was my birthday?

We'd barely made a dent in the stack of papers to be signed when Robert's cell phone buzzed. He glanced at the thing and excused himself from the room.

What was that important . . . or should I ask who?

Fortunately, the queasy feeling in my stomach fleeted away as we signed the last of the legal forms and accepted the keys to the house. Robert refused to take them, nodding in my direction. So this was to be my house?

The symbolism scared me until Robert stepped across the room, pulled me into his arms, and whispered into my ear, "Happy birthday. I love you."

The words were a long time coming, but well worth the wait.

The heat hit me in the face when I exited the building. I beamed at Robert and took his arm as we started down the stairs. Then I heard the shouts, "Happy Birthday!"

My eyes shot to a small crowd across the parking lot and realized this was my crowd. My family. The balloons and signs were for me! My heart almost exploded with joy as we shared hugs and headed for the steakhouse next door.

Stephanie separated herself and motioned me aside. She hugged my neck and kissed my cheek. "I'm sorry about how I behaved at your house, Granny," she whispered in my ear. "Happy Birthday. I love you"

I gave her an extra hug. "Love you, too, sweetie."

My knees weakened. Robert braced my elbow. "Breathe, Biz. Take deep breaths."

The hyperventilating thing was happening again. I leaned against the building, cupped my hands over my mouth and nose and breathed in until I felt my tummy expand with the air. One. Two. Three. Gradually, the dizziness faded.

"You better?"

I nodded, accepting his arm as we began to walk. A new home in the country. A steak dinner and an evening with my husband and family. Life didn't get better than this.

We finished dinner, and then there were presents. Nothing huge, except the fact that my family remembered. I tried my best to appear offended when Morgan presented me with a gym membership and promised to go with me as often as I liked. Truth be told, as much as I detested exercise, I loved the idea of spending more time with my daughter.

We made plans to meet at my house the next morning and drive to the country together. I loved Vickie's idea that we pray over the property and house, amazed at the work God was doing in me and in my family. I was too touched for words, and that, in itself, said a lot.

"You must be exhausted." Robert pulled out of the parking lot. "Shut your eyes, and you'll be home in a jiffy."

I leaned my head back, more than happy to soak up the silence as I replayed the entire evening in my mind and whispered a prayer of thanks. Pure bliss.

CHAPTER 36

My first clue should have been that Robert didn't pull his car into the garage. My second, that he didn't carry an overnight bag into the house. And my third, that he practically rubbed a hole in his jeans as he sat at the kitchen table while I put the coffee on. I saw it all, but missed the significance completely.

Here we sat, husband and wife. I had shared my darkest secrets at the beach, and my husband still loved me. Now I wanted more. I wanted to be best friends. I wanted to know Robert intimately and completely. And I was finally ready to risk totally exposing myself to him.

"Thank you for one of the best days in my life. Any idea when you'll be able to move home?"

His discomfort bounced from the very corners of the room as clearly as a neon sign in the black of night. I struggled to breathe—the air around me clogged with chunks of impending threat. I took one slow breath after another and willed myself to fight the panic surging within me.

He wrapped his trembling fingers around mine, stroking my knuckles ever so gently with his index finger. "I love you,

Biz, and I want to come home. But I need to be honest with you about something first."

I wondered at the serenity trickling into my heart as I waited for his next words.

"There's not another woman." Robert's fingers went still. "I have remained faithful to you. But . . ."

But? Where was he going with this? Kathy Harmin? I looked away as the room seemed to spin around me like bathwater swirling the drain.

"I had feelings for her, Biz. Wrong feelings."

I forced my eyes to reconnect with Robert's and felt strength gush into my spirit that could only have come from God. "Kathy Harmin?"

He nodded. "Her husband left her for a younger woman. She just needed someone to listen, and I honestly thought I could do that without becoming emotionally involved."

"And physically?"

Robert reddened. "Just hugs. I held her hand a lot . . . She tried to kiss me intimately one time, but I stopped her immediately."

I literally sensed the blood draining from my face. My stomach cramped, and I had to hold my breath to avoid retching. "I knew it."

Robert sighed, shaking his head. "She began insisting on my attention the day after you found us together. Showing up in my office at all hours. I confronted her, but she denied all wrong intentions."

"The whole missing report thing at the office. That was her work?"

He nodded. "That's when I finally began to see what was happening and volunteered to take the temporary position in Chicago."

I expected anger but felt only empathy. Easy to understand why my man would fall for another woman's attention when all he got at home was ridicule and rejection. If anger dared show its ugly finger, I could only direct it to myself.

Grace. The word pounded itself into my mind until I could almost imagine the letters stamped across my forehead. God's grace . . . for Robert, and for me. "I'm sorry, Robert. I really am."

Robert turned, and I saw only compassion in his wet eyes. "No, Biz." He knelt beside me and reached for my hands. "I am the one who has failed you. Can you possibly forgive me and give me another chance?"

I thought of my precious Jesus kneeling before his disciples to wash their dirty feet. I was so much dirtier than Robert. So much more at fault. Yet here he was, kneeling before me in total humility. As his love overwhelmed me, I rested my head on his shoulder and wept. "I love you so much, Robert."

We moved to the living room sofa where we held each other, cried and talked late into the night. At one point, when I slipped away to the bathroom, Robert surprised me by ordering a pizza. Even remembered the extra cheese. Not that I was going to fall off the Weight Watcher wagon completely. I would resume my diet the next day. But tonight, there was reason to celebrate. My husband had returned.

Robert followed a deep yawn with a question. "Would you mind if I spend the night?"

"Hmmm, let me think about that." I eagerly anticipated the idea of my husband's body next to mine in the bed. "Not sure I want to get used to something I can't keep."

Robert grinned like a featherbrained schoolboy. "Oh, did I fail to mention that I'd like to move home next weekend?"

A smile started from the depths of my heart and worked its way out. Though I knew I couldn't distance myself from the past completely, I was determined not to ever let it control me again. Instead, with God's help, I would allow it only to remind me how far God had brought me. For that was God's grace.

I didn't realize how I'd missed waking to the smell of freshly brewed coffee. I joined Robert in the kitchen for a scrumptious breakfast of bacon, eggs and pancakes.

"Glad you slept late because I had to make a run to the Piggly Wiggly. Nothing in the cupboards."

I laughed. "Didn't want to move any more than necessary. Rather start fresh."

The gravity of my words seemed to suck the air out of the room as Robert took my hand. We spoke a million thoughts into each other's eyes in a matter of seconds. Until Robert began to pray and my sight became blurred.

"Father in heaven, thank you for placing this remarkable woman in my life. I promise to love and cherish her until death do us part. Place your hand on our lives, Father. Strengthen the bond of love that has held us together through thick and thin. Create in us a bond of friendship, security and intimacy. Make this marriage everything you designed it to be, so that, together, we might enjoy every day you give us to the fullest. Amen."

I squeezed my husband's fingers in reply. "I love you, honey."

He swallowed hard, withdrew his hand, and picked up his napkin to wipe his nose. "Let's eat before this meal gets cold."

We talked about the new house as we ate, and Robert surprised me with landscaping plans he'd made. "I kept a little money back from my retirement account." He pushed his empty plate back. "Thought it might be fun to let the Salvation Army pick up our old furniture and shop for new. We don't need to drag any of the past into our new home. You think?"

Okay. For once I was grateful when the crazy phone rang and saved me from totally falling apart in my husband's arms. Could God really be this good?

Robert answered the phone. Robby and Vickie were running about an hour late. "Good." Robert set the phone down. "I'd like to talk about the emotional ramifications of something before the kids join us."

Emotional ramifications? Those were my words—straight from the thesaurus. I started to panic, until I saw a silly smirk playing at the corners of Robert's lips.

He topped off his coffee. "Another cup?"

"Sure."

Robert set the pot on the table and disappeared into the pantry.

Did I say I was having a good morning? Surely he hadn't found—

"We need to seriously discuss this." Robert reappeared with Kathy Harmin's gift. And the letter I'd written to Kathy.

He had definitely read it. My head dropped. What would this do to our reconciliation?

"You think I'm upset?" Robert lifted my chin and broke into laughter. "This is an incredible piece of work, Biz

McNeely. I'll call the office on Monday morning to get Kathy's address so we can mail the thing."

"Are you serious?"

He nodded, sealing his approval with a kiss. "Do me a favor. Read this letter aloud. I want to hear it in your voice."

I took the note from him with trembling fingers. Was he serious?

"Go on, read it."

"Okay . . . Ms. Harmon, Robert shared his candy gram with me. He knows how I love sweets. You were kind enough to speak my language, so please let me return the favor. I'm sure you sport an extended vocabulary as a professor of English.

"First of all, I want to assert that you must be visually impaired to conjecture that your liaison with Robert was anything but a partisan affair. Short and sweet . . . BACK OFF! Find your own man. There are plenty of fish in the sea. I'm sure there's another piranha out there just waiting to sink his teeth into a voluptuous woman like you. Sincerely, Mrs. Robert C. Beemer."

By the time I finished, Robert was doubled over, wiping tears from his eyes. "A piranha? Really?"

I smiled. "I wanted to call her a voluptuous worm, but thought it might sound a bit too harsh."

"Oh, Biz." Robert stood and pulled me into his arms. "Have I ever told you that it was your spunk I first fell in love with all those years ago? Please don't ever change, sweetheart. I love you just the way you are."

Robert met Robby and Vickie at the door when they showed up around ten. "Hey guys, we riding together?"

"Sure," Robby said. "As long as you don't plan to stay all day."

I climbed into the backseat of the SUV. "Where are the kids?"

"The boys will come later with my parents," Vickie said. "Stephanie is with Morgan. They're going to pick up some lunch and meet us at the house."

I glanced up just in time to see Robby wink at Vickie. "Hey, what's going on, you two?"

"Nothing to worry about," Vickie said. "By the way, I meant to tell you that the business is picking up a lot lately, Biz. We're going to need to hire a bookkeeper soon. You interested in coming back part-time? You could even work at home if that suits you better."

I shivered at the thought. "Oh my, no. Morgan may be interested, though. She said something the other day about looking for something different."

Was it possible that my business could provide a future for both of my children? Nothing would make me happier. Well, other than the fact that my husband just put an arm around my shoulder and shared an inviting smile. I could get used to this life.

As we pulled up the drive to our new home, shock topped my contentment. Marissa and the Golden Oldies stood around long tables covered with red checkered tablecloths. To the side, another table held a multitude of food trays and a huge birthday cake. "Happy Birthday, Biz," the ladies screamed as I stepped out of the car.

"A surprise party?"

Vickie hugged my neck and whispered into my ear, "We love you, Biz."

My body shook. I wanted to laugh and cry at the same time. "I don't know what to say."

Frieda jumped up and ran to my side. "How about, 'Let's eat!'"

I glanced at my friend in surprise. Who convinced Frieda to come?

I watched my family and friends mingle. Something sweet settled in my heart. Behind the masks and misunderstandings, we were good people. Whether blood or not, this was family. The thought of baby Dean tugged at my heartstrings. Danny Cooke, Jr., rather. And he was not a baby anymore. I didn't know this young man, but I wanted to. And I wanted him to know his family. Only as God led, of course. In his perfect time.

Olivia approached me as I finished my meal. "Can I talk to you alone for a few minutes?"

Uh . . . could she just let me enjoy my birthday?

Waiting for Olivia to take the lead, I followed her toward the barn. She paused just outside the doorway. "First of all, I want to tell you that I love your outfit. You're losing weight, aren't you?"

My face went hot. What was this about? "Trying. Not sure what I just ate is going to do for me, though."

Olivia nodded. "Don't worry about it. In fact, there should be a law against dieting on one's birthday, don't you think?"

"Sounds good to me." Where was the woman going with the small talk? My birthday lunch was quickly working its way through my system, pushing breakfast dangerously close to the exit. I had, maybe, ten minutes before I would need to awkwardly excuse myself.

"Look, Biz." Olivia's face twisted as if she had a cramp of her own. "I need to apologize for so many things."

"No." I forced myself to maintain eye contact. "I'm the one who—"

"Please." She held up a bony little hand. "Until you came along, I didn't realize how stuck I was in my life. The idea of change terrified me, and I directed my fear at you. Will you please forgive me?"

Okay, I detested facing the real stuff that went with relationships, but I had to admit that I liked this Olivia. She was so genuine. I probably needed to apologize, too, but I wasn't sure quite how to verbalize what was in my heart, and I sure didn't want to babble stupid in the presence of such beautiful honesty. So I held my tongue and nodded.

Olivia pointed to the barn. "From the first day I met you, you've reminded me of a stallion. I think that's what scared me the most."

I laughed, not sure whether to take her opinion as a compliment or an insult. "A stallion?"

She nodded. "Mac and I train horses for a living. When we get a young stallion, our work is cut out for us. The horse's incredible strength does no one any good until the horse's will is broken and he is taught to submit to authority."

Where was she going with this?

"Mom!"

I turned to find Morgan leading the other guests in our direction. "There's something in the barn you need to see."

Robby pulled the doors open and took my arm as we walked inside. In the stalls stood two of the most beautiful golden-yellow palomino horses I'd ever seen. Someone had braided their creamy manes and added bright ribbon bows. "Happy birthday, Mom."

So now I laughed and cried. "Who did this?"

"Me," Gracie said.

Frieda laughed. "Excuse me? How are you going to try to put your name on my gift?"

"What?" This came from Marissa. "You two know I did this!"

One by one, they all responded. I walked over to the stalls and nuzzled the horse's noses as I waited for the ladies to finish. Then I swallowed my butterflies in order to say a few words of my own.

"Years ago, I vowed never to let myself need another person as long as I lived. I was rejected, abused and betrayed as a child. Well, I've kept my vow, but I've lived a miserable, critical lonely life."

Robert stepped forward. "Honey, you don't need to—"

I put up my hand to silence him. "Yes, I do. In the last few weeks I've realized just how ashamed I am of the life I've led and how much I want the years ahead to be different. God has given me a second chance, and I intend to let him direct my life from here on out.

"A few minutes ago, Olivia told me I reminded her of a stallion. I now understand what she meant. For years I've detested the strong stallion personality I was born with. But now I realize that God created me with the exact personality, skills and abilities I need to do the work he sets before me. It's just that he wants to hold the reins."

Again, Robert started to object, but I shook my head.

"Thank you for your love and patience, ladies. I've a steep hill to climb in my life, but I know that I can trust you to walk beside me. I need you and . . . want you to be my friends."

I paused to regain my composure ... and to work up a bit of courage to say what was still on my mind. "One more thing. I don't like the name of our group. Golden Oldies makes us sound like a bunch of washed-up old biddies who have nothing to do but chew the fat and bide our time. God has a lot of work for us to do, and I think we're more about Partners in Prime—mature Christian women, ready to pass the baton—one friendship at a time."

"Whoo-hoo!" Frieda shouted. "I'm in. What about the rest of you?"

The silly ladies clapped and cheered like I'd just delivered the State of the Union address or something. Come to think of it, maybe I had, in my own personal way.

"So let's go eat some cake. I want to open my presents!"

Lettie wrapped me in a bear hug as we headed away from the barn.

I pulled away and looked into her eyes. "Thank you for being my friend all these years. But why didn't you tell me what a mess I was making of my life?"

She laughed and walked away. "Like you would have listened?"

Hi, Friends.

I hope you enjoyed reading our book. You know, when Barbie first approached me with the idea, I thought she was crazy. Good grief, who would pay good money for such a pathetic story? I insisted we name the thing "A Messed Up Life—Extreme!"

But I guess Barbie saw something more in my life. Like God's grace—healing my hurts, forgiving my failures and changing my hardened heart as I accepted and soaked up his love. Now I prefer the title "A Messed Up Life—Redeemed!"

I'll bet you're wondering what happened with sweet Hazel and Sandy. And did I contact my son Dean? Were Robert and I able to start working through all our baggage when he moved home?

The answer to all these questions is a great big YES! Barbie and I are working on book two right now so I won't say too much. But I will tell you that I soon discover a HUGE secret about Marissa. Frieda has some pretty understandable reasons behind her behavior, too. And Stephanie? Well, she and Lindsey definitely do the teenage rebellion thing. Unfortunately, this leads to a tragic accident. Stephanie is forced to face the consequences of her choices. Pretty tough life lesson. And not just for her.

Oh, there's so much more. We'd better get back to writing. Don't be a stranger—visit us at **www.barbarahaleybooks.com**! Fondly, *Biz & Barbie*

P.S. Would you please help promote our story?
*READ
*REVIEW ... on Amazon *AND* on your Facebook Page
*RECOMMEND ... the book to folks on your email list, at church, in your neighborhood, at the dog park ...

Made in the USA
Columbia, SC
17 June 2018